The Manny

Nina Bloom

Edited by Nina Fiegl at Lingvinis Editing

Sensitivity Editor: Sarah Clark

Cover Design by Aisling at Pretty Indie Book Covers

The Manny

MAE NEEDS A NANNY. Preferably an aging male with a balding head. Too bad the Jedi Knight of Mannies and ovary-charmer, Remi, shows up instead.

Mae, a single mother navigating a male-dominated corporate world, is trying to keep her company from folding. Days are long and nights are stressful. Add an active toddler into the mix, and life is like trying to extinguish a fiery blaze with a watering can. Seeking balance in her life, Mae hires a male nanny but soon realizes giving up control is harder than she thought. And she *really* shouldn't be fantasizing about her child's way-too-young caregiver.

Remi doesn't take himself too seriously, except when it comes to caring for his charges. When a dream job lands in his lap, he's all too eager to take the contract. Only, he didn't realize he'd risk losing that job so soon. By committing the nannies' cardinal sin—fall for the parent.

As they grow closer, Remi can no longer keep his feelings to himself, but Mae is adamant about not adding more complications to her already hectic life. Can Remi's belief in their connection convince Mae that giving him a shot is worth it? Or is she right in thinking this reckless affair can only make them lose it all?

Are the risks worth taking?

The Manny is a steamy contemporary romance stand-alone. If you love humor laced with raw emotion and spicy cinnamon roll heroes, you'll love this new book by Nina Bloom.

Contents

Playlist

IN SOME PARTICULAR ORDER: https://shorturl.at/vGV15

W.I.T.C.H by Devon Cole

Castle by Halsey

Boys Wanna Be Her by Peaches

Lilith by Halsey

Pretty Vicious by The Struts

Fine Line by Harry Styles

The Tradition by Halsey

Sweet Creature by Harry Styles

When You Were Young by The Killers

Music For A Sushi Restaurant by Harry Styles

Nightmare by Halsey

Diamond Heart by Lady Gaga

Golden by Harry Styles

Fall For You by Talk

Grapejuice by Harry Styles

Two Weeks by FKA Twigs

Smile Like You Mean It by The Killers

Sweet Girl by Stevie Nicks

Adore You by Harry Styles

Cracklin' Rosie by Neil Diamond

Desire by Meg Myers

Watermelon Sugar by Harry Styles

Untitled (How Does It Feel) by D'Angelo

Devil In Me by Halsey

The Best by Tina Turner, Bailey Rushlow cover

1121 by Halsey

Control by Halsey

You Should See Me In A Crown by Billie Eilish

Times Like These by Foo Fighters

Paradise by Clementine and the Galaxy

Dedication

DEDICATED TO MR. BLOOM. My best friend and soulmate. You are the calm to my storm. The humor in my angst. The love of my life. You see *me* through all my bullshit, even when I'm not very nice. Thank you for your unwavering support of any cockamamie idea I've ever had.

Even when the stars die, we will still be.

Content Warning

Chapter 1

What I Wouldn't Give For A Goddamn Sleeve of Thin Mints Right Now

Mae

Working for someone is the equivalent of being a servant to Hell. Sure, Lucifer may pay you well, but he'll suck your soul right out of your breathing body.

That was never going to be me. It has always been my goal to sit up in a high-rise, calling all the shots and playing the corporate game like we're all chess pieces on a board and I'm the grandmaster. I'd perch high on my throne, next to my best friend, and we'd conquer the world together, beholden to no one but ourselves.

However, no one told me about the sacrifices. No one mentioned life's curveballs and how to navigate them. When your company is floundering, it's still *your* company. If you don't do the work, no one is there to pick up the slack. There is no fucking around to make the time pass by. Every minute is money, and every lead is an opportunity.

There's no leaving early to have drinks with friends. No spare evening for a romantic date. No free lunch break with subsequent fifteen-minute smoking sessions throughout the day. Which makes me *hangry* with a blood-sugar level of stress. Worst of all, there is no clocking out or days off. Not even when your kid can't go to daycare because she's running a fever.

I want to give my daughter the things I never had. A stable home without financial worries. Healthy meals with substance instead of the TV dinners I was raised on.

She is the driving force that pushes my ambition—this need to be on top of my game, a fierce competitor in the digital marketing industry.

"Elliot, where is the Deximo proposal? I can't find it in the cloud." I try to keep the impatience out of my tone while setting up the highchair to feed my daughter breakfast.

"Mama!" My two-year-old hasn't learned how to use her inside voice yet, and when she wants my attention, she demands it.

I smile at my confident girl as I walk over and pick her up off the floor.

"I'm sorry about that, Ms. Keller." Elliot's on the verge of stammering.

It tells me I need to temper my anxiety, which sounds a lot like irritation. My assistant is great and I don't mean to be abrupt with him, but this is an important deal. It's *vital.*

I sigh, counting to ten in my head. We're in the final negotiations of Ever Heart Digital's biggest contract with a huge player in the sports industry.

If we're counting children, Ever Heart is my firstborn. A company that my best friend and I built from the basement of their home. Now, we sit thirty stories high in a Chicago skyscraper. If all goes well, we'll satisfy our investors and keep all our employees. If not...

Blowing out a breath, I shake my head. I can't even think about it. I just hope everything I'm sacrificing—the lonely nights, the rushed days, the lack of sleep, proper nutrition, my youth, and mostly quality time with my daughter—will be worth it in the end.

I smooth red curls away from Isabel's face as I place her in her highchair with breakfast—a mashed banana and Go-gurt. Her squeal of delight lights me up, and some of the frustration from this phone meeting dissipates.

"It's fine." I wince at my not-so-subtle aggravation and rein it in a bit. "Really, Elliot, you don't need to apologize. I know there's a lot on your plate."

The impatient undertone in my voice makes him stutter. "I-I just got the updated budget. I'll have it ready and uploaded this afternoon."

Regret twists my gut. I'm being too abrasive to someone who doesn't deserve it. I never alluded to what we're up against. People's jobs are on the line. *His* job is on the line, and it's not because of work performance.

Our staff is the backbone of our company, each one interviewed and carefully curated by my best friend and myself. Our people have a strong work ethic and great integrity. We can't lose them and, most of all, I can't let the people that depend on us down.

My hand flies to my forehead and starts rubbing, fending off the impending tension headache. "See that you do."

Shit. That came out wrong. My tone could use some correction. I've lost my tact somewhere in my struggle between pursuing my ambitions and becoming a single mother overnight.

I lighten my voice. "Let's go over the proposal again. It has to be perfect."

"Yes, ma'am."

My shoulders scrunch to my ears. I fucking hate that word.

"With the complete marketing package—"

"Mamama!" Isabel wails and flips her bowl of yogurt off the tray of her highchair. White gooey shit flies and lands on every possible surface, including my silk blouse.

My blood pressure is skyrocketing but eases as Isabel giggles and plays with her food. The stab of anxiety turns into a small sting. I almost smile. "No, Isabel. You have to *eat* your food, not throw it on the floor." My tone is more soothing with her than it is with Elliot. I hope.

Elliot continues talking in the background.

I'm nodding at each bullet point, checking them off in my head one by one, like I've done a hundred times since we first sat down with Dexico.

When I'm in front of Isabel, I tap her nose with a smile and lift a spoon of banana to her mouth, which is the absolute worst thing I could do. She arches her back with a grunt of irritation and turns away from the hand I'm trying to feed her with.

"Nononono, Mama."

"Uhh, maybe I should call you back," Elliot, the ever helpful assistant he is, knows how to read a room. It's one of the reasons I hired him.

By the shade of my toddler's face, that's probably for the best. She's about to turn this peaceful protest into a roaring riot. A blitzkrieg of fury over the most innocent of the utensils—the spoon.

"No," I snap, then a seed of remorse plants itself on my tongue. The shitstorm brewing isn't Elliot's fault. I deliberately temper my voice. "Thank you, but I'll call you." I'm about to say something pleasant when my daughter's face pinches, telling me that her eruption is imminent. "Be on standby." I hit end and right on time too.

Isabel's shrieking emits at a hundred and thirty decibels, and is only increasing by the second.

They say tantrums are a form of expression, the only way children know how to show their frustration, but it's hard to remember patience when I already know this is going to be a long morning. On days like these, I feel like I'm being ripped apart in two very different directions—the need to stay with my daughter and the need to make sure the ship I'm running stays tight.

When I pick up my screeching child, she pushes backwards, almost flinging herself out of my arms. "Mama, maaam. Nooo!"

Working from home isn't ideal because it's hard to think about proposals when I have an active toddler throwing food and tantrums. I need some assistance, which is why I'm meeting a child caregiver from Child Care Connection. They are number one in their industry, and their charges get into the best kindergartens. It's child care and tutoring all in one. And that's what I love about it—its efficiency.

The new nanny can't get here fast enough. Though I'm not one to admit I need help, the kicking and screaming Tasmanian devil in my arms proves I've got some limitations.

"Shhh, baby girl." I try my damnedest to be calm and speak low into her ear, but it doesn't matter. My child can feel the tension rolling off my body, like thermal waves do off asphalt.

My breaths catch in my chest as thoughts race in my head. I have to make sure this proposal is perfect so Dexico will have no choice but to sign the contract. We *have* to get this deal. Once the ink has dried, the threat of laying people off will drift away like a bad storm.

I also have to make sure I don't neglect my daughter in the process. None of this will matter if she resents me as she gets older.

There are so many duties on this long list of "have to". My heart is hollow while my brain is overwhelmed with commitments. Each task is a brick, building a wall between who I am—a competitive player in the business world—and who I want to be—an attentive mother to my child, who deserves the best parts of me. With each layer added, the weight of responsibility sits heavier on my chest.

I slide to the floor, daughter in hand, and give her my phone to play with, hoping it distracts her out of this meltdown. Isabel continues her tornadic activity while I try to rock her and calm this storm. If I had the capacity to cry, I would. Since I don't, I stare at the wall, unblinking and numb.

I wish Brad were here with all his cool and charm. He never buckled under pressure, and it would be nice to have some semblance of support.

As soon as that thought enters my brain, another one takes its place. Only, it's a memory. The kind that stabs you in the gut and makes you bleed out slowly, until you're painfully drained and left with nothing but flesh and misery.

My eyes burn. Before I can muster a glimmer of humanity, the doorbell rings.

"Thank Goddess." I set my daughter on the floor.

Her shrieks turn into hiccups as she focuses on the device in her tiny hands. This should keep her occupied long enough for me to greet our visitor, but as soon as she realizes I'm not next to her, she wails again.

Sliding my eyes shut to block out the need to run to her, I open the door, expecting to find the experienced child caregiver I hired on the other side, but I get something else entirely.

A man-boy stands in front of me. He looks like he's some kind of Boy Scout. A messy-haired one, like he couldn't be bothered to sit still while his mother tried and failed to comb his locks. Tilting his head, his floppy dark hair falls to one side.

He's wearing olive wool pants and a white button-up. All he's missing is a khaki shirt with patches.

But the more I size him up, the more I realize—by the defined angle of his jaw—he's definitely all man. A man scout maybe? Is that even a thing?

I wonder if he has cookies. Damn, what I wouldn't give for a goddamn sleeve of Thin Mints right now. Or is that the wrong troop?

Whatever he is, he's got to go.

"Oh, um, I wasn't expecting any deliveries today." Checking the watch on my wrist, I dismiss the Boy Scout crowding my front stoop. "I'm sorry. I have a meeting, and I'm waiting for—"

"A nanny?" He peers at me with warm umber irises and a smile. His voice makes me squirm, vibrating from my stomach to my knees and making them shaky. It's rough and deep, a rumble of thunder before the loud crack.

It's been a long time since a man's baritone has affected me this much. *Too* long. While my daughter's sorrowful hiccupping chirps behind me, the timber of his voice silences everything else.

I don't like it. Not at all. It's dangerous, attractive, and the very last thing I need in my life—a big ol' distraction.

I check behind his shoulder, thinking this must be a misunderstanding. "I was told you were a college graduate."

Is anyone else coming? An aging, balding anyone else?

"A double bachelor's in elementary education and music with a master's in child psychology, University of Illinois," he says. "Go, Fighting Illini!" He pumps his fist with a smile but then clears his throat, reading my unimpressed face.

He can't be older than twenty-one. Maybe he has one of those high IQs with a membership to Mensa. No, he can't be that attractive using more than three percent of his brain. The universe doesn't work like that. It just isn't fair to the rest of us.

But if I've learned anything in life, it's that the universe *isn't* fair and never claimed to be.

"I'm Remington Arison from Child Care Connection." He raises his hand for a shake. His long fingers are giving me images of him behind a grand piano or strumming a Les Paul guitar. Either fantasy makes me shiver. Wonder if he could get me to sing.

My detour from these thoughts is sharp and swift.

Usually, my meetings start with me charming high-profile executives of Fortune 500 companies. It's never the other way around. Yet here I stand, stupefied, staring at his offering instead of shaking it. If his voice sent me in a tailspin, I can only imagine the horrific belly swoop of actually touching him.

He straightens his *boyish* angular face, drops his hand, and clears his throat. "The agency told me you were seeking a child caregiver." As if he can't help himself, he smirks. "A male, specifically."

My gut punches. I swear that twinkle in his eye has a laser aimed right between my thighs. It's been so long since anyone looked at me like that. The thing I usually get glinting in a man's eye is contempt. Most likely because I have his balls in a vise, but I digress.

I can almost hear B.O.B. vibrating in excitement on my nightstand drawer, down the hall past the screaming child, inside my bedroom. I may be someone's mother, but shit, I still have needs. And I'm lonely. It's tough being a dictator all day and mommy at night. I long for deep connections with other people, like anyone else. There's just not enough time.

Oh God, this is so fucking cliché, isn't it? *He's a child, for chrissakes.*

Well, not a child.

My eyes can't help but sweep down his front, the fit of his shirt molding around his lean but cut frame. A child doesn't have a body like that. But he *is* someone's kid, right? With wild sex hair. And a mouth meant for sucking. Don't even get me started on those long fingers and what they could do. The places they could reach.

I clench. And then self-flagellate.

I'm old enough to be his ... what? Older sister? My age slaps me in the face before gripping my arm and yelling, *you still have a pulse!*

Is it so bad that I crave male company? Most healthy thirty-something heterosexual women do. No matter, I am a mother and I might become his employer.

So I straighten my spine and square my shoulders, holding my invisible crown high. I am still the queen of this castle. "I see. I misunderstood. Accept my apologies. You have a very young face." *Her Royal Highness can shut her trap about now.*

Isabel's cries for mommy become the equivalent of a sonic boom. My shoulders hitch as the sound blasts my eardrums. Here I am, standing before this … nice-looking man-boy, with sweat beading from my temple and yogurt crusting on my blouse. A tantrum of epic proportions going on behind me.

Pre-kid me wouldn't be this rattled, this wound tight. The Mae of three years ago didn't sweat in uncomfortable situations. She didn't blink an eye at pursuing someone. But it's not just about me anymore. I have a responsibility to my daughter, and being reckless would be detrimental to that obligation.

I'm sure he's about to politely get the fuck out of Dodge when he peeks over my shoulder towards the wailing banshee child.

"May I?"

I want to reply, *No, you may not*, but all I want is my child's happiness. So I should at least give him a chance, right?

I stand aside.

His mouth tips a lopsided smile as he waltzes past me. Without a glance, Remington picks up Mr. Snuffles among the sea of toys littering the living room floor. The stuffed dog has certainly seen better days—quite literally since I excised his marble eyes, stitching him up with the finesse of a drunk surgeon.

How does this stranger know it's her favorite stuffy? I'm positive Isabel's father wouldn't have paid enough attention to even care. Brad was only concerned with one thing—Brad.

"Arf, arf, arf." The sexy man-boy gets on all fours and approaches a tear-streaked but cute ticking time bomb.

Holy mother of God, I was not prepared for this new visual.

A lump forms in my throat watching Remington's thoughtful tactics with my baby. It's like he knows exactly what she needs. He crawls over to my daughter, the plump of his ass on full display.

I'm aware that objectifying him is wrong, yet my deprived body betrays me. Redirecting my thoughts, I crack a smile at the nanny's antics.

I can't even call him a "nanny". That word conjures an image of an obnoxious-voiced Fran Drescher with a laugh that grates my nerves into pasta cheese. No, the man before my daughter is nothing of the sort. He's doing wonderful things to my nerves, which are suddenly alive with fluttery wings.

"Why are you sad?" he asks in a Mr. Snuffles voice. Gone is the rasp of his baritone, a goofy slur taking its place.

It's still pleasing to the ears. It makes me want to answer him, *Because I'm alone, abandoned, and drowning in so much work I'm afraid I'll never come up for air.*

The Tasmanian devil laughs like a tiny cherub. My child, who was kicking me ten minutes ago, is completely charmed. And calm. This only adds to the immense guilt I feel over not doing this sooner. She's missing a support figure in her life. Someone who will dote on her and treat her like she matters. Someone strong she can count on to protect her when scared. She has me, but it's not the same.

I know the feeling all too well. My mother was there, but she wasn't present. More often than not, I had to fight through my fears. Monsters under the bed? Too bad. *"Go to sleep anyway because Mommy has to be at work early."* Thunder shaking the whole trailer? *Try to block it out because Mom's not here to coddle you.*

When Remington sits criss-crossed in front of Isabel on the floor, she crawls over to him. He's definitely piqued her interest. And mine, I must admit as I rub my sternum against the warmth blooming in my chest. Watching this beautiful man charm my daughter does something funny to my insides.

Brad couldn't be bothered by her, by us. He didn't want to acknowledge his own flesh and blood, let alone try to form some semblance of a bond with her. He'll never know how amazing she is. I'll never understand.

It's something I don't want to explore, so I mentally slap myself and chant "nanny, nanny, nanny" in my head to tame the lady-boner I sprouted the moment I laid eyes on him.

"I'm Remi. What's your name?" Even though the Scooby Doo voice is reserved for Mr. Snuffles, his deep tone is lighter.

Creeping over, silent as a ghost, I sit on the arm of the side chair, watching the magic before me. This may be his job, but he's not phoning it in. His actions are deliberate and sincere. Which makes my objectification of him that much more egregious.

"Is-bewl," she answers in her sweet voice.

My heart melts at the sound of her name, and for other reasons that are becoming more evident as the scene before me plays out.

"What a pretty name," he gushes, his engaging demeanor fascinating Isabel. "Fit for a princess."

Her whole face alights. She loves Disney movies, especially the princesses.

Remi opens his arms and Isabel climbs on his lap, content as could be. Like they've known each other forever.

And just like that, the man who has the appeal of a hot college jock and is currently holding my world—along with a raggedy stuffy—has charmed his way into a very discerning little girl's heart ... and melted my frozen one.

She reaches for her stuffy. Remington hands it over but before placing it in her hands, he makes Mr. Snuffles kiss her on the cheek. When he rears back with surprise, Isabel giggles again.

"I think he likes you," he says.

I think I like him.

"So, that went well," Remington says when I descend the stairs after putting Isabel down for a nap and changing my yogurt-splattered blouse.

"Yes, thank you for that." I thumb behind me.

We speak at the same time.

"I—"

"You—"

He walks over, standing in front of me with a gaze that makes me swallow. It might be my unruly imagination, but his eyes look heated. When he lifts his hand and reaches for me, I rear back.

"W-what are you doing?" I know I am in no position to be incredulous after my dirty thoughts, but this is too much. Too forward. Too close.

My lashes flutter, and my belly flips. It's been years since an attractive man was this close to me. A wistful thread tugs at my heart.

His smile is disarming. "You have a little something…"

I'm frozen as he glides his fingers through a lock of my hair. His movements are tender, and his stare is intense. All air leaves my chest, and a bullet of desire shoots through me.

I don't know if a man has had this much effect on me before. Not even when I was in bed with Brad.

I almost lean into Remington, but he holds up a gunk of the white viscous shit, reminiscent of the semen scene in Something About Mary.

I'm thoroughly mortified. "Oh, thanks." It comes out a bit too breathy for my liking. I pride myself on being unflappable, but this situation makes me a nervous chicken, flapping and losing feathers all over the damn place.

Not to mention, I've violated this man in my mind every which way since he's been here. If he could read my thoughts, he'd be filing a restraining order against my vagina, stat.

As far as nannies go, I'm sure he's good. He's from Child Care Connection, after all, and Kiara runs a top-notch organization. But there are other nannies out there, right? Ones I won't be attracted to. Ones that won't cause so much trouble.

I need to make him go. It's a bit heartbreaking, but it's the right thing to do.

"Listen, Remington—"

"Remi," he interjects. "Please, call me Remi. Remington makes me feel old." He makes a face.

If *he* feels old, what the hell am I?

I want to say, *Impossible*, but I continue on with my original thought. "I'm sure you're great and all. It's just that I assumed the agency was going to send me someone with more experience."

His lips thin with the tone of his voice. "I *am* experienced. I've read your file and agreed to your list of requirements."

"How long have you been with Child Care Connection?" I ask point-blank because life experience has taught me to spot bullshit from a mile away. If there's probable cause to let him go, I'm doing it. I have no need for this kind of emotional turmoil on top of everything else I'm dealing with.

"Almost two years. But before that, I—"

"Have you nannied many toddler girls?" Rapid fire is the only way I work. *Facts, kid. Just give me the facts.*

"Not many, but I've been volunteering with Big Brother for six years and work with children of all ages."

"I'll take that as a no. Tell me something, *Remi*, what do you know about potty training?"

His cheeks turn a beautiful shade of white panic. I've got him where I want him, squirming like a worm under a magnifying glass. Though, it doesn't feel as sweet as I thought it would. It's as unsatisfying as a salad when I'm craving a steak. The victory tastes pretty sour.

"I'll tell the agency that you were very professional but that we are not a good fit. Thank you for coming today." I walk over to the front door of my brownstone and swing it wide open, hoping he takes the hint before this gets any more awkward.

Remington's face is painted in irritation as he strides towards the door. "Good luck finding someone who meets all of your unspoken expectations, ma'am." He smirks his way past me and out of our life.

His acute observation slices like a papercut, and the word "ma'am" pours acid on the wound. It takes everything in me to not slam the door.

Chapter 2

Crow Feathers and Latte Foam

Mae

My child alarm sounds at 5am. I groan. It's a lot earlier than normal. When I pick up my daughter for a kiss, I know why—her cheeks are burning.

Shit. She has a fever.

An important meeting with our investors is tomorrow, and I need to prepare for it. I'm proposing the changes that need to take place in order to set ourselves up for a lucrative partnership with a conglomerate. If all goes well, jobs will be secured and everyone will get paid handsomely. If the company's taken care of, so are its financial insecurities. It's not dire, but growing up with nothing leaves a nugget of desperation in the back of my mind. All it takes is one wrong move, and I could lose our employees, along with what little time I have with my daughter. *She'll lose, most of all.*

I want to be able to take a step back and make beautiful memories with Isabel, for her to have the charmed childhood I never had. But mostly, I want to have the freedom to be there for her whenever she needs me.

Isabel's sweaty, fussy, and squirmy in my arms. I pull her into my chest, resting her head on my shoulder. My heart knows she needs me home today, but my head is yelling at me to prepare for the conference so that I don't have to make these gut-wrenching choices in the future. I'm the only one who can do it. I leave the art to Jay, but I won't put the burden of this company on anyone else until Ever Heart is secure. People are depending on me to nail this presentation.

It's just one day, isn't it?

One day among a list of many that all add up to neglect. Neglected kids grow up to have behavioral problems, teen self-esteem issues, and trouble forming trusting relationships as adults. I know because I've experienced it. What if she ends up a lonely workaholic like me and like my mother before me?

A rope of regret constricts my neck.

Bouncing my baby in my arms, I hum a lullaby, trying to ease her suffering and mine. Her molars are breaking through, so I run downstairs to the freezer and find her a teether to chew on. I strip her down to her diaper to release the heat from her skin. By the time I get her soothed and settled in her Pack 'n Play, her cheeks have cooled. I take her temperature to be sure, and then it's time to get ready for work.

I'm in the shower when it hits me. The guilt. The grief and the shame.

What am I doing? I'm relieved that my child feels better, but not for the right reasons. I'm relieved because now that she isn't running a fever, I can drop her off at daycare. Pain, sharp and swift, slices my chest.

Did my mother feel this way about me? I used to get so upset when she chose her work over me, but now I realize it's not a choice. It's survival. My father left us with nothing, so she had to pick up the pieces and create a life for us.

It doesn't ease the resentment, though. How ironic is it that I became everything I didn't want to be?

Shame is a dangerous friend. My daughter deserves better than what I'm giving her. She needs to be nurtured with one-on-one attention.

As soon as I step out of the shower, I call Child Care Connection. I still haven't heard back from the agency about finding us a better fit. An unattractive and older better fit.

"This is Kiara, can I help you?"

Oh, good. Just the person I need to talk to. "Hi, yes. This is Miranda Keller. I called a few days ago about finding a replacement nanny and haven't heard anything back. I need someone as soon as possible."

"We've been trying to find a good placement for you, but I'm afraid male child caregivers are few and far between. Remington was the best fit, but since it didn't work out, I'm afraid I need more time." Her voice is polite and full of that customer-service persona.

"I don't have that kind of time," I bite out with clenched teeth. Taking a grounding breath, I try again. "Do you have any connections with other companies that might have what I need?" My voice goes reedy as if I'm asking for something illicit.

Kiara's tone cools. "We are the best agency, Miranda. Our placements are matched perfectly, and our charges get into the most prestigious preschools Chicago has to offer. I don't place caregivers at random. *You* may check with other agencies. But I can assure you, you won't find what you're looking for."

I didn't plan on eating crow for breakfast, but she's right. I've spent countless hours researching and meeting with child care agencies. CCC *is* the best.

I pace the bathroom half naked, leaving drops of water everywhere. "Is Remmington Arison still available?" I'm chewing on my thumbnail because I really want her to say no. As much as I want her to say yes.

"I thought he wasn't a good fit."

I wring out my strawberry-blonde hair with one hand. "I... He was great. Really, he was. It's just, he's..."

"Young?" Kiara offers with a smile in her voice. Yeah, she knows what's up.

"Yes. He seemed too young, and I'm not quite sure of his dependability," I confess with lies because I don't add, *and I'm a perverted lecher, who can't keep her thoughts about him clean.*

"Ms. Keller, let me restate. I do *not* place caregivers haphazardly. Remi is the perfect fit. Young but experienced with all ages and practiced in child psychology. I see his age as a benefit as he will be taking care of an active toddler who needs a lot of physical play and activities."

Crap. I didn't think of it that way.

"You're in luck—he's available immediately. I can send him over right away, but it's your call."

Crow feathers really dry out the mouth.

Isabel's whimpers float over the baby monitor, and they almost sound like, "Please Mommy". In the short time they spent together, she bonded with him. Kiara is right—he is a great fit. If only I can keep my wits about me.

It's not as if I'm going to see him much, right? A little bit in the morning and then he'll go off on his merry way in the evening, and I will be chaste and professional. I can do that.

I note my weary green eyes in the mirror and give in. "Send him as soon as possible, thank you."

I hope I'm not making a mistake.

"I mean, I don't know what they want from us, Jay. We've put the contract together to their specifications. We have our best team on their branding. Why is Deximo still dragging their feet?" I pace my office and let out a frustrated breath.

"Mae, these things take time. Why are you getting so stressed over one potential deal?"

"Because we need it. We have employees depending on us. We can't lose our momentum." If we do, my house, Isabel's private preschool, and the fancy nanny I'm hiring go with it. I won't sit idly by while laying off dozens of employees. It's not right. I'll sacrifice what I can before it comes to that.

"We won't." My best friend steps up to me and places their hands on my shoulders, stopping me from wearing a path in the carpet. "We've got a few good ones in the works. And the accounts we *do* have love us. They certainly aren't going anywhere." When I give them a glum face, they add, "It's a marathon, Mae, not a sprint."

Jay's always been the laid-back one of this partnership. Donning gold hoop earrings, a full beard, and a silk kimono, they're also the talented artist driving Ever Heart Digital to the top tier in the industry. Babies and dogs love them. Hell, the whole company loves them. When an employee wants something, they go to Jay. When they have a grievance, they go to Jay. When they want to pass a message onto me, they go through Jay.

I call it "good cop, bad cop". Jay calls it Beauty and the Beast. I'm the beast in this scenario.

At 6'2" and two-hundred and 50 pounds, their size should be intimidating, but everyone knows they're a big teddy bear.

Jay opens their arms. "Come to me, mija." Whenever they call me "dear", my anxiety loosens.

My shoulders fall with the tension in my chest. I can't help the wry grin that cracks my worried face. Jay has always been like this. They're the peacemaker, the calm in the storm, and my rock. They're also the most innovative digital creator in the Midwest.

Walking over to my best friend, I slump on their chest, their spicy cologne tickling my nose and comforting me. In a world where children are taught to raise themselves, I've always had Jay to help me along. There were many nights I went to my best friend's house after school.

When I was ten, Jay brought me home like a stray puppy. Their family adopted me on the spot and have been there for me ever since. Sometimes, I wouldn't see my mom for days. She never questioned where I was, and I'm not sure she even cared.

"Come to dinner on Sunday. Let the family love up on that baby of ours."

I give them a stink eye. Ever since Jay helped deliver Isabel, they've claimed her. They've been there for us, unwavering and unconditional, and have gotten me through some of the worst moments of my life.

I peer up at them. "Tres leches?"

"You know it."

"Okay, I'll think about it."

Jay ruffles my perfectly coiffed hair, and I smack their hand with a chuckle. They know I'll be there—Mamma M's cooking is the best.

When there's a knock on my door, Jay and I share a look. No one dares approach my office unless they absolutely have to. Jay's the "people person" in this company, whereas I have no bark but my bite can be nasty. My resting bitch face isn't just for show.

The door opens and my assistant, Elliot, advances a hesitant half-step into my office but no more than that. "I'm sorry, Ms. Keller, but Remington Arison is here for you."

That was fast.

Tall, Dark, and a Killer Smile waltzes into the room like he owns the place.

I bristle. This kid is too cocky for his own good.

"Oh my, what do we have here?" Jay sizes up the nanny.

I palm my forehead. I'm never going to live this down. The nanny is hot—there's no denying it—but now, I'm going to have to hear about it from my best friend putting all kinds of shit in my head. I don't need any further inappropriate thoughts about Remi.

"Are you sure you're here for *her*?" Jay crosses an arm over their chest while the other rests on it, pensively smoothing their beard. "She's not normally ... keen on visitors. We could—"

"Jay, this is Remington, Isabel's *nanny*." Flinging my hand towards Remi, I cut Jay off before their mouth gets away from them and embarrasses me.

"Oh, you don't say?" Jay circles the poor kid as Elliot fidgets by the threshold, waiting for an out.

Remington winks at Jay. *Winks!*

I roll my eyes because it's all a fucking scam. I know all about guys like him. Charmers. Lady lovers. Womanizers.

Con men.

Hell, I almost married one.

The only good thing that ever came from my last relationship is Isabel. Brad was just as charismatic as Remi. All sweet smiles and twinkling irises, disguising what he really was—a philandering coward. When things got complicated, he bailed, leaving me—*us*—high and dry. Regardless of what that asshole put me through, I wouldn't trade her for the world.

I'm losing control of the room, which is unacceptable in my position. This man-boy needs to see me as an authority. I call the shots, not him.

I clear my throat obnoxiously. "Jay, I have some business with Remington, if you don't mind." I gesture to the door.

"I bet you do." Jay whistles.

I almost break my face with a laugh. They're so dramatic.

Elliot turns to leave.

"Mr. Hansley," I call out.

My assistant swallows and turns back to me.

"Call Deximo and see if there is anything else they need. I need third-quarter projections by noon. My dry-cleaning is ready to be picked up, so please have it at the house by three. And some caffeine would be great."

Elliot nods and goes to close the door on his way out.

I stop him. "Keep it open." My tone leaves no room for questioning. "Please, have a seat." I point Remington to the chair in front of my desk as I sit behind it, putting a physical barrier between me and the ovary charmer.

"I was surprised to get a call back from you. I thought I wasn't 'a good fit'." The nanny uses air quotes like a child.

That's because he is.

I balk and harden my features. "Let's get something straight. While I may be a client of Child Care Connection, I'm technically your employer." I raise an eyebrow. "You do not get to question me or my motives."

The nanny takes a sharp inhale, sucking in his lips, but stays silent.

"I need a caregiver for my child, and Kiara thinks you're a perfect fit. Who am I to argue?"

Clearing his throat, Remington shifts uncomfortably in his seat. *Good.* He opens his mouth as if he wants to say something, but my question was rhetorical.

I don't need a smartass answer from him, so I lean in and speak before he can. "My daughter is my world. Everything I do is for her." There is a strong note of authority in my voice. He needs to understand who is in charge here. "If you screw up, you won't only lose your job— you'll lose your legs and ability to procreate. Are we clear?"

His pretty eyes widen as he clears his throat and crosses his legs. "Crystal, ma'am."

That fucking word.

Elliot comes in with the magic elixir that is organic King's Reserve Kona Espresso flown in straight from the island and fluffed in a latte. "Thank you." I give him what I hope is a genuine smile and not a grimace, then dive, nose first, into my cup. That initial sip is always the best, and I can't help the little moan that slips out when I swallow.

My moment of grounding is over, and I'm back to business. "One more thing." I grit my teeth. "Never are you to call me 'ma'am' again. Is that clear?"

This amuses him, but he bites his cheek to hide his stupid smirk.

"Something funny, Mr. Arison?"

A bright grin breaks out on his face, revealing not one but two dimples. It's disarming.

I bite my lip to contain my visceral reaction. A swoony sigh will not help the situation.

His gaze locks on mine as he licks his full, pillowy mouth, and I clench my molars to keep my jaw from relaxing. The dew his tongue left behind calls to me like a Cabernet after a shitty day. *Just one sip wouldn't be so bad, would it?* Umber eyes fill with mirth the longer I stare, and I'm caught in some kind of daze. He's a work of art to be admired. A hot, trendy piece I can't afford.

"You just—"

Elliot's voice breaks through my intercom, yanking me back into reality. "Ms. Keller, Corissa Fawlen is on the line."

Perfect diversion.

Composing myself, I stack my walls higher. I slide over the thick binder I prepared for the nanny, outlining Isabel's day minute by minute and all the other expectations a mother would have for her child's caregiver.

"Please familiarize yourself with this." Pointing to the binder in his hands, I add, "You'll also have academic standards to teach to prepare her for preschool next year."

He thumbs the hundred or so pages without looking back at me.

I lose some patience. "Anyway, you'll find the keys and the code to the alarm in there. I expect you to be at the house at 7am to get Isabel ready for the day. My daughter is my first priority and, therefore, yours." Pinning him with a glare, I reiterate, "One small mishap, Remington. It only takes one."

He stands to his full height before leaning over my desk to grab the items, nailing me with a stare. "For what it's worth, I take my role and my charges very seriously." Warm umber burns into me. I swear my cheeks flame. "I can also pick up your dry-cleaning, grocery shop, and cook."

Well, this is a pleasant surprise. Kiara didn't tell me he could cook, which is awesome because I fucking hate it.

"You'll find that I'm quite hands-on." He smirks as if he can't help his innuendo.

I stiffen my spine to stave off the shudder my body wants to release. Giving him a smirk of my own, I pick up the line. "We'll see about that." *Back to business.* "Isabel has been attending Building Blocks Nursery School since she was six months old. She will continue to attend morning sessions on Tuesdays and Thursdays. You'll have those mornings off unless she is sick."

Before he can utter another raspy syllable, I let the phone call through and swivel around to face the window, effectively dismissing the nanny. When I hear the door click shut, I hold my chest and exhale in relief.

"This is Miranda," I greet with a genuine smile. I like Corissa and working with Fawlen Studios. They are one of our favorite clients.

"Hey," she greets, matching my enthusiasm. "I just wanted to personally invite you to our annual customer appreciation picnic. We missed you last year."

I couldn't go because Isabel was sick. Not that I had a sitter on standby, anyway. "Yeah, I'm sorry about that. I have a toddler, and I can't always find a babysitter."

"How did I not know this? Of course, bring her with you. It's a family event. There will be games and face painting." Her voice is coated with excitement. "Please come, I never get to catch up with you outside of work."

My smile is wistful. Corissa is authentic and funny, and exactly the kind of person I would love to hang out with if I had the time. "I know. I promise I'll try."

"Awesome, I'll send the details to your assistant. I swear it's a good time."

A small laugh escapes me. "I don't doubt it. See you soon."

When the call ends, I set the phone down and massage the back of my neck.

When I turn around, I groan at the sight before me.

Jay and their technicolor dream coat are standing there, judging. "You've been holding out on me, baby girl. Why didn't you tell me the nanny—who's actually a manny, by the way—was so hot you could fry an egg with extra crispy bacon on his skin in the middle of a Chicago winter?"

I palm my head for the second time today, and it's not even lunch yet. "I'm not holding out on you. I told you I was hiring a nanny."

"Yeah, but you left out the part where he looks like Enrique Iglesias's hotter younger brother."

"That's because I hadn't noticed." Except I have but if I say it out loud, that makes it real. And now that they've mentioned the Iglesias semblance, it's all I see.

"Bullshit. You may be frigid, but you're not dead."

I bristle, folding my arms over my chest.

My friend's eyebrows raise in a challenging stare.

I deflect with humor, pretending to wipe a tear from my eye. "You're always so sweet to me."

"I know. While you're wiping your eyes, you might want to catch your nose too. There's a little something there."

Mortified, I pull my compact out and shove it in my face. Sure enough, I have a big ring of latte foam on my nose. Now I know why Remington was amused.

"*Crap.* I need him to take me seriously, and he won't do that if I look like a doofus every time I see him." The other day with the yogurt hair, and today with the latte nose.

Jay walks towards my desk, hands perched on their hips. "Sure, you want him to take you seriously. Mm-hmm. It has nothing to do with the fact that he's a hot manny."

"He is not *hot*."

Jay crosses their arms. "Careful with the lies, Mars Bars. You don't want to end up with a nose the size of a Chicago skyscraper."

We have a stare-off with them tapping an impatient toe on the carpet.

A long sigh deflates my chest. "Okay. I admit he's a good-looking kid, but I'm way too old for him and it's inappropriate to objectify him. I don't need a harassment suit on my hands. Besides, he's here for Isabel and that is our first priority."

Jay rears back with their hand on their sternum. "Oww, your nose just stabbed me in the chest. You can fool yourself, but you'll never fool me. I've been your soulmate since we were ten. I've seen it all." With a smirk, their eyes flitter about me. "The fact that you used the word "our" tells me you've been thinking about the hot manny more than you want to admit."

My lip curls. They are too damn perceptive for my own good.

Jay flings their arms out in dramatics, showing off their impressive bell sleeves. "That's okay. Your indiscretion is safe with me. I am the Alcatraz of secrets."

I snort. "Yeah, until someone bribes you with Firecakes Donuts. Don't forget I know all about you too, *Jayden*."

"Gasp. You know the love and care they put into those donuts is special and rare. I can hardly be blamed for it." They sniff. "Anyway, it's nice seeing that someone other than *moi* can get under that steel armor you wear. He might kill you with his sword, but what a way to go."

I bark a laugh, then sober. I haven't been this rattled since the day I found out my baby daddy was an absolute piece of shit. Then, I had my rage to keep me straight.

The new nanny gets under my skin by his mere presence. It's annoying but mostly frustrating, with no real reason underneath. Just my woefully inappropriate attraction. *He* hasn't done anything wrong, except having a face that belongs on the cover of a man-scout magazine and an amiable personality.

I think I might be in some trouble.

Chapter 3

Belgium Waffles and Warm Maple Syrup

Mae

MY EYES BLINK OPEN, sun rays beaming in through the blinds piercing them, so I slam my lids shut again.

Sunlight? The sun's up?

Shit. Isabel. I check the baby monitor screen, but it's quiet, and the lump next to Mr. Snuffles tells me she's still sleeping.

Odd. She usually wakes up before the sun. Something's wrong.

Flinging the covers off, I jump out of bed and scurry down the hall to her room. There's a smokey smell, which amps my alarm.

Is the house on fire? Where is the fire alarm?

I don't see red locks peeking out from under the lump of blankets. "Isabel!" Did she climb out of her crib? I'd be proud of her if I wasn't so terrified.

The house is burning and my daughter is gone, which makes me think she got into something. Cue the guilt and self-flogging. It's my fault this is happening right now. I'm negligent and scatter-brained because there are just too many tabs open in my mind.

With my heart pounding through my rib cage, I run down the stairs, anticipating smoke filling up the foyer and family room. However, all is clear.

The smell is stronger down here, but it's smokey *and* savory, making my mouth water.

What has she gotten into? Is she okay? Did she stick something into the electrical socket? Oh God, is she being electrocuted?

My pace quickens, and like a blood hound, I follow my nose. Which leads me to the kitchen and stops me in my tracks.

Isabel is sitting in her highchair, happily eating a mashed banana.

She's okay. Tension releases its grip on my lungs.

When I turn towards the other side of the room, my salivating mouth dries. The sight before me is better than any dream I've ever conjured. Someone is cooking breakfast on the stove.

No, not just someone.

Him. The hot manny.

Get it together, woman.

He's all lean muscle in low slung jeans hugging his plump ass perfectly. A dishtowel is hanging off of his back pocket, and I've never wanted to be an inanimate object as much in my life. The thin white Henley he's wearing is stretched out over the planes and ridges of his back.

He runs his long fingers through his wavy sable hair before turning his neck towards me with his signature toothy grin. "Good morning, Ms. Keller. How did you sleep?"

I'm so taken off guard I can't form words. My mouth works in all directions, but only spit drools at the cause of the smell—eggs with extra crispy bacon sizzling away on the skillet.

Either Jay is manifesting for me or I'm in the twilight zone. But I get to eat, so I'm all in.

"Ms. Keller, is something wrong?"

"Oh. Um, no. I just forgot you were, like, starting today and ... stuff." Oh my God, why am I sounding like a teenager from the Valley? I do not use "like" and "stuff" to describe things. "Coffee?"

He wipes his hands. "I'll put it on now. I didn't want it to get cold."

I watch in amazement when he proceeds to make me a French press. I didn't even know I had a carafe for that.

"Should be done in about four minutes. Sit, and I'll serve you breakfast."

He's so natural in the kitchen. It's almost as if he belongs there.

"I—" I bite my lip, abandoning the urge to speak to him. I'm rattled, and nothing good will come out of my mouth in this state. He's Isabel's nanny, not my housemaid.

My daughter gives me a cheesy grin as I walk towards her. She looks so cute, rumpled and sleepy. Isabel holds out a squashed banana in her hand to me. She loves to share. *My perfect girl.* And she's absolutely content. All that worry was unnecessary.

I release a breath, pretend to eat her offering and then proceed to be the cookie monster, *nom-nom*ing up her arm to her cheek. Her giggles are contagious, and for the first time in a long time, I'm not rushed. I can take this little moment to be playful with my daughter.

My chest aches when I realize I haven't had the chance to play with her in a while. If I miss it, I can't even imagine what she feels.

Only, I can. Because I've been in her shoes. I always wanted little moments like this with my own mom yet never got them.

Am I doing the same thing to Isabel? Not giving her enough quality time? Always too busy to stop and do the little things that brighten her day?

My heart twists.

Remi's soft voice pulls me from my musings. "I made eggs and bacon, but there are waffles too."

I pinch my arm because I'm sure I'm still dreaming. In a daze, I slump in the dining chair. "You made waffles too?

"Yeah, I wasn't sure what you liked. I got fresh fruit from the market on the way home from your office yesterday too."

Remington—formerly the hot nanny, now known as the scorching panty-melter—sets a full plate of breakfast in front of me, along with my French press coffee and a gorgeous platter of fruit. With a cute lopsided smile, he sets a silver sauce boat next to my plate. "Can't have waffles without warm maple syrup."

I blink several times. *No, I guess not.*

After he's done with me, he brings Isabel a small portion of scrambled eggs and waffles. She squeals with delight.

"What time did you get here?"

"A little before six. I know you said seven, but I wasn't sure of Isabel's routine and I wanted to get the lay of the land, so to speak." He makes a silly face and plays with something on Isabel's tray. She peels with giggles. "I hope you don't mind that I got her as I heard her fuss. I thought you might want to sleep in a little."

Oh. My. Goddess.

I haven't had a decent sleep in two years. It's like I'm in a daze or a really beautiful daydream. Whatever it is, I never want it to end.

"Oh, thanks." Taking a sip of coffee to hide my bewildered state, I slide my eyes shut and moan as soon as rich notes of caramel and chocolate hit my tongue. "This is the best cup of coffee I've ever had." It's not a lie.

I take a bite of waffle—freaking Belgium. Which elicits another obnoxious groan.

He clears his throat. "Glad you like it." Dark umber eyes turn shy, and he lowers his face to hide a small smile.

His bashfulness does something to me and—my God—I want to crawl over this table and kiss his red cheeks. I shove a forkful of eggs in my mouth instead.

"Remington, this is too much. It's really not necessary. I don't expect you to cook or wait on me." I shake my head. "It's much appreciated, but—"

"I like cooking, and I want to." He shrugs a shoulder before giving Isabel some strawberries.

I almost fall over. How do three little words light me up from within? *He wants to.* Not "has to". Not "obligated to". *Wants. To.*

First, I fired him. Then, I was terse when he came back. Yet he's here, cheery as can be.

The ice around my heart thaws a bit. Maybe he's not callous under that prince-charming exterior. His only responsibility is Isabel, and yet he considered me when making breakfast.

Usually, my mornings are a rush of activity with one goal in mind—get Isabel to daycare and then to work on time. This morning is relaxed and stress-free.

"Look, I'm really sorry I was abrupt with you before. It's only day one, and you've impressed me. Which is a really hard thing to do." Because my standards are unreasonably high.

"No apologies necessary. You were concerned for your daughter. Wanted her to have the best." His eyes volley between me and Isabel eating the squished food in her hand.

She offers it to him. The gross, slobbery food that I pretend to eat, he actually chews and makes delightful faces as if it's the best thing he's ever tasted. With every bite he takes from her hand, a confident glint builds in her eye and her legs kick in excitement. He's been with her for less than an hour, and they've already built a rapport.

Tears burn in the back of my eyes. This is exactly what I wanted, and yet it's so much more. His interactions with her ... are magical.

Remington turns to me, catching my stare. "I understand your concerns and admire you for it. A lot of people, especially when stressed, just want to hand the kid off to the first person who shows up. And I don't find fault in that. I don't have to be a parent to know that raising children is difficult. But you're willing to sacrifice for your child, and that's what a parent should do." The conviction in his voice tells me he's seen some shit. "I know you've been on your own, but I'm here now and you don't have to do it all alone anymore."

For the first time since I had Isabel, I feel seen. It's as if my head keeps dipping underwater and I'm on the brink of drowning, but Remi just threw me a life jacket and rope. When I breach the surface of all the things that keep me under, I take a full, deep breath.

That's when I know I'm a goner. The melting ice around my heart turns into complete global warming. It takes everything in me to sit quietly and eat when all I want to do is hug the crap out of him.

"Thanks." My voice is small because I'm still trying to figure out his angle. No one is this passionate about their job. Are they?

I guess I am and I certainly know Jay is, but it's our company. We're steering the ship, but it's on me if it sinks or sails.

"Hey, I wanted to know if you need me on the weekends," Remington says, taking me off guard.

This whole morning has me surprised.

"I was under the impression that those are your days off unless by special request."

"That's how it is in the contract, but I don't mind if you need me on the weekend. I do have a thing on Sundays, but I'm free most Saturdays."

"Really? You're a young guy. I'm sure you have a life outside of work." This is just an innocent observation. I am not fishing. I'm not. Though, I suppose I wonder what this "thing" on Sundays is.

"When you love your job, your job *is* your life."

I'm about to protest when he raises an eyebrow at me. *Touché, Hot Manny. Touché.*

When a foul smell hits my nostrils, I know my easy morning has ended. "Smells like someone needs a diaper change." I go to stand.

Remi stops me. "Finish your breakfast. I can change Isabel. Me and poopy diapers are BFFs."

I make a face because she's my whole heart and it still makes me gag sometimes.

"Yeah, that was a stretch, but seriously" — he gives me an earnest look — "I got this."

When I get up to bring my plate to the sink, he tells me he'll get it later. I don't want to let him because I can do it myself, but his words echo in the back of my mind. *"You don't have to do it alone anymore."*

I decide to let go of the need to complete this small task. Easier said than done because just leaving my mess feels wrong. I hold my plate and hover over the sink as my head yells at me to wash the damn thing and tidy the kitchen before I go to work. The longer the dish sits, the harder it will be to scrub clean later.

This isn't about a dirty dish at all. It's about me needing to have micro control over every aspect of my life. Can't I let it go just this once? Could I trust someone I barely know to take care of it for me? The uncertainty weighs heavy on my shoulders, and I vacillate. It's aggravating.

I've always been so self-aware. Decisive. In control. But this is why I hired a nanny. To make my life a little easier. Make me more efficient.

As it turns out, being selfish and letting someone else do my work isn't without effort.

"Ms. Keller, do you need something else?" Remi's question breaks me out of the intense argument in my head.

Setting the plate in the sink, I will my fingers to leave it and my feet to move out of the room. "No, I'm just going to get changed." I shuffle past without looking him in the eye.

He has me so flustered it's uncomfortable. Letting go of that foreign feeling, I head to my ensuite for a shower. I feel like I'm missing something because my arms are empty. Usually, I have Isabel with me for my morning routine.

I catch my reflection in the mirror and want to drop dead. *Oh, for the love of Saint Lilith.*

In all my spazzy surprise this morning, I didn't realize I was still in my pajamas. I went for absolute comfort last night—Jay's old threadbare t-shirt donning a humanoid hot dog with the phrase: *It's not a party until the wiener comes out.* Rounding out the "I've given up" vibe perfectly are a pair of sweatpants with little Jay heads all over them.

"So you're not so lonely in bed," they said when they gave them to me on my birthday.

I smack my head. If this is ever going to work, Remi has to see me as a professional. There can be no casual encounters between us. He has a job to do, so I can do mine.

"Wee wee wee, all the way home," echoes through the baby monitor.

Curious, I pick up the device and watch Remington changing Isabel's poopy diaper like it's his favorite job ever, singing *This Little Piggy*, wiggling each of her toes. All the while my daughter mimics him, having the best time. Usually, she fights me and I get frustrated. I don't mean to—I'm just so exhausted sometimes.

"What a pretty voice," he praises her effort.

Watching the two of them sing happily does something to my chest that makes it achy and hard to breathe.

I feel like I've finally done something right by my baby. My little girl deserves the best of everything, and Kiara was right—he's the best fit for us. I mean, *her*. The only reason he's here is for her. Isabel is his only responsibility.

The sooner we both realize that, the better.

"As you can see by the numbers projected, when Deximo approves the proposal it will be lucrative, putting Ever Heart on the map with the biggest marketing companies and securing your investment for years to come." And a much needed step-back for me. "We have our best team on this." I stalk around the meeting room on four-inch stilettos and an air of superiority.

Every single eye is on me. Every ear listening to the words I utter.

"You said 'when'," Robert Pingman—our biggest investor slash pain in the ass—pipes up at the far end of the room.

Startled, I turn towards him. "That's right. When Deximo approves the proposal. Which they will."

"But they haven't yet," he points out, and the room breaks into dissenting murmurs.

A sure sign I'm losing control, and I absolutely cannot.

"Mr. Pingman, I assure you the proposal *will* go through."

"Until the ink has dried on the contract, I'm going to have to consider pulling out. Ever Heart missed last quarter's projected earnings by five percent."

"But—"

"No buts, Ms. Keller. Your team is dropping the ball. You've been distracted lately. Maybe your team should think about finding a stronger leader. Someone that doesn't have as many ... obligations. Maybe then, I'll have more confidence in the direction Ever Heart is going."

Fury, mortification, shame, and resentment fall over me like molten lava, and I'm ready to spew fire. I know what he's implying, and it's complete, utter bullshit. If I were a man, he wouldn't be inferring anything, but because he knows of my single-mother status, he thinks he's justified in using it against me in a conference with other men. *Like-minded* men.

"I would highly advise you to watch what you are implying, Robert. You have witnesses." A hawk flies past the window, and I imagine its sharp beak impaling Pingman's carotid. The thought tempers my anger, marginally.

"Whatever I'm implying, Keller, is irrelevant. You need *me* more than I need this fledgling company. When it's my money on the line, I pay very close attention to how it's handled."

I'm going to wrap my manicured nails around his saggy scrotum and squeeze until his balls pop out. Then, I'm going to feed them to him and make everyone watch. This is what happens when you mess with me. My gender will always be my strength, no matter what this imbecile thinks.

Everyone's eyes ping-pong between me and Robert, and I'm determined to have the last word.

"M-Ms. Keller?" The heavy glass door swings open presenting a nerve-wracked Elliot and a cocky manny.

In his Henley and jeans, Remi sticks out like a gorgeous thumb amidst the stuffy suits in the room. He rolls Isabel's stroller in, popping a wheelie like they are motocross racing. They look like best friends, making faces and laughing at each other.

I stand frozen in place because if I allow myself to move, I'll break down. *What does he think he's doing?*

"Mama!" Isabel screeches with all the enthusiasm of a kid high on ice cream.

Robert's creased face turns smug, and all of my aggravation has just found its target.

"Mr. Arison." My bark is sharper than I mean it to be, but I'm freaking out because everyone is watching. "I'll speak to you outside."

Concern etches his features, but he gives me a slight nod before heading back out the door.

Brushing invisible lint off my shoulder, I address the situation. "We're done here. Be on standby when that proposal goes through." I raise my eyebrow at numbnuts Pingman. "Because it will happen at any moment."

Strutting out of the room, I keep my back and head straight. I will not break.

"Mi niña pequeña!" Jay picks up Isabel in a full swing.

She screams in delight.

The conference room is a giant fish bowl with glass on three sides, clear enough that I catch everyone's eyes whipping to the door I just exited. This is getting out of hand.

"Jay, bring her to your office." Remington starts to follow, but I stop him. "Not you." Freezing, he turns back to me. "She's in good hands with them." I flick my finger between us. "We need to get a few things straight first."

Jay's too busy giving Isabel belly raspberries to notice my ire. They never take it seriously anyway, and that's okay. Remi, however, needs to know his place. And it's not here.

"Is Isabel sick?" It's evident in my tone that the question is rhetorical.

He cups the back of his neck and twists. "No."

"Is she too much for you to handle?"

Squaring his shoulders, he clenches his jaw. The first sign of irritation he's ever shown. "Not at all. She's amazing."

I almost soften at the warmth in his eyes, but I remember who's watching, so I keep up my steely resolve. "Then why are you here, interrupting a very important meeting?" I rest my fists on my hips.

"I didn't realize bringing your child to see you at work would be an issue."

"That's the problem. You can't just insert your overzealous personality every-where you go. Especially here." Pointing to the window of the meeting room, I ask, "How many women do you see in there?"

His brow furrows, but he answers anyway. "None." He shrugs. "One, if including you."

"How many men?"

Remi mouths numbers to himself. "Ten."

"Wonderful, you know how to count. So as you can see, I'm outnumbered there. Ten dominant assholes that will cut me off mid-sentence. That do not have a care or responsibility outside of their occupation." My voice goes deadly low. "That will use my motherhood as a strike against me." I walk right up to him and burn him with a scathing stare. "I need them to be confident in my leadership. In my dedication to this company." I point a finger right in his face. "I won't allow anyone to undermine my position. Do you understand my role in this company, Remington?"

He rears back as if I slapped him. "I—"

"I'm not finished. Do you think their nannies bring their children to see them at the office?"

His pretty mouth stays shut. *Good boy.*

"I suppose not. But because I'm a female, you thought it would be a great idea to bring my child here. Go as far as interrupt a conference I'm leading."

He heaves a breath and starts. "Elliot—"

"Is not your boss. *I* am." I shoulder past him to get back to business. "Any surprises you may have in the future, you run them by me. Do you understand?"

He salutes me. "Yes, ma'am."

I could strangle him for that.

"Are we done here?" There is no inflection in his voice. It's like he's unflappable.

What gave it away, the view of my back? "Yes, we most certainly are."

"Great, I'll leave you to it, *Queeny.*" I whirl around, ready for full-on combat. "But you might want to wipe off the lipstick all over your teeth first. Wouldn't want those men in there thinking you were all 'distracted' out here" — he can't help but fuel the fire when he smirks and adds — "with me." Walking away, he throws me a wink.

Bastard got the last word.

And now, of course, I'm thinking of ways he *could* distract me.

Standing there, chest heaving, I don't know if I want to kill him or hump him. He never reacts the way I want him to. It's like he doesn't take anything seriously.

Correction, he's another man who doesn't take *me* seriously. And I can't rattle him like he does me. This whole fucking thing is beyond frustrating.

The irksome feeling follows me as I head back to my office. I fall into my chair like I've been carrying fifty-pound kettlebells around all day, secretly wishing Remi was still here with my girl. I just want a moment to smell and cuddle her. She grounds me. Warms my heart. Makes me remember I'm not a machine. My little gift.

A gift you didn't acknowledge. Couldn't even muster a small kiss before you kicked them out. The thought cuts me deep.

I'm so wrought with anxiety over what that douchebag Robert was saying. If we lose him it will hurt, but we'll be okay if the others stay. I don't need for the other investors to see my maternal side and look at me differently. I've witnessed it in other companies. As soon as a woman has a child, she is no longer considered an asset. She's labeled as a liability because, in their eyes, she'll no longer put the company first. It's not overtly apparent, but I'm not dumb enough to think it isn't discussed in the good ol' boys club behind closed doors and puffed cigars. Pingman's comment only proves my point.

I scrub my face, trying to rid it of the degradation that asshole slung at me. The mouth-watering, lemony aroma of hummus and grape leaves greets me at my desk. I didn't have time to put in a request for lunch. If I want to be a better person, I have to improve my attitude. Be nicer.

I press the intercom. "Thank you for lunch, Elliot. That was really nice of you. I'm famished." The line crackles with silence. "Elliot?"

"Um, it wasn't from me, Ms. Keller."

"From Jay?" They're the only other person I can think of that knows my favorite Mediterranean place.

"No, ma'am. Remington called earlier, said he was meeting you for lunch, and asked if I knew your preference."

Well, isn't that a swift kick in the gut. I hold my head in shame.

"I'm s-sorry I interrupted the conference. I-I thought you knew he was coming."

Elliot sounds scared shitless, and I wonder how horrible of a boss I am that he gets so worked up when talking to me. Sure, I get hasty and short when stressed, but he has to know it's not about him. Right?

I feel terrible that he can't say a single sentence to me without nerves getting in the way of his words. "It's okay. You do a good job. I'm grateful to have you as my assistant." I didn't mean to verbally vomit on him, but I have a war going on in my head.

Am I that cynical that I can't handle a thoughtful gesture? Do I have to be suspicious of every nice thing the nanny does?

Sighing, I close my eyes. I regret treating Remington in such an awful manner. He's good for Isabel, and I wasn't fair to him. To either of them.

It's hurting my heart. I might not show it, but it still beats, reminding me that I need to do better. I need to be aware of how I'm treating those who work for me.

Most of all, I need to apologize to Remi.

My phone rings interrupting my weighty introspection, and when I see who it is, I want to throw the device off the top of this building. With an irritated grumble, I swipe left instead.

"Charlotte." My tone is cool because my mother and I are not that close.

It's just how we've always been. She worked two jobs when I was a kid, and I practically raised myself. We didn't have money for a fancy nanny, so I was either at school or at home … alone.

"How's my sweet girl?" No matter what, she always sounds cheerful. Like she lives in her own little la-la land with her doting husband, whom she has plenty of time for.

My eyes roll of their own volition. I'm a single mother doing a piss-poor job at raising my daughter and keeping my company afloat. "Pretty bitter, actually."

"Now, don't give me that. You are smart and beautiful. And you sit thirty stories up in a Chicago skyscraper. Not to mention my sweet grandbaby. Things can't be all that bad."

Could she be that obtuse? While I tend to avoid personal problems, Charlotte's in constant denial.

She thinks we're the same, but we aren't. One knows the issue exists, and even if they don't want to talk about it, its havoc leaks into every other aspect of their life. And the other … just pretends it never happened. *There's nothing to see here, folks.*

She tries. She really does. I know we're both dysfunctional, but we were never very close. Not the way mothers and daughters should be.

Sometimes I wish we had a stronger bond, but because I couldn't really rely on her for emotional support growing up, I have a hard time with it now. I don't know how to approach our relationship, so I end up frustrated and snippy.

An abhorrent thought runs through my mind. *What if Isabel feels the same way about me someday?*

I take a deep breath and exhale my angst. Mom is right about one thing, though. Things aren't that bad—now. I'm grateful to be able to give my baby a nice home, unlike the trailer I grew up in. And as of today, she has a nanny, so she won't have to go to daycare every day. I know she'll be much happier with one-on-one time with someone she can count on. Someone she knows will be there when she's missing me.

Maybe if I had that as a kid, I wouldn't be such a mess. But I will lose all of it if it comes down to putting innocent people out of work. Talent that took a chance on a new company because they believed in us and our vision. A vision that's slowly fading.

As fast as it went, angst is restored to its rightful place—a knot in my chest.

"Was there something you needed?"

She sighs. "I need *you*. I was hoping I could come for a visit soon. I really miss you and Isabel. It's hard having my girls so far away."

Regret twists my insides. I have my reasons to stay away. "I don't know, Charlotte. Work is pretty busy and I just hired a new nanny, so I'm trying to figure that out."

"Listen, I know you're dedicated to work and I admire you for it, but you and Isabel need family around."

How ironic. I bite my tongue so hard I taste copper.

"Just tell me when, and I'll be there. I can't wait to have my girls with me again. We're going to have so much fun!" she squeals in the receiver.

I pull the phone away from my ear. It's just like her to sweep things under the rug.

"How's Randy going to handle you away from him for more than five minutes?"

After I graduated high school, my mother met a nice guy and got married, and I inherited a thorn in the flesh—my step sister, Aubry. At first, I adored her, but it didn't take long for her claws to emerge. It was awful. A foreshadow of the havoc the girl could wreak when feeling threatened. To be clear, *I* wasn't menacing—my mere presence in her house was.

My mother remained neutral about it while I was in constant turmoil. Yet another example of when I needed her and she wasn't there for me. As soon as I was able, I moved away from the little Podunk town in Indiana I grew up in.

"Oh, stop. You know Randy loves you like his own."

Even though the man didn't raise me, he tried to step in as a doting father. He's always been good to me. That's part of the problem—Aubry's problem.

"He thinks it's a brilliant idea. Besides, he's hoping you'll come for the holidays. We'd love to throw a big Christmas celebration for Isabel." She giggles and it's an abrasive sound, rubbing against me in the worst possible way.

She can't be serious. She knows why I don't go to her place for the holidays. It's the elephant in the receiver that she refuses to acknowledge. Besides, Jay's family has us every year, and Isabel loves going. I won't let Charlotte guilt me into missing out on that because she's having a maternal moment.

"That's never going to happen, and you know why. As far as you visiting..." I shift some papers around to give my agitated hands something to do. "I'll look at my schedule and get back to you." Never, but I don't need to get into an argument with her right now.

"I'm sorry, honey. You're a mother, so you understand why I have to try." Here she goes.

"Right." A smart retort is on the verge of rolling off my tongue, but I count to ten in my head to keep my cool.

"Have you ... talked to her?" Charlotte edges out, knowing I'm prone to shut down when my step-sister is directly mentioned.

"I can't do this right now." I cross my legs, admiring the point of my stilettos—sharp enough to stab someone in the chest. I don't attack from the back like a coward. *Like Aubry.* "Guessing you haven't either since you're asking me."

"I'm not making excuses for her, but how would you be if I abandoned you when you were little—"

"Fine, *Charlotte*. I'd be just fine, like I am now." The audacity. "Gotta go. Got a meeting in five."

"Oh, okay, Honey. Talk soon?"

I hate the hurt in her voice, but she's the one responsible for the state of our tentative relationship. If she had been on my side *just once*, maybe things wouldn't have gotten so bad.

"Yep." I hit end, happy to be done eating her sparkles-and-rainbows bullshit.

Can't things just go smoothly for once? First the Pingman fiasco, then the nanny nonsense, and topping off this shit sundae is a sprinkle of Charlotte. I could do with less fanfare in every aspect of my life.

Chapter 4

Futz Around and You Will Find Out

Remi

FUCKING IDIOT. WHAT IN the hell was I thinking?

I have no idea what Ms. Keller is up against at work. She's superlatively self-aware with a majestic air about her. Who am I to decide what she needs? I should have consulted her first before usurping her day—she's right to be upset.

Tugging at the roots of my hair, I berate myself. I'm not ignorant of corporate culture. Having a cutthroat businessman for a father taught me what to expect in competitive industries: squash the opponent, especially if they are female.

The first lesson he ever preached was that women don't have the capacity to think rationally or for themselves, using my passive mother as an example. It's up to the men to lead them through life. I was ten, and it was the first time in my life I felt rage. It was big, ugly, and barely restrained.

The bitter taste of contempt coats my mouth.

My father could be brutal when defied. But even at that tender age, I was smart enough to understand my parents' dynamic was fucked-up. My mother was a strong, vivacious woman ... until my father entered the room. Then she became as lively as a wallflower, an invisible ornament barely hanging on by a loose screw. Little by little as the years went by, she disappeared altogether.

Pushing Isabel's empty stroller down the hall, my eye catches on the city bustle below outside the window.

Mom loved Chicago and would tell me stories about her old haunts, looking wistful and melancholic. As a kid, I wondered why she seemed sad when talking about her home. As an adult, I understand. This is the last place she was free to be herself.

Fuck, I miss her.

My father broke her spirit, then stole her soul. Her only crime was being brighter and more intelligent than he'd ever be. He couldn't stand it.

I couldn't stand him. So I got on a plane and flew across the country to live closer to my mother's side of the family. To have a piece of her without *his* interference. To remember who she really was, not what *he* turned her into. And to keep true to myself, be aware of the world around me, and be a good samaritan to the people I meet. Exactly how my mother raised me. If I had stayed in California, there's no telling who I would have become. But on the off chance that I would have turned into him...

I'd rather be dead.

Hurtling myself out of this brooding rabbit hole, I shake off the memories. I'm not a guy that dwells on the past. That's done and gone. The present is the only moment that's promised, so I focus on that. What can I do to make this moment count? Sometimes I get it right, and sometimes I fail miserably.

As is the case right now, when I knock on Ms. Keller's colleague's opened door to pick up my charge with my tail tucked between my legs.

Jay whistles a doomsday tune when they find me shifting on my feet just outside their office. "Oh, she bit ya good, huh?"

Rubbing the back of my neck, I stammer, "U-uh..." Yeah, she did, but I deserved it. I should have gotten to know this family dynamic better before I decided on a whim what is best for them.

"Emmie, wook!" Isabel runs up to me with a paper waving wildly in her hand.

Jay and I both grin at the adorable toddler.

I squat down with arms open, showing her that she has my full attention. "What do you have here?"

When she hands me her drawing, she explains her masterpiece of two stick figures holding hands, one with red hair and the other brown. "Dis me and you." She points with her tiny finger.

My nose stings. "I love it, Isabel. You draw beautifully."

She gives me a toothy grin, and warmth fills my lungs.

Caring for Isabel feels different, more important than any other job I've done. My instinct to protect her is stronger.

She's special. Everything she does is utterly adorable. And right now, studying the drawing she made, I'm so proud of her.

I've never gotten this attached to a charge so quickly.

"Whatever happened out there" — Jay tilts their chin to the hall — "it's clear whose side this little one is on."

My grin falls to a grimace as I peer at them. "I only meant to help." I shake my head as remorse threatens to drag my smile to the floor. "I didn't mean..."

I stand with Isabel in my arms, half scared that this is the last day I'll have with her. And that Kiara's going to hand me my ass. Even if Ms. Keller doesn't fire me, do I really want to be someone's punching bag?

The image of an intriguing woman with guarded green eyes and weighed down by the world she carries on her shoulder flashes in my head. Mae isn't a malicious woman. I can see how much love brims in her eyes when she holds her daughter. She's probably just exhausted. Stressed and fucking sick of men like me making decisions for her.

I'm an idiot.

"I know. Mae is my best friend and a pain in the ass." Jay raises an eyebrow at me. "I can say that because I'll tell it to her face." Their stare is challenging as if saying, *I'll kill anyone else who says it, though.* "But under that hard mask of self-preservation is a beautiful soul, who would do anything for the people she loves. If you can break through her walls, you'll see who she really is."

I dip my chin. "I can understand that."

She hadn't been sure about me at first, but she called me back anyway because it was the best decision for her child. It could not have been easy to admit she'd made an error, even to herself.

"I'm pretty good at reading people, Remi. I think you'll be great for them. But *futz* around, and you will find out."

I gulp. She was very clear about exactly how I would find out if I fuck up.

"She's not one to give an undeserved inch, but she is fair. And worth it." They wink.

I don't know Mae well, but for some reason, I believe Jay.

Isabel giggles when I bounce her in my arms and it rights all the wrongs of my snafu today. I can definitely roll with the punches to be able to care for this little one.

And I really want to get to know the woman underneath the hard mask she wears. Hopefully, she lets me stick around.

"Can you copy this?" I'm sitting on the family room floor with Isabel, playing with alphabet blocks and showing her how to spell her name.

Her pink tongue pokes out as she concentrates on finding the letters she needs to match mine, and it's a marvel to watch. "I." She picks up the right one. "S." She has a little trouble with this one, but she's determined and doesn't give up easily.

For all of Mae's harshness, Isabel is a sweetheart. She shares her toys and doesn't fuss at naptime. So far, my job has been ridiculously easy and fun. That's a tribute to her mother, the person Jay sees. Isabel is a remarkable little girl, which makes me wonder about the woman who raised her. I'm determined to meet that woman. Something tells me she's just as incredible as her daughter.

The front door opens, and a cold breeze ushers Queeny in. Cool green irises find us right away.

"Hello," she greets with a timid tremor, so unlike the fire she expelled earlier.

I can see an apology in her stare before she scoops up Isabel and kisses all over her chubby cheek.

"Hi, baby. Did you have a good day?"

I'm sitting on the floor as if part of the furniture, awkward and unsure of my place here.

"Yeah! Emmie play wif me, and we had mac 'n' cheese," Isabel speaks excitedly to her mother.

Mae's chin quivers with some type of emotion. Guilt, maybe? She has nothing to feel guilty about.

I stand and face her. "We had a great day. Isabel is very well-behaved, and she ate every bite of her lunch like a pro." I chuckle, remembering how excited she was with the cheesy goodness. "Ms. Keller, I wanted—"

"I've got it from here, Remington. Thank you," she addresses me without looking at me.

An ounce of frustration simmers in my chest. Is she always going to be like this?

Rubbing my sweaty palms against my pants, I make my exit. "O-kay, I'll just be on my way then."

"Will you come back?" Mae's soft voice cuts through the tension. Her head hangs a little, and it takes every ounce of my being not to tip her chin up. A woman like her should never lower her gaze ... to anyone.

For my job security, I keep my damn hands to myself. "Absolutely." I nod, the tone of my voice leaving no room for uncertainty.

"Good," she clips. "We'll see you out."

Queeny starts for the front door and I follow, wishing I had something clever to say to break the ice between us. I'm usually good with one-liners, but today has me rattled. This is a good contract and I'd like to keep it, so I let Mae lead for now.

As soon as I get to the threshold of the opened door, I turn and say goodbye to Isabel, who is wildly waving, "Bye-bye."

"I just want to say—"

"Can we not?" Mae's brows lift with her plea. It's more of a desperate request than a brush-off, so I let it slide. "It's been an awful day, and I just need some time with my daughter."

Ever polite, I hook up the side of my mouth. "Of course." I lift my hand in a small wave before skipping down the porch steps and walking to the train station.

I don't look back. The past is done. Over.

Tomorrow will be better. It always is.

I'm not a quitter, and I won't give up on this family because something tells me they need me more than they realize.

Chapter 5

Apology Pancakes

Mae

WOMEN HAVE AN INNATE ability for certain laws of nature. Take motherhood, for example. No one really knows how to do it until you pop a kid out and have to learn real fast. But in the grand scheme of learning a new craft—something as complicated and fragile as raising a child—women master this skill at the speed of light.

Before Isabel, I never burped a baby. Never saw a documentary about it. Didn't have time for a baby-gas class. But as soon as I gave birth, I instinctively knew when she needed a pat on her back to release the air cramping her stomach.

There are other things I know from primal instinct alone: when my daughter is going to be sick before the first sign of snot; when she's upset, my arms ache to comfort her; I can tell by the rise and fall of her chest if she's dreaming. However, all my talents are summed up in managerial skills and diaper changing.

When it comes to cooking, I have a charred thumb.

Beep beep beep!

"Fuckshitdamn! Shut up, or you're going to wake up Isabel," I hiss at the smoke alarm as I ineffectually wave a dish towel in the air to dispel the smoke. It doesn't work.

This is the third batch of pancakes I've burnt. A cloying sweet-smoky smell saturates the air, and even if these things do come out less than black, there's no way they are edible.

But I'm not a defeatist, so I whip up another batch. "If you had just apologized last night, you wouldn't be torturing yourself right now."

When I got home after work, I was too ashamed to rehash what had happened. I didn't want to be reminded of how I'd dismissed my daughter. So I gave Remi a short hello, scooped Isabel out of his hands, and pretty much pushed him out the door. I just needed time to decompress.

"But nooooo, you had to go all postal on the hot manny. Who, by the way, is perfect for your daughter," I continue my self-rant, slopping another pile of batter on the skillet. "Did that stop you? It sure didn't. You just—"

"Knock, knock."

My head swings to the threshold of the kitchen, where Remmington is leaning like a cocky Calvin Klein model.

Did he just hear my word vomit?

"Mmm, smells good in here." I'm pretty sure he's being sarcastic, and his gravelly voice isn't helping anything, except for waking up parts of my body. "You makin' breakfast, Queeny?"

"Yes, and don't call me that." I'm as petulant as my two-year-old sometimes.

Bemused, he swaggers over, no doubt mentally taking stock of all the ways he could fix this. How do I know? Because I do the same thing at work.

"Why not? I think having a cute nickname for you is only fair. You just called me, quote: 'hot manny'."

Blood drains from my face, and I want to bolt the hell out of here. *I'm ready, Lord. Taketh my life.* My eyes scan the floor, looking for a hole to collapse into.

"I-I didn't call you that. Jay did, and it stuck in my head."

Remi's smirk transforms into an indulgent smile.

"I'm trying to make you breakfast because I royally fucked up yesterday. I cut you off and practically kicked you out so I wouldn't have to admit my appalling behavior." I'm well aware I'm rambling. "Which is such a cowardly thing to do. You've been nothing but great, and I'm a big bully." I turn the stove off, admitting defeat in more ways than one. "I'm sorry."

The manny's hands casually rest in his pockets as his dark brown eyes sparkle with mischief. He's relaxed as he steps in close.

I back away.

"So you *don't* think I'm hot?"

I twist the back of my neck, staving off the heat of humiliation building there. "Jesus, will you let that go? Didn't you hear a word I said? I. Am. Sorry. Go ahead and gloat because I'm not one to admit I'm wrong."

"You weren't wrong." He shakes his perfect head. "You were right—I should have asked you. I wanted to surprise you with Isabel because I'm sure you don't get to see much of each other during the day."

God, his simple explanation makes my reaction regrettably irrational.

"I overstepped. I'm sorry."

His apology is too much. *He's* too much. *Where did he come from?*

"I grew up in Los Angeles, but I moved here permanently when I went to college," Remi punctuates with a cheeky smirk.

Oh, for fuck's sake, I said that out loud. But I can't stop the next question that slips out of my mouth. "Why?"

Remi, the adorable bastard, starts cleaning the mess I made in the kitchen. "My mom's family is here, my older sister too. When she had my nephew, I knew that this is where I wanted to be."

That's so sweet. "You really do love kids."

A wide grin breaks out across his face. I swear his straight white teeth wink at me. Even they are flirty. "I do. I'm a big kid myself."

"You can say that again." I slam my hand over my mouth. I've never been this loose-lipped, always so poised and in control.

Remi's beatific grin inches higher. He pulls out plates and utensils. "Don't know about you, but I'm ready to eat." Remington scrapes a brown pancake off the griddle, but he loses part of the middle because it's still raw.

Watching on in helpless horror, my shoulders hunch to my ears and my nose scrunches. "You don't have to eat that. I'm a terrible cook."

He chuckles and shakes his head, continuing towards his demise.

"Really. The main thing is I wanted to apologize. Again, I'm sorry. Please don't eat that."

"Why not?" He sits down at the table. "Apology pancakes are the best pancakes, made with my enemies' tears and regret." He scoops up a chunk of "what the fuck" with his fork.

"Wait!"

Mouth open, his utensil stops mid-air.

"Don't you want some syrup on it?" *So you can't really taste how awful my cooking is?*

Remi rubs his abs. "I plan on taking Isabel to get ice cream later, and too much sugar isn't good for you." He throws me a wink before he wraps his pillowy pink lips around a big bite.

I brace myself, waiting for the gag, but it doesn't come. He just sits there, happily chewing and then ... choking.

Oh god! I'm killing him! He's too pretty to die.

"Waahher." He points to the sink.

"*Shit,* sorry. I was too busy being horrified."

I scurry over with a full glass, which he promptly gulps. Being the mother I am, I start rubbing his back, noting his warmth and strength. The fucking horsepower rumbling underneath those muscles. It's then I remember how wildly inappropriate this is and back away like he's going to burst into flames.

Pounding his fist on his chest, he swallows, going back for more water. "Maybe the next time you want to apologize, you can buy me muffins or something."

I raise my eyebrow because he's pushing it.

"Not that these aren't delicious because ... yum. Can I have more please?" A dopey smile forms on his face as he lifts his plate.

I start laughing and almost fall over.

The burnt smell is lingering, and brown mushy pancakes are still piled on the griddle.

His face brightens, even though I know he's suffering. Why is he so freaking cute? No, not cute... Adorkable.

It's all too much, and I snort. I. Flipping. Snort.

Heat tingles up my neck and through my cheeks. My nincompoop nose chose airflow turbulence over the melodic laugh I was going for. *Mother of God, why?*

Jay is going to have a field day with this.

"Did you just snort?"

Hiding my flaming face, I nonverbally admit my blunder.

Remi clears his throat, hiding a chuckle, and I peek at his bemused façade through my fingers.

"You're somethin', you know that?"

Unable to fully confront him, I keep my hands over my hot skin. "You too," I grumble, sulking in my embarrassment. My ears are so scorching I'm afraid they are going to melt off.

"Me too," he agrees.

At his assent, I steal another glance at him.

Umber eyes twinkle in amusement as a sexy smirk creeps over Remi's face. He stands, and it's like the sky opens up, shining its heavenly light but only on him. Emphasizing the way his t-shirt molds around his hard chest and tucks into dark faded jeans that are slung ever so perfectly at his narrowed waist, hinting at abs so taunt a dropped quarter would spring off of them.

My mouth dries. I swallow, trying to encourage proper saliva flow, but the damn thing is arid. *God, he's beautiful.*

The manny walks towards me in slow motion, and I note every muscle ripple in his shoulders, down to his forearms. He's flawlessly cut and devilishly handsome, with a wicked grin on his face. Liquid pools in my mouth at the angle of his jawline. I wonder how sharp it would feel against my tongue.

The thought barges in unwelcome but takes up a seat in my mind anyway. My breaths quicken as he comes closer. When I inhale his clean scent, I almost swoon.

The atmosphere crackles between us, or maybe it's just my audible exhales. Whatever it is, it's drawing me closer to his intense magnetism.

With glittering irises and a small chuckle on his plush lips, he pulls my hands away from my face. His mouth sets into a lopsided smile, and he rubs small circles on the back of my wrists with his thumbs. "Can I have a hug?"

A shiver skitters up my spine, answering for me. He can have whatever he wants.

Lost in the spell he's casting, I peer up at him. "You're asking?"

Is this a friendship hug, a truce ... or—gulp—something completely different? Friendship and truce I can handle. We need to work together. We *should* be friends. There's nothing inappropriate about that. Anything else, however, isn't even a remote possibility.

It doesn't mean the fantasy of him hasn't planted strong roots in my head, though.

Pursing his supple lips, he tilts his head. "Yes, Queeny. I won't hug a woman without consent."

Why does it feel like he's saying something else?

"Yeah." That came out breathier than I wanted it to, so I clear my throat and try again. "I consent, Remington."

This makes him peel with laughter, and something lightens on my shoulders, clearing my head and calming my nerves.

He pulls me to him, still rumbling with mirth. I'm lost in the solace of his chest. He's gentle, comforting, and smells like fresh laundry right out of the dryer. I want to dig my nose into his shoulder and take a big, dramatic whiff like I do with Isabel.

Jay is the only other person I let get close. Even when I was dating Brad, we were never really affectionate outside of the sheets. I was naïve, thinking we would fall in love. Looking back on it, I don't even think I liked the person as much as I liked the idea of being in love.

How could I ever like a man like him? *Stupid.*

I guess I had a void that needed to be filled, so I was blind until I saw the horrifying light. Now that I have Isabel, that hole has healed. I'll never make the mistake with men like Brad again.

But I can't deny that this is nice. That maybe, someday, I'll trust enough to want something more than platonic relationships.

He pulls back, still holding my arms. His irises swirl with liquid caramel as his mouth twists up. "Go get ready for work. I'll get Isabel and make us all breakfast." His voice is low and husky, every whispered syllable tickling my eardrums.

His words are telling me to go, but we're locked in this moment, neither of us making a move to leave. Air zaps around us. I'm surprised my hair hasn't been lifted by the static. As I take in the magnificence of him, my eyes blink slow and dreamy.

The amusement painting his face dissolves into ardor as if to say, *I promise I got you.* Some kind of understanding passes between us, but I can't articulate what it is because there are no words for it. Even though I just met him, there's contentment here. A seed of trust.

When I lick my dry lips, his eyes heat.

Is it my imagination or did his chin inch closer to mine?

His breaths brush across my mouth, arousing anticipation for a kiss. As illogical as that seems—by his demeanor and mine—it's just as possible. It's a pause before the spark that will ignite the inferno consuming us.

The trajectory of my physical attraction unfurls in my my mind—kiss, suck, fuck, bliss. My head is screaming with hurricane warning sirens to evacuate, but my body betrays me as a bolt of desire shoots through my gut. My lids drop at half mast, and I tilt towards him.

Remi sucks in a breath, and his jaw goes slack.

Christ, he's going to kiss me. And God damn it to hell, I'm going to let him.

My daughter's whimpers echo through the monitor, breaking the captivation, and we jump apart. I'm twisting the back of my neck to dispel the arousal thrumming through me. He's scrubbing his face for absurd reasons I won't acknowledge.

Remi puffs out his cheeks with an exhale and, like a mirage, erases all hints of whatever *that* was between us. With a saucy grin, he tips his head towards the family room. "Before I go... Just to confirm, you think I'm hot?"

Dick. I shake my head, clearing away the remnants of desire. He certainly knows how to break the tension.

Eyes rolling back into my head, I push him away with a playful hand. "Get outta here, you cocky little shit. You know you are."

I turn away and start towards the steps because, after what just happened and my subsequent confession, I need to get the hell out of here.

"Queeny," he calls.

Oh, he's going to get it. I sigh in resignation and turn around with a crooked smile. "What, Manny?"

Surprised delight coats his features. "I hope your wiener shirt is going to make another appearance. It's my favorite." Hands on his stomach, Remi cackles like he's the funniest man on the planet. He looks more boyish than anything else.

"We'll see. Only if you're a good boy." I wince. That came out way weirder than I meant.

Mortified, I backtrack until he says, "I can be a good boy for you." He's all charming dimples and glinting irises.

I'm all shifting feet and sweaty palms.

He's as heartwarming as he is body-heating.

And I just know that sentence, with that smile, will live rent-free in my head for as long as I exist.

Welcome home.

When I enter the kitchen for the second time this morning, I'm better dressed and a lot more poised.

"Mickey!" My daughter's exuberant squeal gets my attention.

There, in front of the stove, stands Remi, holding Isabel on his hip while she rests her head on his shoulder and sucks her thumb. *So natural.* She's wearing her little footy pajamas, and they both look so warm and cuddly.

Cuddly? What the hell is wrong with me?

He flips something on the griddle. "That's right, Isa-bea."

Isa-bea? He has a cute nickname for her too, making her a part of the process and having fun. Breakfast isn't just a thing to get through so you can go about your business the rest of the day. No, Remi makes breakfast a bonding experience.

He kisses the top of her head. *Swoon.* "Can you sing the Mickey Mouse Song?"

"M. I. C.—K. E. Y," they sing in unison. Or, he starts and she mimics.

It dawns on me—he's teaching her how to spell. By the second verse, she knows all the letters. *My smart girl.*

Leaning against the counter, I cross my arms with a smile.

He turns with a small look of wonder on his face. "Look who it is, Isa-bea."

"Mama!" She lunges forward, and my arms want to hold her.

"Those look a lot better than what I made earlier."

He walks over and hands her to me, playfully pinching her chubby cheek. "Yeah, but they are not as good as apology pancakes." The flirt winks before returning to the stove.

Isabel starts pulling on my earrings. I don't usually wear them because costume jewelry is frivolous and unnecessary in the office. But for some reason, I had an urge today. Jay will either be proud or mad because the earrings are theirs.

"I don't know what you have planned for today, but will you stop by the office? Lunch is on me this time." I give him a sheepish smile because I'm well aware I tore him a new one over this very thing.

I'm so ashamed of letting assholes like Robert get to me like that. I chose his perception of me over my daughter, and that's unfair to her. Remembering Charlotte treating me this way as a kid gashes me deep.

Of course Isabel comes first—I am a mother. So what? It only makes me fiercer. More determined.

He looks up at me, gauging my intent. "What happened yesterday is okay. We got through it, and I'd never hold it against you. I know you're busy at work."

As disasterly as it was, seeing them yesterday was the highlight of my day. Eating the lunch he so thoughtfully brought me was balm to my aggravated nerves. "I have a confession to make."

He pauses and faces me, holding a spatula in mid-air. A sly grin slowly builds on his face. "Oh?" He stresses the word like he's waiting to hear something salacious.

Like I said, adorkable.

"When I got back to my office after the meeting, I was wishing you guys were still there. My head was so far up my own ass I didn't even acknowledge her." I hold my mouth to her warm cheek because this admittance slices through my heart, making me bleed out. My throat hurts from holding back my emotions. "What kind of mother does that?" Even as I ask it I know—Charlotte.

Remi sets the spatula down and straightens. "Hey."

When I don't look at him, he walks over and takes Isabel, putting her in her chair with some fruit. After he's sure she's content, he comes back to me, placing his hand on mine. His touch sizzles up my arm, and I stare at his beautiful fingers.

"Hey, Queeny. You're doing the best you can. The fact that you recognize it makes you an amazing mother."

"Right, so amazing I can't even cook my daughter a proper breakfast." I pull my hand away and go sit at the table, needing some space between us. "I fed her yogurt and a banana before carting her off to daycare." Looking around the kitchen, I see it with different eyes today. It's a mess, for sure, but it looks more like a home than it ever did. A stranger—a childless one, at that—is a better parent than I ever was. "We never sang while making a meal together. I've never made her a part of anything I did. I just did it. It was more efficient, but it's not right."

Remington sits next to me, scooting the chair closer. "Are you perfect? No, of course not. None of us are. We're learning. That's the magic of life."

I turn to him because ... what?

"Yes, the magic of life is that we can recognize our own ego and change how we approach a situation."

I narrow my eyes at him. He's twenty-six—I may have checked his paperwork for practical purposes. He can't know this from experience.

"Master's in child psychology, remember?"

"Ah, yes. I forgot you went to school to become the Jedi Knight of Nannies."

"Correction—of Mannies." He chuckles. "Truly wonderful, the mind of a child is." Remi's Yoda voice is spot-on. Getting up, he takes out plates to fill them with something delicious, no doubt. "In any case, you recognize it and want to change it."

Still sitting, I look up at him.

His eyes shine with a remarkable belief in me. "You will."

I'm so transfixed, the words are a whisper. "So, you'll come?"

Brown irises melt into honey, and he bites his lip. "Just tell me what time, and we'll be there."

"Jayden Corazon Morales, I'm in so much trouble." I stride into my best friend's office and slump in their papasan chair.

"Yeah, you are! Are those my Cartier earrings?!" Jay says, incredulous.

Reaching up to feel the mentioned earrings, I say, "Finders, keepers." I groan again. "Jaaaydeeen, did you not hear what I just said?"

"Oh my god, have you been abducted by aliens? They didn't probe you, did they?" Jay grabs a letter opener and holds it in front of them on the defensive. "Where is my frigid bitch best friend, and what did you do to her?"

Throwing my arm over my head, I chuckle then moan my misery. "Do not make me laugh. This is not a laughing matter. I'm in real trouble here, and you're making jokes."

"Yes, this is how I deal with uncomfortable situations—inappropriately timed humor. You know this, yet here you lay in all your" — with one hand on their chest, the other one stirs the air — "emotes." When I don't move, they let out a long sigh. "What's wrong, mija?"

I peek at them from under my arm, not wanting to admit what I know to be true. Jay's going to run with this, but they're the only person I trust to tell. I *need* to tell someone. To rid my head of this ridiculousness. I'm not a silly girl anymore. I don't think I ever was.

"Look, you're spiraling and getting your muckiness all over my zen space." Jay picks up a selenite crystal and wraps my hand around it. "Take a deep breath."

Inhale. Exhale.

"Good. Now, on with it. I don't have all day."

"I have a crush on the hot manny." I don't add that I'm in so much fucking trouble because if this gets out, we'll lose him. I'll have to buy out Remi's contract and find a new nanny as amazing as him, which I already know is impossible.

"And?"

And? "Isn't that bad enough?"

"Babe, you're hysterical because of the little lady boner you sprouted for the hot-as-sin baby-charmer. I mean, duh. And, oh my God, you *are* human." Their voice mocks their revelation.

"That's what I'm trying to say. This isn't good. Not at all," I whine like a toddler in a toy store.

"Listen to me, your life guru. Bang him and get him out of your system."

I shoot up, appalled. Though, the devil on my shoulder finds reason in Jay's advice. Something tells me the banging would be a mind-altering experience, but no.

"I can't do that. I'll breach my contract with Child Care Connection." I fling my hand into the air. "He'll lose his job," I shriek. Shaking my head, I temper my inner panic. "Isabel needs him. He's too good for her for me to screw it up with sex."

"See? Problem solved." Jay holds their palms together and bows as if they are the oracle of wisdom, then waves their hand towards the door. "Now, go. I have art to create."

"I snorted in front of him." My tone is glum.

Jay places their fingers over their astonished mouth. "No, you didn't!"

Reluctantly, I nod.

They bust out a big guffaw.

And there it is ... the you-made-an-ass-out-of-your-self-and-I-wasn't-even-there-to-watch laugh. "Oh, God. Make it stop."

Jay's laugh becomes hysterical, and I can't help but chuckle at my absurdness.

"Not helping."

"I— *Bahaha*... I'm sorry, Cruella." Jay wipes the tears from their eyes. "Welp, he's practically family now. There is no going back after that snort, you know that, right? It will be burned in his memory forever."

I open up my arms to them with grabby hands. "Cuddle me?"

Great, now I'm acting like my two-year-old.

Jay climbs up on the papasan and spoons me with the finesse of a grizzly-bear.

"Remember when we used to lay like this? Everything seemed so complicated then, but looking back on it now, it was simple."

There was nothing to worry about except for who got the last piece of tres leches. No "everything we've built is crumbling, and people will lose their jobs". We didn't exhaust ourselves over the future. There were no babies to support. Our only responsibility was to be home for dinner—food we didn't have to buy nor make.

"You mean, when you hogged all the covers and the choices I had were to use you for body heat or die of hypothermia? Yeah, can't forget it," Jay gripes, sounding bitter. They're teasing. If I know one thing about my best friend, it is that they love a good cuddle.

"Do you ever wish we could go back? Be innocent for a little longer?" I'm wistful in my thoughts.

"Never. First of all, I never want to wear braces again. That Justin Timberlake phase is a big blight on my childhood." We laugh because I remember it like it was yesterday. We fried Jay's hair—first with peroxide, then doubled down with perm solution. "Besides, innocence is way overrated. Sex is hella fun. Also, we have our baby and she's everything. I wouldn't trade her for the world and I know you wouldn't either, so where is this coming from? Your little crush?"

I shrug, contrite. "I just want to give her everything I never had. It's all I want. But sometimes…" My chin quivers with unshed tears. I swallow the lump of loneliness in my throat. "I wish I had someone just for me."

"Rude. *I* am just for you."

I smack their arm. "You know what I mean. I'm thirty-three, and I've never had an Ian," I say, reminding them that they do, in fact, have someone just for them.

Jay and Ian are a match made in heaven. Undeniably perfect for each other. I'm so happy for them because they are happy. But if I'm being completely honest, I get jealous sometimes.

"Not even when I was with Brad. There was always something missing between us." I look away, introspective.

What was so wrong between us that he had to resort to such measures to get rid of me?

"I should have known something was off, but I refused to look deeper. I don't think I'll ever be able to trust anyone enough to let them in romantically."

"Whoa, where is all this coming from? Not all men are like your bullshit ex. Brad is a piece-of-shit's shit—the really repulsive kind. The only thing he was good for was providing little swimmers to make sweet baby Isa."

A harsh breath escapes my lungs. While true, it doesn't change my mind about what most men are like—flight-happy the moment things get a little complicated.

"As for Ian," Jay continues. "It's pretty self-explanatory, love. You're not me."

Laughter rumbles through my chest. "Thanks for astute analysis of why Ian and I are incompatible."

Jay pulls me tighter, and I relish in their serenity. They've always felt like home. "I do believe that each one of us has someone out there. To find them, you have to look with your heart and not your head. Love isn't something you can plan or control, Mars Bars. It just happens. Your heart will know when it's time. Have faith."

If only I could. My heart gets me into trouble and my head keeps me out of it, so I tend to listen to logic and avoid emotional decisions. What's scary is that it's not just about me anymore. Whomever I meet has to not only be an amazing person but also fit seamlessly into our lives—before I'd even consider giving him the time of day, let alone meet the most important person in my life.

"I love you, Jay. Don't ever leave me." I squeeze my eyes, holding back tears, remembering the first time I'd ever said that to them.

It was the first time they brought me home to their family, taking me in without question. I have never felt so loved and secure in my life. They welcomed me. Gave me a place to sleep. Always had a plate for me at their table. Forever supportive of anything Jay and I did. When Jay had begun using they/them pronouns in high school Mama Morales didn't even bat an eyelash. She loves and accepts everyone for who they are. Mama still tells me I'll always have a home with them.

A wayward tear slips out when Jay echoes Mama's words. "Even when the stars die, we will still be."

Chapter 6

Bitches Get Shit Done

Mae

WHEN I WAS YOUNG, I believed in wishes. Every night, I'd stare out the window and plead with the stars that Daddy would come save us, whoever and wherever he was. I would daydream about the mansion we'd live in and the family trips we'd go on.

The man had left before I was born. I'd never seen a picture of him, never heard his voice, never known anything about him. Except that he'd knocked my mother up before she graduated high school and left us to fend for ourselves. Not exactly father of the year.

When it came to him, my emotions were a mixture of sadness and curiosity. Charlotte wouldn't talk about him, let alone seek him out for financial support. I'd lay in my tiny bed in my tiny room in our trailer and wonder about what he looked like or if he ever thought about us. Did he even know I existed?

As I grew older, curiosity turned into resentment—a big chip on my shoulder that I wear to this day. It also turned into this drive to do better than my mother did. I promised myself and my future child that they would never be without money, a father, and family trips. I'd attend every recital, spelling bee, and play. Wholesome lunches would be packed every day and dinner on the table every night. I vowed I would be there to help with homework or a cuddle during sickness.

But when I became an adult, reality punched me in the gut. Life never works out the way it's supposed to. If I wanted my dreams to come true, I'd have to chase them myself. Stop at nothing to create the life I want so I could be financially ready when I *decide* to have children.

Turns out, the decision was never mine to begin with. Fun sex turned serious real quick when I missed my period. I was busy building Ever Heart, and Brad traveled a lot for his job. We may have lived together, but marriage wasn't really on our minds. After my pregnancy was confirmed, Brad and I talked at length about our future and what it meant for the life growing inside of me. Despite it being a complete surprise, I was excited and in love ... or so I thought. Brad seemed excited too. He swore he'd be there for us, and he was.

Until he wasn't. I'll never forget the bomb that dropped on me that night. Or the constricting feeling of my heart closing in on itself.

I had to consider my and my baby's prospects, and how I would move forward. It was no longer about ambition. I had to be as strategic and cunning as any man in my position. Past experience has taught me to keep my guard up. However, I'd do anything to make sure my daughter is safe and happy.

Which explains why I'm on the train after work hours, going further into the city and not away from it. Per last-minute request, I'm meeting with Paul Wexford, Dexico's CEO and all around chauvinistic pig. How do I know? He patted my ass on the way out of our initial proposal meeting. I was so stunned, I wasn't even sure it'd happened. We were surrounded by senior staff, but no one batted an eye. When I had time to process, I knew what had happened. I hate that I didn't say anything about it. I hate even more that I succumbed to his request tonight.

My legs feel like lead when I exit the train and make my way over to the steak house. When I get to the crosswalk, I check the street and freeze as a familiar face floats through the moving crowd coming towards me. *Is that Aubry?*

I haven't seen her since she capsized my life, so I shoulder through needing to confront her. Wanting to show her she didn't break me. No one will ever break me.

But as people intersect, the crowd gets too thick and I lose sight of her. *Was she even there to begin with?* I've been working long hours, and I'm exhausted. It's no wonder I'm losing my mind.

Like someone about to commit a crime, adrenaline and paranoia thrum through my veins. Pulling my coat tighter and tucking my chin in the collar, I swear eyes are on my every step to the restaurant.

I'm praying I'm reading the situation wrong, that this is a busy man and the only time he has to talk about our proposal is over a meal. Even as I think it, the pragmatist in me says it's a silly notion. The reality of the situation is far more sinister.

When I enter the restaurant, all the blood drains from my face and the chip on my shoulder falls to my stomach, where it churns in the demeaning feeling of inequality. The first thing I notice is that the atmosphere is far more romantic than it should be for a business dinner. The lights are dimmed, and flames twinkle across glasses of wine and cocktails. A pretentious orchid sits in the middle of every table. A metaphoric red flag, if you will.

"Miranda, thank you for meeting with me. You look beautiful." Paul stands, eye-fucking me from the cloth-covered table, going in for a double cheek kiss.

I bite back a cringe. I do not get personal with business clients. It's inappropriate behavior.

And using your B.O.B. every night to fantasize about your kid's nanny isn't inappropriate? It is, but he doesn't have to know about it.

My lips thin, but I contain my unpleasant retort. My beauty is irrelevant to this meeting. "I'm always happy to discuss our proposal."

Paul's jaw is so square it gives new meaning to the term "blockhead". His weasel eyes light up. "Is that so? I admire your dedication."

It better be worth it. This is cutting into precious time with my daughter.

Jay said they'd come with, but it's their and Ian's anniversary, and they are taking a much deserved vacation. I gave them a pass on this one. I hope I don't regret it. Plus, I never told them about the mishap. Jay would have refused to work with Dexico and would've probably killed the guy. By keeping the indiscretion to myself, I saved this deal and prevented Jay from going to prison.

Paul thinks he's smooth as he pours wine into my glass. "I took the opportunity of ordering us a 2015 Lafite Rothschild. It's nice to unwind after a hard day of work, don't you agree?"

It's nice to go home after a hard day of work and not be subjected to this bullshit. "It's hard to unwind when you are a single mother of a two-year-old, whose favorite pastime is throwing food on the floor."

If this were a professional appointment, I wouldn't be bringing up my daughter at all. Sadly, this is a situation that requires a protective shield from this prick's innuendo. They usually pivot when I mention my single-mother status.

"Well, it's good to have some adult time every now and again." He licks his lips.

I want to vomit. The misogyny is strong with this one.

Leaning back, I cross my arms. "Mr. Wexford, I was under the impression you wanted to speak about our digital marketing proposal that my team and I have worked extensively on."

"Ms. Keller, while I admire your tenacity, can't we enjoy a nice dinner first?" When I'm about to protest, he throws in, "We at Dexico are like a big family. We like to fortify our interpersonal relationships before we do business with a new company. Especially one as young and fledgling as Ever Heart."

There's that word again—fledgling. Has he been talking to Pingman? I want to lunge across the table and strangle him. We might be new to the high-rise block, but we're not neophytes in the industry.

"All work and no play makes Paul a dull boy."

I'm sure he thinks his smarmy smile is charming, but I'm losing my patience here.

And did he just quote *The Shining*? Creepy.

"Yes, well, Jack ended up going insane, so maybe he should have focused more on work."

"Touché, Miranda. But he also blew up with the hotel." He raises an eyebrow.

I'm about to make my exit, when the waiter walks over. "Would you like to order, sir?"

The waiter only looks at the suit sitting across from me. He hasn't acknowledged me at all.

"Yes, William. I'll have the Porterhouse, rare." Putting a hand on the side of his mouth, he makes a joke. "I like my meat red and raw."

Fucking seriously? Does he think this shit turns women on? My skin ripples in skeeve.

"Be careful. I wouldn't want you to catch a parasite." My smile is saccharine. It is a valid warning, after all.

Undeterred, he addresses the waiter once more. "The lady will have the halibut with the arugula and frisée salad."

"The lady can order for herself," I snap. "Unfortunately, I'm feeling unwell. I'll have my assistant reschedule this meeting during office hours." I give Paul a pointed look as I stand.

I am well aware I'm not being nice. But nice has never gotten me anywhere. Bitches get shit done, and I happen to be the queen.

Poor William looks like he's about to shit himself.

"Sit. Down. Miranda. We have business to discuss. Unless you want to tell your partner that you single-handedly lost your company's biggest deal."

As if on a carousel, the faces of our devoted team dance around in my head. I sigh, sit back down, and address the waiter. "I'll have the filet. Medium. And two of your best desserts to go." Leaning forward with a glint of defiance in my eye, I cup the side of my mouth. "I hate fish," I say, wrinkling my nose. "Too slimy for me."

Paul lets out a hearty laugh. "You are a sharp broad, I'll give you that."

Broad.

I finger my salad fork, imagining the various ways I could mutilate him with it, but otherwise remain calm in the face of this pompous asshole. When the waiter leaves, I take control of the situation. "We have our best team dedicated to Dexico for as long as you're contracted with us. We've studied your competition and—"

"Dexico has no competition," he interjects.

He's delusional on so many levels. "I only mean to say that we will keep you on the front page of *Forbes* for years to come. This is why you came to us, is it not?"

The change of his face is subtle, but so is my smirk. *Forbes* is his Achilles' heel. The front he can use to distract his shareholders so they don't realize the company is slowly falling behind their competitors.

"It is. Go on."

Thank God he's dropped the whole "woo the little woman" act. "With Ever Heart, we will build a strong brand identity and reach your target audience. We've done the research. Your profits have been steadily decreasing since last year. I'm afraid you are falling behind the up-and-comers of the industry. Especially the ones with on-trend branding."

Paul stares at me with a bemused look on his face. "You are adorable, you know that?"

A hazy red falls over my vision. I've worked hard to be where I am. No one has ever given me anything in life. I have earned the throne I sit on, and I will not tolerate such blatant, disrespectful behavior. The ass tap came out of nowhere, and I didn't do anything about it then. I admit, that was my first mistake, but I'll be damned if I let another egregious violation slide.

I'm gripping my fork-weapon so tightly my knuckles are white. "I'm missing bedtime with my daughter, so if you—"

"Then let's make this quick." He wipes his mouth and motions the waiter.

Swift relief settles in. Finally, he understands I am not interested in whatever he is offering outside of our business relationship.

I grab my phone and make a quick text to Remi that I won't be much longer. But before I can hit the send button, the piece of fecal matter across from me speaks.

"William, we'll have our meals delivered to the presidential suite. The lady and I have some business to discuss." He winks at the waiter. "In private."

Enough is enough. I pull two hundred-dollar bills from my purse and hand them to William. He looks at them like they're dripping with disease.

"Fine," comes out in an exasperated sigh.

Throwing the money on the table, I address the creep disguised as a gentleman in a three-piece suit. "Let me break it down so your tiny brain can understand. I've seen the dateline episode, so I know how this ends. My body is not part of the proposal. Work with Ever Heart or don't."

Out of nowhere, a sudden urge hits me—I will not go away quietly. Not again. As if it has a mind of its own, my hand grabs my full glass of eight-hundred-dollar wine and throws it in Mr. Sexual Harassment's face. I watch in satisfaction as he huffs in surprise. Red drips down his crisp white button-down. I probably just ruined a three-thousand-dollar suit.

Good.

"You bitch!" Paul, in all his embarrassment, loses his suave disguise and reveals what a swine he actually is.

If being assertive and having self-respect makes me a bitch, then I will proudly wear the label. "That's right, Mr. Wexford. You'll do well to remember that the next time you try this shit with someone else. For the future, if you ever touch me without my permission again, I will go to the press. No amount of rebranding will restore your reputation after that."

I walk away with my head held high ... and a pit in my stomach.

We're going to lose this deal. And our people will suffer because of it.

Tiptoeing into the brownstone, I slip off my stilettos and creep through the foyer down the hall. My toes dig into the soft, plush carpeting—a comfort to my aching feet. A low melody echoes through the space, wrapping around my shoulders and settling in my chest. Lulling me to a calm only home can give. I'm able to release the stress of worrying about the future and focus on the most important thing in my life—my daughter.

Even if I have to sell off everything, I'll still have her. And Jay. That's what matters.

When I get outside of her room, I stand still. There's nothing like watching Remi hold Isabel—my whole heart—in his arms as he tenderly rocks her to sleep, singing a low hum of Harry Styles's *Sweet Creature*. He's been singing the same song to her for a few weeks now. I never heard it before, but now it's my favorite. Remi's voice is ... yeah. It's raspy and resounding, and so fucking soulful I could weep.

I try to catch them in these moments all the time. It's one of the highlights of my day. After tonight's shit storm, I need it.

Even though it was a rocky start, Remi and I have fallen into an easy routine. It's only been a short time, but already he fits. Isabel adores him, and I can see why—he has a way of making you feel special. When you have his attention, it's potent. It's eye-to-eye, breath-by-breath, full-on absorption. The only other person who meets me head-on like that is Jay. It's ... nice.

Refreshing.

Goddamn exhilarating.

Remi can sing the hell out of *Barney* songs and wax poetically about the magic of life. Just the other day, I found myself in a compelling conversation with him about music and the five senses, and how it can be used in therapy to help adults and children alike. The way he sees the world is different. He's fun and engaging, but he's also attentive and reliable—something I didn't think a charmer like him would be capable of.

Remington makes my life easier and he keeps the house serene, a place I can relax and just be. His help with the household duties is immense, and his bond with Isabel is strong. I should give him a raise.

I shiver, fantasizing about all the ways I could give him one.

"I can be a good boy for you."

His words echo through my mind, reverberating all the way to my core and curling my toes. I play it on repeat at night, when I come whispering his name.

Remi spots me leaning against the doorframe and tips a small smile. He looks so peaceful, in his element. Like he was born to be a father.

My ovaries twitch. But as soon as I think about it, a sour taste burns in my mouth. I need to concentrate on my child, the one sleeping peacefully in Remi's arms. The center of my whole universe.

Shuffling to the crib, Remi gently places Isabel next to Mr. Snuffles. He rubs her back to make sure she's settled and then shifts his focus to me. "Hey, Queeny."

His gravelly voice washes over me, and I raise my eyes to his. In this low light, they are dark and devastating.

A deep, cleansing sigh leaves my chest. While I have to be the ice queen at work, I can let down my guard here. My home is my safe haven. I can rest my scepter at the door and just be me, not Miranda Evelyn Keller, co-president of Ever Heart Digital.

"Hi, Manny." I chew on my lip.

Remi swallows, and I watch his throat undulate as I try to hide my fascination. I never thought throats were sexy before ... before the nanny showed up and proved even the most mundane physical traits of a man could be sexy.

His mouth opens to say something, but he stops himself, rakes his fingers through his dark hair, and begins again. "How was your day?"

I know he's just being polite, but damn it feels good to have someone ask. "It was" — I sigh again, looking for the right words to articulate the hell I'm in — "a day. But it's better now."

Remi looks behind him and grins. "I bet. Isa-bea has that effect on people." Turning back to me, he licks his lips. "Takes after her mom."

I die a little. He's devastatingly handsome and heartbreakingly too young for me. What a flirt, though. I can't help the quirk of my lips. I know this is just how he is, but it totally lights me up. He knows how to turn a taxing day into an easy night.

"I don't know about that," I say as I breeze past him and walk over to the reason I breathe, brushing back her baby-soft curls. "How about you?" I look back at him. "How was your day?"

"Well, it was very thrilling. Starting with monsters in the toilet and ending with Mr. Snuffles eating all of Isa's broccoli, which I found squashed under the tray of the highchair." He chuckles softly as he comes to my side and lays an arm around my shoulders.

Ever since that first hug, Remi has been an affectionate friend. We don't shy away from little touches here and there. I should be desensitized to the vortex of physical and emotional attraction Remi evokes. But every time we make contact, my complex feelings for him grow.

Being somewhat tucked into the side of his broad chest does something to me. The air crackles with tension, and I almost imagine him as her father.

My heart clenches. How could Brad have turned his back on her? His own flesh and blood. And for what?

I shake my head because I'll never understand. I'll never forgive either.

Remi stretches, and my eyes rake down his form. His rumpled t-shirt lifts with his arms, and a sliver of his toned abs peeks at me over his low-hung jeans. My mouth goes dry because I'm lying to myself about what I truly want, alas a battery-operated version will have to do tonight.

With a bitter taste in my mouth, I turn away, cutting the tension. My stomach churns with these reprehensible thoughts. Wasn't I just storming out of a restaurant because someone objectified me? And here I am, doing the same thing to Remi. Someone I respect and care for.

I shake my head. "Thank you for putting her to bed. I'm sure you've had just as long a day as I have. You can go."

The manny tilts his head. His sharp jawline practically touches a raised shoulder, fidgeting, before he speaks. "I, uh, I can stay if you want."

I rear back, stunned and pleasantly surprised. Did he just offer to—

"In case Isabel wakes up in the middle of the night or something." The remark was meant to be flippant, but I swear his voice purred on the word "something". "You need your rest." Remi looks away and scratches his head.

Oh, he's just being polite, taking pride in his job and making me feel like we are no burden at all. Even though I pay him well, it isn't easy looking after a toddler all day.

My smile is warm as I walk back into the hallway. It's easy to relax around Remi. "I appreciate it. I have no idea what we'd do without you. But you have a life too, so..." I shrug, not knowing what else to say. All I want is to slip out of my clothes and have a date with B.O.B. in the soaking tub, which includes a bottle of Cabernet.

"Okay, well, you have my number. You can call me for anything."

Something hooks at the base of my stomach, pulling it taunt. He doesn't realize what my "anything" entails—me riding him hard like I'm going for the Kentucky Derby Trifecta. I bite my lip. My "Okay," comes out all weird and breathy. *Damn him.*

Remi pulls on his jacket as he heads towards the door. Hand on the knob, he turns back to me with a cocky smirk. I swear he can read my thoughts sometimes. "Sweet Dreams, Queeny," he purrs.

Once the door is closed, I lean back on it, swooning like a silly girl. I don't know that I've ever been this affected by a man before. No one gets under my skin like Remi does. It's like he has this magical power over everyone he meets.

Jay loves him. He and Elliot have some kind of bro handshake. Just the other day, I caught him chatting happily with Virginia, my persnickety neighbor with too much time on her hands, whom I always avoid. It's like no one can resist his charm. He leaves a little sunshine wherever he goes.

Heading into the kitchen, I grab a bottle of wine and gear up for a thrilling night of getting myself off before going to bed, just to wake up and do some version of this day all over again. After the bullshit I had to deal with tonight, I almost want to take a day off, but I can't. I have to devise another plan to secure our company, keeping all our employees. And I'll need to tell Jay what happened.

Opening the cabinet, I reach for the stemware when a yellow post-it note on the glass catches my attention. In Remi's neat script it says, *Open the fridge first.*

Why does he have to be so fucking cute?

Giddy, I open the fridge and find a wrapped plate of what looks like ground beef, salsa rice, and beans. That's right—it's taco Thursday.

The note on top of the plate says, *Eat me.*

A thrill runs up my spine at his thoughtfulness, though I'm not surprised. He's been cooking almost every meal. If he meets me at work, he brings takeout. Lunch has become the highlight of my day.

Hungrier than I thought, I inhale dinner like it's going to grow legs. His cooking is so good it rivals Mama Morales's. After I load my empty plate into the dishwasher, I pour myself another glass of wine and head to my bathroom for an indulgence hour. Opening the drawer of the vanity, I look at my "tools". Can't say I don't have a variety of options.

Lifting a finger to my chin, I sing, "Eeny, meeny, miny, moe, which one of you will make me moan?"

After today's bullshit, I reach for the rose, needing something to snatch my mind and forget my name for just a minute. Undressing as I run a bath, I set up camp and slide in the moment it's filled. Warm water washes over my sensitive skin, feeling like a cozy blanket. Pulling my hair into a messy bun, I lean back and settle, letting my mind wander.

It isn't long until it conjures illicit images of one hot manny. I imagine running my fingers through his dark locks smooth as silk. The tremble of his breath tells me he likes it. In my head he's groaning, and even though it's a fantasy, it's goddamn potent. My nipples harden, and my skin pebbles. Gliding my hand up to squeeze my breast, I pretend it's his hands with those long fuck-me fingers.

"You feel so good, Queeny."

My back arches, and I whimper.

His sexy smirk is front and center. *"You like that, baby?"*

"Yes," I hiss to the man in my head. "Please."

"Mmm, you look good enough to eat." He lifts my hips out of the water and teases my clit with the tip of his tongue. *"So fuckin' good."*

I'm well aware I'm going insane and this is six shades of wrong, but it doesn't stop the twist of my hips.

He dives in, lapping at me like a starving man.

I adjust the rose to the next setting and rev my impending orgasm.

"I'm going to fuck you so good, Mae. So fucking thoroughly, you're going to forget your own name. Then, I'm going to grind on that little pussy until you only remember mine."

Pressing the silicone toy against me, I explode, breathless and grunting his name.

Chapter 7

Guilty Pleasure

Remi

I USED TO HAVE to hold myself back to try to fit in a box of expectations from my parents and older brother. My father's a plastic surgeon, and his father before that. My brother, Dad's mini me, became an acclaimed reconstructive surgeon and cemented his position in the hierarchy. They live in a dog-eat-dog world I refuse to be a part of.

I'm wired differently.

Sure, they make a decent living, but are they happy? My mother certainly isn't, no matter how many pills she pops.

I never want to be that way. On my deathbed, I want to remember all the adventures I've experienced, the people I've loved, and the mark I've left on this world. *That's* what's important.

No one remembers the amount of money in the bank, only how they lived their life. If you find yourself with regrets, well ... better luck next time. *Maybe?*

If this is the only life I've got, I'm going to make it count in ways that don't have a monetary value. Which is why I'm making breakfast for my favorite little girl and her mama.

As I move around the kitchen, my lips purse in a whistle of the earworm I woke up with. I reminisce about the times my gram and I would play this song—*Hooked On A Feeling* by Blue Suede—and dance around the house without a care in the world. Gram taught me there is no such thing as guilty pleasure. It's a man-made term, inspired by indoctrinated societal norms to keep us from exploring life free from the burden of conformity. Pleasure is pleasure, and I'm not going to feel bad about something that makes me feel good if it doesn't hurt anyone else.

Humming along, I savor the rich smell of buttery toast as the griddle sizzles with maple sausage and scrambled eggs. It's true what they say—breakfast is the most important meal of the day. It also happens to be my favorite.

My phone pings an alert as I'm taking plates out of the cupboard.

> **Cody:** You're still coming tonight, right? Kiara will have my head if not.

I groan. *Fuck, that's right.* Kiara is the owner of Child Care Connection by day and matchmaker at night. I'm her latest project. It's time I settle down, according to her. It's not that I have anything against commitment, I just haven't met the right one. As it is, I'm not sure about tonight. Kiara is a bit uppity, and the woman she wants to set me up with is her friend. Unspoken expectations are already making me feel claustrophobic.

The clacking of heels pulls my attention away from responding to Cody.

"Morning, Remi." Mae power-strides into the kitchen, barely looking at me.

"Mama, Mama," Isabel babbles in her highchair, excited to see her mother.

She's wearing black today. Mae has patterns and routines, each offering nonverbal cues as to what's going on in her head. Red is her power color, and she wears it to important meetings. Blue is the color of her happiness. It hasn't missed my notice that she's been wearing that particular hue less lately. Purple looks beautiful on her, but I don't like when she wears it. Those days, she seems defeated and introspective. But that inky suit she has on? That's the color of her anger.

Heads will roll today, and hopefully mine isn't one of them.

A woman like Mae doesn't need a knight in shining armor. She'll kick ass and take names all on her own. She certainly doesn't need my interference in her battles.

It doesn't stop me from wanting to know what happened ... or wishing I could fix it.

Just focus on your job. That's all this is.

"I don't have time for breakfast. I'm just going to grab some coffee and head out."

Not on my watch, Queeny. Going without breakfast will not do at all.

"No worries. I'll pack it up for you." Whistling, I grab a glass container and start loading it up with eggs and veggies. She loves my double chocolate cookies made with carrots and apples. Hey, when you have picky kids to feed, you hide veggies into everything. I make a mental note to stop by with lunch as I throw the cookies into a plastic baggy.

"Mama, Maaamaaa." By the crescendo of her tone, I can tell Isabel is getting antsy for her mother's attention. "Maa—"

"Enough, Isabel," Mae snaps and then watches in horror as her daughter breaks out in tears. She walks over to pick Isabel up, but at this point, she's arching her back, wailing and pushing Mae away. "Oh, God. I'm sorry, baby. Mama's sorry."

"Hey, hey, hey, Isa-bea," I sing cheerfully to break the tension and get the baby to focus on me.

When she sees me coming, she throws out her arms and lunges for me. A sense of pride fills my chest, knowing Isabel feels safe enough to reach for me when upset. The bubble bursts when I see the hurt and shame in Mae's eyes.

"She just needs a little reassurance, and she'll be fine." I cup Isabel's head to my chest and kiss her hair, singing and swaying until her whimpers settle into hiccups. "Easy, sweet girl. Easy."

Holding out my hand, I silently ask Mae to take it. Children are in tune with their parents, especially when young.

Mae needs to release her tension before she holds Isabel, or she'll fuss. Lucky for her, I'm just the guy who can help. Giving her an encouraging smile, I wait for her to take my hand and mimic my demeanor.

When her small, warm fingers wrap around mine, I try not to concentrate on how perfectly they fit. I exhale an even breath, ignoring the tingled buzz racing up my arm. My glance shifts to a peaceful Isabel wrapped around my torso, and my chest tightens with emotion. She is sweet, smart, and funny. Quite possibly the cutest baby in the world.

The moment my gaze locks on Mae, the feeling in my chest flutters with buoyancy. She's just … remarkable. Strong, intelligent, and so self-aware it's admirable. And quite possibly, the most beautiful woman in the world.

How could I not get attached to them? It's practically impossible. And *wrong*. But it isn't bad that I want to take care of Isabel and support Mae. It's my guilty pleasure.

I can tell the moment high anxiety leaves Mae's body. Her face softens, and her eyes warm. This, right here, tells me they need me as much as I need them.

When her posture relaxes, I gently tug her arm. It is just a gesture of praise, but my heart has other motives. The poor schmuck wants them close and the idiot I am, I concede.

It's worth it when she lets me pull her into an embrace. The three of us link in a little group hug. Something shifts the moment I realize I'm holding space for the both of them. Something I don't want to examine too closely, but it won't be disregarded.

Before I realize it, I'm making a silent vow to always be here for them, holding them together, protecting them and... *Shit.*

Clearing my throat, I shift to Isabel. "All better now?"

Oblivious to my mini panic attack, she rubs her sleepy lids and reaches for her mother. My little sweetheart.

Get a grip, man.

Mae pulls Isabel to her with relief and remorse. "I'm so sorry, baby."

While she holds her daughter, I'm holding them both. No matter what personal fuckery I have going on in my head right now, I will not let Queeny walk out of this house with all that guilt bowing her spine.

Come to think of it, she was short with me last night when she got home too. *What's going on?*

I bet I can make her forget all about it. A plan forms in my head. Yeah, I'm gonna make her smile.

"She knows you love her and she loves you, Mae. Very much." Something about those words makes my chest constrict, but I continue, "She'd never hold it against you. Just please ... don't make her any apology pancakes."

3, 2, 1... Bingo.

Queeny's laughter is the prettiest melody I've ever heard. I try to make her sing it every chance I get. Because damn, that's one hell of a gorgeous smile. The world just got brighter.

I tell myself it's because I want her to be happy. Happy parents create easy-going babies. That's all this is about.

Nothing more. Right?

"What do you think, Isabel, should we listen to Harry or Taylor?" I'm a Swiftie and ain't ashamed about it. *Lavender Haze* is the shit.

"Sussi, Emmie. Sussi!" Isabel shouts, hopping around my legs. She, on the other hand, is one of the Harries. She wants me to play that damn *Sushi* song all the time. I can't blame her—it's a catchy tune.

As soon as the beginning bass riffs that funky beat, Isabel's jumps get higher and more animated. She's adorable, her enthusiasm contagious. Pretty soon, we're cutting a rug around the family room. We dance until Isabel has exhausted all of her toddler energy, and then we go into quiet time.

Grabbing Mr. Snuffles, I settle Isabel on my lap. She nestles in, and I take a moment to breathe her baby scent. It tempers the chaos in my head and helps me focus on what's most important—caring for her. Not being tactual with her mother like a sentimental dipshit.

"Do you want to read about the moon or about the cat?"

"Cat."

I smile. She's decisive, like her mom. It makes my job easy. "Okay, *The Cat and The Hat.*"

Isabel's baby giggle tickles my ears. "Him hat cwazy."

I chuckle. "Definitely."

"Definty," she mimics.

"Very good, Isa-bea."

Halfway through the book, Isabel looks up at me with the most soulful green eyes. *Her mama's eyes.* They both look at me like I matter to them the same way they matter to me. Sometimes, I kid myself that it's just the job that I love. But most times, it's so much more than that. I care in a way that exceeds mere obligation to this charge.

"I want cat." She yanks on my shirt. "Emmie, I want cat."

"Alright, we can talk to Mommy about it." How I said that rubs me the wrong way. Maybe because it implies that Mae and I are together as a couple. It's not appropriate nor allowed. Though, I can't deny the words flowed naturally off my tongue.

Were it up to me, I'd give Isabel anything she asked for. This little girl has me wrapped around her finger.

"We can ask your mom about it, but maybe we can just visit them at the shelter."

"What's ssewter?"

"A place where cats and dogs … um. It's where they live." Christ, I'm not about to get into why there are animals in the shelter—her huge heart would break. I can't bear to witness tears on her cheeks again today.

"Dey, lib dere?"

I love this age because they are curious about everything. Watching her learn about the world around her is the most rewarding thing about this job.

"Mm-hmm. They do, and sometimes they get adopted and get to live with families."

She looks away for a minute. I can practically see the cogs turning in her toddler head. Finally, she peers at me. "We adoded?"

How? How can I say no to her? It's like telling a begging puppy they can't have a treat. They call it "puppy eyes" for a reason.

"Well, cats need a lot of attention and care. Let's finish the rest of the book and see what this cat gets into. We can talk about it after."

Satisfied with my answer, she refocuses on the book. By the time I say, "The end," she's out cold. As soon as I put her down, I scrub my face with both hands.

I need to get a grip because I'm the stray that's getting too attached. So attached that if Kiara removed me from this family, I'd be ... devastated. Worst of all, Isabel would pay the price.

Shit.

I pick up my phone and text Cody back.

Me: Definitely. I'm excited to meet Mandy.

Because if I don't meet someone else, I'm going to fuck up the one good thing I have going for me—this job.

"So, do you like child caregiving, Remi?" Mandy, Kiara's friend and my blind date, blushes every time she asks me a question.

I can't help but flirt with her because it's cute. We're seated in the middle of a swanky restaurant. The lights are low, and classic jazz fills the space around us. It's the perfect setting for a romantic date and just what I need to divert my mind from a certain strawberry blonde.

"I do. There's something about a child learning that is really rewarding for me," I say with a smile and then check my watch. Cody and Kiara should have been here fifteen minutes ago.

This hoity-toity place has Kiara's name all over it, and I'm making her foot the bill. Besides, she knows my salary and definitely knows it's out of my price range.

This is a nice girl and I'm enjoying her company, but if there's to be a second date, I need to temper her expectations.

"Right, how cool is that?" Mandy's face breaks into a big grin. "I feel the same. I teach preschool at St. Mary's. Some days I'm pulling my hair out, and some days the kids do something small, like figure out how to color in the lines, and it's like Christmas came early." She looks away, bashful. "I don't know. You probably think it's stupid."

Not only is Mandy pretty, she's got a good heart too. A dark-haired beauty with big brown eyes. Her red lipstick matches her dress, which hugs her in all the right places.

Knowing we have this common interest loosens my joints, and I relax further into the chair. "You couldn't be further from the truth. I admire your dedication and passion for your job. Teaching preschoolers isn't easy. Believe me, I know. I can relate. I feel the same about Isabel."

"Is that who you nanny for? Isabel?" she asks, genuinely interested. "I bet she's happy to have you to play with." As soon as she says it, she clamps her teeth over her lips. "Okay, that sounded less weird in my head, but you get the picture."

I laugh. "Yeah, she's amazing. She's the sweetest too, but don't piss her off because she'll hand it back tenfold. I get bested by a two-year-old on the daily." My smile is wistful. "Nap times are the funniest. Sometimes, there are monsters in her closet that I have to beat up before she'll go to sleep. She'll call me back several times." I shake my head. "I know I should only give in once, but the way she jumps and cheers me on is adorable. She knows I'll keep coming in for battle." My grin widens. "Once she conks out, though, she'll sleep through a tornado."

Mandy's giggle is cute, and I find myself matching her liveliness.

Yeah, this is exactly what I need.

"Should we order drinks while we wait for Cody and Kiara?"

"Sure. Why don't you get the waitress's attention while I text Cody and see why they're standing us up."

She laughs again. In fact, she finds humor in all my corny jokes. I like that.

> **Me:** How far out are you?

Eyeing the woman sitting across from me, I send another text.

> **Me:** Tell Kiara thanks for the set-up. Mandy's great.

> **Cody:** Don't mean to tell you 'I told you so', but I told you. Says Kiara.

I click my tongue. This chick is always trying to bust my balls.

> **Cody:** We're pretty far out, stuck in traffic. I don't think we're going to make it.

> **Cody:** Have fun, you crazy kids.

My stomach clenches in disappointment. While I'm happy to get to know this girl one on one, my leg starts to jiggle in mini panic. I don't know how I'm going to pay for this meal.

"I'm sorry, Mandy. They are held up in traffic and are probably not going to make it. You're stuck with yours truly for this evening."

"Oh, great." She dramatically tosses up her arms. "Not *you*."

Her sarcasm pushes the chill button on my nerves, and we both laugh. She's easy to get along with.

"I do have a confession to make, though." She nibbles her bottom lip.

"Let the confession segment of the date begin."

She shakes her head, smiling. Blushing. *Cute.* "I'm a preschool teacher, who lives in a shitty apartment because rent is disgustingly high downtown. This isn't really my scene."

My ears perk, and my leg stills. "What is your scene then?"

"I'm more of a beer-and-pizza kinda girl. How about you?"

"Ah, and it was going so well. I prefer burritos and beer. This is never going to work out."

She throws her head back, cracking up. "I'm heartbroken."

"Don't be. Pizza and beer are good." We catch each other's glance. "I can definitely go for pizza and a beer."

We pay our tab, link arms, and head to the pub down the block, chatting as we stroll the sidewalk. There isn't one lull in our conversation. This is probably the best date I've been on in a while. She's really laid back.

"Have you always lived in Chicago?" Mandy asks.

"No, actually. I'm from—"

My phone cuts me off mid-sentence. When I go to dismiss the call, Queeny's name pops up on the screen.

I answer immediately. "Hey, Queeny, what are you doing on this fine evening?"

"Remi."

Her choked panic causes my steps to falter as my chest constricts. I hear Isabel screaming for me in the background. My world pivots. I've never felt such terror before.

"I'll be right there. Tell me everything."

Turns out, Isabel isn't feeling good and she's fussy, which is no surprise. Mae sounded like she was at her wits' end.

I explain to Mandy what's going on when the call ends, and she offers to help calm the mom while I settle Isabel. The great girl she is, she completely understands and comes with me to take the train towards the house.

When we get off the train, we take a taxi to Mae's. Normally, I'd walk, but my baby's in distress and I don't have time to waste. Yes, my baby. Fuck it. It certainly feels like she is. My heart is pounding out of my chest.

Storming into the house, I scan the area until my gaze locks on a sobbing Isabel and an exhausted Mae. Everything else fades away. They are all I see. As if my world is on fire and I'm the only one who can temper the blaze.

"Em-mie," Isabel hiccups, and my heart lurches.

She holds her arms out to me, and I reach for her. "What's the matter, Isa-bea?"

She doesn't answer. She just rubs her nose all over my chest.

Mae bites the side of her thumb as her eyes fill up with tears. "Remi, thank you for coming. I'm sorry to bother you on your night off. I'm just..." She glances away.

Her usually perfect locks are a tangled mess as if she's been tugging and twisting them for a while. She's wringing at the back of her neck, trying and failing to ease her tension. An oversized sweatshirt hangs off her body like it's being weighed down by gravity. Or maybe it's just mirroring her mental state.

When she turns back to me, I can see the vulnerability in her eyes. My ever-confident Queen is stripped raw and needs someone to fix her fallen crown. I want to be the one to do it.

Before I can pull Queeny to my side, my date approaches. "H-hi, I'm Mandy. Remi's, ah, friend."

Mae stares at her, stunned, and doesn't say a word. It's then she takes me in, sweeping her watery green irises from my head to my toes, taking in my dress slacks and white button-up—clothes I rarely wear.

"You were on a date." Her tone is flat, but I hear a hint of something. Accusation, maybe? In a second, Queeny goes from exposed to locked tight. She squares her hunched shoulders. "She was crying for you and wouldn't stop." A crack in the façade appears in her quivering chin. "I'm a terrible mother who can't even handle her own child."

Mae's emotion is catching up with the baby in my arms, who starts whimpering again.

"You are an amazing mother. And you're human." I rest a hand on Mae's shoulder, wanting to hold her to me. She's putting on that tough front because of Mandy, but I know she's hurting just as much as her daughter is.

Mae exhales a bitter laugh and shakes her head. Her gaze catches on my date and hardens before turning to me. "I just gave her a dose of Infants' Tylenol. She'll calm down in a bit." Her voice is robotic. "I'm sorry. You can go."

"How about, instead, you and Mandy get some tea in the kitchen while I get Isabel settled?"

Mae opens her mouth before tightening it into a thin line. "I can do it. It's fine." She sounds anything but.

While I understand Queeny doesn't like to be overruled, I'm not going to give her a choice tonight. A faithful valet doesn't desert his Majesty when she needs him most.

"I know you can." I keep my tone soothing, reassuring. "I want to do it. Please, let me help."

Her head hangs low when she nods.

As if it has a mind of its own, my free hand lifts her chin before reaching up and drying her tears. "There. It's going to be okay," I whisper.

With a sniff, she starts towards the kitchen. Mandy sends me a worried look and goes after her. Sure, our date was cut short, but she understands how important they are to me.

Settling into the rocking chair in Isa-bea's room, I set a relaxing rhythm. "What doesn't feel good, sweetheart. Hmm?"

"Mouff."

Running my hand across her forehead, I can tell she has a slight fever. "New teeth, huh? Yeah, kiddo. It sucks, but guess what?"

She looks up at me with the most trusting stare. "What?"

"Chicken butt." I don't normally do these kinds of jokes, but I'm trying to distract her from the pain.

With tears still stuck on her lashes, Isa lets out the shriekiest giggle. "You says 'chicken butt'."

I chuckle. "Yes, I did. I wanted to make you laugh." I brush her sweaty hair off her red face. *My sweet girl is hurting.* It slays my heart. If I can ease her pain even a little, I'm going to try. "You want me to sing your song?"

Nodding, she snuggles back into me and sticks her thumb in her mouth. We rock, casually, until she's out like a light. After settling her in the crib, I lay a hand on her back, just to feel her breathing.

I keep my voice low when I say, "I know you're not mine ... but I will always be here for you and Mommy. I promise."

Entering the kitchen, I find Mae and Mandy awkwardly staring at the contents in their mugs. Shit, I completely forgot Mandy was here.

"You were right, Mae. Giving her Tylenol was a good call."

Mae startles, and Mandy gives me a shy smile. Two completely different women, and yet I ran towards one without a thought of slighting the other. With this revelation, I inhale a sharp breath that stings my lungs.

"She's settled now, but I want to check on her in a little bit to make sure her fever doesn't rise."

"No, you don't have to do that. She's settled, and I've ruined enough of your night."

I have no plans of leaving this house tonight. Now that Isabel has calmed, I need to make sure Queeny does too. "Mandy, can I call you a taxi and we can talk later?"

Mae's neck turns red—a sure sign she's about to lay into me. "Remi, I said no. Take your date and leave." She rakes her fingers through her hair. She's a mess—a stubborn, beautiful mess.

I know she doesn't mean to be dismissive. Tired adults act just like tired children—cranky.

"With all due respect, Queeny. I'm staying." I lift my chin to my date. "Mandy, I'll wait with you outside."

"Yeah, that would be nice." Mandy brushes her hand on Mae's shoulder, but Mae's tight smile and stiff spine tell me that her walls are firmly stacked.

As soon as I close the front door, I apologize. "I'm really sorry. I just can't leave them like this."

Mandy gives me a sad smile. "It's good to care about people. You're a great guy, Remington."

"I really did have fun tonight before all this. Maybe I can get a redo?"

Her cheeks flush. "Yeah, I'd like that."

"Consider it a date."

The cab pulls up, and it's that awkward moment of should I or shouldn't I.

I'm on the fence. I stall by walking her down the steps, but fuck it. It was a date, after all. I open the cabbie door and give her a small kiss on the side of her mouth before she climbs in. Waving as I walk back up the steps, I rub my lips together.

As far as first kisses go, it was nice. A little perfunctory, maybe—not that I expected fireworks on the first date. But...

No buts. It was nice, and it will be even nicer the second time. I'm determined to date this girl because I cannot—will not—pursue something unrequited. Something that will surely be my undoing. Something I won't recover from.

When I get back to Mae, she's tidying up the family room. There are toys thrown everywhere, so I silently help her.

"Remi, you're amazing. Truly. But I need you to go. I'm tired, and I nee—"

"I need to stay."

We have a stare-off. Neither of us willing to surrender. Both of us wanting what's best for the other.

She doesn't realize how deeply they are rooted in my life. Hell, I didn't realize it until that call tonight.

"Do you have any idea what went through my head when you called? The panic in your voice. The agony in Isabel's..." Putting the last of the stuffies away, I face Mae. "Fuckin' ripped my heart right out of my chest. So please, for my sake, let me stay."

I'll beg if I have to.

But why? They are fine now. Isabel needs me and so does Mae, nothing more.

Stiff shoulders release as green irises glow emerald. "Fine." Even though she relents, there's reluctance in her tone. "There's a guest room down the hall, but I'm paying you overtime." Without another word, she turns off the lights and heads for the stairs.

I'm not ready to let her go. She needs to understand this is more than my duty as a caregiver. Just because it isn't in my job description doesn't mean it isn't my concern. I care ... too much.

"Not so fast, Queeny. We need to talk."

"What about?" She sniffs, halting her steps but not turning around. She's so heavily guarded, but I see it for what it is—fear. She's afraid of relying on anyone outside of herself. Afraid of disappointment.

Mae doesn't know the lengths I'd go to to make her and Isabel happy.

I step in close, my hands ghosting over her back but not daring to make contact. "About you dismissing me earlier, when I said I wanted to stay."

She shivers, and something akin to satisfaction settles in my gut.

"Because you're not obligated to stay. You weren't even obligated to come. I feel like shit for messing up your date." She rakes her fingers through her naughty hair. "You have your own life, Remi. I don't want you to get caught up in mine." By her sharp tone, I can tell she's going to shut me out.

Not this time.

Awareness of what I'm about to do thrums through me. My thoughts are reckless and frantic, my limbs aching with a need so powerful it silences everything else. I yank her back to my chest and wrap my arms around her, almost sighing in contentment. There's that warm, fuzzy feeling again.

She doesn't hug me back, but she doesn't push me away either.

My heart is pounding so hard I'm surprised it doesn't break a rib.

Can she feel it? What does it mean if I don't care that she does?

I fight the urge to squeeze her to me like some stage-five clinger. I've hugged her before, but tonight it feels different, more significant than any other time.

Queeny's frozen shoulder blades melt into my chest as if they are ice dissolving into liquid heat. Maybe she likes being in my arms as much as I like her being there. Every stuttered breath she exhales ripples up my torso, feeding the raucous beat of the silly thing in my chest. I nuzzle her hair, biting back a blissful groan as her warm vanilla scent wraps around me. *Her hair is really soft.* It doesn't escape my notice that my nerves flare alive when I'm this close to her.

Needing to see her face, I turn her towards me and tuck a lock of hair behind her ear so I can see her better. The sorrow in her gaze, breaks me. *Who hurt you so badly, Queeny?*

"That's true. I'm not obligated to come after hours. It's not contractual to cook meals and visit you at work. It's not my duty to comfort you either."

She begins to push me away, but I hold her tight. She smells so damn comforting. Even more than Isabel.

"I need you to know I'd literally die for that baby."

Her stare widens, and her chin trembles. The sadness coating her orbs lightens to hope and trust.

I kiss her temple, lingering … wanting. *Opposite of perfunctory.* "Her mother, also." I meant to say those words in my head, and even though I'm shitting a brick, I can't take them back. I won't lie to her.

Peering up at me, Mae's mouth falls open and her fingers clutch onto my shirt. Her eyes are fathomless pools of sparkling emerald.

"You would?" Her voice is broken and beautiful.

"Never doubt it."

What the fuck is wrong with me? As always, my emotions eclipse any logic in my head. This could end epically bad. Kiara would rip me away from this family so fast my heart would be whiplashed and broken in a single second.

But what if it doesn't? It's clear Mae and Isabel need someone they can rely on. Someone solid they know will never let them down. I'm happy to be that person, fucking elated.

Queeny's forehead tightens before releasing all tension as a small smile grows across her cheeks. It creeps up a millimeter at a time until it's a full-on grin.

Goddamn, she's beautiful.

One by one the bricks fall, crumbling the walls she's built around herself. She curls into me, and her shoulders tremble. Showing her vulnerable side tells me I've earned her trust, and something about that gives me a high. She's a self-possessed sovereign with an iron fortress around her, and yet she's letting *me* in—the poor peasant boy who can offer nothing but himself.

Later on in the guest bedroom, I ruminate on the night. Knowing I did great in some ways and fucked up in others. I like being here more than I should, but I don't want to dissect why. Kiara warned me not to get attached, and I've tried, but I'm pretty sure I soldered them to my being the moment I met them.

Rolling to my side, I punch the pillow under my head. My ears strain to hear any noise coming from the baby monitor on the nightstand, per my request. I think about my date, or at least, I try to. I could, too, if my mind wasn't stubbornly occupied by the woman down the hall. A woman who's so much more than conventional beauty, though she's stunning with curves that could bring a man to his knees. She's ethereal in her majesty and fortitude. She might not need a knight in shining armor, but she and Isabel need me.

I'm good with that. I'll never let her down. Neither of them.

Chapter 8

A Juicy Carrot in a Starving Rabbit Race

Mae

A LONG DARK HALLWAY stretches to eternity before me. Heavy doors made of hardwood and steel line the walls on either side. Opening the first door, there is nothing but black, just an ominous feeling in the air. The same creepy-crawly sensation I had that day. But I'll be damned if I back down. I can face anything, do anything, be anything.

Squaring my shoulders, my eyes narrow, challenging the dark abyss before me.

"I'm not afraid of the dark," I declare to no one. My voice seems to echo a hundred times, each one becoming louder until the sound is unbearable. The piercing howl makes my eardrums scream.

Clutching the sides of my head, I back out of the black and sprint down the hallway, trying to outrun the sound to no avail. The howl turns into my daughter's wails, and now I'm opening every door to find her.

"No, please. Not my daughter."

When I can't find her, I panic and yell her name, but no sound comes out. Over and over, I search and holler, but nothing. My world is closing in, and I'm dropping down a spiral, spinning way too fast. The cries are too loud. I can't get to her.

And then ... I'm caught, and it all just stops. The free fall. The wailing. The panic.

"There you are," a voice coos. "Shh, I've got you."

It's calming and familiar, but I can't place it. I seek it, but the more I strain to listen, the further away it drifts.

"No, don't go," I plead, but it doesn't work. I'm alone in the stillness and silence, but I'm no longer afraid, so I float in this space until...

I fling upright with a breath caught in my throat. Figures. I tossed and turned most of the night, finally falling asleep in the early morning hours, only to have a nightmare.

Collapsing back onto the bed, I stare at the ceiling. Sunlight sprays through my blinds, bathing the room in gold. The hope of a new day feels more like dread. I'm spiraling.

He was on a date. *A date!* It's not that I thought the guy was a monk, with a body that is panty-melting, scorching hot and a smile so disarming he could steal your watch and you'd thank him for it. He probably has a hundred girls lined up for a chance with him. Most of all, his personality and the way he sees the world are vitalizing. Optimistic. He's the fucking pied piper of happiness, and I'd follow him anywhere.

Remi is pure goodness, through and through. He's a young, single, eligible bachelor—of course he's going to date. I just wasn't prepared to confront it.

In my head ... *sigh* ... he belongs with us. He's ours. It's selfish and irrationally possessive, but it is what it is.

And his date, Mandy. I can't even pick on her because she's sweet and pretty, and perfect for him.

Meanwhile, I'm trying to do the one thing I'm supposed to know how to do—take care of my baby. When my child screamed for him while kicking me, I went into a self-flagellation of epic proportions. If I had a whip, I'd strike my own back. A sliver of shame imbeds itself in the soft tissue of my heart.

Isabel's guttural cries became so fervent she couldn't breathe and was making herself sick. I didn't want to call him. I really didn't because the more time I spend with him, the harder it is to not act on the indecent thoughts rolling around my head.

But I did call. And he came. He got here in less than ten minutes—not an easy feat coming from the city.

When Remi walked through my front door, the sight of my daughter lunging for him made me want to whip his ass too. How can I be jealous *of* him and *for* him at the same time? The manny worked his magic on Isabel, and then... *Swoon.*

He's a charmer, that one. I wonder if he knows he has all of us wrapped around his long, fuckable finger. To be honest, though, his appeal is more than merely physical. Last night proved how emotionally attached to him I've become. When he held me, try as I might, I couldn't resist. My body melted right into his.

Closing my eyes, I try to conjure the sensation of being in Remi's arms. The peace and comfort that spread through my limbs. The safety. The conviction that nothing would go wrong as long as he was holding me. It's been a long time since I didn't feel so alone.

"I need you to know I'd literally die for that baby." His statement was already a potent aphrodisiac to my uterus, but then he added, *"Her mother, also,".* Making my ovaries explode all over the damn place.

This shit's getting messy. What was simply lust is creeping into another L category. A category that is nothing but an illusion. It's not real. I know first-hand. It's fickle and fleeting, and has no place in my reality. Like Tina said, what's love got to do with it? Fucking nothing, that's what.

Rolling onto my back, I punch the mattress with the side of my fists. What the hell is wrong with me? I'm so fucked.

You wish.

Yeah, that too.

Groaning, I climb out of bed and throw my bathrobe on because I'm wearing the shortest shorts I own and a cami that leaves nothing to the imagination. I don't want him to think I'm seducing him. Right?

Tightening my belt like it will save my chastity, I head to Isabel's room to see if she's still sleeping. I take a moment to watch her. The soft fall and rise of her chest tells me she's had a restful night. But the rosiness of her cheeks reveals a stubborn fever that will not go away.

Rubbing my groggy eyes, I mindlessly head to the spare bathroom to find the bottle of Tylenol. But when I open the door, I find something else—a wet and whistling hot manny, scrubbing his hot manny chest in the shower. Oblivious to my entrance and subsequent staring.

Every nerve ending in my body flares alive with thrumming need, and saliva pools in my mouth.

I should get out of here. I shouldn't be peeping on the nanny unawares. I should at least cover my eyes.

I do none of those things. My eyes take the decision right out of my brain's control as they slowly sweep down the most gorgeous specimen of a man I've ever seen.

His dark floppy hair is slicked back, showing the full spectrum of his Adonis face. Ripe red lips whistle a tune innocently while I imagine them sucking on me salaciously. I imagine myself all warm and wet inside that shower with him. Would he wash me with those strong hands? Linger on the most sensitive parts as he scrapes his teeth along my skin? Would he try to get those hard-to-reach inside places?

Christ. My pussy puckers, and I clench my thighs together.

I follow the rivulets of water from his head, down his cut torso, to the V of his pelvis, and my lungs expel the last breath they're ever going to breathe.

Holy hell, he's a show-er.

I turn my head sideways to find the tip, and I swear it bounces off his knee as he moves. If that's what he's like flaccid, he's a goddamn murder weapon hard.

I never met one in real life and now that this unicorn is in front of me, I can't look away. I can't help but think how I've always wanted to try one of those—a show-er.

I almost whine in grief at the disappearance of the star of the show. A wet Remi turns, facing away from me. If his front was impressive, his back is fucking mouth-watering. The muscles of his shoulders undulate with his movements. They taper tauntingly down to a narrow waste and the juiciest ass I've ever seen on a man. I can only imagine the nail marks I'd leave on those luscious cheeks after I've sucked him off properly.

My knees knock together, and I almost fall further into the room.

What are you doing? Grab what you need and get the hell out of here before he notices you're a creeper, risk level: one thousand.

I squat-tiptoe in like some crouching-tiger-hidden-dragon ninja shit. I mean to keep my sight on the tiled floor. My eyelids, however, have a mind of their own as they flit up to catch the majestic waterfall pouring from the tip of the manny's long member. Cotton stuffs my mouth, and I'm suddenly greedy for hydration.

Facing me fully, Remi rinses off, completely oblivious that my eyes are firmly focused on the thing dangling in front of my sight—a juicy carrot in a starving rabbit race.

And propriety be damned because I'm gunning for first place. I lick my lips because victory will be sweet...and a little salty.

"*Shit.*" Remi shoves his hands in front of him and clears his throat.

The sound breaks me out of the penis-induced trance and throws me right into mortification. My robe gets caught around my feet, and I fall forward with a yipe. I face-plant onto the floor while my ass stays high in the air, like a public offering. With my lids squeezed tight, I shift upright but keep patting the floor, like I lost a contact lens instead of my goddamn mind.

"Um, don't mind me. I didn't see anything." Throwing my hand over my eyes, I reach around feeling for the cabinet door. "Nope, nothing dangling at all. Not even your knees. No, sir. For all I know, you could be washing up with an elephant trunk in there."

Shut up, woman.

When my fingers trace the corner of the cabinet, I find the nob and swing it open in one jerky movement, which sends the thing careening into my nose. "Fuck."

The hand that was covering my eyes goes to my nose, and I know it's bleeding. Liquid drips onto my lips and as soon as I taste copper, everything goes black.

There is an irritable patting on my cheek. I try to brush it away, but it doesn't stop.

"Queeny, come on. Wake up."

More pat-pat-patting.

I groan.

"That's it. Come back, Queeny."

Isabel's fever. Looking for Tylenol.

Finding a naked man instead.

Staring. Getting caught.

Crap, it's the show-er.

I can't. I can't do it. I won't. "No, leave me be."

"I can't, babe. I need to look at your nose. I don't want you to bleed out on me."

"It's too late. I'm already dead." I throw my arm over my eyes, adding to the cinematic drama that is my life. "The sight of your wooly mammoth tusk killed me."

I feel rather than hear his deep chuckle in his chest. That's when I realize he's cradling me against him. The only thing I want to do is grind on his lap to see if he's still naked. Because if he is, well, that's an invitation I'll RSVP to.

"Well, at least I know you're okay. Come on, up you go."

He lifts me under my arms like he does Isabel. Like I weigh nothing when I damn well know I'm not the lightest by any stretch of the imagination. Setting me on the toilet, Remi brushes my hair back as he tips my head. I can't bear to look at him, especially if he's still naked.

"You can open your eyes now. I'm … covered." I swear I hear the snicker in his tone.

Jerk.

Yeah, well, you're a lecher.

Whatever.

"I can never look at you again after this, I'm afraid. My corneas were burned by the sight of your monster dick." Welp. In for a penny, in for a pound. "It's something no mortal woman should ever see. It's a celestial cock."

He roars a laugh that bounces off every surface, reverberating through my body. "Well, that's a fucking shame. Celestial or not, my monster dick happens to like mortal women." He puts pressure on my nose. "It's stopping," he murmurs, his minty breath sweeping across my cheeks.

When a warm hand lands on my cold shoulder, I freak. My lids fly open and I jerk up, head-butting him in the process.

Remi grabs his chin, staggering back. "Jesus, woman."

With his movement, the towel wrapped precariously around his waist loosens.

My mouth dries in horror as my eyes prepare for their feast.

"Oh god. I'm sorry." Trying to look away, I notice the outline of my hard nips through the sheer cami and place my arm across my uninhibited boobs. "Where's my robe?" I screech.

"It was wrapped so tight around your neck I thought you couldn't breathe, so I loosened it." Looking away with a sheepish smile, he scratches his head. "It fell off when I picked you up."

"I'm appalled..." At my behavior, but he doesn't need to know that. "How dare you?"

"How dare *me*?" He shoves a finger into his bare chest, and I want to lick it. "You were the one creeping in here like a peeping Tammy."

"What the hell is a peeping Tammy?"

His fists rest on his hips. "You know, when someone secretly watches you when you're naked."

I click my tongue. "A peeping Tom, you idiot. And I was not creeping. It's my house."

"You were."

"I was *not*."

"*Yes.* You. Were." He pauses as his stare becomes intense.

The nerve of this guy. "Was. Not."

I'm shivering, even though it's nice and steamy in here.

Remi inches closer and my eyelids flutter at his proximity. I can't think straight when he's this close. It's disorienting.

His arm lifts towards me and I bite my lip, transfixed by its direction. My breath hitches because I know without a doubt he's going to touch me. The soft hair on my arms rises, along with my dimpled flesh, eager and ready for contact.

When he cradles my jaw, tilting my chin forward, my eyes slide shut.

This is it. This is when I come undone. He's going to kiss me, and I'm going to fuck him on the floor. A swarm of buzzing bees vibrates through my belly.

My lips part in anticipation.

He moves my head from side to side.

Is he trying to figure out where to kiss me? I lick my lips to show him where to begin.

He leans in closer. A breath away, and my lungs seize. *So close.*

"Looks like the bleeding has stopped, but let's get some ice on you. Wouldn't want that cute nose to swell up." He tightens his towel and moves towards the door.

I almost cry out at the lost opportunity. Because he can't just tease me like that, can he?

"Where are you going?" I ask instead of whining, *why aren't you kissing me?*

"To put my celestial cock away so I can restore your vision and get ice for your nose." The bastard winks and walks out the door.

Composing myself, I pick up my bathrobe—now stained with blood—trying not to pass out again as I put it back on.

What the fuck do I do now? I totally perved on Remi. I would carve anyone with a dull knife if they ever did that to me.

What if the hot manny did that to you? Well, then I'd have to put on a show. It's only fair to reciprocate.

It's all fine. An innocent mistake. I was taken off guard that I had a naked man in my bathroom, that's all. I haven't had one in a long time—a naked man in the shower. Or in my bed.

I'm just sexually deprived. I've read that sexual frustration can lead to all kinds of mental health problems, including fantasizing about a guy who is totally off limits.

It's just about his proximity. *That's all.*

And maybe the way he cares for my daughter. *Yeah, that too.*

And his cooking is fucking amazing. *I enjoy his meals. So what?*

And he's a really great person. *What's there not to like? Platonically, of course.*

And ... and ... I bet he fucks like a wild stallion with his huge horse cock.

I'm going to hell.

Dressed for the day, I power-stride towards the kitchen to get some coffee before I leave.

I will be cool. It's not a big deal. I've seen dicks before, and I'm a grown woman. I can act like an adult and deny it ever happened ... with conviction.

As soon as I step over the threshold, my eyes catch a juicy booty bent over while its owner fishes something out of the oven.

They're banana nut muffins. Which gives me a flashback to his banana and nuts. Which I'm going to, of course, ignore.

"You clean up nice, Queeny." He smiles widely, and I almost pass out. Like, a real nineteenth-century swoon. Those motherfucking dimples are trying to murder me. I whisper a Hail Mary and turn away.

"What was that?" Remi taunts and saddles up to me at the counter as I pour myself coffee.

"What was what?" I huff. *Tell me he heard that.*

"Sounded like, 'Oh, dear mother of God'." He makes the sign of the cross and places his palms together. I'd laugh if I wasn't so focused on keeping expressionless. "Is there a reason for your impromptu devotion today?"

Yes, to cleanse me from the sin of lust. "Stubbed my toe." I shrug, still not able to face him.

"Uh-huh." He purses his lips, mirth dancing in his eyes. "I could always kiss it and make it better."

Does he know he's playing with fire? Surely not.

"You wouldn't be saying that if you saw my toe-jam." Deflect. Deflect. Deflect.

Remi dips his head close to my ear. His cool breath teases the soft skin under my lobe, and my knees knock together.

"I know what you're doing," he sing-songs.

Um, trying not to fuck you? "Yeah, Captain Obvious. I'm drinking coffee," I mumble, hoping he leaves me here to sweat it out in privacy.

His warm, strong hand glides up my back and tickles my neck. Every hair on my body is alive. For all that lean muscle, he's quite tender in his approach.

"No, you're ignoring the mammoth in the room."

I choke, and coffee sprays on my pristine white countertop.

The jerk chuckles. "We can't avoid talking about it forever."

Watch me. "I have no idea what you're talking about."

He squints, scratching the playful set of his chin. "Okay, have it your way. I'll let you stew on it. You'll come around ... eventually."

"While you were away, two things happened." I hand Jay their coffee before sitting across from them for our Monday morning meeting.

Jay takes an exaggerated sip and moans. "Exquisite," they sigh, then wave their hand. "Go on."

"Right, well, we're probably going to lose the Dexico account."

Jay stops making love to their coffee and focuses on me, concern etching their face. "I know you worked really hard on this, and we did everything we could." They shrug. "Besides, I've always felt they're not a good fit. That Paul asshole creeps me out," they finish with a dramatic shiver.

"I just wanted us to be on top. Landing big accounts, like Dexico, attracts other big accounts."

"I told you—we don't need Dexico." They take another swig. "We are solid with the accounts we already have. There will always be other Dexicos, Mae. With you at the helm, I have no doubt."

My soul dies a little at their confidence in me. Jay is an artistic person—they don't mess with numbers. That falls on me, and it's not looking pretty. I'm not so sure we'll be able to recover if more investors follow Pingman's lead. Sometimes, I wish Jay would take a more invested look into our financial health. If they understood the predicament we were in, they'd understand my concerns.

Setting their coffee down, Jay adjusts their sleeves. "What happened with that meeting, anyway?"

I knew they'd ask, and I know just the thing I can distract them with. "We can discuss it with our team later." Skimming over the issue, I pretend I didn't fantasize about castrating Dexico's CEO. "Don't you want to know the second thing that happened?"

They raise an eyebrow like they're going to call me out for holding back information, but they let it go. "Tell me."

Settling back into my seat, I cradle my coffee in both hands, pausing for anticipation. A sly smirk spreads across my face. "I saw hot manny's monster dick this morning."

They choke on their latte, getting it all over their blue silk kimono. "Jesus fucking Christ, Mae. Give a warning before you paint that picture."

I start laughing. "What picture?"

"Uh, an image of the Inglesias doppelganger with a delectable dick."

My cheeks flare, and I press the back of my hand to them, feeling their warmth. I do not blush. Ever. "It was awful."

"Lies," Jay hisses.

I throw my balled up napkin at them. "I'm being serious."

"Okay, tell me everything. Let your bestie assess the damage."

"He was on a date," I pout.

"Wait, he showed you his jewels while he was romancing another woman?" Jay leans back as their brows creep to their hairline. "Feral."

I click my tongue. "No, you big dummy. Isabel's getting her molars in so she was fussy and screaming for Remi. I had no choice. I called him."

"And he was on a date?"

"Yeah, only I didn't know it until he brought her to the house." I peer deep into the caramel contents of my cup, trying to see a future without ever looking at Remi again. It's bleak.

"And then he showed you his cock?"

"No, let go of the cock thing for now. Would ya?"

"That's what he said."

The next thing I throw at them is a pen. "Be serious for just a second and let me tell you what happened."

"Such a killjoy." Jay waves a gallant hand. "Finish."

"Anyway, he gets to the house within ten minutes of my phone call. Barrels in as if he's S.W.A.T. coming into a raid. I was so preoccupied with the way he was with Isabel, I didn't notice how he was dressed or who came through the door behind him." I take another sip of my coffee and continue, "She's really pretty, Jay. Nice, too." Shaking my head, I resign to the fact that ... she's young, kind, and most likely carrying zero baggage. Unlike the U-haul I transport on my back. "She's perfect for him."

"Back it up, baby girl. Did you say he was on a date and dropped everything to come to your rescue?"

I nod. "Yes, he said he'd literally die for my baby." I turn with pleading eyes to my best friend. "Die for her," I whisper again. "So he settles her down and I tell him to leave, but he doesn't."

"No? Wasn't he on a date?" Jay's incredulous.

"Yes, and he called her a taxi. Said he was staying and wouldn't take no for an answer. Then he said something else that shook me to my core."

"Oh, man, I see the ice around your private parts is melting."

With a leaky nose, I nod. "'Tis true." Staring out into space, I relay the rest of the evening. "When he said he'd die for Isabel"— my brows push together as I try to swallow the lump of emotion caught in my throat —"he added, 'and her mother, also'." I blow out my cheeks and repeat it just so I can hear it again. "Her mother, also." My nose stings. "Like, who says that, Jay?"

"Someone who wants to show you his monster dick."

"No, he loves his job too much to fuck it up. Fraternization between caregivers and guardians is strictly prohibited. It nulls the contract, and both parties would be responsible for paying hefty fines to the agency." My vagina whispers, *worth it*. My brain threatens to dry her out if she says anything else. "I'm pretty sure he was just being a good guy. I know how much he cares about Isabel, and me by extension." Pulling my hair high on my head, I wrap it into a sloppy knot, not caring who sees me like this. I have more important things on my mind. "He's probably going to get a restraining order put on me. We'll have to exchange custody of Isabel in a police department parking lot."

When I look over to my friend, they're not commiserating with me like I thought they would. Jay's face is turning red because they're biting their cheek so hard, trying and failing not to laugh at me.

Whatever.

"Don't you roll your eyes at me, Mars Bars. You wanna know what I think?"

"Does a bear shit in the woods?" I click my tongue against the roof of my mouth. "This is why I come to you with all my life's problems. So you can fix them for me."

"Job be damned, he's probably happy that you saw his monster cock. In fact, he probably can't wait to show you how it works." Jay proceeds to act like they're riding a raging bull, lassoing me with an imaginary rope. "Yee-haw, baby."

"You're so full of it," I huff, then a smile cracks over my face before I burst out laughing.

My best friend may be a jokester, but they're rarely wrong.

They predicted that Aubry would follow me to Chicago. She did.

Then there was the time they told me my new boyfriend would turn out to be a dirty jagoff. It was Brad, and he did.

Most recently, they knew I was having a girl before gender was revealed. I did.

I sober.

If I want to keep Remi, it's going to have to be up to me to hold a respectable distance from my daughter's caregiver.

I'm not going to steal little moments and watch him. I'm not going to speak to him unless it's absolutely necessary. I'm not even going to call him Manny anymore. It's too personal.

If none of that works? Well, then I'm going to bring my A-game—make myself as unappealing and revolting as I can.

Easy peasy.

Chapter 9

Queen of Hearts

Mae

As the rainy spring evaporates into summer, the sun isn't blocked by heavy clouds as much and the city parks come alive with activity.

"What do you think, Isabel, you want to go to the festival?" We had an easy Saturday morning, and I'm dressing her so we can go out for the day.

"Yeah!" She jumps, raising her arms so I can put her shirt on. "Emmie?"

"No, sweetie, Remi is off." After her head pops through the collar of her shirt, I smooth it back. "Your hair is crazy today." I boop her nose, and we laugh.

"Caw Emmie?" She's a persistent little shit.

But I get it because I feel his void too. The house feels homier when he's here. "Maybe later. Let's go play some games first, deal?" I hold out my hand, and her little chubby one takes it.

"Deah." She nods.

Well, that was easier than expected.

Twenty minutes later, we stroll into the festival at Centennial Park. There are bouncy houses, carnival games, face painting, and small rides. It smells like sunshine and yummy food. My stomach grumbles.

"You want some French fries, Isabel?"

"Yeah," she squeals.

I don't usually feed her fried food, but this is a special occasion.

While standing in line, a creepy-crawly feeling skitters down my back, and I have an odd

feeling I'm being watched. Pulling Isabel's stroller closer to me, I look around, but I don't see anyone or anything out of the ordinary.

"Can I take your order? Miss?" The food truck guy is trying to get my attention, but my spidey senses are on alert.

I place my order and then look around again. Either something is off or I'm being paranoid. Considering the stress I've been dealing with lately, I'll go with paranoia.

When our order is ready, we go and sit under the dine-in tent. There are many tables set up and people around. I feel less exposed here. I don't know what is going on, but I'm not going to let my worry ruin this beautiful day with my daughter. Winter seemed like it lasted five years instead of five months.

"Fwy, Mama." Isabel makes grabby gestures with her hands, and I give her a soft French fry.

"Chew it good, sweetie."

Her eyes grow big and she grins wide, showing all her baby teeth. She's too cute. "Good."

I giggle. "Sure is."

" Emmie!" she shouts, and I give her another fry so she gets her mind off the nanny.

"Honey, I told you... We'll call him later, okay?"

She pushes my hand away and looks around me. "Emmie!"

"Shhh, Isabel. He's not here."

"Who's not here?"

I swing my head around and my eyes drag down his form, taking in every inch of him like he's a mirage and going to disappear any moment. Remi is classic, wearing a plain white V-neck stretching deliciously across his chest and dark denim jeans, faded in all the right places. With black Ray Bans sitting perfectly on his face, he looks like James Dean reincarnated.

It's only been a day, but my heart leaps as if he's been missing for decades. I want to run into his arms and bury my nose in his neck. The need shocks me.

The leaping organ plummets to the ground when I see Mandy's hand wrapped around his arm. He's not alone.

"Hi." She gives me a weak wave. While her smile is pleasant, it does nothing to tamper the hot streak of jealousy scorching through my chest.

"H—" I swallow the ball in my throat. "Hey, what are you guys doing here?"

"We're just here on a date." Mandy smiles.

My stomach clenches around the fries I ate and roils. It's an obvious truth, yet she needed to emphasize that this isn't just a friendly outing. Of course, I interrupted it ... again.

"Emmie!" Isabel lunges for Remi.

The great guy he is, he picks her up and swings her high in the air. "How's my favorite girl?"

Isabel's giggle is adorable but heartbreaking. Someday, she'll outgrow having a nanny and he will move on to another family. Just the thought leaves me grief-stricken.

Remi sits next to me with Isabel on his lap. He eats some of our food and then offers some to her, oblivious to the tension building between me and his date.

I'm not that girl. As much as I want this guy, it can't happen between us. He's here with another woman. She's good too. He deserves good.

Wiping my mouth and hands with a napkin, I stand up. "It was really great seeing you guys." My smile is stiff, but it's all I can muster. "Come on, Isabel. Let's let Remi and Mandy enjoy the rest of their date."

When I reach for my daughter, she clings on to Remi.

"It's okay. Right, Mandy? We can all hang out. Besides, I want to see this little one take a ride on the kiddie coaster." He smiles at Isabel, melting my heart and resolve.

This guy will happily halt his date with a beautiful woman just to see my daughter have fun.

I turn to Mandy and mouth, *I'm sorry*. If I was here with him on a date, there's no way I'd want to share him with someone else.

Mandy waves her hand off like it's no big deal, and that's how I know she's the better woman for him. She's kind and generous. While I have my strengths, I am neither of those. I'm a bitch, selfish with her time.

We walk around the park for hours. Remi insists he take Isabel on all the rides and snaps a million pictures—some of her, some of them, and some of us. The first time she went on a ride by herself, I could swear his eyes turned glassy with pride.

"She's getting so big."

"It's amazing how fast they grow," Mandy chimes in. "Pretty soon, she'll be off to school full time. When are you enrolling her in preschool, Mae?"

"Not for a while," Remi answers as he watches Isabel on the kiddie roller coaster like a hawk.

"Excuse me." I nudge him with my elbow. "She'll be taking AP calculus next year. We hope to get her into a good university."

Remi and Mandy laugh. They are easy together, and I wonder how serious they are. They seem like they've been dating for a while.

Loneliness hollows my stomach. I wonder if I'll ever have that.

"Funny, but you're going to wait until she's ready, right?" There's some kind of desperation in his eyes, almost like he's asking for reassurance.

"Yeah, of course. But except for potty training, she's done everything early. So, who knows?"

The ride stops, and Remi jogs to pick up Isabel from the cart. He's not on duty, but yet he seems like he is. Maybe caregiving is in his blood and he can't help himself. Isabel's talking to him a mile a minute, and he listens with rapt attention.

"He's going to be a great father someday," Mandy says, drawing my interest away from them. She's looking at him with hearts in her eyes, and for some reason, I want to cover them. I don't like her looking at him like that.

But it's okay for you to do it? I do not.

"Yeah, he's great with Isabel." Shifting my gaze towards Remi, a small smile forms on my face but then drops. "Have you two been together long?" I'm making conversation, not fishing for information.

"We're new, but it feels like we've known each other forever." She smiles dreamily at them, then turns to me. "Some things are just meant to be."

"Right." I don't mean to sound cynical, but it's better than vomiting all over the place. *Why am I being like this?*

"I big girl," Isabel announces, raising her chubby little arms in the air.

"Yes, you are." Remi hands my daughter back to me, but he doesn't go far. With one hand still attached to her, he wraps the other one around me. "We're so proud of you, Isa-bea."

A surge of emotion bursts through me. Of course *I'm* proud of her. But to hear the sentiment from him, saying "we" as in he and I—a unit— is everything I ever wanted for my daughter. And for myself. How can something that feels so right be horribly wrong?

"What a sweet little girl you have." An older woman walks up to us. "She was riding next to my granddaughter. They were so cute together."

"She's amazing," Remi and I say at the same time.

"Jinx," he calls, giving me a wink.

"Yinks," Isabel echoes.

"I love seeing young fathers so involved in their child's life. In my day, that was all women's work."

My mouth dries, and words escape my brain.

"Oh, he's not—" Mandy interjects, but Remi clears his throat, not letting her finish.

No matter. Our moment is gone as a strange distance forms between us.

"Fathers should be in their children's lives without question." His voice is soft yet earnest. "This little girl deserves all the love in the world. Caring for her is an honor." With his large hand splayed across her back, he holds Isabel close and presses a kiss to the top of her head. A sweet smile curves his lips as if she is perfection personified. When his gaze turns to me, his umber irises glow with flecks of gold and ... fervor.

Reality falls away as I zero in on the man holding my daughter. A month ago, I labeled him a womanizer, a charismatic con man. Shame slithers through my veins as this moment punches the truth into my stomach—Remi is one in a million.

He's thoughtful in everything he says. Genuine in everything he does. He's the one good thing in this world. How could I not feel something for him?

"How wonderful," the woman praises, patting Remi's arm. "It was nice meeting you, Isabel. You have a great time with Mommy and Daddy." She smiles and walks away like she didn't just thrust me and Remi in the most awkward position possible.

His eyes watch mine, but we don't say anything. What is there even to say?

We're locked in a moment as if no one else exists besides the three of us. A little family. We both know he's not her father. It was a silly mistake. But still.

"That was crazy, huh?"

"Insane," he breathes.

His lips look so pink and soft, and the urge to kiss him zaps through me.

He inches closer and—like a magnet—I do too.

"Remi? We should probably get going. The movie starts in half an hour." Mandy's soft voice is the equivalent of nails on a chalkboard, yanking me out of the illusion I'm wrapped up in.

He's on a date with someone else. We accidentally bumped into each other. No matter what Jay says, Remi only cares for Isabel. That's all this is.

Remi startles and looks at his wrist. The corners of his mouth dip down. "Oh, shit. I didn't realize it got so late." His eyes are apologetic, if not a little sad, as he straps Isabel back into her stroller.

"Ssit."

To ease the tension, I give Remi a playful glare, and he sends me a sheepish smile.

"Isabel, I think Remi should give you a dollar every time he swears."

Pulling cash out of his wallet, he hands a single to Isabel, but she's not quite sure what to do with it so she just waves it around, making him chuckle. "You be a good girl, okay?" He softly pinches her chubby cheek.

My baby's bottom lip sticks out. It's soul-crushing. "You weave?"

"Isabel, Remi is going to hang out with his friend, and we are going to have a girls' day. Do you want to get your face painted?"

"Emmie?" With that lip still pouting, she reaches her hand out to him. Ooh, she's playing dirty.

He squats in front of her. "I know, sweetie. Listen, I'll call you later and say goodnight, okay?"

Isabel looks down and nods dejectedly, tears forming in her eyes. Man, she's pulling out all the stops.

"Hey, none of that, Isa-bea." Remi tips up her chin. "What are you going to get painted on your face?"

She puts on a brave front. "Cat."

"Like *The Cat in the Hat*?"

She nods, forming a small smile.

"That's awesome. Make sure Mommy sends me pictures, okay?"

"Kay. Bye bye, Emmie." Isabel waves.

With a kiss on Isabel's forehead, Remi stands and faces me.

"Thanks for hanging out with us," I say to Remi and Mandy. Ugh, even their names sound cute together.

"I'm really glad we ran into you." With warm eyes, Remi gives me a lopsided smile. The way he stares at me drives me insane. It's as if he can't bring himself to look away.

And Christ on a kiddie coaster, I can't either. All thoughts of the Become Unappealing Mission are far away in a distant galaxy called *I Forgot*.

"Anytime," Mandy replies, tugging Remi away.

After they walk a short distance, he looks back at me with a wistful smile.

I grin back, hiding the ache throbbing in my chest. The further they walk, the more my heart begs me to follow.

Isabel sits still as the artist paints whiskers on her face. I watch her, actively capturing this moment as a memory. She's going to be a grown woman someday, and I hope she remembers times like this—us having fun together—instead of me leaving her for something work-related.

Now that we're alone, I feel like something is missing. Or someone, rather. My thoughts turn melancholy. If I don't loosen up, I'm going to be alone and miserable once Isabel is grown and living her own life.

It's time I have a little fun, so I decide to be silly and get my face painted too. When the artist asks me what I want, I opt for the Queen of Hearts make-up. I do have reddish hair, after all. When he's done, I look completely ridiculous, but I haven't felt this carefree in a long time.

It's been a long, happy-filled day and I'm exhausted. Isabel was fast asleep before we even got on the train to come home. After settling her into bed, I find a smooth Cabernet and fill my glass.

I'm too exhausted to even contemplate hanging out with B.O.B. tonight, so I snuggle on the couch and scan Netflix for a good movie. Before I have a chance to make a selection, my phone chimes.

Remi: You home yet?

Crap, I forgot to call him so he could say goodnight to Isabel.

Me: We got home a few hours ago. Isabel fell asleep on the way. Sorry I didn't call.

Remi: What are you doing?

Me: Cuddling with a glass of wine, looking for a movie.

Remi: Lucky glass.

Is he being serious, right now? I don't even know how to respond to that.

Remi: Queeny?

I contemplate ignoring it because nothing good can come out of this conversation. Besides, he was out with another girl yet he's flirting with me. I don't want to lump Remington into the "lying, cheating bastard" category. And I'm certainly not a member of the man-stealing club.

Just as I'm about to turn my ringer off, there's a knock on my front door.

My head shoots up.

Remi: If you don't open it, I'll just use my key.

Leaping off the couch, I run to the entrance and swing open the door. There stands Remi, holding up a six-pack of beer.

"Hey, Queeny. Up for a movie?"

"What are you doing here? Weren't you just on a date?"

He dips his head. "Yeah, I was. But…"

"What?"

"I had a lot of fun today."

I almost slam the door in his face. I do not want to hear about his amazing date. "Happy for you. Why are you here, then?"

"Because I didn't want it to end. Can I come in or do you want to talk out here?"

"I—" Can't find the rest of the sentence.

He skips up the front steps and slides past me into the foyer, giving me a panty-melting smile as he brushes by. "What do we have here?" Remi picks up my wine glass and sniffs it.

I go to pull it away from him, but he holds it up in the air, making me growl.

"Hey, get your own."

He laughs at me before biting his lip illicitly. "What if I want yours?" His voice is pure velvet, brushing across my sensitive skin and beaconing the desire I'm desperately trying to ignore.

Setting my hands on my hips, I give him attitude. "Too bad. You can't have it."

"Sure about that, Queeny?" Without taking his eyes off me, he takes a sip of my wine, staining his pink lips red. "Mmm, delicious," he purrs.

I want to die, only to be raised from the dead so I can watch him do that all over again.

"Where's Mandy?" If he's playing her—he probably is—I'll lose all respect for him. *Please, Universe, not him too.*

Handing me back my glass, he walks to the kitchen and proceeds to look for a bottle opener.

"Remi?"

"Mae?"

"Where is Mandy? You know, your *date*." I'm trying to keep my tone from becoming spastic, but the longer he stalls, the more my temper flares. "The person you should be with right now."

He raises an eyebrow before clipping off the cap of a beer and taking a deep sip, pinning me with a piercing stare like he's trying to transfer a subliminal message into my psyche. "Is she really the person I should be with right now?"

I want to yell, *Of course she isn't!* But I can't because she's more suited for him than me. As much as I hate the idea, he should still be out with her.

"You didn't call or send me pictures." He looks dejected, then studies me for a minute. "Are you wearing blue eyeshadow?"

My hand flies to my face. *Jesus*. Why does he always have to see me at my worst?

"I asked you a question first."

"If I answer, can I stay?"

I set my fist on my cocked hip. "That depends."

Remi lets out a long sigh. "Our date ended early for reasons I'm not ready to talk about." Picking the label off his beer, he continues, "I didn't want to leave you guys and go with her."

Well, that's certainly something. My heart hammers in my chest, but reality stabs it to death because it's actually nothing. It has to be that way. He has fun with Isabel, but he has to understand that he has a life outside of us.

The manny lifts his chiseled chin at me. "Your turn."

"I got my face painted as the Queen of Hearts." I smirk.

He smiles back. After a moment, Remi takes another sip, leaving his lips wet and suckable. "Mandy's a really nice girl." Introspectively, he tilts his head from side to side. "She's pretty and sweet. Down to earth."

"I get it—she's perfect for you." I don't want to stand here and listen to this. *Do not cry. Do not cry.*

When I go to refill my glass, he pins me with a stare—it's the only thing holding me in place.

"She's perfect for me, huh?" His face dips with a humorless laugh. "Answer this for me then." There's a hint of frustration in his rasp. "Why was I waiting for *your* phone call when I was supposed to be enjoying a movie with her?"

I shake my head to stop him from saying anything else. "Rem—"

"Why do I forget she's with me when I'm with you and Isabel?"

"You care about Isabel. That's all." My eyes are pleading with him.

I want him to want me yet I don't, because if he doesn't, I'll be able to keep up the pretenses of a strictly platonic relationship. But if he does, all my iron-clad restraint will turn to dust. I'll fall for him, landing so hard my heart will shatter into a million pieces. Because someday he'll leave, and I don't want to be the reason for his departure, for Isabel's loss.

"Yes, that's part of it. But Isabel has nothing to do with why I was so anxious to leave my date to come here." He swallows. "And see you."

"Remi, don't." My words break in my throat and come out disjointed.

What I really want to say is, *I wanted you to stay with us too. It feels unnatural when you're not around, and I miss you. We miss you.*

In another life, he'd be perfect for me. A man who isn't threatened by my independence. A partner who loves my child as if she were his own. A lover who is kind and genuine, spreading happiness wherever he goes. My pessimism doesn't stand a chance against his sunny optimism. He makes me a better person and mother. Most of all, he makes Isabel happy. That's why he's too important to squander for a momentary indiscretion.

Our eyes stay locked, pleading for different reasons. Mine for established boundaries. His for blurred lines.

"I'm sorry. I'm trying, Mae." His voice cracks, melting the ice between us that's supposed to be keeping us apart. "I promise I'm trying."

It's the first time I've ever seen him this open and vulnerable. I don't know what to do about it.

"You're trying what?" I study his face, trying to decode what he's really saying.

"Not to think about you the way I do."

His words are the devil's serpent, slithering between my thighs, flicking my clit, and wrapping around my heart. Claiming every place they touch.

Red splotches bloom on his cheeks. "It's what made me go out with Mandy in the first place."

Christ, am I drunk? This can't be real. Squeezing my eyes shut, I chant, *Wake up, wake up, wake up.*

When I open them again, he's still standing in my kitchen bemused at me. "You done?"

"Apparently not because you're still here."

A dangerous smirk creeps up one side of the manny's gorgeous face.

One word comes to my mind when I see the devil's mischief written all over his demeanor—trouble. I don't know if I want to be his partner in crime or arrest him before this situation gets out of hand.

He stalks towards me, one salacious step at a time. His movements are calculated and deadly, and so damn hot they scorch the space between us. Sweat beads between my breasts. The air is thick with musky pheromones, and my lungs wheeze, trying to take in the air he's stolen. When he's a breath away, a swarm of butterflies takes flight in my belly.

"You really want me to go? Hmm?" The low tenor of his tone is full of gravel.

With rigid muscles, I back up to put distance between us, but it's futile. Remi chases me at a snail's pace, until the marble countertop digs into my back and I'm left with no place to go. Not that I'm in a hurry to get out of here. He pulls my glass out of my hand and sets it next to his beer behind me.

His teeth graze across his lip as he studies me like I'm the most fascinating piece of art he's ever encountered. The thirst building in his gaze tells me I'm examining him the same way. Because he's everything wonderful carved into a beautiful specimen of a man, which makes him virtually irresistible. Though, I must find the strength to resist.

Cold fingers tuck a lock of hair behind my ear, and I shiver.

I place my hand on his hard chest to keep him from getting any closer, though all it does is make me more aware of the heat emanating from him. "We can't."

Remi swallows hard, his mouth ghosting over mine. "You want to."

His words are whispered seduction, trailing over my lips and trickling down my clavicle, painting a vivid picture of what his soft kisses would feel like there.

My heartbeat pulses in my neck, wrists, and core. "I didn't say that."

He shakes his head and cages me in with his arms. "You didn't have to." His minty breath is laced with malt.

I'm dying to fucking taste him. My traitorous body sways closer, and the pulsing turns into an agonized throbbing. "I'm serious. We can't do this." My voice cracks with desperation—to give in and to flee. "You'll lose your job. And I'll—" Everything in me aches for him. "I mean, *we*'ll lose you."

He rubs his nose against mine, the simple touch an aphrodisiac so potent I nearly drop to the ground. He's fucking crack cocaine, and I'm jonsing for a hit. I've never experienced such a visceral reaction to other men. This is more than mere desire—it's longing, sanctuary, and affinity. My heart rattles against my ribcage, screaming his name.

"I know this could get messy, but we don't have to let it. We can keep it between us." Remi's voice is soft and sexy, uttering syllables to seduce or reassure. Maybe both.

"I've done the casual thing, and I lost. I can't do this to Isabel." I search his eyes to see if he gets it. "My daughter has to come first." The tone of my voice is desperate.

The manny covers my hand still resting on his chest, his thumb brushing soft circles across my knuckles. "She does, always. But for me, you do too."

"Remi, listen to me, please." My eyes are burning with tears. I want him so badly, but it's not right. It will lead to nowhere except him out of our lives, and I can't bear it. "Do you like Mandy? She seems really nice."

Remi's features pinch and tighten as he steps back. My hand falls away, bereft.

"She is nice. Yeah, I mean…" Blowing out a breath, he rakes his fingers through his hair. His stare shifts up as he chews on his cheek in rumination. It's only a few seconds, but it feels like an eternity before he comes to a conclusion in his head.

I'm hoping he came to his senses, but it's clear all rationality has left the vicinity as he encroaches my space again. The manny brushes his fingers along my neck, and it takes micro control of every nerve of my body to not dive in.

"I see the way you look at me." His other hand falls to my waist and squeezes.

A shiver runs through me.

"I feel it." His Adam's apple ripples down his throat. "I want it," he purrs.

It's been so long since someone has wanted me like this. With Remi, it's not just about a physical need but so much more—a bond. Something so significant I'm not sure I'll heal if it breaks. That smacks me out of this seductive trance.

"You don't know what you're saying." This isn't me. I do not crack under persuasion. I push him back, but he doesn't go far.

His frustration simmers in his ticking jaw. "I know exactly what I'm saying."

"We've been in close proximity. We're good friends, Remi. That's it. We have Isabel in common."

"Do you think I'd come and put my career on the line on a whim? Do you think I'd jeopardize my responsibility with Isabel?" Dropping his arms, he leans back. Cool air tempers the heat between us. "I love that little girl."

"I know you do." I raise my hands in a placating manner. "I just think you're getting caught up in something that's not—"

"Don't you dare." He points a finger in my direction. "Don't patronize me, Mae." Umber eyes turn desperate, pleading, and Remi's face contorts in torment. "I can't stop it."

All air leaves my lungs and seeps out of the room. The walls are closing in, and electricity snaps off the shrinking space, charging the air between us. Our breaths mingle, turning into magnetic vapors pulling us closer.

If I don't do something, we'll be fucking on this counter and I'll be tied to him in more ways than one. There will come a day when he'll break that tether and I'll be the one hurtling to the ground, taking my daughter with me. That. Can. Not. Happen.

"Go home, Remi. Call Mandy and ask her out again."

Instead of turning the other way, he moves closer.

"Please," I beg.

It doesn't deter his advance, only makes him grow bolder. He cradles my jaw and stares at my mouth like it holds the key to life's greatest mysteries.

"Go." I choke on the word.

A man with something to prove, he doesn't budge.

"You say you care about me, and I believe you. I care about you too."

Lips parted, he leans in.

I press back, turning my head away. "As a friend."

Remi's trembling body stiffens, and his gaze flickers to the side. He won't face it. *Stubborn.* When he looks back at me, the devastation coating his eyes slays me. *Fuck, he's beautiful.*

Without thinking, my fingers curl around his chin and draw him towards me. This is probably the last time I'll have him this close and personal, so I give him a little and take something for me. With the soft pad of my index finger, I trace the hollow of his cheek then move to his plush lips. His mouth opens as his breathing becomes faster. By the trembling of his fingers, I can tell the rope restraining his impulse is fraying. It's time to end this flirtation, or whatever it is.

"I'm putting Isabel first. I need you to, also. If you can't..." I sniff. I'll need to do the right thing and cut him loose. The thought is soul-crushing. "Don't make me say it."

Indecision and frustration tick in Remi's grinding jaw. He wants to resurrect this dead horse, but I'll only beat it down again. I'm resolute in my decisions, and I won't back down—even for him.

126

Strong shoulders sag the moment he resigns. He gives me a sad nod and turns away, twisting the back of his hair as if he's stuck in an awkward situation.

I need to diffuse this weirdness between us, so I move off the counter and embrace him, laying my face against his chest. Strong arms immediately envelop me. So warm, so safe.

A voice haunts my mind. *"There you are. Shhh, I've got you."* It's the voice from my dream the other night. It was *his*.

When his lips rest on my head, I squeeze back tears. This is hard, but it's worth it. I need him in our lives, and sex will ruin everything. I've learned my lessons, and I won't make the same mistake again.

"See you Monday?" I peer up at him, my voice weak and unsure.

With red-rimmed eyes and a wavering smile, Remi gently squeezes the back of my neck. His other arm is wrapped around the small of my back, anchoring me to him as if we're in a cyclone and he's afraid I'll be ripped away with a gust of wind.

"Yeah."

Chapter 10

Show Me Your Boobs

Mae

I've always been a resourceful girl. With a little elbow grease, if there was something I wanted to accomplish, I've always come through slaying any milestone in my life.

But Jay was right about Remington, so now I'll have to launch plan B, which is ironically called "A-game".

Sighing, I twist my hair into the most obnoxious rollers I can find. I slather an egg-avocado-oatmeal mask on my cheeks. It looks like Isabel threw up on my face and I covered it in absorbent sawdust—the kind the janitors used to clean up vomit in grade school. Finishing off my new style is the black-seed mustard oil that I dot around my neck, making sure that I smell as repulsive as I look.

"There. That should do it," I say to my reflection, almost gagging. The stuff on my face really looks horrid.

Wearing raggedy pants and a smirk, I walk down the steps to greet Remington in the kitchen.

"Good morning."

He flips something on the stove before turning. His words die on his lips, and he blinks several times before he manages a greeting. "Hey there, Queeny. Tryin' something new?" Remi's eyes don't linger on me like they usually do.

I should be happy about that, yet it doesn't make me feel as satisfied as I thought it would.

Isabel takes one look at me and starts crying. As high-pitched as a fire alarm, she starts screaming, "Hulk!" Only it sounds like "fuck" because she can't pronounce her Ls.

Oh, hell, I didn't realize I'd scare her off too. Running over, I go to pick her up.

She starts screaming bloody murder. "Fuck! Fuck! Noooo!"

"Hey, baby, it's okay. It's Mommy."

Her panic only escalates. "Mama fuuuck."

"Okay, Isa-bea. That's enough of that. Mommy's wearing a Hulk mask, that's all. She's playing a game." Remi gives me a full body scan. "A really funny game. But she doesn't scare us, right?" He winks at me like he knows exactly what I'm doing. "We're tough."

I can tell my baby is terrified, but she's trying to put on a brave front for Remi.

"Remi's right. Mommy's just playing."

She points an accusing finger towards me. "Don yike fuck, mommy. No fuck."

Girl, I'm trying to "no fuck". Will you work with me here?

Remi is holding her away from me. "Queeny, you might want to wash your face before you scare our baby any more here."

Our baby?

The mayhem that has been spinning around the room comes to a screeching halt. Nothing moves. Not my stare, my limbs, nor my heart. "What did you just say?" I need him to clarify. Why would he say such a thing?

He closes his eyes and deflates, confirming my suspicion. "I just meant the baby in the room. She's not mine—I know that." Setting her back in her high chair, he straps her in. "Shit."

"You sword, Emmie. Ssit," she repeats, thrusting her hand out for her reward.

With a nervous laugh, he pulls out his phone and a dollar, handing it to her. Her tears dry, and she's no longer swearing in my direction.

Then Remi is on me. His hand is at my elbow, pulling me away from the kitchen.

Dried avocado and oatmeal start peeling off my face, and a piece lands in my eye. "Ow, crap." I really didn't think this through.

Lifting a finger, he swipes up goop off my eye and pries my lid open to assess the damage. "Look, I know what that sounded like, but I didn't mean it like that." Helping me up the steps, we go into the spare bath, which I've renamed to "Cinema Show-er". "Let's get you washed up before you go blind. Isabel's already going to have nightmares." Remi grabs a towel, wets it, and gets in really close.

When I can finally see, I notice red blotches all over the manny's face. Then he starts coughing ... and doesn't stop.

"Oh my God, what's wrong? Are you choking?"

"Mustard," he wheezes out.

"What about it?"

"Allergic."

Christ, I only meant to deter him, not kill him.

"Oh no. Do you need an ambulance?!" I'm freaking out because I'm swimming in uncharted territory. Is he hive-slash-cough allergic or anaphylaxis allergic? These are things I need to know. My face is streaked green and it smells putrid because of the raw egg, and I'm running around in circles because I have no idea what to do. "Please don't die on me. You're too pretty to die."

I make Remi swallow Benadryl, drag him down the stairs, and call an ambulance. All the while Isabel is chatting into Remi's phone, oblivious to the fact that I'm murdering her nanny.

Two hours later, Isabel is down for her nap, I've changed back into normal-people clothes, and Remi is resting in the guest bedroom.

"Knock, knock." I tap on the door frame. I know I'm going back on my plan, but I almost killed the man ... again.

"Don't come any closer, you. First you tried to poison me, then you head-butt me, and now you tried to kill me. I didn't realize you were a psychopath when I started."

"It's in my file. It's your fault you didn't read it." I sniff.

He rolls his eyes and pouts. "Now, she has jokes."

"You're fine. Quit being a big baby." I still can't get him to look at me.

Isn't that what you wanted?

Yes. No. I don't know.

"You have to know how sorry I am. How was I supposed to know you're allergic to mustard?"

"I guess you didn't read my file either," he says, petulant.

"Oh, but I did." I scratch my cheek. "Just not that part," I admit. An awkward silence falls around us, and I hate it. "Let me make it up to you."

"Please don't cook for me."

Cocking my hip, I set my fist on it. "But you've never had my pineapple surprise cake."

"I don't like pineapple." He's really milking this.

"That's good because there isn't any pineapple in it."

"Then why is it called pineapple surprise cake?"

"Surprise," I say meekly, wiggling jazz hands.

He throws his head back with a laugh.

Blowing out a breath, I take him in. His Adam's apple is jumping with the baritone notes of his laugh. One hand is resting on his taut stomach while the other is holding his wavy hair back. Then there's his face, boyish and manly at the same time. A five o'clock shadow enhances his jawline. His full lips stretch over his perfectly straight teeth. He really is spectacular.

"Forgive me?"

Remi crooks his finger, calling me closer, and I'm next to him in two steps.

"Sit." He pats the side of the bed.

I cautiously sit next to him.

"I know how you could make it up to me."

"Anything." I mean it.

His face is dead-serious. "Show me your boobs."

I rear back. "What? I'm not showing you my boobs." Shaking my head, I berate him some more. "For the love of Lilith."

"It's only fair. You got to see mine." He wags his eyebrows, but I'm not budging. "You almost killed a man, Queeny. The least you can do is slip me a nip."

I can't believe he's asking this. "I—"

For the first time in my life, I'm speechless. Scrubbing my face and raking through my hair, I squeeze the locks at my roots. When I can't think of a single rebuttal, I sag in resignation.

Grr. He's right—I watched him shower, fully aware it was terrifically improper. And I almost killed him. It is only fair.

It's not like you don't have a nice set. Right, but it doesn't mean I should flaunt my assets willy-nilly.

You literally salivated at his hard, wet, naked body in the shower while he was completely unaware. I saw it all. It was brazen and crude ... *and so hot it's branded on your memory for whenever you need it.*

As if my brain needed to show me evidence, the image emerges in vivid detail. My thighs clench together.

I didn't do my due diligence with this stupid plan, and I almost killed the guy. This whole situation is completely on me.

Taking a deep breath, I reach for the first button on my blouse.

"Oh my God, you were actually going to do it?" Remi busts out laughing. His face is red, and he won't stop cackling.

I jerk up. "Looks like you just lost your chance to see my rack. It's pretty magnificent, if you ask me, but too bad you'll never know."

"Mmm," Remi hums, placing a finger on his chin. "I bet I will…" His eyes twinkle a wicked dance. "Eventually."

"I bet you won't," I say, snapping my neck. I'm so bratty at this point I'm surprised I don't stick my tongue out.

"Do you know how adorable you are when you're annoyed?"

"You chauvinistic, patronizing…" Shaking my head, I smack his chest, but he grabs my wrist when I go to pull back. His warm hand is strong while gentle fingers brush against my knuckles.

All humor washes away as his face settles in sincerity. He murmurs, "Stay."

"Do I have to show you the girls?"

"Nah." His thumb continues to brush small circles against the back of my hand. "Not unless you want to."

What I want to do is lick that smirk right off his face, but I divert the topic instead because this conversation has gotten way out of hand. I need to rein in this sexual tension and lock it away forever.

"Listen, one of our clients is having an event this Saturday, and I have to go and represent Ever Heart."

"Do you need me to stay with Isabel?"

No matter how many times I've accidentally tried to maim him, he's still so willing to be there for us. "Yes and no." I bite my lip as if I'm about to ask him to prom. "Do you want to come?"

"I'm not upset, Mae. I don't need a pity invite."

"It's not a pity invite." Okay, I am totally asking him to prom, but my version—a work outing. It's important. *He*'s important. I'm happier when he's around. "I want you to come."

The side of his mouth lifts. "Yeah?"

"Yes. And if Isabel has a meltdown, I'll need your calming skills." It's a joke, but I instantly want to shove the words back into my mouth as the light in his eyes dims a little. "I'm— Seriously, I want you there."

"It's okay, Mae. I get it. I'd do anything for Isa-bea." The stare he's burning me with tells a different story.

I gulp. "Great."

What am I doing? *The exact opposite of what you should be.*

Another Saturday, another outing with Isabel, and this time we'll have one hot manny in tow.

I went with a 50s pin-up look: high-waisted sailor shorts, red polka-dot halter top, and matching lipstick. The look is classic and shows my curves off beautifully. As I style my hair into victory rolls, I tell myself it's just because I'm representing Ever Heart, but I know deep down that's only partly true.

I dress Isabel in a little sailor jumper and pull her hair into pigtails. She looks adorable. We're playing with playdough when Remi comes in.

My mouth drops open. I'm a teething baby with drool dripping from my mouth.

Remi is wearing plaid golf pants and a white linen button-down. His wavy hair is styled perfectly, so unlike the sexy mess he wears every day. While golf pants easily make a woman gag, the hot manny pulls them off flawlessly. He could wear a trash bag full of dog poo and still be edible.

"Well, well, what do we have here? Two of the prettiest girls in the land."

"Emmie!" Isabel shouts, holding up her latest masterpiece—something resembling a pink dinosaur.

He gasps, kneeling next to me. "That's an Isa-raptor."

She gives him a toothy smile as he inspects it closely. "It *famoghinuts*, siwwy."

Remi turns to me. "Translation?"

I bark a laugh. "It's how she says 'flamingo'."

"I see." He gives Isabel a kiss on her forehead before planting a quick one on my cheek. Pulling back, he winks at me.

A thrill shoots through my belly. "Stealing kisses now, are we?"

"A man's gotta eat," he rasps, shrugging one shoulder.

I could give him plenty to eat. By the growing smirk on his face, he knows exactly where my mind is. The flare of his nostrils tells me he's imagining the same.

"Kiss, Mommy. Kiss." My kid points a finger at me and then Remi.

Oh, Lord, did he rope her into this?

Remi inches closer, pointing to his impossibly high cheekbone. "Yes, Mommy. Kiss."

Rolling my eyes, I begrudgingly touch my lips to his cheek, rubbing against the manny's smooth, freshly shaven skin. Hints of leather and spearmint tickle my nose. The desire to take his mouth is throbbing in my gut. It takes pure iron will not to give in.

When his hand holds the side of my neck, keeping me in place, I almost do. With him this close, I can't think straight. Trying to keep hold of my restraint, I exhale a sharp breath against his skin. He shivers, and I swear I hear a small whimper from the back of his throat. Before I do anything reckless, I stand.

Red splotches dot Remi's cheek as he dips his head, hiding a bashful smile. Regaining some composure, he raises onto his feet before scooping up Isabel. I snap a picture of them on my phone, loving that he's wearing my kiss holding my daughter.

They are mine. As unrealistic and untrue as it is, the thought rolls through my head like an avalanche—impossible to ignore, much less survive. But I don't say anything about it as we walk out the door.

"You have an epi pen handy, right?"

"Yes, smartass. I'll be carrying a first aid kit everytime I'm around you."

"Oh, good. There's a bunch of other shit I'd like to try." As soon as I say it, I cover my mouth.

What was that? Freudian slip?

A sexy smile forms on his face. "Yeah? Like what, Queeny?"

I hold my fist to his face to get him to stop with his innuendo. "Like what you'd look like with a broken nose."

He licks his plush bottom lip before pressing it against my knuckles. "You would never."

I feign indifference. "Try me," I breathe, fighting a shiver.

"You like my face too much to mangle it. What is it that you call me?" He taps his temple. "Oh yes, Hot Manny."

That breaks the spell. I shove him away with my hip. "You're so full of yourself."

His eyes are roguish. "I'd really like you to be full—"

"Don't you dare finish that sentence." This is getting into dangerous territory.

Pushing Isabel's stroller, I power-walk ahead of him. His deep chuckle follows me, making my mouth quirk up without my permission.

I'd really like to be full of him as well. The image of me deep-throating his celestial cock comes to mind. *Stop that, libertine.*

The waterfront is decorated in bright oranges, blues, purples, and yellows with world's fair nostalgia. There are clowns with balloons, kiddie rides, and what looks like a beer garden. The smell of charred meat wafts in the air. It's a proper shindig. There's also what seems to be a mixture of cosplay and everyday garb.

We walk past a guy wearing a sailor hat, with short shorts and a striped tank. He gives me a nod and a wink.

With a grimace, I wave back. Did I unknowingly dress for comicon?

"Mae, is this a costume party you forgot to tell me about?"

"I had no idea Isabel and I were coming to represent the sailor sector of comic-book heroes." I should have known. The company throwing the party is Fawlen Studio, and they sell all kinds of movie props and costumes.

"Another missed opportunity to strut my stuff in my Princess Leia bikini."

I almost choke. "That would have been a sight. I'm glad I didn't tell you. You would have burned the corneas of women everywhere." My hand flies over my loose lips.

Remi cackles like an obnoxious goose.

"Miranda, you made it." Corissa Fawlen, the owner, comes over with a couple of other women I've never met. "This is Kelly and Pandee. Girls, this is Miranda. She and her partner are our digital marketing mavens."

We all exchange pleasantries, and the women fawn all over Isabel.

"She is just precious," Pandee gushes. "You must be the daddy." She twirls her dark hair and blinks at Remington.

His cheeks flame. "The nanny, actually," he says softly.

"That is just wonderful," Corissa chimes in.

Pandee inches closer to Remi, and Kelly licks her lips. It takes all the power in me to not laugh. Remi is clearly uncomfortable to have these women overtly ogling him, but he's too good-natured to snub them off.

"A-ah..." he stammers, pulling Isabel's stroller in front of him like it's a pheromone shield. "Let's go find something to drink, Isabel." He turns to me. "Can I get you anything?"

The women lay their hands on their chest, swooning.

I suppress a smile. "I'm good, thanks."

"Okay." He sighs. "Let's see if there are any IPAs I can drink and complain about."

When he's out of hearing range, three sets of bugging eyes pin me in my spot.

I step back. "What?"

"Don't 'what' me, woman," Corissa huffs. "Where did you find him? I might need his services."

Kelly smacks her friend's shoulder. "He's a nanny, not a sex worker, Corissa."

"So?"

Pandee throws her friend under a fast-moving bus. "You don't have any kids."

Corissa looks at me. "Can I borrow yours?"

We all crack up.

"Can we not objectify my daughter's caregiver?" I interject because A: I don't want them looking at him like that; and B: I don't want them to know I objectify him on the regular. This is a professional outing.

"Oh, shut it, Miranda," Corissa snaps at me playfully. "You can't tell me that you have *that* walking around your house, carrying your baby all day, and not think about what he'd look like making his own."

A coughing fit overwhelms me because ... yeah, I do.

"I knew it," Pandee accuses.

The light atmosphere darkens when the creepy-crawly feeling that someone is watching me skitters down my spine. Why do I get paranoid so suddenly? Looking around, I don't recognize anyone and nothing looks out of place, so I shrug it off.

"What's with the costumes?"

"My brother is big into cosplay." Corissa rolls her eyes. "He's twenty-eight going on twelve."

Just then, my ears tune to my daughter's shrieks. Turning around, I see her little chubby arm pointing at—

Oh no.

"Fuck! No! Fuck!" Isabel is pointing to a person dressed as the Hulk—a very realistic one with a huge mask and hands.

Remi is in front of her, trying to calm her down.

"Is that your daughter yelling 'fuck'?" Kelly asks.

"She is scared of the Hulk, but she can't pronounce her Ls, so it sounds like—"

"Fuck!" she screams, pointing behind Remi as if he's in imminent danger.

"That," I finish my sentence.

The girls double over.

Kelly slaps her thighs. "That is the best thing I've ever heard."

We watch on as Remi gets the Hulk to take off his mask and show Isabel that it's just a costume. She doesn't look convinced, so she tucks her head and hides her eyes.

Picking her up, Remi comes over to where we are. "It's okay, sweetie. He's nice. The Hulk helps people."

I pull her into my arms, brushing her tears away.

She peers at me with a puffed bottom lip and watery eyes. "No fuck, Mommy."

"Unfortunately, babe, 'no fuck' is right." I don't know where that came from or why I even said it.

Remi jerks. His eyebrows shoot towards his hairline as a grin spreads across his face. Two flirty dimples dig into his cheeks.

Everyone peels with giggles. Isabel sees everyone laughing, so not to miss out, she joins in. Welp, at least her tears have dried.

After she catches her breath, Corissa pats me on the shoulder. "I think we need to hang out more often."

"Oh, well, between work and Isabel, I don't really have time to do much hanging out."

Remi butts in. "What she means is that she'd love to." He softly pinches the back of my neck, and goosebumps coat my skin. "I can stay with Isabel if you want to have a girls' night."

I haven't had one of those since college, when I actually had girlfriends. Once Jay and I started building Ever Heart, I drifted away from most of my friends and fun. They got married and had children, and I had work, then Isabel.

"You're such a great guy, Remi. I wish all nannies were like you," Kelly simpers, not even hiding her obvious attraction.

"Well, unfortunately, I'm a rare breed. And this little one owns me." He splays his hand on Isabel's back while I'm holding her.

They all swoon ... again.

"So, that was pretty funny, wasn't it?" Now that we're alone, I want to know if he was affected by the way Corissa, Kelly, and Pandee were openly flirting with him.

Did he like it? Did he want to flirt back? Did he catch feelings? The bigger question is ... why do I care so much?

After a burger and a couple of beers, the girls and I exchanged numbers. They made me promise that I'll go out with them one night. After much encouragement from Remi—otherwise known as blackmail—I agreed.

"What was funny? Isabel shouting 'fuck' or the way those women were eye-fucking me?"

A giggle bubbles in my chest. "All of it." We get on the L and settle in for the ride out of town. "Don't lie and say you didn't love it." In my experience, all men are flattered by female attention, even if it's uninvited. "In fact, I think you were trying to pick one up." I almost punch myself for that lame joke.

What am I doing, grilling him on something that is none of my business? "Never mind, I'm teasing. That was way outta line."

"Oh, I don't know. There might be one lady I'm interested in."

My heart stops.

This is what I want, though, isn't it? Why does it feel so awful to hear him say he's interested in someone? *Because you think of him as yours, but he's free to date anyone he wants.* Just because my world is small doesn't mean Remi's is. My heart is a goddamn troublemaker.

"Queeny?"

My eyes travel to his. "Yeah?"

"Is it working?" Heat flares in his gaze.

My belly flips a triple lutz, and my skin flames through my cheeks like a warning: *Mayday, mayday, mayday.* I need to shut this down fast. If I don't cool off, I will slip up and say something that will only fuel his fire.

Nothing can happen between us, and I care too much about him to lead him to think differently.

"You…" I wave my hand in a dismissive manner. "You're always ribbing me. You like riling me up or something?"

He leans forward, that smirk looking red and ripe. "Or something."

I wonder if he tastes as hot as he looks.

"Maybe I just like to see you smile."

Warmth blooms in my chest, melting my frigid resolve. "Mission accomplished."

"I aim to please."

"I bet you do."

Remi's eyes darken as he slowly peruses my body, his gaze landing on my lips as he bites his. His insinuation is intentional, and it elicits its desired effect. With slow and sensual movements, he reaches up and twirls a loose lock of my hair back into place. Calloused fingers graze down my cheek. His concentration is intense and full of erotic promise.

Arousal pools at my core by this simple touch alone, and I rub my thighs together.

His mouth twists up with a smug expression.

Cocky bastard.

Christ, I'm in so much hulking trouble.

Chapter 11

Are You Going To Spank Me Now?

Mae

SOCIETY SAYS WOMEN ARE meant to be soft, the more compassionate of the sexes. The latter might be true, but the former can go fuck itself. How could I ever be soft when I'm so fucking angry?

While I knew Dexico was not going to sign with us unless I let numbnuts Paul into my underwear—Pingman likely to pull his assets—I didn't expect three other investors to follow.

"We're going to have to lay people off, Jay."

"We don't need Pingman and his ass-kissers. We have us. We don't give up—we never have." They sit back, opening their falafel. "Does it suck that we may have to lay off people? Royally. But would it be so bad to downsize a little bit?"

"How can you say that? It's everything we've worked for."

"No, it's everything *you*'ve worked for. I was fine freelancing, working remotely."

What are they saying?

"It's our dream." It's all we talked about when we graduated college.

Setting their wrap down on my desk, they pin me with a look. "Our dream was to make enough money to travel and see the world."

I shake my head.

"Yes, Mae. *That* was the dream. Not dredging ourselves in corporate-America bullshit until we croak."

Tears burn behind my eyes. If I was a man, this wouldn't be happening. Powerful men respect other powerful men, but when it comes to women, they are hard-wired to think about nothing but what's between her legs.

"Maybe you should hire another partner. I'm failing you." My chin dips with my mood. "Maybe a guy would do better in this position."

Jay's face hardens. "Miranda Everly Keller, do not make me come over there and shake you." They sigh. Warm, kind eyes erase the anger from their tone. "Why would you say such a thing? Ever Heart is you and me, end of. If you're out, then I'm out. As simple as that."

"It's not simple though, Jay. You and Ian want a family someday, don't you? I have Isabel, and we have a hundred other employees depending on us for their salary." Meeting my best friend's eyes, I plead, "I can't look at them and tell them it's over."

"*If* we have to lay anyone off, we'll do it together." Jay's mouth moves without words as if they want to say something of delicate nature. They draw their shoulders up, confessing, "If that was our only option, I'd rather lay off a hundred employees than lose a single you."

I suck in a breath because that's not the business ethos we should practice.

Jay raises their palms. "Look, I know what I said is inconsiderate, but it's how I feel."

"That doesn't mean it's the best decision for Ever Heart."

Jay's demeanor hardens. "We work well together—you have my back, and I have yours. You kill it in the boardroom. In my opinion, you're a better leader than most people I know. Why on earth would you think a man would be a better fit than you?"

My shoulders slump because I have to tell them what happened, even though I really don't want to. I was able to distract them with the Hot Manny Peen Gate incident, but I can't put this off anymore. "Because I won't put out, and if a man was in my position, he wouldn't have been propositioned. Dexico would sign on because you are the most talented graphic artist out there."

They raise one perfectly threaded eyebrow. "Is there something you're not telling me?"

I bite the inside of my cheek because I can't say it.

Jay crosses their arms in front of them. "Out with it, or I'm telling the hot manny you want his monster dick."

Pretty sure he already knows. Blowing out my cheeks, I spill, "That night, Paul wasn't interested in talking about the proposal."

Their forehead creases. "Why in the hell did he request a meeting?"

"Because he wanted to negotiate between my legs instead of in a conference room." My words feel like bullets, sniping any man who ever took without asking. Any man who'll gleefully hold a woman under their thumb. Especially those who want to maintain the good-ol'-boys'-club exclusivity.

My best friend's six-two frame is imposing when they stand at full height. "I'm going to fucking kill him."

I rush to Jay's side and hold onto their arm with both hands. "You can't kill him. I already threw a glass of wine in his face in front of the whole restaurant. Told him I'd talk to the press if he ever tried this shit again."

"Why the hell didn't you call me and tell me that night?"

"Because you were with Ian. I didn't want to spoil that."

"You know what, Mae? That's complete bullshit. Just because I met someone doesn't mean I'm not here for you. I can't believe you didn't tell me." Jay is a ray of sarcastic sunshine. They rarely get upset with me, but by the ticking of their jaw, I can tell they're ready to give me a lecture. "We're a team. We've always been a team. Even when we are committed to other people, we're still going to be a goddamned team."

My throat prickles as tears threaten to spill. "I know."

"Mija, I love my job, what we've built, but I don't want to do this at the expense of your well-being." They look around my thirtieth-floor office in the heart of Chicago's business district. "Do we really need all this?"

I back away. "Are you saying you don't?"

"I was happy when it was just the two of us in a fucking room with a broken desk chair. You had all these goals, and you were excited. Of course, I'd follow you anywhere. But lately..." They look away.

My chin quivers. "Finish that sentence."

"You don't seem happy anymore. You're snappy and angry. I hate it."

How dare they? Everything I've done was for us. "You hate it."

Jay wraps their comforting hands around my arms. "I just want you to be as happy as I am here at Ever Heart. This thing doesn't work if only one of us is fulfilling their dreams."

"I am." If I'm being honest, making the leap from their basement to a high-rise was a bit more of a curveball than I realized. I just saw us up in the sky, where we always talked about being. But I had Isabel and my world shifted. My time was no longer my own. "I know I'm spread thin right now. But once Isabel goes to school full time—"

"Honey, that's what I'm saying. We've been following my dreams for so long you forgot your own." Always soothing, Jay's hands rub up and down my arms, but it's of little help.

All my hopes and sacrifices were for nothing. If this isn't what they want, then what the hell am I doing here?

But this is my career. It's all I know. I wanted this before I wanted children, but life doesn't work that way. You can't control fate, and I found new meaning when I had Isabel. If I don't have this, then what do I have? Who am I outside of this building? Everything I thought I was is gone.

I remember something. Just as I don't want to be defined by motherhood, I don't want to be defined as a hard-nosed manager with zero people skills. Jay is right about me being angry and snappy. The more we accomplished, the more pressure built to succeed, to do better than we had the year before. When things don't go precisely my way, I micromanage, resenting the people I oversee because I have unrealistically high standards I can't even meet.

I'm not a leader—I'm a dictator. It's everything I never wanted to be. It's a harsh truth, shooting a bullet between my eyes, leaving me bleeding out with mental anguish.

"You're right, Jay."

Their head whips up. "Okay, now I'm really convinced aliens have kidnapped my real best friend because the Mae I know wouldn't admit that." Reaching over, they press the intercom on my phone. "Elliot, I would like you to make a note that, on this day, Miranda Keller told Jayden Morales they were right. Thank you."

"I'm having an existential crisis, and you're over there gloating. Nice, Jay. Real nice."

"Don't snap your lips at me. I keep it real, darling. I'll always have your best interest at heart."

I slump back into the chair in front of my desk. "I know. I'm just not ready to make the call yet. Can you understand that?"

"I can, only if you promise me that you'll come to me if this shit ever happens again."

We challenge each other in a stare-off, but it's me who breaks first. "Ugh, fine."

Jay raises their chin, smiling in victory. "I'm glad you see it my way." They wrap their falafel back up. "Now, I'm going to finish this delicious wrap, and then I have work to do. So, if we're done here..." They stall, waiting for my answer.

"Go, we're done." I'm not, though, because I have jobs to save. All this conversation did was make me more determined to patch the gushing hole in our boat. Sink or sail.

With an "I've got my eyes on you" gesture, they waltz out the door, silk fabric blowing airily behind them—like my career in the wind.

When I'm sure they're out of ear range, I page Elliot.

"Yes, Ms. Keller?"

"I need last year's P&L statement and this year's projected. Plus all the leads we've collected over the last two years." I don't care what Jay says—I'm determined to save this company in its entirety. Once it's on steady ground, I'll be able to step back and figure out what it is I want to do for the rest of my life. Aside from raising my child, nothing has ever felt this important.

Numbers and letters dance together in a blur on the screen. I'm exhausted, but I will not rest until I figure this out. Are there any overhead cuts that can be made? If layoffs are looming, how do I mitigate the damage to a possible few?

Of course, we have an accounting team, but it's up to me to find these "opportunities". No one else—besides Jay—has skin in the game.

"Hey, Mae?" Remi's soft rasp startles me as he walks into my home office.

"Yeah, you got to take off?" I asked him to stay a little later, but I can't expect him to spend the night.

"No, I was just seeing if you want something to eat. You haven't had dinner yet."

"I'll eat in a bit, thanks." Dismissing him, I turn back to my laptop.

Not easily deterred, he comes and leans against the lip of my desk. His fabric-softener smell entices me to curl into him and sleep.

"You said that two hours ago, when the food was still hot. You can take five minutes, Mae." He peers behind him to my screen. "Whatever this is can wait."

Rubbing my tired eyes, I nod. "Yeah, okay. Will you heat it up for me? I know I'm asking a lot of you, but—"

"It's fine," Remi cuts me off with a smile. He's lucky he's cute or I would have cut his balls off.

Fuck, I'm doing it again—thinking like a dictator.

"Meet you downstairs?"

"Yeah, thanks."

Before he stands to leave, he reaches over and touches the hollows under my eyes. "You need rest, Queeny."

Nodding to appease him, I resume work, vowing that I will stop to eat and put Isabel to bed. All too soon my tired eyes blink slowly until they fully close. *I'll only rest them a second before getting back to work...*

There's a jostling of my arm.

"Hey, Queeny?" Remi's voice is distant.

I feel like I'm drowning and he's my life raft. "Hmm, swim there."

His soft chuckle makes me smile. "You want to swim to bed?" After a few precious seconds of peace, the jostling continues. "C'mon, let's get you to bed. You're drooling all over your laptop, and I'm pretty sure it will be fried by morning if you don't get up."

Rudely, I'm hoisted in the air.

"What the hell?"

"You are not sleeping at your desk, and don't even get me started on you missing meals. I'm not happy, Queeny."

He's sexy when he's all bossy, so I lay my head on his chest and enjoy the ride. "Are you going to spank me now?" Blame the twilight state because I have no idea why else I would say that.

"Thinkin' about it." He gently settles me on the bed.

I roll onto my side with closed eyes, still half asleep. "Over my pants or bare-cheeked?"

Remi pulls the blanket over me. "Christ, woman, you sure know how to torture a man."

"I won't sleep with him for a business deal."

"What?" His voice sounds further away.

Even the tugging of my shoulder doesn't bring me back.

"Why would you say that?"

I don't answer because I have no idea what he's asking. All I want to do is drift back off to oblivious bliss.

Tonight, I don't sleep to dream.

The next morning, I drag myself to the kitchen to find an IV needle to flood my veins with caffeine. I haven't bothered brushing my hair or teeth yet because I'm too tired to care.

Entering the kitchen, rich smells of butter and pancake batter hit my nose, and my stomach churns.

"Hey, sleepyhead."

"Why are you always so goddamned chipper in the morning?" I gripe.

He leans back with his hands up in surrender. "Whoa, someone woke up on the wrong side of the bed today."

Without saying another word, I shuffle over to the coffee maker and start loading the top with beans to grind.

"Sit and eat. I'll make the coffee."

I ignore him.

"Mae."

He's really starting to piss me off. "I can make my own damn coffee."

Remi swears under his breath, and it sounds like, "So unbelievably stubborn."

"Yeah, well, you're unbelievably pushy. Forgive me if I don't roll over with your every command."

"I'm just trying to help, Mae."

Filling up the water container, I still won't look at him. "I hired you for Isabel. Not me. I don't need your help."

He steps closer and lays a hand on my shoulder, which completely sets me off.

"Stop. Whatever it is that you're doing, stop it. This is the exact opposite of helping, Remington."

Remi's mouth pops open. "Well, *Miranda*—since we're using full names—I'm trying to be a friend." He sneers, shaking his head. "It looks like you need one because you're not taking care of yourself."

Turning away, I scoop coffee grounds into the filter. "What, you want to take care of me? Do you have a daddy complex or something?"

I feel rather than see Remi scoff. "Wow, okay. Carry on, Queeny. Forget I even asked."

Opening the cupboard above, I pull a mug down, but my motor skills haven't caught up with my awakened state yet and I lose my grip. To save it from shattering all over the ground, I do some awkward, twisty move to catch it, but it only causes my wrist to bend in an unnatural way.

"Ow, shit." Pulling my hand into my chest, I cradle it with my other.

Remi turns me around to face him, pulling the blasted thing from my hand and setting it safely on the counter. "What is it?"

"Nothing but me being a clutz. I just twisted my wrist. I'm fine." I wiggle away from him, but he just follows.

"Let me see." Not hesitating, he pulls my wrist towards him. His touch is gentle. He starts massaging my forearm, working his way up to where I'm tender.

His touch feels like warm honey, and I'm the biscuit he's covering. Transfixed and completely under his spell, I forget all about my irritation.

Now, I understand how he gets Isabel to settle so fast. What would it be like if I just let go and let him take care of me?

"So soft." The words leave his mouth in a breath, and I'm not sure I was meant to hear it.

"W-what?" I ask like an idiot anyway.

A sheepish smile forms on his pretty face. "Oh, uh. Your skin. It's really soft." He drags his thumbnail down the underbelly of my forearm and watches the movement.

I shiver, and my pelvic floor involuntarily Kegels. His touch is soothing, and his fingertips leave a trail of heat wherever they trace. My mind runs wild with how they would feel in other places of my body. Arousal thrums in my veins, cranking up my internal temperature.

When he looks up at me, his brown eyes darken to black. "How does it feel?"

The soft rasp of his voice slides down my back and makes my knees weak.

"Hot," I breathe.

"Hot?"

"Um, I mean is it hot in here?" I pull my arm back and shake off the remnants of pain, turning it into a dull ache. "Thanks. Good as new."

This earns me a stink eye. "You know, I have a special magic trick to heal all boo boos in record time." He's such a tease.

I smirk. "Uh-huh, sure." It's really hard to stay mad at the guy.

"I do. Isa swears by it."

He knows just how to take the cynical right out of me. "Well then, by all means." I shove my hand towards him. "If my two-year-old swears by it, it must be the real deal."

Holding my arm by my elbow, he lifts my wrist before paralyzing me with the heat of his stare. I watch, mesmerized, as he presses his red, soft lips to my pulse point. When he exhales, the air sweeps across my skin, raising the tiny hairs on my arm. I never believed in erogenous zones before. I stand corrected. A shiver wracks through my body, and I shudder a breath. I could die right here.

I'm still staring at my wrist when he lifts his chin and that delectable mouth twists in a smirk. "There, all better."

"Y-yeah." I scramble for words, peeved that this man has me so flappable. "I mean, yes. Thank you."

"Anytime. It's my specialty." He winks and turns back to the stove. "Now, go sit at the table and eat."

Pouting, I do just that and get some bites in. As always, it's delicious, but my stomach isn't having it. "I'm going to wrap this up and take it with me." When he turns to me with uncertainty in his eyes, I reassure him, "I'm already running late and it's really good, so I don't want to waste it."

Even though he nods, he doesn't look convinced.

Sliding out from the table I walk up to him. "I'll take my coffee to go too, if that's okay?"

His lips quirk in a crooked smile. "Yeah."

The next thing I do is so out of character for me that I surprise myself. Raising on my tip-toes, I press my lips to Remi's cheek, lingering. His arm wraps around my back, anchoring me to him.

He closes his eyes and releases a steady breath through his nose as if savoring my innocent kiss. A sneaky thumb dips under my sweatshirt and swipes across my bare skin.

Remi swallows, his Adam's apple rippling down his throat before his head rests against mine. We share the oxygen between us, trembling, anticipating. It's like when he was massaging my arm—I was the center of his universe for that moment as if the sun was shining only on me.

It feels incredible.

I think about it when I get ready for work. When I give Isabel a quick snuggle before I leave. I think about it on the train. I think about it the rest of the day.

It's been so long since I've been touched with such care, that I've felt such need. In all of my past romantic relationships, I've gotten the bare minimum and was fine with it. When you go through life with the mundane, you're not even aware there is something better, something extraordinary. That's what Remi feels like, so unlike anything I've ever known. Now that I've gotten a taste, I don't think I'll be able to go without.

Remi isn't careless in his attention—he's all in. Every move is thoughtful, every touch deliberate. It leaves me questioning why I'm resisting this so much.

If we're both consenting, would he really lose his job?

I'm still thinking about it when I finally lie in bed after a long day of fantasizing about the hot manny. My belly flutters as I run my hands down my body, trying to replicate the feeling. It's a poor substitute, but it will have to do.

"How does it feel?" His words from this morning echo in my mind, but it's a different scenario I'm imagining. Soft fingers trace my swollen slit and languidly circle the bundle of nerves peeking out.

"So good," I whimper.

"You want more, Queeny?"

Twisting my hips, my circles become firmer. "Please."

"You're soaked, baby. All this for me?"

Using my own arousal, I slip one finger inside, then two. "Yessss."

"That's it, baby. Fuck my fingers. Make yourself come."

Pretty soon, my rhythm becomes erratic and sweat beads on my forehead. "So good, so good, so good," I chant.

"I'm going to fucking worship you."

I clench tightly around my fingers, letting my orgasm take me to a place where responsibility and propriety can't reach me.

As soon as I come down, guilt washes over me, pulling me into a riptide of regret. He's Isabel's nanny, for chrissakes. I shouldn't be imagining his innocent touches as something indecent. I shouldn't be wishing I was a young twenty-something girl with no responsibilities. And I certainly shouldn't be objectifying my daughter's caregiver.

"Fuck me," I groan and throw my arm across my eyes. Suddenly, I jerk up. "I mean, no, don't fuck me. That's not what I'm saying."

Sheesh, can I just let it go?

Chapter 12

My Fetish is to Feed You

Mae

"I HAVE AN ULTRASOUND appointment on Friday. I thought we could go and make a day of it. We can shop for baby furniture."

It's an early Wednesday morning. Brad and I are lying in bed. I'm hoping for a quick round two since he fell asleep before helping me finish round one last night.

Hesitating, he scratches his five-o'clock-shadowed chin. "Yeah, sure. What time?"

"At 11:30am." I run my fingers through his moppy blond hair. "I'm thinking about inviting my mom for a visit."

"Well, give me a heads-up. I'll be scarce."

Chuckling, I smack his chest with the back of my hand. "No way. She'll insist on seeing Aubry too while she's in town, and I'm telling them about the baby." I shudder to think of Aubry's reaction. Maybe a baby will soften her to me, call off the games that I'm not even playing. "I need you to be there as a buffer in case things get ugly."

"Your mom's not staying here, is she?" I detect a note of panic in his tone.

A long sigh leaves my chest. "She might." I don't really know, though. My apartment is small. Like, munchkin-cubby-hole small. "She could always stay with Aubry."

My step-sister has a penthouse in West Loop, compliments of Daddy. I swear she moved here just to antagonize me. She thinks I care that she lives like a queen while I live like a farm-plowing peasant. Joke's on her because everything I have, I've earned.

156

I wouldn't take shit from her father, which garnered his respect. Something she hates and still punishes me for.

Brad gets up and, much to my disappointment, pulls on his boxers. "I'm going to shower and head out."

"Oh, okay. I thought you didn't have anything today. We have enough time for a quickie." I wag my brows and "accidentally" let the sheet tumble from my shoulders, enticing him with my assets.

"Can't. I have golf with the guys." Without a second glance, he kisses me on the head and waltzes into my bathroom, leaving me bare-chested and alone in bed.

Shaking my head, I hope to toss out the memory. I'm not sure why I'm even thinking about it. I didn't see the rejection for what it was—a forewarning. Brad never made the appointment, so instead of furniture shopping, I went home right after ... and found out why he never showed.

My stomach churns. Jumping up from my desk, I vomit into my wastebasket. When I stand up, stars float around my head and the room is spinning. If I believed in immaculate conception, I would've thought I was pregnant again. Maybe I'm coming down with the flu.

Ugh, I hope not. It's the worst possible time to be sick. Not that any other time would work better.

I page my assistant. "Elliot, can you bring me some tea and saltines?" Without thinking, I add, "I would be so very grateful. Thank you."

"Of course, Ms. Keller."

Ten minutes later, I'm lying on the floor of my office with my arm over my head. I'm still nauseated, and now I have a migraine. I'm totally winning today. If it didn't hurt to move my eyes, I'd roll them.

"Ms. Keller?" Elliot stands over me, with a steaming mug and a box of crackers in his hand.

Sitting up, I reach for the mug. The lights are off, but the sun is beaming in through my windows. I have to squint to look at him. "Will you set those on my desk?" I point to the package he's holding. "Thanks, E. You're the best."

Instead of leaving, he just stands there. Or more like shuffles foot to foot.

"Is there anything else?" My tone isn't as harsh as it usually is. I don't have the energy for it.

"You look pale, ma'am."

I wince. "Cut the 'ma'am' shit, would ya? You've been working for me for two years. You can call me Mae, you know."

His green eyes widen. "Yes, ma'— I mean, Mae. Do you want me to get Mx. Morales?"

"No!" I spit, hating that I snapped. Taking a deep breath, I try again. "No, thank you, Elliot. I'll be okay."

"Let me know if you need anything else, Ms—" Elliot clears his throat. "Mae." He gives me a small smile, and it dawns on me—it's the first time I've ever seen it.

Two years. Seven hundred and thirty days. Seventeen thousand five hundred and twenty hours. And this is the first time I've ever seen him smile. All because I've only considered him as my assistant. I never looked past his role, never examined the human inside the employee. What makes him tick? Does he like his job? Does he have a happy home life? He's been my right-hand man for two years, and I know nothing about him outside of his work performance.

What have I become?

Sharp pain stabs at my head.

Two hours later, I'm in the same position. I have no energy to get up. Just the thought exhausts me. I shouldn't have skipped dinner and breakfast.

My cell phone starts ringing, but it's on my desk across the room. I need to make sure it isn't about Isabel. Even though everything inside screams for me to lie back down, I crawl over to answer it.

"Hello?" I clear my throat because it sounds like I have a frog stuck in it.

"Queeny?" Remi's soft dulcet tone soothes the ache in my head.

My lids start falling. "Hmm?"

"You okay?"

"Peachy."

"You sound more prickly than peachy," he teases.

I click my tongue, but there's no real irritation behind it. "Is there a reason you're calling?"

"Eggs are on sale." Is he crazy?

I pull back, giving my phone a dirty look. "You have a weird fetish for breakfast."

"It *is* the most important meal of the day."

"Smartass." My chuckle sends a stabbing throb through my temporal lobe. Digging the heel of my palm into my temple, I swear, "Jesus Christ."

"What's wrong?"

"Headache. It's fine. Elliot got me some turmeric tea." I wave it off because it's not a big deal.

"Sounds ... yummy." The way he says it sounds anything but. "Promise me you'll come home if it doesn't go away."

God, why does he have to be so caring? It makes ignoring my attraction to him really difficult. He's got to get over whatever it is he feels for me, and I need to reclaim my sanity. I've been feeling off-kilter since he started. I'm not inappropriate, or flighty or fun, or any of those other F-words. I'm a single mother and a workaholic. I get shit done, and I'm good at what I do ... or at least, I used to be.

I bite my lip. *This guy.* "I will, Manny."

"Thank you, Queeny." The smile in his voice makes my lips quirk up.

The call ends, and I feel marginally better, so I muster the gumption to actually get some work done today. Climbing onto my desk chair is like scaling Everest without a rope, but I manage it.

My cell lights up again, and without looking at the bright screen, I accept the call. "Did you forget to mention any other discounted dairy items?" I quip, hoping my humor eases Remi's concern, but all I hear is breathing.

It's not heavy, per se, just eerily there.

"Remi?" Did he butt-dial me?

I pull my phone back and look at the screen. The number comes up "Restricted" and now I'm creeped out. If it was Remi, it would say "Manny". Holding my cell in front of my mouth, I stare at the screen as if it's playing a horror movie.

"Who is this?" I demand.

All I get is a dial-tone in response, leaving me baffled.

Maybe it was just a robocall. Great, those bots are like vultures. Once they know a live person will answer a number, they'll sell it to the highest bidder. I'm now on a call list. *Wonderful.*

Shaking my head, I get back to work.

The rest of the morning, I crunch numbers until the pain behind my eyes turns into head-splitting agony. But I can't stop now. I'm sure the solution is right past this hurdle. There's got to be a way to keep this company profitable. We just need a little something for us to gain momentum. But the longer I sit here researching, the more I end up with nothing but my skull splitting apart.

My cell phone chimes again, startling me.

> **Corissa:** We're going out for drinks Saturday night. You in?

Rubbing the tired out of my eyes, I think about my response. It's not that I don't want to go. I just don't want to abandon my responsibility to have fun. It feels wrong ... like Brad.

> **Me:** I don't have a sitter. Another time maybe?

> **Corissa:** What about that hot nanny?

Smirking, I shake my head. He's certainly popular with the ladies.

> **Me:** He's been working overtime. It's his night off.

I am not going to take up any more of his free time.

My phone goes off again, but I silence it. I need to stay on top of my game, and blowing off steam with girlfriends isn't going to help that.

I've found it. The golden ticket. The solution to all our problems. I was right to keep looking for it. I'm tenacious for a reason.

I blink through my double vision before I hit the phone number. "Hi, I'm Miranda Keller from Ever Heart Digital. I'd like to make an appointment with Mrs. Williams." Cold-calling isn't usually my style, but it's a chance I have to take.

"Hold, please."

My heart is hammering through my chest. This appointment will mean business if I can speak to Amala Williams woman to woman. She happens to be an executive director at Pür Innovations, the parent company of toy and baby stores across the nation. While they are not as big as Dexico, it's something substantial.

"Miranda?" Her receptionist gets back on the line. "How is this Friday at 4pm?"

"Perfect." Even if it was the eighth day of the week, I'd make it work.

"Great. Amala looks forward to meeting with you."

My stomach settles with that sentence. My shoulders drop, and the tension that holds my head in a vise grip loosens to a dull ache. I calmly lay my phone on my desk, then jump up and cheer, "Yes!"

My palm flies to my temple as my head gives a grumbled throb at my sudden movement, but it doesn't suppress my burst of excitement. We might just make it after all.

With hope igniting my energy, I run over to Jay's office. They're sitting at their art station, looking uninspired.

I'm about to make their day. "Hey, look alive. We have work to do."

Jumping to their feet, they press a hand to their chest. "You can't just barge in here like the Kool-Aid man. You almost gave me a heart attack."

"Sit."

"So bossy."

When they are seated, I start massaging their shoulders.

Jay lets out an exasperated huff. "Okay, what do you want?"

"Can't I just be nice to my best friend?"

"You're hardly nice."

I smack the side of their head. "Harsh."

They twist and raise an eyebrow at me.

"Fine, we need to put a proposal together for Pür Innovations. This could be it, Jay. This could be our golden goose."

Jay narrows their eyes. "And if it isn't? What are you going to do?"

"It is. I can feel it. I have a meeting with Amala Williams on Friday, and I want you to come with me."

"No way. I'm the talent. You're the shark."

I give them my best Isabel's puppy-dog expression, lip sticking out and everything. "Pwetty pwease, oh, powerful one."

Jay purses their lips as their face settles to stone.

I squeeze and bat my lashes, trying to muster up a tear—mostly from eye irritation—but a tear is my friend's weakness.

They roll their eyes and huff a breath at my antics. "Argh, fine. Keep massaging. I got a kink in my neck. And a pain in my ass, named Miranda Keller."

"Shush, you love me."

"You're lucky I do. Now, let's put something together that will blow Am's mind."

"Am-ala," I correct.

"Whatever."

The rest of the day is spent designing the shit out of Pür's proposal. By the time I sit on the train to go home, I'm confident that we'll nail this presentation. The brass ring is within reach, and I'm going to take it.

All the nausea and head-throbbing from earlier have dissipated, and it's like I'm walking on air as I make my way up the sidewalk leading to my brownstone. Stopping in front of it, I raise my palm to the sky as gratitude swells in my chest.

I'll be able to keep it.

I don't want Isabel to grow up in a shitty apartment or trailer, like I had to. I want her to have a permanent home. A place she can always come back to, no matter how long she's gone. Though, if it came down to losing people or my home, an excruciating decision would be to sell the house.

Skipping through the door, I spot Remi and Isabel playing with building blocks on the living room floor. It fills me with a sense of satisfaction knowing I'm giving my daughter everything I never had—stability, quality time, and beautiful memories.

"Very good, Isa-bea." Remi points to his blocks, then to hers. "You spelled 'cat' just like I did."

"Cat," she repeats, pride written all over her face. "Adoded cat?"

"Uh…" He busies himself collecting the blocks, fidgeting with the wavy hair at his forehead. I almost laugh at Remi's hesitation.

She's hard to say no to, so I save him from it. "Not today, Isabel." I point to the manny. "And *you* don't let her rope you into something that will get you both in trouble."

"Who, me? Never." He turns to Isabel. "We are precious angels, aren't we?"

Isabel looks up at me. "Pre-sus."

So smart. Walking over, I pick up my daughter and hold her to me, smelling her unique scent. If I could combine her aroma with Remi's and bottle it, I'd be a billionaire. The opiate effects are potent. "How's my sweet girl?"

She gives me a toothy grin. "Good."

I laugh because she says it with such enthusiasm, showing me she really is doing well. "Great, baby. It's all Mommy wants."

Remi looks up at me with concern. "Are you feeling better?"

He remembered. My heart whoomps. "Yeah, thanks." I bite my lip to hide the giddiness coloring my face.

"Cat?" Isabel won't be distracted from her request. She's shrewd and tenacious, like me.

But no cats.

"We'll talk about it later." I boop her nose before setting her in Remi's lap. "I'm going to get changed, and then we're ordering dinner. What are you in the mood for?"

As soon as I ask him, I want to smack my forehead.

Right on cue, that signature smirk forms and the devil dances in his eyes. "Whatever you want to feed me, Queeny."

Fighting a smile and losing, I shake my head and shuffle up the stairs. My buoyed mood follows me all the way to my room as I hum the song Remi sings to Isabel. Going to my dresser, I find my softest yoga pants—that I do anything *but* yoga in—and a top. A sly grin graces my face when I look in the mirror.

Skipping down the steps, I find Remi and a tired Isabel cuddled in his lap on the couch, and there is nothing I want to do more than curl up with them. My limbs go limp, agreeing, but I can't just sit with them, can I? That would be blurring the line I've drawn.

I shift on my feet, playing with the hem of my shirt. It's not like we're going to lay down. Remi's sitting upright with his legs stretched out in front of him. His arms are occupied with my daughter.

When he catches my stare, he pats the cushion next to him. Longing tugs at my heart.

What the hell is wrong with me? There's nothing wrong with sitting by the manny. He's holding my child, whom I've missed. And we *are* friends.

Awkward as an emu, I settle on the couch close to them, tucking my feet under my butt. This position inches my body closer to him. While I'm not actually touching Manny, I feel the heat waves rolling off his skin.

When he notices what I'm wearing, his eyes sparkle. "I do believe you are trying to seduce me, Ms. Keller."

I break out in laughter. He knows just how to make everyone comfortable around him. "You love my wiener shirt that much, do you?"

"I do. It tells me everything I need to know. 'It's not a party until the—'"

I smack my fingers over his mouth. "I just got my sight back. Please don't take out your dick." Flinging my hand towards it, I ask, "Do you even have a permit for that? It should be a registered weapon."

Umber eyes light up, taking the bait I didn't mean to cast. With a sexy smirk, he holds his hands over Isabel's ears. "As a matter of fact, I do have a concealed carry permit for it."

My gaze drops to 'it', and flames lick up my neck before I regain sanity.

"Don't swear in front of the baby."

"Oh, because you abstain so well." I pick up my phone and search through the food delivery service.

A cheeky, crooked smile creeps onto his face. "I will admit, abstaining is quite difficult around you."

Oh, he plays dirty.

Ignoring his dangerous innuendo, I start spouting off takeout choices. "Ooh, Ranchito Burrito sounds amazing. I haven't had good carnitas in awhile."

Something about that statement wipes the playfulness right off of Remi's face.

"Let me guess, you hate burritos. I'll never understand you. How about—"

"I love them."

I'm still looking through my phone, so I'm not sure what he's talking about. "Hmm?"

"I want burritos. I love them." He sounds really reverent for making a food choice.

"Okay." I make my selection, then hand him my phone. "Order what you want. I'll put Isabel to bed."

"I can do it."

"I know." I give him a sweet smile. "But I want to." I pull her from his lap, and she's already rubbing her eyes. "C'mon, sweets. Mommy doesn't sing as good as Remi, but I'll try."

Isabel digs her nose in my neck, and I hum their tune again as I take her up to her room.

"Pretty, Mommy."

Oh my heart. She is the cutest. I know I can't hold a tune, but she's giving me the encouragement to keep singing. It's something she learned from Remi. A sudden burst of emotion fills my chest, and it's hard to swallow. "I love you, Isabel."

"Wovvu too."

It's not long before she's fast asleep, but I'm not ready to stop holding and rocking her. As I inhale her scent and kiss her hair, I promise to be better. I promise to be there for her whenever she needs me. I want to be a homeroom mom, to pack her lunches and take her to school. I want her to feel like she can come to me for anything, good or bad.

After Ever Heart is stable for the future, I will do just that.

The doorbell rings, which means the food is here, so I set Isabel in her crib. It's time she gets a big-girl bed. She's growing so fast. It feels like yesterday that Jay was holding my leg and chanting, *"Shaahh, push it. Oh, baby, baby."* A lot of mothers get classical music in the delivery room. I got Salt-N-Pepa.

I meet Remi in the kitchen, where he has us set up next to each other on the island.

"Mmm, smells good in here."

Remi lays my plate in front of me with fanfare, then settles in next to me. "Check your phone. You got a text when I was ordering."

When I unlock it, I see the messages I missed from Corissa. One I ignored this afternoon and one a little while ago. I know she means well, but she's being a little pushy.

"Yeah, Corissa wants me to go out for drinks on Saturday. She's not taking no for an answer."

"Why are you saying no? Do you not like Corissa and her overly flirty friends?"

My head throws back with a laugh. "I like them. I just have responsibilities here. Plus, you're off on the weekends. We already hog all your time." I take a big bite of the soft flour tortilla, and the tangy taste of salsa verde explodes on my taste buds. I moan. "Man, I forgot how good these are."

Remi has yet to take a bite of his food. His focus is solely on me.

"What? Do I have food on my face again?"

He swallows, and I swear the gulp echoes around the room. "Uh, no. I'm just waiting for you to take another bite."

"Jeez. You *do* have a food fetish. Too bad for you I'm shit in the kitchen."

"Maybe my fetish is to feed you."

I almost choke on my next bite, but I don't otherwise acknowledge his flirting.

"You said you had a headache earlier. Did the tea help?"

Chewing my porky goodness, I nod. "Are you going to eat that or can I have it?"

He scoffs. "No, it's mine, woman. These things are bigger than your head. There's no way you'd be able to eat two."

"Try me." I smirk.

Making a spectacle of taking his first bite, he rubs his belly and hums. "This is so good. Too bad you're not getting any."

Balling up my napkin, I throw it at his head. He catches it and tosses it back, bopping me in the side of the face.

"Jerk."

"How was the rest of your day?"

"Good. I found a hot lead, and we're meeting with the company on Friday. If we get this account, we won't be too affected by investors pulling out."

Getting up, he pulls out a beer from the fridge and pours me a glass of wine.

"You are so good to me."

Remi hides the grin that wants to break free, and the tops of his ears pink. "Is that why you've been so stressed out lately?"

Wiping my mouth, I respond, "Yeah, I'm just trying to keep it all together, you know. If I can set Ever Heart on stable ground, I'll be able to step back and be there for Isabel whenever she needs me."

Taking a long pull from his bottle, he sits back down. It doesn't escape my notice that he scooted closer. *Smooth, guy. Real smooth.*

"It sounds like a noble plan."

"I just want to be there to support Jay, and for my daughter. Be the mother I never had."

Catching me off guard, he wipes something off the side of my mouth.

My face gets warm. "Thanks."

"You and Jay are close."

"Yeah, my mom was always working when I was a kid. Jay's mom stayed at home. They always shared their lunch with me because mine was always a bit sparse." It's something I never want my daughter to struggle with. I want her to be the one to share her lunches with others. "One day, Jay took me home for dinner and we've been inseparable ever since." I'm thoughtful as I pick a stringy onion out of my burrito. "I owe Jay so much."

"Is that why you work yourself to death? Because you feel you owe your best friend?"

"No," I snap. Taking a breath, I set my burrito down, looking at it as if it has all the solutions to my issues, then getting pissed because it doesn't. "Yes," I deflate. "I don't know. We're a good team. I love working with Jay—they're the best. I'm good at what I do. It's just..."

"What?" Remi has dropped all pretenses of eating. He's just blatantly staring at me, watching me hammer a burrito like it's a piñata filled with gold. Which is both flattering and unnerving.

"Is this my dream job? I don't know." My shoulders scrunch. "I love conquering goals, but sometimes the race to the top is..." I hesitate, not wanting to voice my deepest discontent. "Soulless." And lonely.

"Don't you think if you told Jay how you really feel, they'd understand? I've seen them with you—they adore you." He takes a sip of beer. "They're also very protective of you. I'm sure if Jay knew that's how you felt, they'd want you to find your own path."

"Jay needs me just as much as I need them. If I go, then who's going to take care of them?" It's my job to make sure they're happy, healthy, and thriving. They've done it for me all these years.

Remi leans closer, his fresh laundry scent swirling around me, pulling me under his spell. "What about you, Mae?"

"Don't." My demand isn't as forceful as it sounded in my head. If anything, it's a weak protest—one I'm struggling with. A protest that I don't believe in because ... what about me? When you're everyone's anchor, sometimes you drown in the tide.

Maybe it's the trembling of my voice or the drop of my shoulders. Maybe it's my lack of conviction. Whatever it is, it invites Remi to run a hand up my spine—to comfort or seduce, I don't know. But it's not unwelcome in the least.

My head sways back when he starts gently massaging the tendons there. It's an innocent touch.

Is it? I was just massaging Jay's shoulders a little while ago.

When Remi moves to pull my hair back, I freeze. My brain doesn't want him making these moves, but my body is begging for him. I don't pull away. Maybe I even sway closer.

He smirks like he can see exactly what I'm thinking. The hand that was rubbing my neck has moved to my head. The soft, strong squeezing is exquisite. I can't help but groan at the sensation.

"Let me take care of you," Remi whispers, a millimeter from my ear. He nuzzles my hair, and his exhale slides across my sensitive skin, leaving goosebumps in its wake. "Let go."

I feel the heat of his other hand as it slides up my thigh. The air siphons out of the room, and arousal pools between my legs.

My breath hitches. "Rem—"

"Let me." Remi brushes the pad of his thumb across my lips before cradling my jaw, tipping my chin towards him. "Mae." It's a whisper, a plea. A promise of what's to come.

Lust and yearning wrap around me, around us. Pulling us closer. Our skin is magnetized and charged, begging for a spark. I'm so lost in this moment. His breath drifts across my lips like a whispered secret, scandalous and delicious.

Goddess help me. I'm trying to not give in, but every fantasy I've ever imagined since he's been here is at the forefront of my mind. Each one fighting to take first place.

Do I fuck him first or let him fuck me? I certainly have plans for those fingers. Oh, and that tongue. Though the thought of physical sex gives me a high, the emotional pull is what sends me fishtailing towards the moon.

Would he hold me after? Could I let my guard down and let him in?

My heart aches, telling me that this is more than needing to get off on a hot body. I want intimacy. I want it with him.

I inch in, practically tasting the malt on his breath.

"Bab—"

"Emmie! Mommy!" Isabel's voice shrieks through the baby monitor. It's an alarm bell: *Warning! Warning! Abort mission and run for your life!*

So I jump up and do just that, shoving right through the hazy tension between us. His soft curse is the only indication he's somewhat affected.

"We're not finished," is all he says as he breezes past me towards Isabel's room.

Chapter 13

Meet Cody

Remi

KIARA STARTS ON ME as soon as I walk into her kitchen. "I talked to Mandy the other day, and she says you haven't called her back. I thought you two were getting on."

"You do know that I'm a twenty-six-year-old man capable of navigating his love life, not needing his big sister to butt in, right?" I snicker, pulling a brownie off the counter and popping it in my mouth.

"Is it so bad that I want to see you with a nice girl?"

Swallowing the thick chocolate, I reply to her rhetorical question. "What if I don't want a girl, Kiara?"

My sister snaps her head at me. "Oh." Her eyes widen. "I might know some guys that are available."

I nudge her arm with my elbow. "That's not what I meant." I bite my lip because … how do I tiptoe around this? How can I feel her out without tipping her off that I'm attracted to my client? "I'm not looking for a girl. Maybe a woman is what I want."

"Really, Remi? Semantics." Even though Kiara is over thirty, she still rolls her eyes at me. "Mandy is a nice woman."

"What if I was interested in someone older than Mandy?" *Tiptoe. Tiptoe. Watch out for landmines.*

My sister narrows her eyes. She doesn't miss a thing. "How old are we talking?"

"Forty years."

Kiara pushes me in the chest. "What the fuck is wrong with you?" Her voice is a high shriek, letting me know the bomb fuse has been ignited and if I don't let her in on the joke soon, I'm dead meat.

But I'm having fun, so... "Yeah, she's one of Gram's friends. You remember Ruth, right? She's on the younger side."

Kiara's shoulders relax as she catches on. I get pushed again. "You're such an asshole. You don't deserve Ruth."

We laugh, and I flick her in the forehead. "Seriously, though. Would a ten-year age difference piss you off?" I bite my thumbnail, waiting for her answer. Even though my sister is important to me, her opinion wouldn't matter anyway. You can't help who you're attracted to.

"I don't think that's too bad. I mean, Cody is eight years older than me and as much as it pains me to say it, you're pretty mature for your age." Wow, a compliment. "Don't let it go to your head, dipshit."

Wrapping an arm around her neck, I give her a nuggie. "You love me. Admit it."

She throws a donkey kick and misses my balls by a centimeter. With my hands in the air, I jump away.

Kiara snickers. "I don't care who you date, as long as it isn't one of CCC's clients. And since I know you wouldn't, I have nothing to worry about, now do I?"

"Ne—" My words get caught in a cough. "Nope."

"Perfect. Go downstairs and drink beer with Cody. I've got to pick up Jackson from baseball practice."

Opening the basement door, I tromp down the steps and see my brother-in-law sitting like a king in his mancave. When I say king, I mean a rabid baseball fan wearing socks he hasn't washed since the beginning of the season.

"Who's winning?"

"Cubs. Six to one, bottom of the fifth." Cody takes a sip of his beer as his eyes stay focused on the game in front of us.

I grab a frosty mug and fill it at the bar. It's going to be a Guinness kind of night. Sitting next to Cody, I make shapes in the frost on the glass, not really paying attention to the television.

"Sup?" My best friend turns to me. "You look a little ... pale. Your sister kick your balls into your stomach or something?"

"If I tell you a secret, can you keep it to yourself?"

His brows slide up his forehead as he pauses the game. The man loves gossip. "You know I will."

"I know you will. But *can* you?"

"The fuck I just say?"

I let out a sigh. "Even if I say you can't tell your wife?"

"You have chlamydia?" With wide eyes, he shifts away from me a little. "I know a good doctor, man. They have pills for that stuff now. Shit." He blows out a breath and runs his fingers through his hair like I told him I had terminal cancer. "Was it Mandy?" His whisper is so low it's comical.

In a fit of laughter, I die. "What the fuck, man? I say I have a secret, and the first thing you think is that I have an STD? You for real, dude?"

"I-I-I..." His mouth flaps up and down, but no words come out. "I don't know. You're young. You're probably banging, like, five—" He looks me up and down. "I mean, a couple of chicks a week. It's not impossible."

"First of all, I've never *banged* anyone without a condom, and I get a check-up every six months. So no, no STDs here."

Cody relaxes next to me and nods. "Good. That's good."

"I'm attracted to someone I shouldn't be attracted to."

He shifts away again. "Dude, I love you like a brother, but you gotta know…" What the hell is he getting at? "You're good-looking, don't get me wrong, but I don't look at you like that. It's cool if you do and everything, but—"

"Are you fucking kidding me? What is it with you and my sister thinking I'm gay? Even if I was, you think I'd have a crush on *you*?" Dude is so full of himself.

"I mean, why not? I'm not that unfortunate-looking. Your sister thinks I'm hot." While his forefinger taps his chin, a smirk forms across his face. "What does she like to say to me all the time? Hmm…" He pretends to think for a minute, and I know I do not want to hear the next sentence out of his mouth. "Oh, yes. 'You're so sexy, baby. Make me co—' Oww! What the fuck, man?" The whiny bitch rubs his chest where I karate-chopped him.

"Do *not* tell me what my sister says to you in bed. That's just wrong." I shiver off the heebeegeebees. "I'm trying to have an adult conversation. Are you capable of that?"

"Yeah, of course." He waves his beer in my direction. "Come on. Tell Dear Cody what's on your mind."

I give him a stink eye and almost clam up. But I need to tell someone, and shithead or not, Cody is my best friend. "I'm attracted to Isabel's mother, Mae."

Cody's face drains of all color, and he whistles the single note of "oh, damn". "Dude, you're in so much trouble."

"I know, but if Kiara sees how happy I am with Mae, you really think she's going to be pissed?" Even as I ask it, I know. My sister is going to gut me like a cold fish.

This isn't the first time it's happened to her with one of her caregivers. When you're working with someone in such close proximity, there's bound to be some feelings that evolve. Unfortunately the last time, the man's ex-wife found out and put Child Care Connection on blast. Kiara had a hell of a time cleaning up the mess and recovering her losses. I couldn't believe how many families cut ties over something irrelevant to them.

Cody turns back to the TV and picks up a wing sopping with buffalo sauce. He doesn't turn the game back on, which tells me he's shaken. "You remember the last time this happened? It's Kiara's reputation on the line, man. When it comes to that, she's ruthless." *Sounds like someone else I know.* "You of all people can't do this." No longer interested in this discussion, he turns the game back on.

"Why me of all people? If anything, I should be the exception. Kiara knows me. She knows I'm not some psychopath."

"You're right—she does know you. Which means she'll be harder on you than anyone else because she expects more from you."

I look on as Cody shoves the whole top of a drumstick in his mouth and pulls it out clean, eating the gristle and everything. *Gross.*

I cringe. "Why do you do that?"

"That's how you eat a wing, asshole." He goes for the flat wing next, twisting and pulling until one bone pops out. Then he inhales it like he did the drum.

"Fuckin' barbaric, man." I shake my head, and grab the celery and blue cheese from the coffee table. For whatever reason, I love this combination—the cool crunch of the celery with creamy, tangy blue cheese dressing. It's the stuff dreams are made of.

"No, what's barbaric is you eating the celery and white shit, like some chick. *And* wanting to bang the MILF." His fists fly up. "Yeah, homerun! Take that, Yankee suckas!" Cody's hoots and woos are loud enough for the both of us. In fact, he isn't even pretending he's listening to me anymore.

Which is fine by me because I don't need another person telling me this won't work out. It's more than wanting to "bang the MILF", though the idea is fucking appealing. I'd give her a night she'd never forget and make her breakfast the next morning, and every day after that. That's how serious this is.

I need to strong-arm my sister to see things from my perspective. For the first time in my life, I want someone. Someone spectacular. That shouldn't be a bad thing. Maybe if I get Kiara to see my side, Mae will give in. It would be nice to keep my job too. It's not too much to ask, is it?

"I need to tell Kiara."

This gets his attention, and he whips his head towards me. "You better give a guy a warning before you do, so I can be in Alaska, off-grid. She won't think to look for me there."

I bark a sharp laugh. "What? You hate the cold. You bitch about moving every winter."

"Precisely my point. I give her epic orgasms, and she still scares me."

I almost gag. "Don't paint that picture for me, please."

"You are her pain in the ass. You should be terrified."

Wrestling with a napkin, I wipe my mouth and reminisce. "She used to kick my ass when we were kids, so I know how hard of a punch she throws. Thing is, I'm more terrified of losing Mae." I pin my friend with a look. "She's important, Cody."

"Okay, she's important. More of a reason to not get involved romantically. If this doesn't work out, everyone gets hurt—you, Mae, and most importantly, Isabel. You know, the little girl you're supposed to be caring for?" Cody rolls his eyes then goes eerily quiet as the next hitter steps up to the plate.

"Yeah, bu—"

"Shhh!" He holds a hand up to my face while facing the television. When the batter hits it out of the park, my friend jumps up and roars like he's actually on the field with the players.

I stick my forefinger in my right ear. "God, you're going to worry the neighbors. They probably think you lured me here under false pretenses, only to cut me up into tiny little pieces."

"You don't have to worry about me, man. Once Kiara finds out what you're doing, she'll take care of your ass for me." Bases are loaded, and Cody's fist pauses mid-air, waiting for a grand slam.

A ball of dejection drops in my stomach. I couldn't care less about who's winning what. "And what is it that I'm doing?"

"Making a horrible mistake." The pitch is hit out of the park, and all three runners make it to home base. Cody is jumping up and down like he won the game single-handedly. He grabs me by the collar and pulls me into a victory hug. "That was fuckin' awesome!" He shouts another shrill "Woo!" before sitting back down. "I have some good advice, though. You want to hear it?"

"That would be fucking nice. I'm out on a limb here."

He looks like he's ready to impart some sage guidance, so I lean in with open ears. Because right now, I need all the help I can get.

My best friend grabs my shoulder and squeezes. "Call Mandy."

Standing there like Goddess Venus, rifling through her bag, Mae plucks out some cash, her ID, and phone, then slips them into a small wristlet. "I can't believe you talked me into doing this."

My eyes feast on her ass, lick down her legs, and salivate over those fuck-me heels. "I'm really glad I did."

She looks over at me with a smile, most likely thinking I want her to blow off some steam. I do, but there is another reason I'm glad she's going out with the girls—seeing her in that dress. When she first walked down the stairs, I almost bit my palm to hide the soft groan vibrating in my throat. She's wearing a black bandage dress that looks like it was painted on her.

"Do I look okay?" She does a small turn. "It's been a long time since I've had a girls' night with adult women." While she's not an insecure person, new situations make her uneasy. For Mae, this is a big deal.

Mae's got curves for miles, and the soft fabric hugs her skin in all the right places. Lines of black boning accentuate ample hips I want to squeeze, and wrap around a plump, juicy ass I want to bite.

"You're stunning." I don't even hide the heat in my voice. I know Mae isn't ready for what I want to offer her, but that won't stop me from letting her know I'm available whenever she is. She wants to keep us platonic because of Isabel, and I understand her reasoning. But she also doesn't realize how good we could be together. We're a synchronized team taking care of Isabel. I'm so invested in their lives it's sometimes hard to remember this is only a job. My life is entwined with theirs, and I'm better because of it. Mae won't admit it, but she is too.

Her loneliness is palpable, but she isn't selfish. She only sees this situation as black and white—pursuing me would take away from her child. Maybe it's because of how I grew up, but watching Mae sacrifice everything for her daughter is why I fall harder every single day.

A shy smile forms on her beautiful face. "Thanks."

Mae tugs the bottom of the short hemline, which is made of lace overlay, giving her an exaggerated hourglass figure that Jessica Rabbit would be jealous of.

As I stare at the black lace, my pants tighten when I wonder if she's wearing matching underwear. Or any underwear at all.

"Are you sure you're okay staying the night? I know you have a thing on Sundays, so..." She looks away.

"Of course I am. That bed is way more comfortable than the hard lumpy futon I usually sleep on."

I'm living in a bachelor pad with a futon that acts as a couch and a bed. My apartment isn't an apartment, per se, more like basement storage under a Chinese food restaurant. It's not as if I couldn't afford something better. I could if circumstances were different. But they aren't, and it is what it is—a futon-couch bed.

Big green eyes flash to me, taking me in. "You sleep on a futon?"

I nod. "I might not have much, but what I do have is mine. Paid for with my own money." My teeth clamp over my lips. Nothing like telling the woman I have feelings for that I have nothing to offer her, except for my cooking skills ... and my monster dick. She seemed fond of that.

Concern etches her features. "Remi, are you struggling?"

"No, you pay me well, Queeny. I'm a guy that doesn't need many material things." I wink, reverting back to flirting.

It's not a lie, but I don't want to be another person she feels obligated to support. She's spread far enough and not in the way I want her to be.

An image of her lying on the bed, legs splayed open for me, flashes in the forefront of my mind. My mouth dries as I look for a place to hide my pelvis behind.

Then she does something that really tests my willpower. She puckers her pretty lips and coats them with a ruby red lip gloss, looking like the most forbidden fruit and the biggest sin a man could ever commit.

"You know you can stay here any time."

I swallow because I don't want her to know how badly I want to take her up on that. It's a terrible idea, of course. Being here twenty-four-seven will make it that much harder to respect her friend-zone boundary. But I also hate leaving them at night. Do they miss me as much as I miss them?

"Thank you for the offer. I might just take you up on it." My lips quirk up at her blush.

"Okay, don't hesitate to call me if you need me to come home. I won't be out late, but you don't have to wait up for me." She's a walking wet dream as she sashays towards me, lifting onto the tips of her toes and giving me a cheek kiss. It's innocent, and yet a bolt of desire zaps through me, making my dick twitch.

When she goes to pull away, I clasp an arm around her back. I'm at a loss for words. All I know is that I'm not ready to let her go yet.

The need to leave my mark on her—so that every fucker who comes within a mile radius of her knows she's mine—shocks me. The world around us disappears, and the urge to kiss her thoroughly fires through my cerebral cortex. I've never been a possessive guy, but I'm different with Mae. Everything with her is a new experience. Sometimes it's invigorating, but most times it's torture. Like right now.

I want to do nothing more than peel this dress off her body and show her how good I can be to her. That she's never met a man like me before. Show her all the tricks my celestial cock can do.

"What are you doing?" Queeny's words are breathy, and she's trembling. In her head, she's running for her life, but her body is calling for me to come closer.

I tuck a lock of red hair behind her ear and trace my thumb down her soft cheek. "Lookin' at you."

Her breasts are firm against the side of my chest. I'm not going to lie—I'm a boob guy, and Queeny's got a perfect set. Buxom and bouncing, they greet me every morning, and yet I've never given them a proper hello. So many times, I've fucked my fist imagining I'm fucking them.

I almost grind against her so she can feel how much she affects me. When she doesn't pull back, I get bolder, watching her face for any sign of reluctance. Her chest heaves with a breath, like an invitation. However, that's not what's driving me mad at the moment.

As if they have a mind of their own, my fingertips brush down her neck and feather over her clavicle. I've never before looked at a woman with such rapt attention to notice an ordinary thing like that on her body.

But every part of Mae is sexy. Her elbows and knees. Ears and chin. Her snorts and sneezes. Fucking everything. She's smart as hell too. The complete package.

Screw what Kiara wants or what Cody thinks. This is my life, and I stopped letting other people make decisions for me long ago.

"Be safe and come home to me." I didn't mean to say it, but I don't want to take it back.

Smokey-lined lids blink dreamily and slowly as her lips part, releasing a quivering breath. "I will."

I'd fight wars to have her wear that dress for me one day.

"You have no idea what you do to me." My voice is low and husky.

A hint of heat flashes in her big green eyes before they cool. "You're right—I don't. Otherwise, I wouldn't have to try so many times to incapacitate you. I'm learning, though. Next time, I'll make sure to get you good." She smirks.

"I hope you do."

Queeny tilts her pretty head. "You sure about that?"

"Yep," I say, popping the P. "So you can nurse me back to health. You still owe me a nip slip."

Her laugh is the most contagious sound in the world, and I love hearing it.

She swats my chest before pushing me away. "Alright, Prince Charming, I'm going to be late if I don't leave soon."

I let her go because as much as I want to keep her all to myself, she needs this—a night she can be carefree Mae and not Mom.

As soon as her cab arrives, I walk with her outside and open the passenger door. "Have fun."

Her eyes linger on me a bit, tempting me to kiss her so thoroughly that she'd rub her supple lips together all night, savoring the ache.

"I will, thanks to you." She pulls the door closed, leaving me standing there and watching until the yellow cab turns the corner.

I miss her already.

Chapter 14

Adore You by Harry Styles

Remi

Isabel woke up early from her nap, which meant she fell asleep early for the night. I've never interacted with a toddler as easygoing as Isabel. She listens, and even though there are times she pushes her boundaries, she has a sweet way of doing it. I'm not saying she doesn't throw tantrums because she does. Every child does. But Isabel is quick to forgive and amend. She's also hilarious, which makes my job ridiculously easy and fun.

Whoever Isabel's father is, he's a fucking idiot for disappearing. Kiara told me he was a deadbeat dad, but Mae never talks about him. Selfishly, I'm glad. The piece of shit doesn't deserve them. Call me an asshole, but I'm glad he's scarce because if he was around, I would have never met my girls.

When my phone chimes with a text, I smile.

> **Queeny:** Having so much fun. Thank you. You are just the best.

She has no clue what her words do to me. It's the equivalent of rocket fuel blowing me out of the stratosphere. No one has ever affected me this much.

I start typing back.

> **Me:** I'm glad. You deserve it.

My fingers pause, before I say fuck it and add something I probably shouldn't.

Me: Beautiful girl.

I watch as three little dots blink in and out, telling me she's writing something. I'm hoping she's a little flirty. The wait is painful, and I almost send another text but stop myself. The ball is in her court. It's her turn to pass it back.

I try not to be too disappointed when the dots disappear with no more words from Queeny.

Sighing, I set my phone aside and shuffle through Netflix, trying to find a good movie that will help me forget about all the scenarios that are now running through my head.

Will she meet someone tonight? She looked smoking in that dress. I'd be an idiot if I thought men wouldn't approach her. I certainly would.

Then there are other things like: Is she dancing? Who is she dancing with? How are they dancing? Who's touching her right now?

If Isabel wasn't sleeping upstairs, I'd probably put an APB out to find her, so I could throw her over my shoulder caveman style and bring her home.

These thoughts are becoming more intrusive and inciting by the second, so I pick an action movie to forget all about the beautiful woman who is so far out of my league she might as well be living on Mars.

A loud bang, followed by a fit of giggles, jolts me awake. I open my eyes and find myself lying on Mae's couch with some random show playing on the television, and I wonder if that's what woke me.

A glass object shatters on the floor, making me fling upright.

"Ow, shit."

"Queeny?"

"I din'n mean to wa-ake you. Fuuck, I loved lat tamp. I mean, lamp." She giggles at her misspoken words. "I said 'tamp'." More giggles, followed by hiccups.

Drunk Mae just might be my favorite. Her hair is a little wilder than when she left, and she looks like sex on stilettos, which look like torture devices. How she's still walking in them is beyond me.

Holding my palm out, I warn, "Stay right there, and I'll clean this up."

She gives me a mock salute and kicks her shoes off.

Pulling the broom and dustpan from the pantry, I clean up the mess, making a mental note to look for another lamp just like this one. She did say it was her favorite. "So, I see that you had a good time with the girls."

"I diiid." Hiccup. "I felt like I wass twenty-years old again. I nevver wanted it to end." Hiccup.

Once the shards of glass are thrown into the garbage bin, I turn to her. "It doesn't have to."

"It's too late." She whines so dramatically it's comical. "I'm already h-home. Back to the griiind."

Turning on the home audio receiver, I play the music Isabel and I were dancing to earlier.

"Ooh, I looove this song." She starts an enticing swivel of her hips, and I almost bite my palm for the second time tonight.

God, she knows how to move 'em.

"Danccce witt me, pleeease." She pulls me to the living room.

I'll never say no. "Okay. I'm only doing this for your entertainment because I'm praying you won't remember this part tomorrow." Dancing in front of Isabel is one thing because my moves are as graceful as a toddler's. I don't do it in front of people. Ever.

Queeny grabs my hands, pulling me to her, all the while swaying her hips to the rhythm. "Oh, I don't think there's anything I'd forget about you."

She does a move that would bring any man to his knees. Turning around so her back is against my chest, she grinds her ass onto me. It feels so good I don't even try to hide the raging boner she's teasing.

"That so?"

"Ummhmm," she confirms before sliding down my front like warm honey.

Fuck. I swear all my blood rushes to the head of my cock, making it throb and twitch. If she wanted to kill me, she's succeeding. Shimmying back up, she turns and lays a lazy arm across my shoulder. The new position has her heat pushing against where I'm aching for her.

The track changes to an upbeat song about a man who would risk it all for the woman he wants. How fucking appropriate. My mouth dips to her ear, and I sing the lyrics because it tells her everything she needs to know.

"Yoour voice is sooo fugging ssexy." She moans and—moving to the sensual beat of the music—drops her head back. Her throat is as inviting as a popsicle on a sweltering day.

I just want to suck it. Taste her. Drive her as wild as she drives me.

"Yeah, you like it?"

Queeny nods and focuses on my mouth like she's under hypnosis. Her lips are stained red from her gloss, and they look so soft. So ripe. So fucking juicy.

"I drannnk apple marinis all night."

"Marinis, huh?" A low chuckle rumbles in my chest.

"Yep. And I coulnt help but wonner if you'd taste the sssame." Her lids drop to half-mast. "I bet you're ssssweet and tart, and ssso fugging egi—" Hiccup. "Edble-ible."

Her pink tongue dips out, calling my name and putting pressure on my resolve. I swear the damn thing is saying, *Pssst, Remi. Don't you want a taste? Just a little one is okay.*

"Why don't you find out?" I'm so fucking close to licking those lips that mine part in anticipation. I'm going to kiss her like she's never been kissed before. So fully she'll know exactly how much I feel for her.

My chest aches with the profound emotion I'm trying to restrain. She's everything amazing, beautiful, and right in the world. The fucking center of my universe.

But she has to make the first move. She's made her boundary clear—if she wants to breach it, that's on her. I'll happily oblige.

Queeny's chin raises, asking me to take the bait. The wait is pure agony, but she goes for it, brushing her bottom lip against mine.

Oh God, so fucking good. The hairs on my arms raise, pointing straight to her. Inside, I'm dying of suffocation, my ribs tightening around my lungs, and my stomach swoops. Every nerve ending in my body is celebrating. An exhilarating buzz zips down my spine to my groin.

I'm about to go in for more, when she jerks back with wide eyes and runs upstairs.

Well, I've never had a woman run from me before. Stunned, my eyes blink rapid fire. What the fuck just happened? One minute we were hot, but in a split second she went cold on me. I can't believe one small kiss has her so spooked.

Raking my fingers through my hair, I contemplate how to fix this. That's when I hear it—violent retching.

"Shit." I run after her and find her in the spare bathroom on her hands and knees, head hovering over the toilet bowl. "Oh, baby." I wince, holding back her hair. "I got you."

She's going to have one hell of a hangover tomorrow. So will my heart.

Mae

Agony, stab, throb. My pounding head rudely wakes me before my alarm does.

"For the love of God."

Pinching the bridge of my nose, I scrape my tongue across the back of my front teeth. My mouth tastes like sour milk and goat farts. Gross. Hoisting myself up into a sitting position, I realize I'm still in my dress from last night. What in the world?

My ears strain to hear anything coming from the baby monitor, but it's off. However, sticking to the top of the device is a note with Remi's neat script.

Relax. I'll take care of Isabel.

By the time I shower and dress, my head feels a bit better but my stomach is roiling in sour emptiness. It's amazing how fast I got used to being fed every morning. Before Remi, I sometimes didn't eat until lunch. I brush my teeth a second time before heading downstairs, finding Remi holding Isabel as he's stirring something on the stove.

"Good morning." I pull my daughter from Remi's arms and give her a snuggle.

"Mommy," she squeals.

Remi looks at us with a devastating smile. "Morning, Queeny." He points to his cheek, leaning towards me.

When I get close, I smell his warm scent and wish it was me he was holding. He's such a greedy flirt, but I'm happy to oblige.

Remi side-eyes me, gauging my hangover status, no doubt. "You doin' okay?"

"Peachy." Walking over to Isabel's high chair, I set her in it and pull her closer to the table, next to me.

"Stawbaby?" Isabel asks.

I boop her nose before heading to the fridge to find her some strawberries. She loves her fruit. Cutting it up, I place it on her tray and sit to watch her eat.

"I apologize for anything stupid I did last night. I don't remember much, but I'm assuming you put me to bed."

I don't recall much after we hit the club. One thing I do remember is the way Remi was staring at me before I left for the night, undressing me with his eyes. When he held on to me… My heart does a triple flip, heating my cheeks just thinking about it.

"You have nothing to apologize for. You were a perfect gentlewoman." Remi winks, sliding a steaming cup of coffee in front of me.

"My hero." Picking up the mug, I cradle it with both hands, savoring the warmth.

"Does that make you my Lois Lane?"

I wrinkle my nose. "No, you're more of a jokester than a nerdy Clark Kent. So, I guess that makes me your Harley Quinn." I almost smack my hand over my mouth. I forgot all about the post-drunk-stupids after a night of inebriation. Basically, I just told him I'm legit obsessed with him.

Remi saunters over and starts massaging my shoulders. My head falls back, and I moan. He's so good with those hands.

"I may be a jokester, but my feelings are very real."

I freeze. I'm physically and mentally weak, and I'm definitely not ready for this conversation. Are we doing this? Right now? When I twist towards him from my seat, his hands fall to his sides.

"Remi…" I shake my head, unsure of what to say.

"Eat, Emmie." Isabel holds up her mushy offering. "Stawbaby." I'll have to reward my baby with a treat later for saving me from this discussion.

Without missing a beat, Remi eats the squishy thing. He never ceases to amaze me.

I continue to drink my coffee like we weren't about to have the most awkward conversation known to man.

"Do you remember anything from last night?"

Damn him. He's not easily deterred.

Let's think for a minute... I have a huge crush on him, and I'm pretty certain he feels the same about me. Alcohol and confidence were involved.

"I woke up in my dress, so not much could have happened."

Remi lets out a long, tired sigh. "You're right there—nothing much happened." His hand rakes through his wavy hair and twists the back of his neck. "Look, I'm not going to pretend *nothing* happened. Because something almost did, and I wanted it to."

Did I come on to him?

He pins me with heated eyes, immobilizing me in place. "Drunk or not, you did too."

Yep, I totally offered up the goods last night.

"What almost happened?" I whisper, unsure if I really want to know.

I wait. Every muscle in my body freezes as a myriad of mortifying things swirl around my head.

He sits next to me and stares at the table top, pensive, like he's thinking through every word before saying it. I almost kick him under the table for an answer.

"We kissed."

My breath halts, and I suffocate. Holy fucking shit. How can I not remember such an epic event? *Shame on you, inebriated brain.*

"After that..." He mulls it over.

"After that, what?" I shriek. I'm sitting here, sweating like a person who annihilated two bran muffins and four black coffees right before getting stuck in bumper to bumper traffic. In other words, I'm about to shit myself.

My god, man. Spit. It. Out.

"You came home a bit sloshed." The manny scrapes his teeth across his plump bottom lip, fighting a smile. "You broke the orange-bust lamp, by the way."

My hand presses against my chest, and my eyes fly to the console table next to the back door. "No! Not Ruth Bater Ginsburg."

"May she rest in peace." He closes his eyes and makes the sign of the cross before clamping his palms together. "Anyway, you didn't want the night to end, so I put on some music. We danced a bit. Then…" He scratches his forehead, looking a bit uneasy. "You barely kissed me before bolting up to the bathroom, where you puked until about 3am."

My head falls to my hands. This is so much worse than anything I imagined. "I puked in front of you?"

Remi tamps a laugh, telling me I did. "Technically, I was behind you, holding your hair back, but yeah. You were in pretty rough shape last night."

"I'm never drinking again," I whine, then panic when I can't find a black hole to suck me into. Barfing is not a Hallmark moment. Even if you're the most beautiful woman on the planet, it isn't a good look. Still gripping my forehead, I curse, "Jesus Christ," under my breath.

Not only did I assault him, but he had to be privy to the half-digested contents of my stomach. The manny stayed with my daughter so I could have one night of fun, and I repaid him with vomit. Awesome. "I'm sorry I hit on you, Remi. You shouldn't have to be subjected to that."

Drawing my chin up with one hand, Remi's other pulls my fingers from my head. "Hey, I'm not sorry. Only that you felt so sick. You deserve to let loose and be crazy for a night, Mae." Brown irises sparkle with mirth and desire. "If you wanted to let loose on me? Well, who am I to argue?" His smirk is deadly sexy.

I shiver and look at my mug. "I'm sorry anyway."

Waving away my apology, Remi places a yellow smoothie in front of me. "Banana, pineapple, coconut water, and ginger. A certified hangover cure." He flashes me his beautiful white teeth.

Cautiously, I take a sip. All the flavors coat my tongue, and the coolness soothes my burning throat. "Mmm, that's perfect."

Two dimples wink at me. "Glad you like it."

Sip by sip, the smoothie fills my stomach until it stops churning.

Breakfast is mostly quiet. Plus, the atmosphere in the room is weird. Or maybe it's just me being awkward because I sexually harassed the manny before puking my guts out. Not my best look.

"You good here? I need to take off in a bit," Remi says, breaking my self-flagellation.

"Yeah, fine. I know you have a thing on Sundays." Scraping back my chair, I take my plate and mug to the sink. "Must be really important if you never miss it."

I refuse to look at him. Besides, I'm just making conversation, saying words to fill the uncomfortable space. Right?

"She *is* really important."

Oh, *she*. Wasn't he just flirting with me two seconds ago, and now he's talking about seeing a woman he cares about?

I bristle. "Well, don't let us keep you from whatever plans you have today."

"Queeny?" Remi coos.

I'm stubborn, with a bruised ego. I start washing the dishes, praying he leaves without further discussion so I can overthink in peace. It isn't until I feel his heat at my back that I falter.

Strong arms snake around my front while soft breath sweeps across the back of my neck. "You jealous?"

"No." I'm petulant.

"Admit it." His voice is low and husky. It tickles down my spine and puckers my pussy.

Of course I'm jealous.

"When I was thinking about you last night, in that fucking dress that hugged every inch of your curves..."

My ass is firmly against his front, and I literally feel him harden against me. My mind screams to run, but my feet have grown roots. They're not going anywhere.

"You are so fucking beautiful, and all I kept seeing in my head was someone else's hands on you." Gentle fingers squeeze my soft belly, and it jumps in anticipation. "Touching what's mine."

Gulp. What?

"Rem—"

"You gonna deny it, Queeny? Hmm?" Manny noses my temple before kissing my head. "You gonna pretend we don't want to go crazy on each other?" He grinds against me, and I whimper. "That's right, baby. Tell me all about it," his raspy voice purrs in my ear.

Curious fingers creep up my rib cage, and deft thumbs brush the sides of my breasts. A bolt of lust zaps through my stomach and pulls lower. I've never in my life so badly wanted a man to get to second base.

"Just the thought of another man touching you makes me furious. Makes me want to mark your skin with my mouth and brand you as mine."

As mine.

Oh my ... fuck. Abandoning the dishes, I completely surrender, the back of my head resting against his shoulder.

"You want that, don't you?"

"Yes." I almost moan the word because, let's face it, last night boundaries were busted and I'm not too motivated to put them back into place. Not when the promise of a heavenly psychedelic orgasm trip via one hot manny's celestial cock is right in front of my face... Er, I mean, right behind me.

But then I remember he has plans with a very important someone. A female someone. I stiffen and pull away, not looking at him. Not wanting him to know how hurt I am by his games.

"You have plans." A man played me a fool once—I'll never let it happen again.

He deflates with a soft curse. "Fine, I have plans. I want you and Isabel to come with me."

I whirl around, facing him. "What?"

"Come with me, my jealous queen." He gives me a wry smile, and he's just too adorable to reprimand or lie to. Because I am. Jealous, that is.

And curious. *This could get interesting.*

And still a bit hungover.

And turned the fuck on.

I pick up Isabel out of her chair and race upstairs to get her ready for our outing.

"Okay, but if it's a drug run and we get busted, it's every man for himself."

Chapter 15

Cumbrellas

Mae

Twenty minutes later, Remi picks us up in his pink Cadillac, and I try not to laugh. I'm not making fun of his vehicle. It's just so odd seeing this hot-as-hell guy in a frilly grandma car.

"Emmie, Emmie, Emmie," Isabel blathers on about her favorite person.

He gets out of the car and pulls Isabel from me. "Quit biting your cheek. You're going to get a sore. But if you laugh at Aretha, she will get mad. You don't want to get on her bad side. Trust me."

Not able to help it, I burst out laughing. "You call your old-person car Aretha?" I shake my head, trying to catch my breath, wiping tears. "You never cease to amaze me."

Opening the back door, he straps my daughter into the car seat I gave him. "Well, to be honest, her name was already Aretha when I inherited her. I promised to keep her happy and healthy. So I tell her what a good girl she is every day."

How? How does he turn a silly conversation into something that flicks my nipples and clit at the same time? "I bet she's a really good girl for you." I'm trying to be funny, but I can't help the heat that warms my tone.

"She is." He opens up the passenger door for me, and I slide in. "I know just how to tune her up right." He winks, and I pass out from lack of oxygen.

Remi settles in the driver's seat, looking in the rearview mirror to make sure Isabel is content, before driving down the road. "What do you want to listen to, Isa-bea?"

"Sussi!"

Fighting a grin, he shakes his head. "Of course."

"Where did you come up with her nickname?" I've been curious for a while. Is it just something that rolls off his tongue or is it more than that?

Remi lowers the music. "What? Isa-bea?"

I nod.

"Bea means bringer of happiness." He turns to me, brown eyes catching green. "That's exactly what she does."

Oh, my heart. My hand flies to the left side of my chest, and my eyes turn glossy. Before I let myself get emotional, I deflect. "Is that why you call me Queeny, because I'm a bossy bitch?"

His quirked lip lifts his cheek. "When we first met, you were pretty cold towards me." He shrugs. "So yes, initially I called you Queeny to get under your skin." He takes my hand, folding his fingers around it.

I just sit there and stare at our skin touching. My breath hitches, and goosebumps dot my arm. It feels so right, even though I know it's wrong. "And now?" I whisper.

"You're not ready to hear it. That's okay." His crooked smile lights me up. "I'll wait."

Isabel takes this moment to shout the lyrics from the back seat like I'm in some kind of Disney movie and the characters are trying to set the tone for a romantic kiss. "You know I wuv you, baybe. Rewwy wuve you, baybe."

Remi chuckles and lifts the back of my hand to his lips before letting me go. Now, my hand feels cold and lonely.

We drive towards the outskirts of town, where wheat and corn are more prominent than skyscrapers and city lights. It seems so peaceful here. Pretty soon, we're pulling into a parking lot for Hope Village Assisted Living.

"Oh, wow. Is this where Aretha lives?"

Manny's chuckle rubs me in all the right places. "No, but her previous owner does."

Once we park, Remi gets Isabel out of the car seat and—holding her—grabs my hand again. "I've never brought anyone here." The reverence in his voice lets me know that this is significant.

If I continue through the entrance hand-in-hand with Remi, our relationship will change. It's terrifying because I don't know if I'm ready for this. And it's thrilling because I'm not opposed to finding out.

Once we step through the heavy doors, we're greeted by the front desk nurse's wide smile. "Is it my favorite day of the week already?"

Remi winks at the older woman, and she blushes. "Seeing you anytime is my favorite day." Their banter is more playful than flirty. "Hattie, this sweet girl is Isabel." Remi smirks and holds my daughter to the nurse, showing her off like a proud papa. "And this is her mother, Mae."

"H-hi." My greeting is weak because something is stabbing me in the chest, and it's not heartburn.

Somewhere between me keeping my hands to myself and Remi at arm's length, I didn't realize his role in our lives has become more significant. I hate forgetting he's only Isabel's nanny, but I can't help it sometimes. Their bond is so natural, and he just fits perfectly. With him, everything just feels so complete. Like a family.

Hattie pinches Isabel's cheeks, and she squeals in delight at the attention. "You know you're going to make her day, right? She's been floating around here, telling everyone about—"

Remi's shoulders tense, and his eyes widen. A plastic grin crosses his face. "Okay, well. It's great seeing you, Hattie. Are you coming to the show?"

The nurse winks at him. "You know I wouldn't miss it." She presses a button on her desk and the doors swing open, revealing a big room where about twenty senior citizens are gathered.

"Remi!" they all cry in unison, and I feel like I'm in a rerun episode of *Cheers*.

Remi goes around the room with handshakes and high-fives, greeting everyone. "Hey, Jack." He even flirts with them. "Did you get your hair done, Ruth? I like it."

Ruth pats her coif as her cheeks flame. "Thank you."

A crotchety old man in a wheelchair points a crooked finger at Remi. "You better play some Frank Sinatra. No more of that Ed Sheeran bullshit."

"You got it, Charlie." He just takes everything in stride—talking, introducing Isabel, and giving human touch to everyone he sees.

An overwhelming warmth blooms in my chest and spreads throughout my body. It's so immense I'm afraid it will heat the whole room. I put my hand against my mouth to hide my quivering lips. Watching him show off my daughter is everything I've ever dreamed of. In another life, he could be her father. We would be a family, happy and whole.

An older woman, maybe in her early eighties, with eggplant-colored hair and dark red lipstick, walks into the room. "It's about time you got here. I was ready to— Oh my, who do we have here?" She reaches up to Isabel. "Aren't you just the cutest?"

Suddenly shy, Isabel hides her face in Remi's shoulder.

"Gram, this is who I was telling you about."

Gram?

"This is Isabel, and this" — he grabs my hand and pulls me next to him — "is her mother, Mae."

Wise brown eyes size me up as if I'm the prized pig in a luau. "Nice to finally meet you, Queeny."

I give Remi a stink eye, and he just shrugs me off.

"Nice to meet you too…"

"Gram," she finishes for me, and I can't help the cheesy smile on my face.

I'm getting déjà vu from when I met Mama Morales. She is Mama, period. That's who she is to everyone.

When Gram comes at me with open arms, I go with it. I'm not usually a hugger, but that overwhelming feeling inside me won't subside. She's important to Remi, so that makes her important to me. Him bringing me here to meet her is significant.

"You listen to me, missy. If he gives you any trouble at all, you send him to me and I'll kick his ass for you."

My head throws back with the force of my laugh.

"Traitor," Remi hisses before whispering something into Isabel's ear. The syllables suspiciously sound like "sushi" and "cat named Harry".

I snicker. Those are my daughter's abracadabra words.

Isabel perks up. "Gam!" she exclaims, throwing her arms out to a woman she was just hiding from a second ago.

Gram picks my daughter up like she's done it a million times. "We finally meet, Isabel." She turns to us. "I got quite the earful from this one the other day."

I tilt my head. How?

"Ah, yeah about that. I have some explaining to do," Manny interjects.

I'm more confused than ever.

"Emmie hewp mommy fuck face," Isabel explains, which means she literally announces it to everyone with a hearing aide.

Cackles and catcalls echo around the room. I look for the emergency exits and panic when I realize they are down a long hallway. They'll be on me before I can make my escape.

Remi coughs in his hand. "It was the day you almost killed me with mustard oil. When I gave Isabel my phone, she inadvertently called Gram. Giving her a play-by-play."

"Of course she did. I'm number one on your speed dial." Gram shakes her purple head. "I tell ya, the kid is a needy shit. It's 'Gram this' and 'Gram that'. I seriously doubted he'd ever bag a birdie."

I swear my face resembles a tomato. "Oh, I'm not with— I mean, we're friends. Just that." She's still looking at me expectantly. I hold my hands up in surrender. "Friends."

"Uh -huh, I knew it." Her eyes narrow at her grandson. "Couldn't land the plane, eh?" She nudges him with her elbow. "Why, your grandfather used to use the blue pill to get it up. I tell ya, honey, it's one hell of a ride." She cups her mouth towards me. "If you know what I mean."

"Okay, then. Grandmother, there are children in the room." Remi's voice is a bit shrill, and red splotches blot his cheeks.

"How do you think they got here?"

Remi looks like a ripe pomegranate. He hands Isabel to me and motions us to sit on a chair in front of a makeshift stage. "Thank you for the biology lesson, Granada. Why don't we start?"

"Oooh, you used my full name. I'm shaking in my slippers." Making a mockery of her grandson, Gram wiggles her fingers in front of him before grabbing a bag from a side table. She proceeds to start passing out feather boas to everyone.

I laugh when Charlie wraps his feathers around his shoulders like a burlesque dancer. "Yeah, more singing and less yammering." Who knew the salty guy liked the color pink.

Isabel and I settle next to Ruth, who's eyeing me like she knows a secret I don't. When I turn to her, she just nods at me and says, "You remind me of when I was younger."

I give her a wobbly smile, unsure of what she means. She knows nothing about me. "Oh, thank you?"

"Yeah, I miss my combrillas. As I got older, I lost them."

I have no idea what she's referring to. She probably has dementia or something. "Um, I'm sorry about that."

"Me too." She sighs wistfully. "Your lashes are so nice and full. Helpful little tools. Sperm in the eye burns like hell."

If I was eating something, chewed bits of saliva-infused food would be sprayed across the room right about now. Oh my god, did she mean cumbrellas? Like, cum-umbrella?

"Best days of my life," Ruth waxes poetically about her dick-sucking years.

Before I can come up with a response, Remi tunes his guitar and Gram pokes the mic to make sure it's on. They are sitting on a pair of stools behind microphones, and Remi is holding an acoustic guitar.

"Alright, you old farts, let's show these youngsters how we do." Gram pumps up the audience, who hoots and hollers. I even hear a "Whoop, whoop, whoop!" from the back of the room.

Remi starts the guitar riff to *Cracklin' Rosie,* and Grams does her best Neil Diamond impression, with her grandson on back-up vocals. They are having a blast, and as I look around the room—bouncing Isabel on my lap—everyone else is raving too. Charlie has the ends of his boa in his hands, flinging them to and fro—even he's having fun.

My chin trembles.

It's Remi. He brings so much joy to everyone he meets. He'll gladly give up his free time if I need him. And on his days off, he visits his gram and they entertain the residents here. Every time he looks at me and gives me a sweet smile while he strums away, dazzling everyone, these feelings intensify.

The eclectic set list goes from Neil Diamond to Frank Sinatra—Charlie's favorite—to Lady Gaga. Rounding out the encore is an acoustic version of *Blister in the Sun* by Violent Femmes. With each song, this thing in my chest gets stronger.

I've been floating on the denial river with a gaping hole in my canoe since he started. There is no way my head can rebuff my heart anymore. In the end, the truth always comes out.

I'm falling for him. Hard.

Chapter 16

See How Good I Take Care of You

Mae

"She's down." I meet Remi in the kitchen after putting a very sleepy Isabel to bed. "All that dancing really took it out of her."

"I know." Remi gives me a half-moon smile while he heats up a dish of leftovers for dinner.

Pulling out a wine glass, I offer one to Remi and grab the Cabernet. "Thank you for bringing us today. That was ... something." Amazing. Fun. Pure joy.

"It was." After setting the timer on the warmed oven, Remi pops the cork and pours us both half a glass while we wait for our food. "I've been itching to take you and Isabel. I just wasn't sure how you'd react." He looks into the red liquid as if he's deciding on what to say next. "If you'd reject the idea or—"

"We had a lot of fun." The wine is smokey on my tongue, making me warm. "You and Gram are quite the pair. Have you always been close?"

He told me once that he moved here to be with his sister and that his mother's side of the family lived here. Assuming Gram is on his maternal side, I wonder where his mom is and if he's as close to her. Though I don't want to pry, I'm tempted to ask.

"Yeah, she's why I'm passionate about music. She taught me how to play piano growing up." His eyes drop to the ground. Dark eyelashes fan over high cheekbones, and I wonder if they are as silky as they look. "My father didn't like it. He said starving artists don't build empires."

"Well, that's a shitty way of putting it. Has he ever heard of famous musicians? They build plenty. If you're passionate about what you do, who cares what anyone else thinks." I almost slosh the wine from my glass. I'm so incensed that a parent would tell their kid that.

Remi sniffs out a small laugh. "He said they were the exception and there was nothing exceptional about me."

A red haze falls over my vision. How dare anyone say that to Remi? He's utterly remarkable in every way. I don't need to personally know the man to surmise that the only thing his father's exceptional at is being a fucking douchebag.

"He wanted his sons in his practice." He shakes his head. "A happy little family business." Even though his face is soft, his tone has an edge to it. "Problem is, I'd never be happy there. I hated Los Angeles."

Don't ask, don't ask. Do. Not. Ask. "What about your mom?" Fuck, I asked.

He stiffens, and I know I'm prying too deep. We've been orbiting each other. Gravity pulls us together, but reality is what keeps us apart. After the atomic bomb disguised as an epiphany I had today, all of my boundaries have been breached.

I give him an out. "You don't have to answer. I'm just ... trying to get to know you more."

"No, it's okay." Remi sucks in a breath, like he's been waiting for something and it's finally here. "We used to have a close relationship when I was little. I was her baby. She coddled me, and my father resented me for it." He gives me a wry twist of his lips. "He hated a lot of things, and he wasn't afraid to attack anything he didn't agree with." His eyes drop, pensive. "Usually, he's just plain mean. It's when he's being nice that you have to watch your back. That's when he's in the mood to be cruel. He knew exactly how to manipulate everyone around him so they felt inferior," he spits out. "Dirt under his shoe." His usually bright features darken. "Especially when it comes to my mom." The oven timer beeps, and Remi pulls two plates out of the cabinet before removing our food from the oven. "After so long, she grew tired of it. My mom went from a vibrant woman to an ashen ghost." He stares at our dinner, but he's not really seeing it.

I hate the look on his face, so I go to him and gently rub his back. That's when I realize Remi runs around giving joy to everyone he meets all the while keeping his pain to himself. He could be as bitter as me if not more, yet he doesn't invite his past into the present. He's eight years my junior, but I've learned so much from him. I want him to know he doesn't have to go through it alone. Not anymore.

Remi's taut muscles loosen under my hand, so I deepen the massage to soothe all that tension away. His eyes slide shut, and he purrs like a cat. He takes care of everyone, but it makes me wonder who takes care of him.

"You can talk to me about it if you want."

He peeks over his shoulder at me, his chestnut irises a storm of want and hesitation.

"I'm here for you, Remi," I murmur.

He clears his throat. "She broke her ankle during a tennis match at the country club." I trace a finger down his spine. "That was her first introduction to the love of her life." His tone is acerbic—a voice that doesn't sound like him.

Anxiety creeps into my chest. "Who was it?"

"OxyContin," he replies with so much hurt and remorse in his tone that I want to wrap myself around him. He steps away, pulling out utensils and napkins. Plating our food, Remi sets them on the counter and we sit close to each other. "Gram left Chicago to help Mom when I was born. It got so bad she moved back, and when she did, my sister left to live with her." He uses his fork to play around with the food on his plate. "Gram pushed me to follow my passion for music and education. My sister pushed me to move here, and when she had my nephew, this is where I wanted to be. I hated leaving my mom, but I was slowly deteriorating as a person. She saw it and begged me to go." He swallows.

I want to pull him to me. With one arm around him, I lay a hand on his forearm like I'm shielding his body from a sniper attack. "I'm sorry."

"Don't be." His head turns towards me, and I realize how close we actually are. "I'm really grateful that you gave me a chance, Mae. I'm happier than I'd ever thought I'd be."

A bubble of hope forms where the anxiety was. "If it's worth anything, Isabel thinks you hung the moon…" I wait until he's looking directly into my eyes. When he does, I confess, "I think you're pretty exceptional."

"Yeah?" He's all soft words and small smiles. It closes the space between us and fills the moment with intimacy.

"Absolutely." Remembering his words from earlier, I swallow a ball of regret in my throat. "About what you said earlier, about me being cold towards you. I'm really sorry about that. You have to know it wasn't about you. It's just…" I take a deep breath. I'm trying to be a better person—part of that is owning my flaws. "I know I can be a bit abrasive, but I am working on it." My eyes widen with a plea. *Please be patient with me.* "Just know that whatever I say in my moments of frustration isn't real. Not that it's an excuse because it's not, but I'm a work-in-progress." I take a sip of wine, gathering the courage to say the next part because it's uncomfortable for me to acknowledge that I can't do everything on my own. "I appreciate you, Remi. You have given Isabel and me so much. It's not just about a nanny position anymore. We need *you*, and that's really hard for me to admit."

Remi's cheeks color, and he nods. "I need you both too." His voice is so low I'm not sure I'm meant to hear it. But my ears picked up every syllable and telegrammed my heart: *We matter to him.*

I stare at the counter, tracing the veining in the stone as if it will lead me to a future where we are free to be together and everything is wonderful. I lose my path because life is full of twists and turns, and the simple fact is, daydreams are called dreams for a reason. There's hardly any tangible evidence of them coming true.

Remi pulls my lip from my teeth and searches my face. "Where are you, Queeny?"

Walking down the aisle towards you, my brain replies, but I shake the thought off. "I'm here." I smile. "With you."

He's still cradling my jaw, stroking my chin with a soft thumb. "Do you want to know why I still call you Queeny?" His words come out velvety, coating my body like butter.

"No, let me sit here and stew about it." I meant it to be a joke, but it comes out breathy and more seductive than humorous.

Plush lips widen into a grin. "Smartass." His giddy demeanor shifts to fever as he pins me with a stare. "You can come off as cold, but I see who you really are." He takes my hand for the second time today. "How can I not? You're amazing and beautiful, and *regal*."

My lungs expand, absorbing his words. "You can't be serious right now." I go to pull away, but he doesn't let me.

"Remember this: every time I call you Queeny, I'm telling you that I see you. How you hold your kingdom together." He gently squeezes my fingers. "How I know you are lonely but not selfish enough to consider your own needs." Umber eyes turn to warm caramel, dripping over my skin. "How I dream of worshiping you." His voice turns low, husky. "In every. Single. Way."

Oh. My. Fuck. My pussy clenches because she got the memo first. I open my mouth to say something, but the damned thing is full of cotton and unable to utter a single syllable.

"At a loss for words, Queeny?"

A nervous breath releases from my diaphragm. "What do you think?"

With one leg placed on the ground behind me, he scoots his stool closer with the other until all I see, smell, and hear is him. I'm inside a Remi cocoon, and I never want to leave.

"What I think is, you don't want that rubbery chicken on your plate." His mouth drops to my ear, and he noses my hair. My breath hitches. I feel him everywhere. "No. That's not what you're hungry for."

"N-no?" It's a weak plea to my libido.

Remi cradles my face, and his eyes read mine. "Definitely not it." He barely brushes his thumb down my cheek, and my heartbeat floods my ears. His blinks are slow and bewitching. His dark eyelashes are so long. Their softness continues to tease. "Bet I can guess what will fill you up to satisfy that hunger."

Without my brain's permission, my hand lifts with greedy fingers, lightly touching the forbidden fruit.

His lids drop, and he murmurs, "Let me, Mae. Let me feed you where you are starving."

Everything about him is begging me to take with wild abandon. But I'm still standing at the precipice, afraid to jump into dark waters. I can't see the bottom, and I won't take for granted that there aren't sharks circling, ready to devour me.

"Remi," I whimper.

He leans his forehead onto mine. "God, it would feel so good—sliding inside of you, hearing your needy little moan." Our breaths mingle and turn to vapors, dancing a seductive waltz around us. Strong hands wrap around my waist. "Have you thought about it, Queeny? Hmm? Have you thought about all the ways you want me to feed you?"

I can't deny that I want him because, yes, I have thought about it. Only, it's me feeding him. Making *him* lose his ever-loving mind.

"Because I have, so many fucking times." His rasp is desperate. Brushing my hair to the side, he sweeps his lips over the sensitive skin under my jaw. "Christ, baby, you're all I think about."

My legs spread without my permission.

He's a mere breath away, trembling beside me. "Tell me you want this as much as I do. I won't take something you don't want to give."

I can tell he's trying very hard to be patient, but he needs my consent. It's up to me to give him access.

I'm utterly terrified. My desire is too much, too big for me to control any longer. No doubt someone will get hurt here because, in reality, what future could we have? He will lose his job if this gets out, and eventually, I will lose him to someone younger. Someone who doesn't bear the weight of the world on their shoulders. Someone more dependent.

Brad constantly nagged about how me making more money emasculated him. I wasn't stopping him from climbing the corporate ladder—he just didn't have the gumption. Still, toxic patriarchy is alive and well in today's society.

Remi's puffs of breath tickle my ear as he runs his fingers over my ribs. His persuasion tactic is very distracting to my logistical analysis of all the ways this relationship would fail. Sure, the manny isn't like that *now*. I'm off limits. A challenge. A conquest. When he gets tired of taking care of me while I'm off conquering my ever-ambitious goals, he will bail. It won't be pretty.

Men do all kinds of things to reclaim their masculinity. They lie. They cheat. Make promises and then snap them in half when life gets complicated. They fucking bail when you need them the most.

How ironic.

I depended on Brad for one thing. He knew how I grew up, how I resented not having a father, and yet he walked out the door without ever looking back. It's been two and a half years since I last saw him.

Every time Remi exhales, a shiver runs down my spine, baiting me. A temptation too strong to ignore.

Disregard the past and don't worry about the future. All you have is right now. A small moment, the devil on my shoulder says. *Sex is just sex. It doesn't have to turn into a relationship.* The throbbing between my thighs helps with the devil's persuasion.

Maybe if I fuck Remi out of my system and we both get what we need, this thing between us will lose its luster. Hopefully, we can still be friends after the fire has cooled.

"Say something," he begs.

All the blood rushes to my core. The million reasons restraining me from his seduction fade into the background. I want to show him exactly what he does to me. But it has to be on my terms and under my control.

"Anything," Remi purrs into the shell of my ear—a request I can't resist.

Fuck, he's killing me.

It's only sex, whispers the devil.

"This stays between us and no matter what happens, you'll be here for Isabel. I can't lose you, Remi." My voice cracks because I already know—once I let him in, he'll leave.

His eyes burn into mine as he cradles my face like I'm a porcelain doll. "Listen to me. I'm not going anywhere." Vehemence colors his features, and I want to believe him with every fiber of my being. "You and Isabel are the most important people in my life." He swipes a thumb under my eye. I didn't realize I was crying. "It stays between us." I almost sigh in relief, until he adds, "For now."

I nod and whisper, "Between us," under my breath as if to convince myself sleeping with him will be harmless if we keep it a secret.

As our breaths mingle, tension and passion fill the small space between us. He's too far away. I need him closer. Every cell in my body is screaming for him and my heart, the poor thing, is about to give out.

"Kiss me?" My voice is so desperate it doesn't even sound like me.

Soft lips crash onto mine.

Jesus Christ. Good thing we're sitting because my legs turn into spaghetti. In my three decades on this Earth, I've never been kissed with such wild abandon. His kiss is intense, desperate, and he tastes like the most decadent chocolate cake made by the devil himself.

One of Remi's hands plunges into my hair while the other one pins me against him as if I'll disappear. Wanting more of him, my tongue wraps around his silky muscle with a provocative twist. His moan rumbles from the back of his throat, and I feel it reverberate down to my core throbbing with arousal.

My lips travel, tasting every bit of skin that has teased me from day one. My teeth sweep over his sharp jaw before I take a moment to suck his neck. His skin is the perfect amount of salty and sweet.

"Shit, baby. Feels so good," Remi whispers, encouraging me further.

I fist his t-shirt and tug the neckline down as I feast on his Adam's apple and nibble the underside of his chin. His soft grunts and small whimpers drive me crazy.

I need more, and I don't hesitate to beg for it. "Please."

The look in his eyes is pure fire, igniting a coil deep in my gut. "Please what, baby? Hmm?" His voice is muffled by the skin of my neck. He sucks deeply, curling my toes and making me putty in his hands. "Do you want me to bury my face between your legs and make you come so hard you forget your own name?" I'm trembling. He's white hot and ready for me to stoke the flames. "Or..." He pulls his lips from the sensitive skin of my neck and tilts his head. His lips are swollen and so fucking suckable.

I wait ever so patiently for option two because I know it will be just as appealing as the first, if not more.

"Do you want me to be at your mercy? Lay back and invite you to do whatever the fuck you want to me?" His eyes smolder as he watches my face flame, revealing my deepest desire. Knowing he's voiced my every fantasy, a sexy smile forms on his face. "I must say, Queeny. I'm partial to that as well."

He takes my mouth again. So languid. So sensual.

"Want you so badly," I murmur over his perfect kiss as my hand creeps over his abs, heading for his holy member—that magnificent cock. When I glide my hand over him through his jeans, he hardens while my underwear turns to goo. "Been thinking about tasting this since I stumbled upon it."

Remi's rumble of laughter breaks through his moans and grunts. "I've been thinking about it as well."

His fingers travel up my ribs too slowly, and I'm screaming for him to hurry up. I swear my nipples reach for his hand as they harden.

When I can't take any more teasing, I arch into him. "Touch me."

Strong hands dip under my top and brush against my midriff, ascending higher until they reach the underside of my breasts.

"Fuck." He stalls there, and I whine in impatience. "There's no going back after this, baby. I'm already on the verge of losing control, so if you are unsure about this, stop me now."

I'm not sure about this at all, but my head is screaming to fuck him thoroughly and get him out of my system. My skin is charged, and my nerves are firing off in every direction. My blood blazes, and my flesh pebbles across every surface he caresses. His touch is kinetic, and electricity snaps between us.

"So sure about this." Drawing back, I push at Remi's hard chest, feeling the thump of his racing heart.

His face almost looks downcast until his gaze follows the path of my hands as they lift my top off and away. My hair swings against my bare back, making me shiver. His unwarranted dejection turns to radiance as he stares at me standing proudly in my lacy balconette. The top of my breasts rise in invitation with every breath I heave.

"Christ, you're so beautiful." He reaches for me with shaky hands like I'm a precious piece of sculptured art.

Calloused fingers tease the lace against my skin. My breath hitches when his forefinger dips inside my bra and swipes across an aching peak. Growing bolder, Remi leans forward and wraps a hand around my back. Finding no reluctance from me, he deftly snaps my clasp open before he cups his prize with both hands. Mesmerized, he pulls off the garment and circles his thumbs around my puckered areolas.

My gasp is audible.

"You like that, baby?" With his lids half-mast and a crooked smile, Remi looks drunk on lust as he takes me in.

"Feels so good." Arching into him, my body begs for more.

He raises a brow. "If you want more, all you have to do is ask."

Licking my lips, I tip up on my toes and whisper in his ear, "I want all of it. Every." Lick. "Fucking." Lick. "Inch of you." My teeth find his pulse point, and I graze them against his skin.

"Fuck." With that, the levee breaks on Remi's control and he rushes forward. One hand wraps around my throat as he kisses me savagely. "Take off your leggings," he pants as he grips my bottom lip with his teeth.

I wriggle out of my clothes but leave my Cheekys on. In one smooth move, Remi swipes his arm across the counter, sending our plates careening to the floor with a satisfying crash before hoisting me up onto the cold surface. It stimulates my overheated skin.

Thank Goddess Isabel is a heavy sleeper.

This is a side of Remi I have not seen, and I can't help but giggle in surprise. I was fully prepared to take control of this, yet I love how dominant he is. It tells me he's just as ravenous as I am.

"Spread your legs for me." His voice is deep, demanding.

With a coy smile, I part my thighs. My skin is so hyper-sensitive I can't help but glide my fingertips over my breast and tweak a nipple. My head falls back in pleasure. I straighten back up just in time to watch him loosen his jeans to grip himself.

"Christ, look at you. So fucking sexy, Mae." His face twists in pleasure. "Put one foot on the counter. Open wide, baby. Show me that pretty pussy."

I do exactly as I'm told and swivel my hips in frustration. "Remi," I whine. "You're too far away."

He grips the collar at the back of his neck and pulls his t-shirt off. The taut muscle and solid planes of his pecs ripple as he stalks towards my parted thighs. My mouth waters as I imagine my tongue traveling over one of his rigid nipples only to bite the other.

He dips his index finger under the lace between my legs, easily sliding along my slippery slit. "All this for me, baby?"

"Yes," I hiss.

Tilting his head with a smirk, he advances. "Since I ruined dinner" — he eyes the broken plates and food scattered on the floor — "I am a bit hungry." He aims a blazing stare at me. "I'm going to have to find something else to eat."

My hips twist—an invitation to feast.

His grin turns lascivious. "You read my mind, Queeny."

My mouth dries as I watch him watching me, squeezing that magnificent cock straining his jeans. Not taking his eyes off me, he wraps a foot around a leg of the stool and pulls it in front of where I'm dripping for him. He sits in front of me and leans back a bit, putting on a spectacular show.

"You want to know how many times I fucked my fist to this very image?"

I nod because ... duh. Of course I want to know.

"Too many times, baby."

Remi lifts his chin and tentatively runs the tip of his tongue over my peaked nipple before taking it between his teeth and nibbling. As he's working my breasts, he pulls the fabric at the apex of my thighs taut, trapping my clit inside. When he starts pulling the lace in an upward motion, I shudder. It's abrasive and intense in the best way. My body drowns in pleasure, begging for more.

I don't realize my eyes are closed until Remi brushes his thumb across my lashes. "Open your eyes, beautiful."

When I do, I find his gaze adoring and fervent. I want to look away. I don't need his adoration mucking the waters of what this actually is—just sex. But as hard as I try, my eyes refuse to leave his.

Not taking his attention away from my face, his fingers hook onto my waistband and tug my Cheekys off. I lift up to help expedite the process—I'm efficient that way.

Once I'm completely bare, his gaze travels down to the landing strip of hair that barely covers my crease. He leans in, nudging my wet slit open with a knuckle. When he takes a deep inhale, he groans from the back of his throat.

"So fucking good." Lifting his head, he catches my attention. "Watch. See how good I take care of you."

Chapter 17

The GOAT

Mae

WHEN IT COMES TO oral sex, you have two species of pussy eaters—the "tippers" and the "all-inners".

The first are the ones who use the tip of their tongue and give a flick here or there while their fingers do most of the work. Giving the minimum effort to get it over with and then expect a deep throat reciprocation. Uh-uh, that shit doesn't fly with me. "No fuss, no nut" has always been my motto.

Then you have the all-inners, the ones that nosh muff like they haven't eaten in three years and this is the last meal they will ever have on this green earth. With his whole mouth latched onto my honey pot, Remi is definitely an all-inner.

"Ohgodohgodohgod," I chant, bowing my back off the countertop and gripping his hair. It's almost too much. His sucks and bites are intense. Relentless. I'm not sure how he's even breathing.

"You like that, Queeny?" Remi asks before biting and sucking my inner thigh. "There's plenty more where that came from."

A soft touch of his fingertip teases my entrance. I squirm for more. "Yes, right there."

He moans, and it reverberates up my torso and skitters down my spine. "You've been wanting this, haven't you?" What gave it away—the jaws-of-life clamp I have on his head or the way I'm literally humping his face? "Gonna take good care of you, baby."

One long, slender digit slides in against my inner walls. The soft hook of his fingertip massages *the* spot. What would take centuries and a longitudinal map for some, this bastard finds in seconds. My toes curl, and my legs shake.

A second digit follows the first, and his soft hooks become taunting tugs and strokes. My gasp is sharp, cutting away from my lungs. A coil of dynamite ignites in my lower belly. I'm trying to stave off my impending orgasm because even though I want one—badly—I want to make him work for it. I want to know how much of the intensity I need he can endure. I'm not sure how long this affair is going to last, so I'm going to make it count.

Remi, though, has other plans. Withdrawing his hands, he spreads me wide. Slick fingers dig into the soft flesh of my ass. He has a panoramic view of the land where the sun doesn't shine. It's been such a long time since it's gotten a glimpse of light and felt the breeze of fresh air that it's not displeased one bit. In fact, my insides contract at the filthy exposure.

"Eyes, baby." Remi's low voice grazes my skin, leaving goosebumps in its wake.

My gaze locks on him, and when he's sure he has my undivided attention, he sends me a wicked grin before diving low. Like, way low. Like—

Oh fuuuck! I jump when something not entirely unpleasant plays with my back entrance.

"Shhh, trust me." Remi splays a hand across my stomach to keep me in place before exploring the unknown again. The hot, wet smear of my arousal coats his path. After a few more languid licks, he swipes up my slit, spearing his tongue inside my core, sending me spiraling.

"Don't stop."

He starts growling and shaking his head like he's possessed by the pussy monster. Then he switches up tactics and laves my bud.

"I-I can't take— Rem. I—" I'm panting so hard I can't finish a sentence.

He slows down, barely licking. Definitely teasing.

"What are you doing?" My cry is frustrated.

I. Need. To. Come. Like I need my next breath.

He chuckles into me, knowing exactly what he's doing. Two fingers tease my core again, and his ministrations become more deliberate. The man muff-dives like it's a sport, a competitive game and he's going down in the Head Hall of Fame. The GOAT.

A growl of frustration rips out of my throat, and I feel him smile against me. The jerk. Then he does something that makes me want to kick him—he stands up.

"You want to come, don't you?" His thumb thrums my clit, and he keeps me on edge.

"I'm going to fucking kill you if you don't get back down there and finish what you started," I growl through my teeth, not the least bit ashamed that I'm threatening his life over a climax.

A dopey grin spreads across his shiny face. "Yeah, not if I kill you first."

He goes back to tormenting me with his mouth before shoving three fingers and giving a harsh yank. At the same time, he sucks my clit so hard I think it detaches from my vagina.

My soul leaves my flesh and floats to kingdom come—literally. Screaming his name, I come for what feels like an eternity.

Remi is a considerate lover, easing his licks and helping me ride out the high of spectacular gratification. Somewhere, there is a woman humming nonsensically and it isn't until my spirit drifts back into my body that I realize it's me.

Wrapping a hand around the back of my neck, Remi pulls me to him, holding me. "You came so good for me, baby." He nips my lips.

I'm not one to need praise, but damn, it feels good. He pulls my hair off my shoulder, and his soft touch brushes across my shoulder blade. I purr.

"So fucking beautiful." Soft lips take mine.

I taste myself on him. It's as if I scent-marked him, warning anyone else that he's mine. A wave of possessiveness rolls over my being, and I wrap my legs around his waist, pulling him closer. The rough seam of his jeans brushes against where I'm sensitive, but I only want more.

Remi brushes his tongue along the soft skin next to my ear. "When I told you I'd be a good boy for you, I meant it." The syllables tickle the little hairs beneath his mouth.

"So good." Squeezing a hand between us, I slip under the waistband of his jeans and grip his erection. It twitches in greeting.

Remi grunts, dropping his head to my shoulder. He calls me Queeny, and he's about to know what it means to be my royal subject.

"I'm going to take you upstairs." Stroke. "Lay you on my bed." Squeeze. "And fuck the cum out of you." Stroke. Squeeze.

"Jesus," he hisses.

"After that..." I flick my thumb over his tip and spread his precum.

"Mae, *please*."

The satisfaction that settles in my chest at him begging me is heady and erotic.

"I'm going to take your cock down my throat and milk you dry." Grabbing his hair from the back of his head, I pull him up to face me. His eyes flash with a blaze of desire, and his nose flares at my rough touch. "Would you like that, Remi?" I damn well know he will, but I need to hear that he wants me.

"God, yes," he breathes, lips teasing mine when he speaks.

"I'm not a woman easily satiated, baby." I suck his tongue into my mouth. "I have some proclivities." It's a warning because when it comes to sex, I crave passionate ferocity. I also like to play with my prey before I devour him. "And lots of time to make up for it." Running a nail across his hardened nipple, I relish in his shutter and ask the million-dollar question. "Can you handle a woman like me? Would you let me take from you?"

He bites his lip and breathes a harsh breath through his nose. "Anything. I'll be anything. Do anything, just— I'm going to implode."

Reluctantly pulling my hand from his erection, I cradle his jaw. "Go to my room. Strip and lay on my bed with that celestial cock standing proud."

With closed eyes, he drops his forehead to mine, nods, then peels himself away from me. When I hear him tromp up the steps two at a time, I ease off the counter. It takes immense control on my part to creep through the first floor before heading up the stairs. I want him waiting, but I want to see him, how beautiful he is. Lying there, anticipating me.

As I pass Isabel's room on the way to mine, the haze of lust clears. An ice-cold bucket of guilt falls over my shoulders.

I'm naked. Remi's naked. All thoughts of my daughter are so far away they might as well be on Jupiter.

Why am I doing this? What in the hell are we doing?

With a sad sigh of resignation, I grab a towel from the spare bathroom and wrap it around my body. Every step towards my room feels like I'm walking the plank to my destruction, and my salvation—I can't decide what's worse. When I'm standing at the threshold of my bedroom, I take a moment and curse God. Prone on my bed is the most beautiful man I've ever laid eyes on.

Why would the universe put Remi in my path if I couldn't have him?

He's the steady mentor in Isabel's life. He's so good for her, and she loves him. I've seen her flourish under his care, and I'm going to fuck it up. When sex enters the dynamic, everything becomes increasingly complicated. If he loses the job he loves, we'll lose him. I'm terrified he'll resent this moment—me—for the rest of his life. It's just another reminder of how selfish I am.

I take in the man so ready to give himself to me. My mouth waters at the sight of his length and its angry red tip. The least I could do is get him off, reward him for his spectacular pussy-eating skills.

"Mae?"

Lost in my head, I didn't notice Remi pick his head up from the pillow.

"Hey." He gets up and comes over to me, concern etched in his eyes.

I hate it, so I shove him back on the bed and kick my door shut. That stupid "talk to me" look is on his face, and it aggravates me. It makes it impossible to categorize this need as mere desperation for an orgasm. I know he wants more, and in a different life, I'd pursue it. But I can't right now, so I unceremoniously drop my towel and fall to my knees in front of him.

"Queeny, I—"

"Stop talking." Reaching up, I cup him, testing the weight of his scrotum.

He's perfect, and I'm the fiend that's going to take advantage of him. With my palms around his shaft, I link my fingers and stroke him root to tip, thumbs swiping over his meat. I increase my grip at each pass. His stomach tightens as he restrains the urge to pump up into my hands.

"You're so fucking sexy." Tossing his head back, he gets lost in the sensation.

He's putty in my hands, but I tamp down my excitement and compartmentalize my emotions. After I make him come, we can't do this again. No matter how much we want to. Because we'll want to, and then this situationship will evolve into a relationship.

Remi is affectionate as a friend. I can't imagine the amount of doting he'll express if we're committed. It would be incredible and detrimental because our relationship will get out. The truth always does.

With one hand at the base of his cock and the other cupping his balls, I flatten my tongue and drag it from root to tip before taking the mushroom head into my mouth and sucking.

"Fu—Fuuuck. Fucking hell."

When he tries to caress my hair, I grab his wrist and hold it onto the bed.

As much as I want it, I can't let his intimacy turn this into something it's not. We'll lose ourselves in each other. Sure, it would be extraordinary living in paradise with him. But it's only temporary because when we come up for air, reality will cut us off at the knees. This is a means to an end. Period.

Before he questions the sudden change in my mood, I hollow my cheeks and rise on my knees, taking him all the way in and partly down my throat, swallowing. A little trick I learned in college.

"Christ, Mae," Remi hisses, and deep sounds of pleasure erupt from his diaphragm. He sounds like pure ecstasy.

I'm practically a dripping faucet of arousal listening to him. Then I'm sucking, alternating between bobbing my head and swallowing around him. I gag, drool dripping over my chin. It makes me rabid, so I go faster.

"Fuck, ba—S-slow down. *Shit.*"

I'm so lost in my head I don't realize his hands are free. Not until he pulls me off of him and I fall back, gasping for breath.

Devoid of emotion, I raise my eyes to his. "You didn't come."

Chest heaving in big gulps of breath, his brows pinch and he reaches for me.

I dodge his advance. "Don't," I say, wiping the saliva off my chin with the back of my hand.

"What happened between the kitchen and your bedroom?"

My chin dips because I know I'll sound like a broken record. Because it's not what he wants to hear. Because I know I'm leading him on.

When I don't answer, he gets impatient. "Miranda. What. Happened?" The frustrated growl of his voice shouldn't turn me on as much as it does.

Swallowing a ball of regret in my throat, I answer him honestly. "I walked past Isabel's room." My eyes burn when they reach his. "I can't do this to her, Remi. I can't."

"So … what? You were going to get me off? Tit for tat. Even Steven." He rakes his fingers through his hair. "I thought we were on the same page." Sliding off the bed, he kneels in front of me, his cock half-mast but still impressive. "I want you. I know you want me."

"That's beside the point. We're playing with fire. Before we know it, the whole house will be nothing but ash." I bite my cheek to keep my chin from trembling.

When Remi reaches for me, I let him because I need him. I'll always need him.

Pulling me towards his chest, he leans against the side of my bed frame, with me straddling the thing I'm trying not to become addicted to. He brushes the sweaty hair off my face and tucks it behind my ear. His eyes are intense, glowing burnt umber with a spark of something else I don't want to recognize.

"I'm not leaving you, and I'm certainly not leaving that little girl." The soft pad of his thumbs draw circles on the top of my thighs. "Unless you kick me out, I'm with you."

"Someone's going to get hurt. Regardless of who it is, Isabel will pay the price."

Gathering me in his arms, he pulls me in tight. He feels so good against my bare skin, and it doesn't escape my notice that he hardens between us. I sigh and liquefy against him.

"I don't know why you're so adamant this won't work out. You can't project onto me the things that piece-of-shit deadbeat did."

I freeze. It's the first time he's ever brought up Isabel's father. I certainly don't talk about him. So how can he pinpoint my fear with uncanny precision?

You know the answer. You just won't admit it.

He kisses the top of my head, then finishes his thought. "He doesn't deserve to breathe, let alone have either of you."

Tears fall from my eyes, and I shudder against him. He said everything I didn't know I needed to hear.

Remi kisses my bare shoulder then whispers in my ear, "Let me in."

Pissed that I'm crying or maybe relieved that I'm able to lower my guard a little, I seek his comfort and curl further into his embrace. "Promise me something."

"Whatever you want."

"Don't catch feelings for me." I lean back to face him. "I'm serious—don't. This isn't a relationship. The minute it starts to feel like one, I'm out."

His eyes dim before he collects himself. "Fine," he spits. "But as long as we're sleeping together, we're not seeing anyone else. Understood?"

"Yes, that's fair." I sound like I'm negotiating a business contract.

"Now…" Remi takes my mouth and bites my bottom lip, not too gently. My need flares to life. "Fuck me like you said you would. Like I'm the last man you'll ever have." He grinds against me. "I'm dying for it."

His words amp the heat in my core, and my pussy clenches, feeling oh so empty. There's a throb between my legs, pulsing in time with the rhythm of my heart.

Reaching for my nightstand, I open the drawer and grab a condom.

"I know you're on the pill."

I give him an incredulous look, and he just shrugs his shoulders like it's no big deal he knows the most intimate things about me.

"I'm clean if that's what you're worried about."

"As important as it is, that's not why we're using a condom." I know a guy like Remi isn't careless, and I haven't had sex since Brad, but I open the packet and slide the rubber on his length anyway. "It's great that we're clean. However, we're not a couple. We don't fuck bare."

Remi jerks back as if I slapped him. "Noted," he gripes, pouting until he's notched in my entrance.

Inch by excruciating inch, I slide down, taking all the time in the world. The stretch is exquisite. His eyes widen as his mouth falls open. When I'm fully seated, his chest caves as oxygen rushes out, as if he's been holding his breath for an hour. Feeling him fully inside of me is incredible. I feel so full. So whole.

His hands grip my ass to control the rhythm, so I stop, clenching him inside me. *God, that's good stuff.*

"I set the pace, and you come for the ride … but only when I say so." I give him a wicked smirk as I rock slightly. Taunting him. Revving him up.

With my hand under his chin, I grip his cheeks and thrust my tongue in his mouth, and nip at his lips. He tries to catch me, but I don't let him. The rock of my hips is slow, but I'm assaulting his mouth.

His growls and pants tell me he wants more. On the edge is exactly where I want him because the moment I give him permission, I want him to come so hard that the memory of this night will burn in his soul.

I stand abruptly, keeping him on the brink, and delight in the bounce of his cock. The look of surprise on his gorgeous face is priceless.

"On the bed, Manny."

Scrambling up, he takes the position I first found him in, that pretty phallus pointing at the ceiling. When I climb on top of him, I don't go to where he wants me most. I shimmy up and hover over his face. Remi's strong hands immediately cradle the round globes of my booty.

"Get me nice and wet. I've been waiting to fuck this face since the day you knocked on my door."

"God, yes. Please," he begs, trying to extend his neck to get me.

Grabbing the front of his hair, I give a warning tug. "Patience, boy scout." I laugh at my inner joke, then lower down on that eager tongue.

Remi moans at first taste, and he pulls my cheeks apart as he presses me further onto him. I'm afraid he might smother. There's a lot of flesh down there, but the way he's sucking, growling, and snorting like a wildebeest, holding me to him, tells me he's better than fine.

"So fucking good." My diaphragm heats, and I know I'll have to pull off soon because I want to come on his cock this time. "You know how to use that pretty mouth of yours," I pant. Leaning back, I balance my hands on his chest behind me, and I feed him my cunt until I'm on the crest. He's not ready to let me go when I try to lift off of him. "If I come on your mouth, you don't get to come at all."

That does it. I knew it would. His dick is practically weeping for release.

Shimmying down his torso, I rest my slippery heat on his rock-hard member, but I don't put him in yet. Taking his mouth, I kiss him thoroughly then wipe his face with the bedsheet.

"Tell me how badly you want inside this pussy." I swivel against him.

Dilated pupils roll back in their sockets. "So badly. You have no idea."

I swivel against him again. "Oh, I have some idea."

His cheeks are red, and his eyes are wild. "Please. Mae, *please*."

"I love when you beg me. Hands above your head and don't move them, no matter what." I wait for his eager nod. My mouth finds his peaked nipple, and I savor an indulgent suck while flicking the other one with my nails.

"Ahh, shit. Fucking hell, woman." His dark areolas become tighter.

I relish in his responsiveness. He'll be sore there before I'm through with him. It's only fair. I'm pretty sure I'll be limping the next three days.

He didn't move his hands though.

"Good boy."

Squatting on my feet, I pull him inside of me, shallow at first. A plump vein slithers across his forehead, and for some reason, this makes me feral. I drop down fully onto him, and he cries out.

"That's it. I want to hear you."

I set a ruthless rhythm, and the bed is shaking against the wall. His soft lips utter harsh curses and beg me for more. When his whine goes up an octave, I settle. Remi's chest heaves as he blows harsh breaths through his nose. The look he's giving me could kill, but that's exactly where I want him.

"Remember the little stunt you pulled downstairs?"

He licks his mouth. "It was worth it."

My giggle is sinful. "We'll see about that." Arching back, I ride him hard. The pressure of my orgasm is building to a feverish pitch. His cock twitches, and I slide off.

"Argh!" He punches the bed at his side.

"Tsk tsk, you moved your hands." I pinch his nipple in punishment.

"Shit," he hisses, stomach contracting. He's beautiful to watch.

The pheromone of his growing need hangs heavy in the air, and I want to savor it.

"No one's ever fucked you like this, huh?"

He hitches a brow at my teasing.

"I can tell. You can barely restrain yourself." I reach between us and softly squeeze his balls before gliding my fingertips across his length.

Remi shivers at my touch. "You win. You'll surely kill me first." There's something in his voice—an undertone of torture.

Of course, *I'm* having fun. This is the most I've ever been turned on in my life, but I don't want it at the cost of his pleasure.

I trace my name across his chest. "Do you want more? Or do you want to come?"

"More. Always more." He lifts his arm from above his head, then hesitates.

Good boy.

I nod and reach for his hand, linking our fingers. His other reaches for my breast and twists my nipple with the same ferocity I would. Remi smacks my tit, and I jump in delighted surprise. That's when I know he's perfect because I crave the same intensity as I want to give. I don't want to be treated like glass. I want bruises from his mouth, his fingers. Between my thighs. For the first time in my life, I'm not going to have to ask.

"I'll happily die inside of you." With a smirk, he waves a hand to where we're joined. "As you were, *Queeny*."

Leaning over, I ride him hard. My hair cascades around us, and the tips of my breasts drag across his chest with every thrust. He has a vise grip on my ass, and his fingers are daringly close to my tight hole.

"I'm going to plug this ass." Those close digits press in, and one breaches. I see stars. "Mmm, you like that idea." He's topping from the bottom, but who in the hell cares. It's fueling the fire burning deep inside of me. "I'll fucking savor easing it in."

With each thrust, he slides further in, giving me a taste of what's to come and winding me into a tight spring aching for a powerful release.

"I'll shove my cock into that pretty pussy while your asshole is throbbing." He chuckles between breaths. I'm going to come soon if he doesn't stop talking. "But don't worry, darling. I'll make sure that ass is nice and ready before I fuck it too."

My head tips back, and my breasts push out.

His voice. His words. His filth. I don't know who I'm kidding with this one-and-done bullshit. I'll never get enough of him.

A haze of lust falls over me, urging the next sentence out of my head and into my mouth. "You're mine," I gasp. "Come."

He bites my tip so hard I constrict around him, and we both cry out in elation, rapture, and euphoria. After the pulsing subsidies, I lay limp against him, my skin melting into his. Soft breaths tickle my ear, and sensual fingertips glide up my spine. I've never been so, so … satisfied.

Remi wraps his arms around me and squeezes.

My lips seek out his in a soft kiss.

A reward.

An apology.

"Can I stay?" There's a hint of vulnerability in his tone.

A simple request that I know I should deny. We can't have more of this. We shouldn't indulge because it will be excruciating when he leaves my bed for someone else's. And yet…

"Yes."

Chapter 18

Remi's Monday

Remi

HOLY HELL AND THE devil's deeds. What just happened?

Fucking mind-blowing sex, that's what. I'm still trying to collect my thoughts as I lazily stroke Mae's back. Her skin is satin under my fingertips.

My body is buzzing with bliss after the unrelenting tension my muscles endured. Talk about torture. I honestly thought my balls were going to explode. The tight ache that kept me on the precipice of climax until Mae decided it was time for release was agony. I'd do it a thousand times to come like that again.

How? How could she ever think I can go back to casual sex with random women after experiencing the fuck of my life? After having *her*.

Nuzzling the strawberry cloud that is Mae's hair, I sigh in utter contentment. No one has ever made me feel this way. I'm stunned, awed.

"Don't catch feelings."

Too late. I can't say she didn't warn me, but I already had strong feelings before this. Now? This horse has been lassoed. I'm one-hundred-percent owned by this goddess that took me through hell only to show me how incredible heaven can be. I'm so in love with this woman I could fucking weep.

I'd do anything to keep her. Sell my soul and my kidney, just to always have her like this. I wish I could stay with her forever. Never leaving this bed, never not touching her skin.

Relishing this moment, I almost whine when Isabel cries for her mother. A faint snore tickles my ear, and I can't help the grin that spreads across my face. "Mmm, Queeny."

Isabel's cries become louder.

Giving Mae a gentle nudge, I sing in her ear, "Queeny."

"Shh, Queeny's sleeping."

I chuckle, rolling us over so I can see her face and kiss her lips. Her touch is delicate and tender, no longer rough and desperate. There's a small smile on her face, telling me she's completely sated. My chest would puff out if there was any space between us.

"Isabel is calling for you, and I should probably clean up the mess I made downstairs."

"Probably," she mimics, playing with the back of my hair, not eager to get up.

Another cry for Mommy reverberates through the door.

"How about this... You get Isabel before she tries to climb out of her crib while I clean up downstairs and whip up something to eat."

Alabaster arms reach over her head as she savors a languid stretch, like a cat bathing in a sunspot. "Only if you meet me back up here after, so we can do *that* again."

I take her mouth and give her tongue sweet strokes, getting my fill of her taste. "I'll have to think about it." I know damn well I'd meet her anywhere, at any time.

She smacks my ass. "Watch it, Boy Scout." There's a wicked gleam in her eye. "I wouldn't want to have to punish you."

I want to act up to see what Queeny's punishment entails because something tells me it will be a sublime experience. I stiffen against her just thinking about it, but I know I don't have time to fuck her properly, so I raise on my hands and knees and give her pretty pussy a wet kiss before I get off the bed. She squeals and giggles, watching intently as I strut naked around her bedroom looking for my clothes. At the approval in her eyes, I stand a little taller.

Finding my boxers, I throw her my t-shirt. She catches it in one hand and holds it up to her nose, taking a big inhale.

"What are you doing?"

I'm slayed when her cheeks flame. The woman who could wear out a bull in a rodeo fucking blushes at getting caught smelling my shirt.

She shrugs. "I like the way you smell."

My dick twitches in appreciation. "Yeah? Feel free to sniff me anytime." With a wink, I hightail it out of there before I pin her down and fuck her within an inch of her life.

Looking through the fridge, I make a mental note to stop for groceries tomorrow. There isn't much here, but I can work with anything—it's from living on my own and adhering to a strict budget. After a month of eating ramen noodles, I needed other nutrients, so I began experimenting and found out I'm actually pretty good at this cooking thing. However, grilled cheese and tomato soup is the best I can do with the limited ingredients I have.

Just as I'm plating the sandwiches, Queeny enters the kitchen, fiddling with the hem of her shirt and looking hesitant. Like she doesn't know if she should sit or come to me.

Just seeing her in my clothes does something to my insides. With a throb in my chest, I make the decision for her. Turning off the soup, I stalk towards my beauty with one thing in mind—kissing the hell out of her ... and then sliding back inside of her warmth. Okay, so maybe two things. With one arm around her back, the other reaches low to grip her ass, pinning her to me. It doesn't escape my notice that she isn't wearing underwear.

Her eyes are endless pools of desire and uncertainty. So I take her mouth and show her there's nothing to be insecure about. I swallow the small, sexy sound she makes before her stomach decides to grumble, angry that it's empty.

She smiles against my mouth. "Sorry, it smells really good in here."

"Don't worry, baby. I'm gonna feed you actual food this time." I give her what I hope is a panty-melting smile and usher her to the table.

She still seems a bit shy, and it's turning me on as much as confident Mae does. Knowing how she is in everyday life, I'm sure not many besides Jay get to see this side of her. It tells me she trusts me with her vulnerability.

Placing our plates and bowls on the table, I sit next to her and watch her bite her lip. It's maddening.

"What is it?" My voice is low and tender. I want her to know she can tell me anything.

"Are you—" She clears her throat. "I mean, was that okay? What I did?" She peeks at me from under her eyelashes.I brush her hair back so I can see her better. "No, I'm not okay."

Her shoulders hunch, and I want to punch myself in the face. She needs reassurance and here I am, teasing her.

I lift her chin. "Mae, I'm fucking spectacular."

A beatific grin spreads across her face. "Really? You liked it?"

I nod. "You mean the mind-altering orgasm you gave me or the life-changing sex? You're incredible, baby. You ruined me for all other women." I bite my tongue because I said too much, too soon.

Queeny swats at my shoulder. "Stop. I'm sure you've had better." She rolls her gorgeous eyes, downplaying what just happened between us.

That won't do at all. Burning her with my stare, I tell her the truth. "I've never had anyone like you before."

"Oh." It's a small sound.

I chuckle at her surprise. "Yeah, 'oh'." Mae gives me a shy glimpse of her Mona Lisa smile. "Now, hurry and eat so I can bend you over this table and fuck you while you're wearing my shirt looking like a walking wet dream."

Picking up half her sandwich, I feed her. To my amazement, she lets me. We share her meal and mine. In between bites, I'm stealing kisses and touches while she steals my heart.

After we finish our late dinner, I make good on my promise. I'll never see the kitchen the same again.

Oh, God.

Soft ... wet ... heat ... slides over me.

Mmm. My favorite kind of dream.

I reach down, digging my fingers in a thicket of silky hair and purr, "Fuck, don't stop."

It's the kind of dream I live for, but it's distressing at the same time because I know it will all disappear when I wake up. Something soft contracts around my cock—once, twice, three times.

"Feels so fucking good."

A wicked giggle echoes in my head. Nails, harsh and biting, dig into my thigh, adding the perfect amount of pain to the pleasure.

"Shit."

Teeth scrape up my length as something velvety tickles behind my groin. That's new.

"Mmm, boy scout, I could do this all day."

I know that voice. That name. Please, please, please be real.

My eyes crack open, but my head is still swimming in pleasure somewhere in the twilight state.

"Morning, sleepyhead." There is no mistaking the mischievous glint in Mae's eyes as she holds me to her pouty lips and swirls her tongue around my tip.

"Fuck, so real." My nose flares with the impulse to come down that beautiful throat.

I clamp it down. Queeny will tell me when she wants me to release, and I'll happily obey. She owns all my orgasms now.

"You want to come, beautiful?" Her lids widen in innocence, then narrow indecently. "I bet you do." She continues the most sinuous torment.

"God, yes," I hiss as she sucks deep.

No one has ever taken such care with my cock before. Mae sucks dick like she invented it. And she won't stop until she knows she's squeezed every last ounce of pleasure from me.

"Fuck, I lo—" I clench my teeth.

Even though it's true, I'm not going to tell her in the middle of a blowjob. She's not ready to hear it. So, I bite my tongue as she quickens her pace and rolls my balls in her downy-soft hands.

My stomach burns and tightens. My hips fight the urge to thrust and fail.

"Go ahead, baby. Fill my mouth."

A growl rips through my throat as I pulse between her lips. Mae takes me deep and milks my cock with her uvula, extending my orgasm until I see other dimensions. I never knew sex could feel like this.

She raises on her knees, proud of herself. Her full breasts bounce with her movement, enticing me to touch, twist, and suck. She's fucking magnificent. Real Mae is far more extraordinary than anything I could conjure in my head.

Sitting up, I pull her to me and kiss that pretty mouth.

A "thank you".

A "no one has ever given me that".

An "I can't believe this is real".

I taste myself on her tongue, eliciting a feral streak to hurtle through me. She's mine. So fucking mine.

When I go to deepen the kiss, she pulls away, leaving me in a state of neediness.

"I'm sorry, baby." She kisses my head, a bit patronizing and a lot cute. "I woke up and realized I didn't make good on my promise. We can't have that, can we?"

"N-n—" I clear my throat. "No."

"Believe me, I want nothing more than to play with my new favorite toy all day, but I have to shower and get to work." She winks and waltzes into her bathroom.

Dumbfounded, I watch on. *Favorite toy?* A roundhouse kick KOs my heart.

While I don't mind flirty names in bed, I'm not sure how I feel about that one. It reduces the epic night we shared to pretty much nothing. I don't like it. Not at all.

I don't have much time to analyze because Isabel's cries for Emmie echo through the door.

After changing Isabel, we head down to the kitchen to see what we have for breakfast. Oatmeal and fruit will have to do today.

"We have to go grocery shopping. What do you say, Isa-bea?"

She holds up her slice of banana like she's cheering for her favorite team. "Yeeahh."

Mae enters the room like a breath of fresh air, picking up her daughter straight away. She's all smiles and giggles, and I gloat a little knowing I'm the one who made her that way.

"Sit, I'll make your coffee."

"Don't have time this morning. I already had breakfast." She smirks my way as she bounces Isabel in her arms. It's a beautiful sight.

"We're going to go to the store today. We could stop by your office for lunch?" I can't help the note of hope in my voice.

"That's really sweet of you, but Jay and I will be at Pür most of the morning, so we'll probably just grab lunch after." Setting the baby down, she grabs her purse and pulls a couple hundred dollars out. "Here. I haven't had a chance to replenish your spending cash since last time." She hands the bills to me.

I hand one back. "That's too much. One is plenty."

Mae sticks the money in my pants pocket. "Get something nice for yourself then."

Last night, she brought me to new heights. I soared without care because I didn't realize the fall was going to be so harsh.

She kisses me on the cheek and strides out the door, leaving me feeling like a gigolo.

"These freaking eggs should be made of gold," I grumble to Isabel.

She looks up at me while sucking her thumb and holding Mr. Snuffles as I push her down the dairy aisle. Mae loves coffee creamer, so I grab a couple of different flavors.

Isabel points to the pudding. "Yeyyow. Yeyyow."

She calls everything jiggly Jello. So I throw a couple of those in the bin.

"Isn't she just the cutest!" a woman squeals, coming up to the cart. She looks to be about my age and on the short side. A Louis Vuitton purse hangs from her elbow. She's a little overdressed for grocery shopping.

It always goes like this. If I was actually looking to date someone, Isabel is the perfect wingman. Women love her and want to pinch her chubby cheeks. Usually, I don't let people get too close to Isabel because you never know someone's intentions, but since we're in an enclosed public place with cameras, I ease my overprotectiveness. A smidge.

Isabel waves, uncharacteristically not shy with a stranger.

"How old is she?" The woman hitches her purse onto her shoulders and tosses back her dark hair. A classic flirty move that I have no response to.

"She'll be three in December." I can't help but smile when I answer because she's getting so big and learning new things every day.

"Look at you. Aren't you lucky to hang out with your daddy all day?" the stranger gushes.

"Actually, I'm her caregiver." I hate correcting people. One, because I don't want Isabel to ever think I wouldn't claim her as mine, and two, because I desperately want to claim her as my child.

"Is that so?" She inches closer to the cart.

Nervous, Isabel holds out her hands to me. "Daddy."

Oh shit. I gather her in my arms to ease her anxiety.

The woman raises her brow.

"Uhh, a lot of people assume. I'm sure she's picked up on it." A nervous laugh punctuates my reasoning.

The woman's face relaxes. "I'm sure." She addresses Isabel, "What's your name, sweet girl?"

Before I have a chance to dodge the question, the little one answers. "Is-bewl."

"What a pretty name! My name is Bree."

Okay, this is taking up too much time. We have a fun-filled day planned and parks to play at.

"Nice to meet you, Bree." I start to push forward, but the woman grabs the cart. A bit too forcefully for my liking.

"Wait, here's my number." She totally doesn't read the severe set of my chin or clenching jaw when she thrusts a ripped receipt my way. "In case you want to meet up by the cheese again." She giggles. It's grating and nothing like the swan song that is Queeny's laugh.

"I'm sorry, but we really need to be on our way. I might be in the store, but I'm not on the market." I give her a robotic smile.

Isabel and I head towards the check-out line. I'm careful to look around to make sure we're not being followed. By the time we're done with lunch and making our playground rounds, it's time to go home. Isabel is fast asleep before we even make it up the driveway.

Chapter 19

Mae's Monday

Mae

I'M NOT REALLY SURE how I got to work this morning. Possibly floating on a cloud of coitus high, reliving last night's—and this morning's—events in my head.

Remi was incredible. So much more than I could have ever imagined. My body tingles at the memory of his touch.

His submission.

His responsiveness.

He met me thrust for thrust. Challenge for challenge. It was carnal. Feral. Fucking transcendent.

My body is a feather floating in the breeze as Jay, Elliot, and I take the elevator up to Pür Headquarters. The image of Remi's sleepy surprise at his morning wake-up now lives rent-free in my head. I hide a giggle behind my hand.

Jay's narrowed eyes study me. Oh shit.

"You seem ... happy?" they start.

I bite my cheek and hide the grin that wants to split my face. "Happy" is such a simple word for the way I feel. I had the best sex of my life last night, and we're about to secure our company with the Pür Innovations account. This is going to be huge for us.

I'm more than happy. I'm fucking rhapsodic.

Being friends for over twenty years, Jay can read the expression on my face quite easily. I can practically see when the lightbulb goes off in my best friend's head. "Oh. My. Goddess in a falafel. You— Oof."

I elbow them in the stomach and nod towards my assistant. "We can talk about this later, Jayden," I say through a tight smile.

Elliot shifts on his feet, nervous. I'm not sure if it's because of my and Jay's exchange or because this is the first time I've required him to come to a meeting outside of the office. But this is important, and my assistant is clever, smart, and charming. He's the perfect person for this job.

I can't help the pep in my step as we walk through the sliding doors into the front reception area of Pür.

"Good morning, Ms. Keller and Mx. Morales, so nice to see you again," Felicia, Amala Williams's assistant, greets us. "And this is..." She eyes the man beside me.

"Elliot Hansley, the backbone of Ever Heart," I announce proudly, not missing the way she's subtly checking him out.

Elliot's eyes are so wide I'm afraid they'll pop out. "Thank you, Mae."

I wave him off.

"Follow me. Amala is looking forward to this meeting."

"So are we," I tell her, unable to hide my enthusiasm.

Our initial consultation went really well. Amala, Jay, and I built a rapport effortlessly. I knew she'd call for a second meeting, and here we are.

Felicia shows us the conference room, and we sit in plush Italian leather seats. The cushion threatens to swallow me as I sink down in its poofy softness.

"Mae, we need chairs like this." Jay swivels as they settle in place.

If this all works out, I'll be the Oprah of extravagant chair gifting—every employee will get one.

Elliot, the ever studious assistant he is, sets up camp with his laptop, iPad, notepad, and graphs. I'm going to promote him and give him a hefty raise after this. He deserves it.

I can't remember the last time I felt this … magnanimous. Who knew all I needed was a night of unforgettable sex.

Amala waltzes in the conference room with a radiant smile. There's an air about her. She knows who she is, and she owns it. Her team follows after her, taking up the rest of the seats around the conference table. It's refreshing to see the women executives outnumber the men. Everyone passes pleasantries to us.

"Miranda, Jayden, Elliot," she greets with a wide grin. "I've been waiting anxiously for this meeting. Your pitch impressed me, and I hope we can build a relationship that will last a long time." She pulls down a projector screen. "Before we get into discussion, I want to show you who we are at Pür Innovations. This way, you can get a good grasp on what this company's about."

Elliot is poised to take notes as Jay gives me a look I dismiss. If they want to toot their own horn, I'm not going to protest. It will give us a better idea of what their media looks like and how we can improve it.

The promotional video goes through all subsidiaries of Pür, and it dawns on me how huge this contract will be. From baby products to food manufacturing—they seem to have spoons in a lot of bowls.

We're probably going to have to hire more graphic designers.

As the video closes, the table claps and we join in. It's great that the personnel are so enthusiastic about the company they work for.

"As you can see, whoever collaborates with us will have their work cut out for them. We're on a global level, and we compete against aggressive companies. Our image is everything." Even though her face is amiable, I detect a bit of calculation behind her eyes.

"Our team is aware and eager to show you just what they can do. Elliot, will you give Mrs. Williams the stats of the companies we work with?"

"That won't be necessary. I already have what I need," she says dismissively. Leaning in, she folds her perfectly French-manicured fingers in front of her. "Can I be candid with you?"

"By all means," Jay answers.

The person to Amala's right hands her some documents. "Robert Pingman is on our board of directors. When we expressed interest in working with Ever Heart, he advised against it."

My stomach drops. This is one hell of a curveball, and one we may not hit out of the park. *Fucking Pingman.*

"Ever Heart is on the verge of a major... adjustment. If one more investor pulls out, you're toast." Amala is so matter-of-fact, and I don't appreciate her flippant words nor the saucy way she delivers them.

I rear back in my seat, indignant. "That's not true."

"So you didn't lose three major investors last quarter?" She stands tall, striding over to us. The documents she's holding are plopped in front of me in all their financial critical-care glory.

My stomach churns because she has us. Conglomerates like Pür do not make business decisions with struggling companies.

"May I enlighten the room with context?" I interject, unable to keep the note of anger out of my voice. Which sounds a lot like desperation.

Ten pairs of eyes land on me. I don't sweat under pressure, but as I sit here, beads of moisture form at my temples. The future of Ever Heart rests on this deal, and we've just been tagged out a yard before hitting a home run.

"Yes, we lost a few investors because our ideals are contradictory. I'm a single mother, and some think that my daughter is a liability when, in fact, she is my strength. She's why I work so tirelessly to make sure this company is in great standing."

If Jay's surprised I'm talking about Isabel in a corporate meeting, they don't show it. Elliot, on the other hand, looks like he's about to shit a brick.

Amala grins. "Children are wonderful motivators, aren't they? I'm a mother too, and sadly, I know all too well the challenges we face in a male-dominated business world." She spreads her hands wide, gesturing to the executives in this room to prove her next point. "We, at Pür, are trying to change that. We want to work together with parents to create products that will benefit their and their children's lives. We are the best in our industry, and despite what your investors say, we think you are too."

Swift relief falls over my shoulders and releases the rope around my chest. "Thank you. We absolutely are."

I look over to Jay, who is smiling at Amala. Elliot is furiously taking notes.

Amala pulls a chair over to where we are and sits. She is the picture of earnestness as she folds her hands on the table. "That's why we want Ever Heart to be a part of our family."

The thrill of victory thrums through my veins. "Thank you, Amala. We are so excited to work with Pür. We will have a team dedicated to you and your needs. Rest assured, your branding is in good hands with us." I open my tote bag. "Should we discuss the contract so we can agree on a proposal that works for you?"

"I have something different in mind," Amala explains, the tone of her voice hinting that it may be something ... atypical. "We want Ever Heart."

"Of course. We're here for whatever you need."

"I think you're misunderstanding me." Amala holds out her hand, and the guy next to her hands her another stack of papers. "We have our own proposal." Sliding our financial records aside, she sets the package in front of me.

Jay shifts so they can look over my shoulder.

My brows touch. I don't understand. I've never heard of a company creating their own branding proposal. That's something *we* provide. It's how we show them what we can do for their company.

"We want to buy Ever Heart, Miranda. We want you as a division of Pür Innovations. We want your most valued talent to work *solely* for us.'

All of my blood drains to my stilettos, and my mouth turns to cotton.

"What?" Jay's the one who asks.

I'm the one hoping I heard her wrong.

"Evan, pull up the numbers on how we will logistically absorb Ever Heart." She turns towards the front.

Even though I see Evan's mouth moving, his arms gesturing, and sounds uttering, I'm not listening.

No thoughts enter my brain.

Not a single nerve ending fires.

This is a nightmare. A grotesquely disturbing nightmare.

Polite words are exchanged between Elliot, Evan, Jay, and Amara. But I don't utter a single syllable.

"I'll give you some time to think about it, but our board of directors would like an answer by the end of the month."

End of the month? That's less than thirty days. How can something that took years of blood, sweat, and tears to create dissolve into something else in such an insignificant amount of time?

"...of course, everyone would keep their jobs and Jay will still be head graphic designer. Miranda, we hope that you will take on the role of Chief Marketing Officer."

"Chief Marketing Officer?" I repeat, more to myself than anyone else.

Amala drones on, not reading or acknowledging the pallor of shock on my skin. "There are only a few minor changes we would require."

"Which would be?" Elliot is holding his own while I'm floundering. I'd be proud if I wasn't so stunned at the swift pivot of this morning's events.

"Since we will be your primary financial backing, you'd have to cut ties with other investors."

Okay, maybe that's not so bad. No more pandering to chauvinistic assholes like Pingman. My ears open up to the possibility a bit.

"While we want Ever Heart's core employees on Pür's marketing, you'll need to hire more talent for the clients you currently work with." Not a terrible request. Creating new jobs is a good thing. *And* we get to keep our dedicated employees. The heavy weight I've been wearing around my neck lightens. "We want you to have a floor in our building." Not having to pay rent on our own would be a blessing. "And we want to change the name 'Ever Heart' to 'Elite Digital Design and Marketing', a division of Pür."

Somewhere outside, car-brakes shriek to a halt—like my reasoning. The request wraps around my throat and squeezes. I can't breathe.

She wants to take everything we've worked for and label it as their own. They will erase Jay and me from the company we started and reduce us to mere employees of Pür. We'd be selling out. Big time.

It's unthinkable.

The next thing I register is Jay is pulling out my chair and tugging on my arm. "Don't mind her. She hasn't had her coffee today."

Amala laughs, and it's the equivalent of nails on a chalkboard. How can someone talk so candidly about pissing all over someone else's dream?

"I understand. It was a bit of a sharp pivot on our part, and I'm truly sorry to blindside you like this." She lays a hand on my shoulder, but I can barely look at her. She knew exactly what she was doing. All I want to do is get far, far away from here. "Please, seriously consider it. We will benefit each other in so many ways. This could be the start of something huge, and it will secure Ever Heart's future."

I almost spit, *that's bullshit.* But I know I need to keep a level head, even though I'm about to blow a gasket. My pulse speeds as my heart pounds. I stand in one jerky movement and twist away from my best friend's hold.

"We definitely will," Jay answers for me.

"Thank you for meeting with us today. We'll be in touch, I'm sure." There's warmth in Elliot's tone, and I commend him for doing the thing I can't right now—remain calm after a surprise attack.

Both Elliot and Jay usher me into the mirrored elevator. I look at my reflection and note the sickly green tint to my face.

"Be calm, Mars Bars. We'll talk about this at the office." They turn to Elliot. "Will you organize a meeting for the end of the week? It will be mandatory for all employees." Elliot is diligently typing into his phone. "Oh, get that great Italian place to cater it." They're planning this meeting like it's going to be a festive event and not a massive layoff.

I don't utter a word. Not in the car. Not as we walk into our building. Not even as we converge into my office.

"Earth to Mae. Earth to Mae." Jay's approach is insulting.

"How can you be so unruffled at a time like this?" I practically screech like my toddler, sitting behind my desk, where my laptop whirs to life.

"At a time like this? This just might be the solution to our problems," they say, as diplomatic as ever.

My head swings towards them. "What?" I sneer. "Why would you say that?"

Jay raises defensive palms in my direction. "Because we are struggling. Because there are a lot of zeros on that point-of-sale contract." They fling a hand my way. "You are killing yourself. But with the turn of events, a new opportunity presents itself." Jay takes an indulgent breath. "The universe provides."

"Stop with the new-age bullshit, would ya? The only thing it provides is an opportunity for another company to steal ours." I can't keep the bitterness out of my voice.

Jay's palms turn to fists, resting on their hips. "That is certainly one way to look at it, Ms. Pessimistic," they mock, jutting their chin out, thinking they're funny.

I'm not the least bit humored. "You talk like there is a way to see this as anything other than selling out."

They scoff. "We're not selling out."

I give them a deadpan look.

"Okay, so we are. It's better than laying off half of our employees. Or losing Ever Heart altogether."

The set of my stubborn chin announces my aggravation.

"You'll keep your role and, hell, you might even be able to take a much-needed vacation." When I won't look at them, they go in for the kill. "Wouldn't it be nice to truly clock out at the end of a work day and have the rest of your evenings free for Isabel?"

Jay's right, of course. It would be nice, but by the steam blowing out of my nose, I'm still pissed. "Don't you dare use my weakness to manipulate me into something that will ruin everything we've built."

Jay expresses a long, suffering sigh. "As always, your pigheadedness shines through."

"You know what, Jay? Fuck you." Standing, I get right up in my best friend's space. "I've been the one working to exhaustion trying to keep this company afloat while you get to make pretty pictures and go on holiday with Ian." I can't stop the diarrhea from exploding out of my mouth. "Then you come here, waving your crystals thinking it helps. Spoiler alert—it doesn't."

Impassive, Jay steps back. If the realization that I hurt them wasn't tearing up my heart, I would have known by the ice in their eyes.

"I-I didn't mean that, Jay." I close the space between us, but they hold up their hand.

"I have been asking you for *months* if this is too much. Your happiness is my only concern." They dig a finger in their chest. "I have been there for you each and every fucking time. Picking you up off the floor when you hit rock bottom. Without insult. Never once did I reduce you to a mere accessory in my life."

My eyes burn, but the tears won't fall. "I'm sorry. I'm just angry."

"You're always angry lately." They walk towards my door.

I run after them. "Don't go, please. I'm so sorry. You said you wouldn't leave me."

They whirl around. "I'm not leaving you. Christ, Mae. You're my fucking soul mate. What don't you get about that?"

I sniff. "You have Ian."

They sneer. "This again? Yes, I fell in love with someone. I'm crazy about him. What a goddamn crime." Their eyes are red-rimmed. "But our bond" — Jay flicks a finger between us — "is on a cosmic level. And you just shit all over it. If you'll excuse me, I need some space from you." They walk out my door before they slam it.

I jump at the sound. It ricochets off the four walls and shatters my heart.

Remorse rips through me. Why in the hell did I lash out at the one person who loves me more than themselves? *Because you know they'd never leave you.* My chin quivers. I don't deserve them, nor the pedestal they put me on.

Slumping in my chair, I wallow and replay the conversation in my head. If I would have just talked to Jay like an adult, we wouldn't be at odds right now. I have the emotional maturity of my two-year-old sometimes. The thought cuts me deep and shame seeps out, covering my skin in slimy regret.

For the next hour, I can do nothing but look out the window to the horizon. Something that used to look so bright is now gloomy.

The soft swish of my door opening is like the thrill of a new day. I swing around to confront it.

"Jay, I'm so..." It's Elliot with lunch. "Thanks, E. You can just set it on my desk. Jay's in their office, if you don't mind delivering theirs." I don't recognize the weakness in my voice.

"Everything okay, Mae?" Concern etches Elliot's blue eyes.

I give him a sad smile. "Not really. But I want to tell you how proud I am of you. You did an amazing job in that conference room today." Bashful, he stares at the floor. "I'm serious. I froze, and you jumped right in without missing a beat. I'm so grateful to be able to work with you."

He smiles. "Me too. I learned from the best, Mae." Elliot gives my arm a small squeeze before leaving me with my chicken salad.

His words echo in my mind, and I snap a bitter laugh. I used to think I was the best, but these days ... I've only been at my worst.

Remi

Before I start dinner, I settle Isabel in the pack 'n play in the living room because I like to keep an eye on her. I've never met a toddler that slept so soundly. When she's out, an earthquake won't wake her—pots and pans clattering are probably more like white noise to her than anything else.

At this age, she should be sleeping in a toddler bed. I'm surprised she hasn't attempted to climb out of her crib, and the thought of that possibility terrifies me. Most likely, Mae has been so busy she hasn't had time to reconfigure the bed. I'm going to offer to set it up because I'd love to help. I want to be a part of this milestone. I want to be there for all of them.

Setting up the emulsifier, I add all the ingredients for the salad dressing. I want to make Mae something special tonight, to subtly tell her how I feel. On the menu: Green Goddess Salad, Marry Me Chicken, and Italian Love Cake. I'm many things—cheesy is one of them.

Turning on some muted music, I dance around the kitchen. I'm going to knock Mae's panties off with this meal. My phone rings, interrupting the Taylor Swift song I was jamming to.

"Hello, beautiful," I answer, breathless and happy. A smile immediately forms on my face.

"Hey." She sounds tired. Defeated. The impulse to go to her is strong. "Can you stay a little later tonight? I'm sorry. I hate asking, but..."

My heart sinks to my feet. I eye all the ingredients on the kitchen island and decide to make it anyway. I can feed it to her when she gets home. Whatever time that may be.

"It's fine. Are you okay?"

"Yes. No. There's just a lot of shit going on at work, and I need to take care of it." There's no mistaking the tension in her voice.

"I have everything handled here. You focus on work, but when you get home, you're mine." I add a hint of wickedness, hoping it will make her smile. I'm going to tell her just how much I want her.

"I look forward to that. You have no idea how much." Her sultry voice wraps around my dick and squeezes.

"Yeah? I'm going to make you—"

"Listen, I have to go. Thanks again, Remi."

Click.

"Anytime," I whisper into dead air.

For the second time today, my heart is bruised.

Chapter 20

All Good Things Must Come to an End

Mae

WALKING INTO MY HOME, I take a deep, cleansing breath. It smells incredible in the kitchen and my stomach grumbles, asking what delicacies Remi made for dinner. I hardly ate lunch, and I'm ravenous.

The house is silent as I creep into the family room, spotting one sexy manny slouched on the sofa, sleeping peacefully. His arms are crossed over his broad chest, and his lips form a soft pout as he softly snores. I wonder if it's creepy that I want to take a picture so I can look back on this moment when he's no longer in our lives.

All good things come to an end. If today's shit storm isn't a prime example of that, I don't know what is. My heart lodges in my throat, and the dull ache in my hollow chest turns to painful anguish.

Pulling the plush faux fur throw blanket from the armchair, I cover him up, brushing his hair back and kissing his forehead as he snuggles down in the warmth. Grabbing a bottle of Cab, I tiptoe back into the kitchen to find dinner. When I open the fridge, I'm surprised to see it full.

There is a covered plate resting on the shelf, with a note on it: *For my queen.*

I thrill and bristle at the words. While I'm certainly his, I cannot claim him. It isn't right. We have no future together. Even though it hurts, it's the truth, and I have to be the one to define our boundaries. Remi is a great guy with a huge heart. It's what helps him make decisions. It's also what will get him hurt.

"Hey."

I startle, standing straight at the rasp of his sleepy voice, hoping he can't read my thoughts on my face. "Hi, I see you've made a feast." I smile, lifting my plate. "Looks amazing."

Remi's cheeks ruddy, and something pulses in my core. "Yeah, tried something new. It came out okay." He scratches the back of his head. "You want me to heat it up?"

"I can do it." I smile, showing him how much I appreciate coming home to this. To him.

"Okay, I guess I'll head out then."

Disappointment stabs me in the gut, aggravating the festering wound there. From our conversation earlier, I thought he'd want to stay again. The thought of having him all night is what kept me from drowning in misery today.

"You could stay," I whisper, hating the plea in my voice. I want him to stay because *he* wants to, not because it will make me happy.

"I don't think I should," he says on a thick swallow.

Disappointment turns to sadness, making my stomach cramp. He got what he wanted, didn't he? So did I, I guess.

I keep my voice light so he can't tell how much I'm hurting inside. "Sure. Yeah. Sounds good."

There's something somber in his eyes, and my shoulders drop. It's something else I need to fix. Shutting the fridge, I place my plate of deliciousness on the counter.

"You okay, Remi?" Eager feet shuffle closer to him, and I brush my thumb across his lip.

It quivers while his stare heats. He nods.

"Do you need some time off?" I hope he says no, even though he deserves it.

I can't believe I've become so dependent on someone else. It's not just about Isabel's care. It's about the comfort I feel when he's here. The way my house feels like a home because of him. It's about our blossoming friendship, aside from our sexual attraction.

He's become as important to me as Jay. He doesn't realize his mere presence—especially now—is significant to me.

Without thinking, I wrap my arms around him. It's not the kiss of passion I was hoping for, but it's something. If he's leaving for the night, I just want to savor his warmth a little.

Kissing the top of my head, he extricates himself from my embrace. "Goodnight, Mae."

I stand frozen in place as ice-cold blood runs through my veins at the brush-off. "Night." It's short, but what else is there to say?

Dejected, I turn so he can't see the emotion on my face. It's been a dumpster-fire of a day, and I'm too tired to put up pretenses. When I hear the soft click of the door behind me, I throw my plate of dinner into the sink. It shatters, and creamy sauce splashes everywhere. I'm shocked at my outburst, but when my nose burns, forewarning tears, I pull a glass out of the cupboard and throw it against the wall. With the satisfying smash echoing in my ear, I go for another plate. And another.

I now understand Adele's mood in *Rolling in the Deep*. My tirade amps with a frustrated howl, and more breakable things are thrown.

When there are no more plates to shatter, I survey the mess with maniacal laughter. What the hell is wrong with me?

Sliding down the wall, I hang my head to my knees and crack wide open.

Chapter 21

Give Me All Your Worries

Remi

Just keep walking. You can leave her for one night.

Climbing in my car, I start the engine. The draw to go back to Mae is strong, but I need to preserve my heart. I'm fucking crazy about her, and the more time I spend with her, the worse it's going to be for me when she decides she's had enough fun. Enough of me.

I'm not going to tell my sister. What's the point? All it would do is get her pissed at me and remove Isabel from my care. I promised that little girl I'd always be there for her. It's the one thing I won't mess up.

But even if Kiara would be okay with my relationship with Mae, what type of future could we have, anyway? What the hell was I even thinking? She'd still be footing the bill for Isabel's care. It's my only source of income and if I don't have that, I have nothing to offer a woman like Mae. Someone who deserves an equal. Someone she can find common ground with. Even though she doesn't need it, she deserves a man who could financially support them if anything ever happens to Ever Heart.

I'm not that man. *Unless you go back to medical school.* I can't believe the thought entered my mind.

Your father would gladly welcome you back in the fold. My chest tightens. I want to be as far from "the fold" as possible. *Even if it meant having Mae?* The devil's advocate has a point. I'd do anything to have her, to be worthy of her.

When I pull up next to my apartment building, I don't have the desire to turn the car off, so I sit there, looking at the darkness of my place. It's sparse.

Lonely.

Cold.

Just like my life without Mae and Isabel.

I hate it.

Without another thought, I throw Aretha in reverse and she squeals out a *u-ey*.

Mae asked me to stay. She had a shit day and asked me to be there for her.

I fucking bailed because I can't handle my stupid feelings. When did I become a moody asshole?

I hightail it to Grayson Street, to the modest brick house with my two favorite people on Earth inside. I dial Mae to give her a heads-up, but she doesn't answer. It only makes me more anxious to see her. She seemed okay when I left, but something clouded her gorgeous green irises. Despondency, maybe.

I punch the steering wheel, and the horn fires, cursing me as I'm cursing myself. Dammit, I can't believe I left her like that.

I whip into her driveway and almost rip my door off getting out of the car. Running up to the back entrance, I hear the most awful, keening sound. Sobs—loud and piercing—slice through my chest and rip out my heart.

I shove my key into the deadbolt and yank the door open. My stomach drops to the concrete at the sight before me.

Shards of glass cover every surface of the floor. My queen is crouched in the corner, bawling, as broken as the glass surrounding her.

"Jesus Christ." Bile sears up my throat. I can't believe I left her. Grief-stricken, my limbs turn too heavy for my weak bones.

It's absolute destruction. Glass crunches like gravel under my shoes as I make my way to Mae. It seems as if it takes forever to get to her, but when I do, I wrap my arms around her and pull her onto my lap, resting her body against my chest.

"Shh," I soothe like I would a child.

She digs her nose into my shoulder and melts against me, choking on her sorrow.

"I'm so sorry, baby," I croak, my throat crimped tight. I shower her temple with butterfly kisses, trying to comfort her through it. "Why didn't you say something?"

She shrugs, ripping my heart out and pulling me under a swell of despair with her. I know it's hard for her to depend on someone, but she already has me, regardless if she needs me or not.

"Mae, look at me."

She shakes her head against my chest. So stubborn. Queeny clutches my shirt as she wails into it. Her tears, warm and unrelenting, soak through, and I wonder how long it's been since she's let herself break down. I survey the damage around us. This must be what years of pent-up hurt, anger, and frustration look like.

"Baby, please," I beg because this is killing me.

Needing her eyes, I wrap my hand around her jaw and pull her chin up to face me. Her blister-red cheeks are stained with white streaks of salty tears, and snot is running out of her nose. Even in this state, she's so fucking beautiful I would sell my soul to keep her. I wipe away her tears with my thumb and use my shirt to dry her nose. My movements are slow and gentle as I clean her gorgeous face.

Her sobs quiet to hiccups, and even though her heartbeat is erratic against mine, the hurricane of emotions seems to have abated.

I need her to relax, so I ease the tension a little more. "Did you not like dinner?"

A loud laugh breaks through her tears. I can't help but smile in return, dripping a sweet smooch on those soft lips.

"Tell me," I encourage, keeping my voice soft and low.

Mae takes a deep breath and leans further into me. I know whatever it is, it's going to be difficult to talk about, so I wait patiently until she's ready.

"I'm losing"— she chokes on a sob — "everything." Her face crumples on the last word. The way she clings to me tells me I'm part of her "everything". She couldn't be more wrong.

"Everything I worked for. All the things I sacrificed." She wipes her cheek with the back of her hand as new tears fall. "All the time I missed with Isabel." Her lids squeeze shut as if she doesn't want to see too far into the future. "It was all for nothing."

The crack in her voice tears at my flesh. Her pain is my pain. I wish I had the solution to all her problems, but I only have myself and my unconditional devotion to this family.

"I'm so sorry, Mae."

New moisture forms in the corner of her eyes and falls like fat raindrops down her cheeks.

I smooth her silky hair off her face before tucking her head under my chin. "Shh, it's going to be okay. You're smart and tenacious. You will get through this and be better for it."

Mae pulls back to look at me. "How can you say that? I fucked up. Jay counted on me, and I ruined them."

"Hey, you are only human. I can't imagine a scenario where you were solely responsible for your company. It's even harder to fathom that Jay would hold anything against you. They're just as responsible."

She shakes her head. "You don't understand."

I don't. But she doesn't either. She has no idea how much the people in her life love her. We'd do anything to make her happy, especially Jay. I've seen them together. Jay lifts her high on that pedestal, like I do. And rightfully so—it's where she belongs.

The mess around us is a reminder that Queeny's kingdom is in shambles, so it's time to change locations. I try to slide out from under her so I can pull her out of the hell she's in, but she has a vise grip on my shirt.

"Don't go." Her words are wobbly.

Never. Never again.

"Hey." I drop down to catch her stare. "I'm not, okay?"

She looks so lost, so vulnerable. I want her to know she'll always have me. For as long as she wants.

I brush my lips over hers, giving the slightest suction. The hand that was holding onto my shirt slides up the back of my neck as she gives into her need.

"Never," I whisper.

She lifts up on her knees to deepen the kiss, but there's something I need to do first.

"I'm going to take care of you. C'mon." While one arm holds her to me, the other slides under her knees and I stand. She relaxes in my arms as I pick her up, surrendering to her exhaustion. Needing me to be strong when she is weak. "That's it, baby. I've got you."

She buries her face in my neck, her tears coating my skin and her hands clasped tightly behind my back.

Guilt twists around my lungs again. I shouldn't have left her.

We make our way upstairs, and I peek in on Isabel—who is still contently sleep-ing—before taking Mae to her bedroom and setting her on the bed.

"Wait here."

Going into the ensuite, I turn on the warm water in the claw foot tub. My body reacts to the thought of giving Mae a bath, but I tamp that shit down. Tonight is about her—making her feel relaxed ... and loved.

Walking back into the bedroom, I go to my girl. There is a shift in her eyes. Downstairs, they were filled with darkness. In here, they lighten.

"Give it all to me. Just for a moment." I pull her into my arms. "Give me all your worries," I murmur in her ear before granting her the deep kiss we both have been craving.

She liquefies right into me, and I can physically feel the moment she lets everything go. Everything except me. Me, she clings to.

I'm the luckiest bastard in the world.

I deftly unbutton her shirt with one hand. She wants to reciprocate, but I shift away. "No, tonight is about you."

She freezes, not wanting to give up control. But she has to. She has to know what it feels like to have someone carry her burden so she doesn't have to do it alone.

I wrap my hand around her neck and brush my thumb across her chin. It's a possessive move, but I'm in charge tonight. "Give. It."

On a shaky breath, she nods. *Good girl.*

"I'll make it all better, baby. I promise." I push her blouse off her toned shoulders, grazing my lips over each one. Next to go are her slacks, and she holds onto me for balance as she steps out of them. *That's right, hold onto me.*

I reward her with a peck on each knee, staying clear of the obvious erogenous zones. Tonight, I'm showing her my intentions are pure. I'm a child learning to walk. For the first time in my life, I'm irrevocably in love with a woman, and she needs to know she's special.

Without letting my hands linger on her luscious body, I remove her bra and underwear, though I can't help but take a moment to appreciate her naked form. She's absolutely stunning. A Venus De Milo in the flesh.

Without words, I usher my queen to the steaming bath. Gripping my arm, she sinks into the tub and hisses. Fuck, she knows how to torture a man.

"Too hot?"

Leaning back against the porcelain, her eyes slide shut. "Just right."

The tips of her dusty rose nipples peek out from the water. My mouth dries.

Trying to distract myself, I grab her shampoo and conditioner, kneeling beside her. "Dip your hair back."

When her ears are half submerged, I trace a finger along her graceful neck before cupping my hand and wetting the top of her head. The erotic hum falling from her lips sends a thrill up my spine. I squeeze a dollop of shampoo on her strawberry hair and massage her scalp.

Mae's sigh is decadent. "Feels so good." Her vanilla lavender scent swirls around us—enticing and seducing.

"I love the way you smell." Gravel coats my voice. Twisting her hair up, I make sure to get her ends. "I just might have to start using this shampoo."

Queeny chuckles and it seeps into my chest, warming me from within. "You want to smell like a chick?"

I bend over to her ear and purr, "I want to smell you on me."

"Oh." She shivers. Her nipples harden into pencil erasers.

For the love of God. She tests my restraint at every turn.

"Let's rinse," I choke out.

She tips back her head again, and I make sure to get all the soap out of it before getting her conditioner. I smooth the moisturizer through her tresses and marvel at the way my fingers slide through the silky strands.

"Mmm, you are good at this."

I smirk. "You'll find that I'm good at a lot of things."

"Oh, believe me. I'm well aware." She gives me a little whimper, and my pants become painfully tight.

Once all the conditioner is rinsed out, I grab a washcloth and dip it in the water. The tinkling of droplets resounds around the room as I lather it with soap.

"Lean forward."

Mae gives me a look of longing as she rests against her bended knees.

I know, baby. Me too.

I squeeze the washcloth against her back, letting the warm water trickle over her alabaster skin. "Feel good?"

"Yes." There is no mistaking the desire in her voice.

I take my time, cleaning every inch of her down to her tailbone. Cleansing her of this horrible day. When I'm done, I guide her back against the tub. The way she's watching me, with half-lidded eyes and rosy cheeks, calls to every fiber of my being, telling me to take her. Her mouth is slightly open, so I go for it, washing between her breasts and up across her collarbone.

"Remi, I need…" Her forehead falls against my shoulder resting on the back of the tub.

"Shh, I know exactly what you need." Reaching around her, I massage her breast, careful not to touch her over-stimulated tips.

She bites my shoulder and mewls.

"Open your knees." It's a command she obeys. Water sloshes in a wave at the movement.

Losing the cloth, I soap my hands and glide them up her body. Her eyes roll closed as she licks her lips. Satisfaction settles in my chest that it's *me* making her feel so good. My fingers knead and massage her soft globes.

Her head falls back in pleasure. "Your hands are" — sigh — "amazing." Her gravelly voice wraps around my cock and strokes.

My hands become greedy as they slide all over her flesh, and I mentally have to calm myself down. *Baseball stats. Ruth in a thong. Kiara kicking my balls.* I tickle her sides playfully and she squeaks out a giggle, further dissolving the anguish from earlier. Ever so slowly, my hands glide up her torso and cup her pretty tits.

I touch her where she's aching. Taking her stiff peaks between my fingers, I roll and twist them until she's writhing under my hands.

"Can you come like this?" The way she's trembling, I'm almost positive she could.

"I-I … never—" Her words cut off with a grunt as my stimulation becomes more intense.

The dusty pink color of her nipples deepens to red as they swell. It makes my mouth hungry. Rinsing her off, I wrap my lips around the bud closest to me while I flick the other with my thumb.

Mae's hands slam on the lip of the tub, keeping her steady.

"Oh God. This." The sweet sounds she's making tighten my balls.

Turns out, I could come like this too. I moan and bite, and pull and suck. My cock is trying to break out of the prison of my jeans. It's excruciating.

She starts rocking her hips to no avail, water rippling, splashing over the sides of the tub, soaking through my clothes. My overly sensitive skin heats.

A whine of frustration comes from the back of her throat, and I decide to have mercy on her.

I slowly slide my hand from her nipple to her lower belly. It jumps, and I smile against her flesh.

She's aching. Mae tries to flex her pelvis, seeking my touch, and I give in. A little. My index finger barely brushes against her pearl before exploring deeper.

A shudder rips through her diaphragm. "Right there," she chokes.

"You're so slippery, baby." Her arousal coats my fingers, and I tease her slit before slipping inside, my palm resting against her clit.

She tries to widen her legs, but they are held hostage by the sides of the porcelain. I shallowly fuck her with my finger while she white-knuckles the tub. Mae's flushed body is trembling, begging for release.

Gathering more cream from between her legs, I cross two fingers and ease them in, finding the spongy spot that drives her wild. I tug and tease, feeling it swell under my fingertips.

"Mmm, God." Her chest caves with a heavy breath. She grinds against my palm, telling me she wants more without using words.

"You like my fingers in your pretty pussy, don't you?" I growl as my carnal need heightens.

"Need more," she whines.

I give her what she wants, adding a third finger. I fuck her slow and deep.

"Shit, yes," she hisses, then gives me a lazy smile. "You sure know how to use those long fingers of yours."

My mouth reaches for hers for a decadent kiss. It's messy and wet. Our teeth clash together, and our mouths barely stay sealed. It's lips against lips and breath against breath. Reaching around her again, I pinch and flick her hard tip. When I pull roughly, a deep guttural groan emerges from her beautiful throat.

"You like that, huh? You get off on the rough." I pump my fingers in and out, smashing my palm against her. "I see you, Mae. And I want it. Every" — lick — "part" — suck — "of you."

She moans and begs, "I need you inside me, please."

I love a woman who knows what she wants and isn't afraid to demand it.

"Not tonight, baby. Tonight it's all about you."

Sharp nails dig deep into my forearm—it stings. It's going to make me come in my pants. When she contracts, my dick twitches.

"Fuck, I can feel you clench around me. How does it feel?"

"Delicious" — gasp — "ache." Exhale. Her hips swivel faster. She's chasing her orgasm, and it's a magnificent sight.

I slam my fingers in and out, smacking her swollen clit each time. Water sloshes everywhere. I'm surprised there's still some left in the tub.

"That's it. Take what you need," I whisper against her lips. "Tomorrow, I'm going to eat that sweet pussy before I fuck it raw." I hook and tug. "You want that, don't you?"

Arching, she cries out but doesn't give me what I'm asking.

"Say it," I demand through clenched teeth.

When all she gives me are pants and groans, I pull out and give her tit a swift smack. A red hand print forms on her pink skin, and precum leaks in my boxers.

Mae jerks against me. "Yes, *fuck*, please. All of it."

"Exactly what I want to hear." I shove my fingers back in her battered hole and pinch her clit at the same time.

Her back bows, and she explodes. "Remi," she cries out my name over and over.

Euphoria swells inside of me with the burning in my gut. Like a virgin schoolboy, I come in my pants, not the least bit upset about it. It's the way she gave herself to me. The way she let me work her. The way she screamed my name like she was crying out for her Lord and savior. A call I will always answer to.

Relaxing back into the lukewarm water, Mae lays her head on my arm, and I caress her with a tender touch.

"Stay with me." Her request is small, but it means everything to me.

"I'm here with you as long as you want me to be," I admit, kissing her head over and over. "I fucked up by leaving you. I won't be doing that again." I search her gaze, hoping she feels what I'm saying. "I'm sorry, baby."

Mae looks up at me with dreamy eyes. "You came back, though. I needed you, and you came." Her tone is split between disbelief and awe.

I know it's just about the epic orgasm I gave her, but I want to believe it's because she feels something for me. "Come on, let's dry off before you turn into a prune."

She lets me towel her off, then helps me out of my clothes.

"I need to rinse off real quick." I wink.

Queeny gives me a cute giggle before planting a wet one on my mouth. "I'll warm the bed for you." She sends me a feline smile, turns, and sashays out of the room.

Just like that, my dick stiffens again. I shake my head. This woman is going to be the death of me.

After cleaning myself up and draining the tub, I find my girl sound asleep in bed. Throwing my jeans back on, sans dirty boxers, I tiptoe out of her room. When I get to the kitchen, I survey the damage.

"My God, Queeny. What happened today?" I mutter, hating that she was so torn up inside. By the looks of it, Mae will need another twelve-serving plate setting, along with tall tumblers and a set of wine glasses.

As I clean up the shards of glass and broken ceramic pieces, I realize just how much she's been dealing with—silently, stoically, and all alone. My throat prickles, and my nose stings. Her hurt manifests and grows inside of me. I hate that she has so much weighing her down.

Making my way to the trash under the sink, I note that she didn't eat dinner. My frown deepens. *Skipping meals isn't going to help, baby.*

When the floor is free from debris, I wipe down the counters and backsplash, which has dried sauce stuck on it. As much as she doesn't want to admit it, she needs someone constant in her life. Someone she can come home to, count on. I know she has Jay, but they have their own life to live.

The more time I spend with her and Isabel, the more I know I belong with them. My life feels so complete when we're together. It's as if we've always been this way, and it seems strange—not to mention depressing—imagining a future without them in it. I know Isabel won't always need a nanny, but she'll need me. There is no written rule that I can't find another job teaching. Kiara might be pissed, but she'll be upset either way.

Creeping back up the steps, I check on Isabel again. She's sound asleep, sucking her thumb. I leave her door open a crack and go to the place I never want to leave—Mae's bed.

She's just as knocked out as her daughter, and I steal a moment of admiration. Her face is clean and serene, making her look more peaceful than I've ever seen her.

Her arm stretches to the other side of the bed. "Rem..." she mumbles, still asleep.

My breath stops, and my heart swells. She's looking for me.

Stepping out of my jeans, I lay them on the chair in the corner and climb into bed. I take her hand and wrap it around my side as I gather her close.

"I'm right here," I murmur against her ear.

"... love ..."

Did she just...

My eyes squeeze shut, wishing to all that is divine that it's true. Even if it's only a dream, she's dreaming about loving me.

I pull her tighter against my naked form, savoring the way her silky skin warms mine. It's a bare whisper, but I can't hold back the words. "I love you too."

Chapter 22

You're All I Want

Remi

"Oh God, yesss."

Soft... Warm...

Delicious weight rests on my pelvis, and I reach for the supple skin that I know and love. "Mmm, Mae."

Her hips circle languidly, and it's the best kind of torture.

"Just like that."

A giggle drifts around me, and it's enough to tempt me into consciousness. I love that giggle.

When I open my eyes, I'm mesmerized, watching the woman of my dreams rock against me, taking her pleasure and amplifying my own.

"Mornin', baby. You sure know how to wake up a man."

With closed lids, a sleepy smile forms on Queeny's face. She lays against me, her breasts brushing against the soft hair on my chest.

"Your dick woke me up first." She gives me a lazy kiss. "It was only fair that I got to play with it."

I dig my fingers into her wild hair and hold her to me. "Mmm, yeah. It's only fair."

"I want you to come inside of me," she breathes against my mouth.

My world pivots on its axis when I realize I'm not wearing a condom.

This is it. This is her giving herself to me fully. She wants me bare, just as much as I want her. My balls tingle and my cock lengthens, sliding against her soft walls. I'm so high on love for her I'm surprised my body doesn't levitate.

Mae seems casual about it, but to me, this is monumental. I've never had sex without a condom before Queeny. I'd never even consider it, but she is the only woman I'd go bare for. She's the only woman for me, period.

She notices the change in my demeanor and pauses. "I'm sorry. I thought it would be okay. *Shit.*" She goes to lift off.

I wrap an arm across the small of her back, pinning her in place, and thrust up against her, fucking her from the bottom. She's a warm silk glove. Fucking divine.

"It's more than okay. I never want anything between us." Hope, euphoric and intoxicating, floats around us.

"You felt good before, but this is ... sublime."

I couldn't agree more. I don't just mean how I can feel every muscle in her pussy. Mae accepting me, accepting *us*, fills my chest with so much emotion I could explode and weep at the same time.

With our mouths pressed together, she pulses around me, and I release into her warmth. The thought of her walking around all day carrying a piece of me inside her makes me wild. She's so fucking mine.

All too soon, her alarm chimes. It's time to leave this little cocoon of heaven and join the rest of the world.

I have the morning off because Isabel still attends nursery school on Tuesdays. Usually, I use the time to clean up the house and do laundry.

"I don't want to get up," she whines, and I couldn't agree more.

I squeeze that ass I'm so fond of. "Go ahead and get ready for work. I'll get Isabel off to school."

When I move to get up, she catches my arm. "Manny?" She bites her lip, unsure.

I slide back in next to her. "Queeny?"

"I'm thinking about taking the morning off." She looks away. "Maybe we can spend some time together?"

The woman who woke me up riding my cock suddenly turns bashful. It's adorable.

She's taking time off—something she never does—and wants to spend those precious moments with me. Is this a date? Or is it about making good use of this bed? Either way, I'm all in.

"Yeah, we can definitely do that." I play with the ends of her hair. "We can drop off Isabel together. Get some breakfast after."

"Sounds nice." She presses her lips against mine.

"Come on, let's get dressed before I'm tempted to slip back inside of you." My tone is joking, but my twitching dick is dead-serious.

We go through our morning routine together at her double-sink vanity—brushing our teeth, fixing our hair, exchanging dopey smiles. It feels very ... domestic, like something I want to do every morning for the rest of my life.

Mae takes care of Isabel while I prepare a small breakfast for her. When they meet me in the kitchen, I wrap my arms around them and give them both a kiss. *My girls.*

"Morning, Emmie," Isabel's cute voice greets me.

"How's my favorite little girl? Are you ready to play with your friends today?"

"I not whittle. I big girl." She lifts her arms up to the ceiling, and I tickle her belly.

Mae is beaming. So different from the broken woman I found on the floor yesterday.

"But we don't want you to grow up. Mommy wants you to be her baby forever." Queeny bounces Isabel, and tiny cherub giggles fill the room.

It's a beautiful morning. Isabel eats every bite of her banana and yogurt like a champ.

It isn't long before we are heading to Building Blocks, Isabel singing "Sussi" at the top of her lungs the entire way. She's definitely a morning person.

"I'm so sick of this song," Mae whines, making me laugh.

When kids like something, they really like it. It amazes me how they can watch or listen to something ad nauseam.

Mae's fingers are folded through mine over the console of Aretha. Holding her hand and taking Isabel to school feels so natural. So right. We drop Isabel off at Building Blocks. Both of us walk her to the classroom, where she runs to her friends, forgetting all about us. It warms my heart to see her so well-adjusted.

Walking back to the car, I wrap my arm around Mae's shoulder. I can't seem to keep my hands to myself. "Where to, my queen?"

"I can really go for some waffles." She wags her eyebrows.

"Waffle house it is."

"Do you want to talk about yesterday?" I pour maple syrup all over the perfectly fluffy stack of pancakes the waiter just delivered.

Mae stops buttering her waffle and looks at me. "I don't want to burden you with my problems, Remi. You have enough to do."

"I just want to help." My face is soft and open, hoping she can see I'm sincere and trusts me enough to let me in.

Her cheeks flame. "Oh, I think the bath you gave me last night helped immensely." She shakes her head. "Besides, you cleaned up the aftermath. A mess you didn't create." Looking away, she shreds her poor napkin into a thousand pieces. I can tell she's beating herself up about it. "You shouldn't have to be subjected to that."

I grab her hand from across the small table. She doesn't understand—I don't want to be just a distraction any longer. I want to be her partner. I want to carry the weight with her.

"I care about you. You have to know that." She doesn't pull away, so that's a good sign. "Is it so bad that I want to help you through a difficult time in your life?"

"No, I just... I'm used to handling things on my own." Her eyes shift to the left for a moment. "I mean, Jay has always been there for me, but they're in love. I can't keep running to them every time my life blows up."

"I'm sure they would still want you too, though." I take a sip of coffee and wince at the bitter taste.

"You're such a coffee snob." She picks up her mug and gives me the same face. "Yeah, it's pretty bad."

"Talk to me." I'm on the verge of begging.

She blows out her cheeks with a long sigh. "Ever Heart has been struggling since last year. We grew too fast, and I was too far into my ego to slow down. To take things a moment at a time. I have been combing through every angle I can to keep it afloat. Last month, I single-handedly lost a huge contract." Her lips dip down.

"I'm sure it wasn't single-handedly. Jay is your partner."

"They were away with Ian, and I didn't want to bother them. I met with a CEO on my own. And..." Something dark passes over her face.

An echo floats through my brain, dropping a lead ball in my stomach. "'I won't sleep with him for a business deal.'"

She stiffens. "What? Why would you say that?"

"I didn't. You did." Her mouth drops in horror as rage flares inside of me. It takes every ounce of effort to keep my voice conversational. "The night you fell asleep on your laptop and I helped you to bed. You mumbled, 'I won't sleep with him for a business deal'. Is that why Ever Heart lost the account? Because you wouldn't drop your morals and disrespect yourself?" I hope Mae can't see the murder scene unfolding behind my eyes.

Shaking her head, she turns away, waffle forgotten.

"Because you know the value you bring to the table, and it has nothing to do with what's between your legs." I know I'm pushing her, but she's blaming herself for something she'd never forgive herself for. She would have compromised her standards.

"It's disgusting what powerful men get away with. Because they do, they think they can proposition every woman that crosses their path," she bites out, crossing arms in contempt. "It's fucking degrading."

I clench my jaw, reining in my anger towards the bastard because it's the last thing Mae needs. If I ever meet this guy in a dark alley, I will kill him with my bare hands. "I'm sorry that happened to you. I'm sorry that it happens at all." She has no idea how much.

Half of her mouth quirks up. "Thanks for not going all toxic masculinity on me."

I scratch my head, trying not to look sheepish because that's exactly what I did ... in my mind. "You can handle yourself, Mae. You do it with grace. You don't need me to solve your problems for you."

"Thank you for saying that." She fiddles with her fork. "We lost the account, and three investors followed. We could still manage with the accounts we did have, but we'd have to do a major layoff. There's nothing worse than telling someone they're done through no fault of their own." Her mouth opens and closes as if she's hesitating.

"What is it?"

"Before I let even one person go, I will sell my house first. Isabel will lose her private nursery school." Her chin quivers, and she pins me with a stare. "And her incredible nanny."

God, how selfless could a person be? She may not say it, but she cares about her people so fucking much. It just makes her that more admirable. "If you have to lose those things, you'll figure it out. You are a resourceful woman. But one thing you can be sure of is that you'll never lose me. I promised you I wouldn't leave Isabel, and I keep my promises." I'd sell my soul to her if she asked, but I'm hoping she'll someday settle on a signed document that says Isabel's mine and a wedding band. Someday soon.

This makes her angry. "You can't work for free, Remi. If I let you, what does it say about me?" A mirthless laugh comes out of her mouth. "It would make me no better than Paul Wexford."

Jealousy surges through me. "Who's Paul Wexford?"

"The disgusting CEO."

Oh no. "Baby, listen to me. You are not and could never be a rape-opportunist. You respect me more than that. As far as my pay, let me worry about that."

Her stare is challenging. "You wouldn't be saying that if you knew how many times I objectified you. I mean, the first day you came to the house, I fired you because I was too attracted to you."

What? My thoughts swarm around my head, but the one that is recurring is: "Did you do anything with that objectification? If so, I really, *really* want to know more." I lean in, resting my chin on my fist.

She throws a straw wrapper at me. "I'm being serious."

"So am I." I can't keep the smile off my face. "I'll tell you if you tell me. If it makes you feel any better, I wanted to bend you over your desk after your little tirade about cutting my balls off if I did anything to hurt your daughter. All while wearing latte foam on your nose."

"Shut up!" She laughs. "You're just trying to make me feel better."

"It's true. I fucked my fist to that image that very night. You had me from day one. So please don't compare us to the bullshit that asshole did to you." I pick up her fork and make her eat a bite of waffle that's probably cold by now. "You didn't eat dinner last night. I expect you to clean your plate."

"Oh, really? What are you going to do if I don't?" She gives me a flirty smirk.

"Spank your ass." I can't keep the possessive growl out of my voice.

Her mouth opens as her cheeks pink. My baby likes the idea very much. *Same, Queeny. Same.*

"Anyway, you were completely professional until I broke your boundaries. I'm the culprit here. Not you."

Her finger taps her chin. "That is true." She raises a wicked eyebrow. "Maybe I should spank *you.*"

My dick's ears perk up, and I squirm in my seat. "You can do whatever you want to me." I smile. "I'm all yours, baby."

Mae bites her plump lip. "You really mean that, don't you?" she asks like she can't believe it.

I'm done hiding the way I feel. It's deep and intense, and she needs to know that.

I sear her with a look. "Hand to God, Queeny. You are all I want. It's not just about your body, though you're a fucking goddess." I give her a wicked grin. "It isn't about that thing you do with your throat either, although I've never felt anything like it before." Like the force of my feelings, I cannot stop the next words from leaving my lips. "The way I feel about you, I've never felt about anyone. Ever. The day you tell me you've had enough" — I choke at the possibility — "I'm not sure I'm going to survive it."

I watch as her throat undulates under the weight of my confession. She doesn't say anything, and it's excruciating. My heart—the fool—is ready to give up.

Mae's phone rings, killing the moment, and I want to throw the thing across the room. Her brows knit together when she looks at the screen before placing it at her ear. "Hello?" Tension builds in her forehead, and I stiffen. "*Hello,*" she bites out impatiently. She startles, looks at her screen again and shoves the offending object in her purse.

"Everything okay?" I'm on the edge of my goddamn seat.

"Fucking robo calls," she gripes before her face relaxes and she gives me a small smile. "Anyway, I don't think..."

Here it is, the big brush-off. My face heats with pre-humiliation. I should have known a woman like Mae would want someone with prestige, not a fucking nanny. From the start, I knew not to fall for her—a woman impossible for a humble guy like me to attain. I'm a daydreamer and a hopelessly-in-love nitwit.

"I don't think I'll ever get enough, Remi."

Wait, what?

"I wouldn't survive it either." Her voice is small and sweet, but it hits me with the force of a sonic boom.

My mouth drops to the floor. "But I thought…"

"It was selfish of me to go after you. You're so young, and you have your whole life ahead of you. I'm married to my job and when I'm not there, I'm spending time with Isabel. I didn't want to tie you down to me. I thought…" She shakes her head then looks away.

I'm literally dying inside. No, that's not true. I'm already dead. This is heaven, and she is my gift. What I did to deserve her, I have no idea, but I won't look a gifted horse in the mouth. I'm just grateful.

"I thought you'd resent me. Resent us. Then, there's your job." She nods. "There's still the matter of your job."

"I could never resent such a beautiful gift." I wink, my mouth twisting to one side. "My job is trivial compared to what I feel for you. I'm sure we can figure it out together." I take both her hands in mine. "I need you to know that you and Isabel are all I want. I can't imagine this 'whole life ahead of me' without *you*." I brush my lips across her knuckles. "Please, don't make decisions you think are best for me, and I won't for you, deal?"

She's radiant. With glossy red hair gathered over one shoulder and soulful green eyes glowing with adoration … for me. "Deal. But what are we going to do about your job? Do you want us to go to Kiara together?"

I can't believe she's ready to out us. I can't believe she's truly mine.

My sister won't have a choice if she wants to stay in my life. "Yes, let's go to Kiara together."

"We're really doing this." With a giddy grin stretched wide, she squeezes my fingers. She seems so much younger today than ever before.

"We really are." I kiss her hand. Something dark passes over her features. "What is it?"

"I just…" Her mouth dips down. "My first thought is, *I can't wait to tell Jay*, but we're not really on good terms right now."

I'm guessing that's primarily why all of her plates are destroyed. "Whatever it is, you both will get over it because you have something between you that will always win."

Her forehead creases. "What will always win?"

It's simple, beautiful. "Love."

After I make sure Mae has cleaned her plate, we pay the bill, and I decide to walk her to work. It's gorgeous out, and not just because the sun is shining and there is a nice breeze in the air. It's because I'm walking down the busy street holding Mae's hand, not caring who sees us. It's freeing. Everything is right in my world, and by the enigmatic smile on her face, Mae is pretty happy too.

"So, you go kiss and make up with Jay. Then tell them about us because I'd like to go on a double date soon."

"Really?" She peers up at me with one closed eye.

"Yes, really. I want to meet Ian and all the people in your life."

"Okay. You'll love the Morales family. They are crazy, but in the best way." She has a thought and skips a little. "We can bring Gram too." I've never seen Mae this … giddy. It's adorable, and I see where Isabel gets it from.

Wrapping my arm around her, I pull her to my side, loving that I can touch her however I want, show the world she's mine.

All too soon, we reach her building. I pull her to me and brush my lips against hers—once, twice—before she swipes her soft tongue against mine. We liplock like teenagers in the throes of new love. It's hard to let her go, but then she stiffens.

"What's wrong?"

Mae looks around us, seemingly paranoid.

"Kiara isn't going to pop around the corner if that's what you're worried about."

Her brows touch. "No, it's not that. Every once in a while, I get this weird feeling that someone is watching me." She does a dramatic shiver.

My buoyed mood dips, and I scan the area but don't catch anything suspicious. I'm about to ask how many times "every once in a while" is, when her voice pulls me from my survey.

"Maybe because I'm happy, I'm waiting for the other shoe to drop."

Bees swarm in my stomach at her saying she's happy with me. "Maybe it's all the guys watching, wishing they were me. You are stunning, baby."

She gives my chest a playful smack. "Stop."

Pulling her back to me, we rock together, grinning like fools. "It's true, but they can't have you, can they? You know why?"

"Because my apology pancakes are a choking hazard to unsuspecting men?"

This cheeky girl.

I place my lips on her ear and purr, "Because you're mine."

A faint moan comes from the back of her throat. "Alright, Casanova. When you pick Isabel up, come back here. We'll have lunch."

"Can't get enough of me, hmm?" Is it needy that I just want to hear her say it?

"Maybe Jay will take the baby, and you can fulfill that 'bending me over my desk' fantasy." Oh, the minx.

"You're so mean. Sending me away with that tease."

She winks and pulls away, our hands staying connected until they physically can't any longer.

For the next hour, I literally skip around town, with the cheesiest grin on my face.

I dial my sister. "Hey, booger face."

"God, you're such a dick." I hear the clickity-clack of her working on her computer. "What do you want? I'm busy."

"Good to talk to you too, sis." More click-clacking. She certainly doesn't make it easy. "Remember the older woman I was talking about. The one I'm into?"

"Yeaaah," she draws out the word.

"I want to introduce her to you guys. Will you be around later tonight?" The line is silent except for the clicking, of course. My sister is such a ballbuster. "We'll bring Giordano's."

"See you at seven. Bye." She hangs up.

I laugh, whistling my way to Isabel's school. I make a mental note to pick up Aretha from the waffle house later.

As soon as Isabel spots me from the playground, she runs to the fence with her teacher trotting after her. "Emmie! Emmie!"

Opening the gate, I swing her in the air and hug her to me. "How's my girl? Did you have a good day at school?"

"Yeah. Owiver twied to kiss me. I pushed him."

"Attagirl. You tell them boys to leave you alone until you're thirty." I wave to Miss. Deidre as I leave the school.

"Tirty?? Dat..." She holds up her hands, trying to count her fingers. She's too cute. "Too many."

I kiss her forehead. "That's the point." Setting her on the sidewalk, I keep hold of her hand as we walk. "We're going to pick up some lunch, and then we're going to visit Mommy at work." She swings my hand. "How does that sound?"

"Gweat!" She skips a little in excitement. Just like her mama. "Cat, Emmie. Cat!"

Isabel points her chubby finger in the direction of a caged-in area on the sidewalk, confining a few cats. There are balloons and tables set up with a sign that says, *Life is better with a rescue cat.* It must be some kind of adoption event at the shelter.

"Cat!" She's full on pulling me now, and there's no way I'm going to be able to deter her from the meowing puff balls. *Tenacious, like her mother.*

"Okay, okay. Slow down." I manage to get her to stop dragging me. "We can pet the cats, but we can't have one."

"Why not?" Her nose is scrunched, and the stink eye on this one is a killer.

I crack up. "Because we have to ask Mommy first. You don't want to pick a cat without Mom around. We don't want to leave her out." I'm praying she sees reason in that. She likes everyone to always be together.

"Okay. We look. No adoded."

When we get to the kitties, Isabel is vibrating in excitement. I'm going to have to convince Mae to get a cat. I cannot bear to say no to this kid.

"Well, hello there," the rescue woman greets Isabel. She's a bit older, with a kind face. One of those people who are passionate about animals—the best type of person.

"Hi! Pet cat?" Straight to the point.

The woman looks at me. "You must be the daddy. Is it okay if she pets the cats? They've had a health workup and are up-to-date on vaccination."

I point to myself. "Caretaker, and yes, as long as we don't go home with one. As in, please help me if this little one gives me sad eyes."

The older woman laughs. "Gotcha." When she bends down to open the cage door, one of the cats darts out, causing mayhem on the sidewalk. It's as if the poor thing is on an escape mission from a high-security prison.

"Noooo! Cat!" Isabel screams.

The rescue woman goes after the cat, but it's agile, parcouring off of the sidewalk and dashing into the busy street.

The next moment happens so fast, and yet I witness it in terrifying slow motion. Isabel yanks free from my hand, and to my utter horror ... runs after the cat.

I don't think. Except for the memory of when I first met her, crying on the floor, and the instant bond we formed.

I don't breathe. Except for a desperate gasp when I remember the moment I knew she and Mae were my entire world.

I don't hesitate. Because if I do, my world will stop turning, implode, and obliterate Mae with it.

"Isabel!"

I chase after my baby because her life depends on it, and I meant what I said—I'd die for her. Thank God people have the wherewithal to pull over, and although I saw Isabel's life flash before my eyes, I'm sure I'm going to get to her in time. Still, my legs break full speed. She's so small, it amazes me how fast she is.

A blue sedan comes into my peripheral view, heading straight for Isabel. It's not slowing down. In fact, it's accelerating. *Jesus fucking Christ.*

White-hot panic bursts inside of me, and my breath incinerates my lungs. Terror, heavy and potent, falls over me, straining my heart.

"No!" I bellow so loud my throat threatens to close.

I barely reach her, and there's not enough time for me to pick her up out of danger. So I push her out of the way as much as I can. She may get hurt, but at—

Pain, acute and excruciating, radiates up my spine as I'm flung face-first onto the asphalt. My head bounces like a ball with the force of the impact. There's a whoosh in my ears and a roar filling my brain until it feels like it's going to explode.

Something heavy is on top of me, and I can't move. It takes a magnitude of effort to see if Isabel is okay, but I manage.

She's screaming bloody murder, but... The rescue woman has her.

That's good. She's going to be just fine.

It's with that realization that my brain decides it's had enough. My body goes limp, and my fuzzy vision fades ... to nothing.

Chapter 23

The Other Shoe

Mae

LIGHTER THAN AIR, I breeze into our building and the elevator whisks me up to the thirtieth floor. My first stop is Jay's office because I can't stand this distance from them any longer. I fucked up, and now I have to take responsibility for it. Ever Heart wouldn't be possible if it wasn't for Jay and their incredible talent.

I'm relieved and nervous that their door is open, leaving me no time to prepare what I want to say, but I'm happy they are here.

"Knock, knock. It's your sorry sap of a best friend coming to grovel, oh mighty one."

Jay looks up from their seat at the graphic design table, unimpressed. Shit, I should have brought Firecakes Donuts.

"You may enter and keep talking." When I walk towards them, they raise their palm in the air. "Stay close to the door in case I need to kick you out." They wave their hand to the side. "Now, proceed with the groveling."

"I'm sorry, Jay. You have to know how sorry I am. Ever Heart wouldn't be anything without you. It's your talent that got us here, and I can't believe I said that awful stuff to you. You don't deserve it." I fidget and twist my fingers, waiting for their response. Why didn't I bring those damn donuts?

They sit still, staring through me, and tiny beads of sweat bloom on my temple. They aren't making this easy, are they?

"Can we talk like adults about the Pür offer?"

I gulp. My Achilles' heel. "Sure, we can talk about it." We can talk for the next three years, but I won't sign away our dream. Jay may think it's the answer to our prayers, but if we take the first offer that presents itself, we'll never know if something else could have worked better. "Can we also discuss restructuring and what that would look like?" My plea is weak. I'm well aware I'm not in the position to negotiate here, but I hope they will look at all angles when deciding the future of this company.

Jay stands and walks over to me. Today, they are wearing a kelly green silk kimono with small chandelier earrings. They shaved their beard because "summer, duh". They look younger like this. Beautiful.

"If we can also talk about you shagging the manny in detail." They crack a smirk.

My face flares because, of course, they know. "I'd never keep that kind of information from you." I bite my lip. "He wants to double date with you and Ian. He wants to meet the family." My smile stretches ear to ear.

"Oh, well. I didn't realize this became so serious."

They are finally in front of me, and I inhale freesia and comfort. My arms ache to wrap around them.

"My first thought was to call and tell you, but..." Tears form in my eyes. I don't even try to stop them from falling. "Please don't be mad at me anymore. I can't take it. I'm so sorry. You have to know how much I love you."

"I love you too, Mars Bars. I couldn't stay mad at you if I tried." When they pull me to them, I cry into their chest. They shift my face away from the kimono. "Watch the Italian silk, will ya?"

They hold me tight, and it feels like coming home after a long, arduous trip. I squeeze my best friend and cannot wait to hash out every detail of my blossoming relationship with Remi.

"Come on. Let's cuddle, and you can tell me all about the hot manny's monster cock."

I laugh as they help me onto the papason. They situate themselves behind me.

"You're the big spoon to my little spoon," I tease.

"Yeah, well, it's better than being a fork. I can hold all the tea, so spill it."

Settling in, I sigh and tell them all about Remi, how he makes me feel … and the things he can do with his mouth and fingers, and monster dick.

"So, this is you stepping out of your carefully curated box and finding love?"

Well, when put like that. Jay has always called a spade a spade. It's unnerving, but it isn't any less true.

"Yeah, I guess it is."

"Did you tell him yet?"

"Tell him what?"

"That you're in love with him."

I play with the soft material of their sleeve. Thinking about telling Remi how deeply I feel has a million butterfly wings fluttering in my stomach. "No, but I'm going to. He and Isabel are coming for lunch." I twist my neck until I'm almost facing them. "You want to join us?"

"Sure, a person could eat." A beat of silence, then, "Oh, wait, you're going to ply me with food so I take Isabel while you and loverboy do filthy things in your office." They know me so well.

I chuckle. "Would you be opposed to babysitting for an hour?"

"Heck no. Me and my baby bestie are going to terrorize the whole floor. Just make sure you give Elliot the afternoon off. He just started being comfortable around you. You don't want him to go back to calling you 'ma'am' again, getting your granny panties in a bunch."

Indignant, I smack behind me. "They are not granny panties."

"Oh, it's on now, Mars Bars." They start tickling me, and I'm laughing so hard I can't breathe.

"Gonna—" I cackle so loud I'm afraid I'm shaking the whole building. "Kick your—" *No, not under the armpits.* "A-s-s."

Our juvenile moment comes to a halt when Elliot clears his throat inside Jay's door. We get up and compose ourselves.

"Sorry, we just..." I thumb between my best friend and me, not knowing how to explain our wacky relationship. As if we just got caught horsing around in church.

"What she's trying to say is that I won the tickle contest and therefore—"

"I'm sorry to cut you off, Mx. Morales, but there's someone here to see Ms. Keller. It's important."

Elliot's face is grave, and something heavy drops in my stomach—the other shoe.

I race out of Jay's office, and they're right on my heels.

Is it Isabel? Is she okay? *My baby.* My heart is pounding so erratically I'm afraid I'm going to collapse.

In my office, I'm met with two female police officers. Both are stoic and unreadable.

"Are you Miranda Everly Keller?"

"I am." It's hard to get the words out because my mouth is full of cotton. I'm not sure why they're here, but my heart is ready to pound out of my chest.

"I'm Officer Taylor," the brunette introduces herself.

Her blonde counterpart steps forward with her hand extended. "Detective Gracyk."

After a short handshake, I reach for my best friend behind me. Without hesitation, Jay grabs my hand.

"First, I want to say that your daughter is perfectly fine. She's with someone from Child Care Connection," Officer Taylor says.

That doesn't make sense. Why? With whom? What does "perfectly fine" mean? There is nothing "perfectly fine" if Remi isn't with her. He wouldn't leave Isabel with anyone else. Unless...

The thing in my stomach becomes unbearably heavy, threatening to pull me down.

"There's been an accident," Detective Gracyk explains. "Remington Arison was hit by a car this afternoon. He's in critical condition," she finishes in a grave tone.

Shock punches me in the gut, but it's dread that yanks me from Jay's hold and knocks me to my knees. *Oh God, no!* We were just eating breakfast, happy, excited, and so in love we couldn't keep our hands to ourselves.

The organ in my chest fractures, each fissure creating a hole in the muscle, welcoming glass slivers of anguish and panic. Each thud of its beat is more painful than the last.

"No, you're mistaken. He's supposed to meet me here."

The weight of everyone's stare is on me. No one says a thing.

A rope of despair wraps around my throat and tightens. I claw at my neck.

We were going to tell Kiara so we could really be together. He's everything I've ever dreamed of in a man. And he's mine—*ours*— We can't lose him ... not ever. We're going to be a family.

I choke, shaking my head unceasingly as if this will all go away if I keep saying "no" in my mind. I can't breathe.

"No."

A scenario of the accident unfurls in my mind. All I see is Remi laying in a pool of blood under a car. My hand flies to my churning stomach and squeezes, but it's too late. I vomit on the floor next to where I'm kneeling.

Jay's on me in an instant, pulling me up and away from my mess.

"Tell them they are *wrong!*" I grip his sleeve. "Jay, *please.*"

Isabel. I need Isabel. She must be terrified.

Remi.

This is going to devastate her little heart. My baby.

"I'm sorry, Ms. Keller." Officer Taylor is calm, but it does nothing for the chaos in my head. "He's in surgery at Northwestern Hospital. His sister is there with him now."

Pleas for Remi ricochet around the room. I don't realize they are coming from me until Jay stops me.

"You are not helping him like this." Holding my arms, they shake me. "Snap out of it, Mae."

Tears blur my vision, and I can't see anything except the conjured image of Remi's lifeless body on the ground, followed by Isabel screaming in terror. It runs in a sick, merciless loop around my brain. Despair explodes in my head.

"No, no, no, no, nooo," I wail.

I don't remember leaving the office. Or riding in the back of a police cruiser. Or stopping at a brownstone I've never seen in my life.

"What are we doing here?" Where's my daughter? Where's Remi?

"Isabel is here, Mae." Jay's voice is soothing.

The officers help me out of the car and when we go to the front door, a man with dark hair, about my age, opens it and ushers us in.

"Your daughter is here. She has a minor scuff on her hand, but other than that, she's perfect."

My panic doesn't subside. That's the second time I heard that word today—perfect. There's nothing perfect about this. Nothing at all.

"Where is she?" I ask, barreling my way through the house in a raging storm. "Isabel!"

"She's in the kitchen, playing with my son, Jackson," the man explains, hot on my heels. He takes my elbow and steers me in the right direction.

Struggling for air, I search for my beautiful baby girl. As soon as I spot her, I'm finally able to take a full breath.

When Isabel notices me, big fat tears form in her eyes. "Mommy!" She drops whatever it is she's playing with and runs to me.

I kneel and catch her in my arms. Relief is sweet but fleeting. She buries her face in my neck and screams for her Emmie.

"Shhh, he's going to be okay, baby. Shhh." I rock and comfort her, keeping a leash on my emotions. Isabel needs me to be strong, and I can do anything for her.

Jay wraps us in their arms. "Everything is going to be alright."

Isabel cries harder.

"Unty Jay has never lied to you before, right?"

With her face still buried, she nods.

"I promise, everything will be just fine," Jay reassures. I wish I had their faith.

I continue to soothe and sway Isabel in my arms. A tornado of emotions tears through me: relief that Isabel is okay, distress because Remi is not, love because it fucking hurts, and anger because I want to find out who did this. Who was so careless that they practically ripped my world apart?

Eventually, Isabel quiets and falls asleep.

"Jay, will you call a cab? We need to take Isabel home." And I need to get to Remi.

The man who greeted us at the door carefully approaches us, looking grim. "You can stay here until we get news about Remi."

"W-who are you?" I ask, still clinging to my baby.

"I'm Cody, Kiara's husband and Remi's best friend. He wouldn't trust Isabel with just anyone. I hope you don't mind that I brought her here. "

"Where's Kiara?" I ask robotically as we make our way down a hall and into a living room. My nose won't leave Isabel's hair, her scent and the weight of her against my chest comforting.

"She's with her brother."

My mind is foggy, and nothing makes sense.

"When can we see him, Dad?" The young boy who was playing with Isabel seems to be about eight or nine. I wonder if he's Kiara's son.

"As soon as he's out of surgery, Mom will call, bud." Cody pulls his son under his arm.

I don't want to wait for a phone call. I need to go now. "Really, we should be going."

Cody turns to me, still holding onto his son. "He told me about you."

"I don't understand."

"You're the one he'd risk his job for," Cody says with a smile. "You're the one he loves." Even though his voice is soft, the word "love" reverberates like the hum of a ghost fiddle.

Instead of feeling elated at this news, my face crumbles. Remi should have been the one to tell me, not his best friend.

Isabel starts to whimper, and Jay tries to pull her from me.

"Mija, I let Ian know where we are, and he's coming to pick me up. Let me take Isabel to my house," they implore. "She can stay with us for as long as you need."

Sniffing, I hold onto my baby, not wanting to give her up but knowing she'll be okay with Jay. I'm no good to anyone in my state right now, and every emotion I feel, she'll feel too. Remi taught me that. He also taught me there is magic in the dawn of a new day.

Each memory leaks out of my eyes in despondent tears. It seems so long ago now. Another lifetime.

"Yeah, okay." I wipe my eyes before brushing Isabel's hair from her face, waking her up. "You want to go to Unty Jay's house? Ian's coming, and I bet he'll make you cookies."

"That, he will. What do you say, cariño?"

Rubbing her eyes, she gives them a little nod and they pull her from me, giving her a big kiss on her chubby cheek.

"You be a good girl for Mommy, okay? Think about all the fun things you want to do when Remi gets better." Because he will get better. Life can't be that cruel, can it?

I kiss and rub her back several times before Jay leaves, holding my heart in their hands.

With my arms empty, the gravity of what's going on pulls me down again. A riptide of agony is what holds me under.

"He was supposed to meet me for lunch." My voice is full of woeful bewilderment.

How did this happen? We had plans. We're supposed to be enjoying burritos, and now he's lying on a hospital bed somewhere, fighting for his life. How did fate turn so cruel so fast? I feel robbed, cheated, inconsolable.

"I can't believe this is happening. I need to go to the hospital. I can't sit here and wait for a phone call." I don't mean to be so impatient, but my heart is going into cardiac arrest.

"It's okay. I understand. There's nothing you can do while he's in surgery, and I need to stay with Jackson," Cody says. "Remi wouldn't want you to be alone."

Even though he's right, the pull to be closer to Remi is the equivalent to the force of Saturn's magnetosphere—powerful and unrelenting.

"I just feel so helpless." I check my phone for something to do, as if Remi is going to call any second and say this was all a big misunderstanding.

Cody grabs some shot glasses from the cabinet and pours us both a finger of Gentleman Jack. He slides one over to me.

"Thanks." I twist the glass around on the counter.

"I'm sorry. Did they tell you what happened?"

"No. I'm not family," I say, dejected.

We *are*, though. We're the perfect little family. We take care of each other, share our lives. Remi is our missing piece.

"In Remi's eyes, you are family. You and Isabel are the most important people in his life. I guess that's protocol, but..." He shrugs a glum shoulder before holding up his glass. "To Remi's speedy recovery. May he be back to his normal pain-in-the-ass self in no time."

It's a cute joke and if I wasn't so upset, I might have laughed.

Cody takes his shot and so do I, letting the burn coat my churning stomach, saying a private toast in my head: *To the long life we will have together.* When he goes to pour me another shot, I hold out my hand. "Thanks, but I need to be clear-headed for when they discharge Remi. I want to be there to pick him up. To bring him home ... with me."

Remi's best friend gives me a sad smile. "You know, he saved Isabel's life."

As if this situation wasn't already fucked up, I now get the image of my baby laying lifeless on the ground, her lips blue and rosy cheeks ashen. Her stare vacant, the inquisitive twinkle in her eye snuffed out.

My world shatters, and a new wave of grief falls over me. Bile races up my esophagus, burning away the resolve holding me together.

"Tell me."

"There was some kind of cat rescue event set up on the sidewalk by Isabel's school. She wanted to pet the cats."

I give a bitter laugh. "She's obsessed with them."

"When the rescue person opened the gate to help Isabel inside, one of the cats darted out and ran into the street. Isabel yanked herself away from Remi and chased after the cat."

Of course she did. She'd save a spider in trouble.

"Remi ran after her." Blowing out a breath, he continues, "Here's the part that's messed up though." He scratches the top of his head with the back of his thumb. "From what the witness said, the few cars that were moving along the street pulled over and stopped. But one came flying down the street. It didn't slow down. The witness said it was as if the car was purposefully going after someone."

I stop breathing and almost pass out. "What? Why would someone…" Why would anyone want to hurt an innocent person? It's unfathomable and vile.

Unless … purposely targeted?

All the times I felt like I was being watched come to the forefront of my mind. In one way or another, I was with Remi each time. Was someone aiming for Isabel, knowing Remi would go after her? I can't imagine he has many enemies, just as I can't fathom anyone purposely hurting a baby.

"Did the person stop? Do they know who it is?" My thoughts won't stop racing, but when I glance at Cody, I'm shocked still at the answer in his sad and disapproving eyes.

"No, the fucking bastard ran off," he spits. "Remi barely got to her in time to push her out of harm's way. The car hit him head-on."

Clutching my chest, I double over, having trouble finding oxygen to breathe.

"I'd literally die for that baby."

"Oh God. Oh no, no, no." The back of my hand presses against my mouth, but I can't keep the sob from bursting out of my diaphragm. I need to see him. I need to go. I can't just sit here.

I pace the kitchen like a caged dragon, ready to raze the town to find whomever is responsible for this tragedy. This abominable moment changed the course of my, Isabel's, and Remi's lives forever.

We were destined for happiness and love. Movie nights with popcorn and stolen touches. Family vacations and school plays. Sunday concerts with Gram. Flirty dinners, blithesome breakfasts, and quiet moments just after waking.

The days ahead were supposed to be the sickly sweet honeymoon phase of first love. We're supposed to nauseate everyone around us and laugh about it. Tell Kiara and Isabel the good news.

Instead we got this—pain, misery, and suffering. Darkness eclipsing a bright future.

"If we ever find out who did this, I'm going to kill them." Cody's threat faintly pierces through the haze of sorrow.

How could this have happened? Who would do such a thing?

Fury rips through my veins, blistering my blood. "If I don't find them first."

Though it was only a couple of hours, it felt like years waiting for Kiara to call with news. Cody brought me up to speed on who Kiara actually is to Remi—I can't believe he didn't tell me she was his sister. He alluded to it earlier, but it didn't penetrate the fog of shock I was in. *Am* in.

Cody said it's something Remi feels funny about. Like he couldn't get a job so his sister had to hire him, which couldn't be further from the truth. Remi is a damn excellent caregiver to Isabel and me. Hell, to everyone he meets. He's the exception. The sparkly diamond in muddy waters. The ray of hope when everything goes to shit. Solid, reliable, and the best person I've ever met.

When Cody gets off the phone, he relays the message to me. "He's still critical in the ICU, but he has his own room. They are only allowing two visitors at a time. I know he'd want to see you."

I nod. I need to see Remi for myself, and yet I'm scared. How can I stay strong when I see him battered and bruised, hooked up to all these tubes? What if his prognosis is poor? Could I handle watching the man I love die? Grief threatens to obliterate me.

He was strong for you the other night. Now, you have to be strong for him. He deserves optimism, patience, and encouragement. Three things I struggle with, but for him I can rally, no matter how dire the circumstances. Regardless of what the doctors say, I'm in his corner, rooting him on. I won't count him out. Not ever.

"I need to see him too."

The first thing I notice when we enter the hospital is the nauseating smell of antiseptic and death. There's an ominous feeling, but I refuse to give in to negativity. Remi needs me to be positive. Just like he is every day of his life.

It's crazy how beautiful this day started compared to its horrifying ending. One moment, I'm in Jay's office laughing, the next I'm barely breathing standing in front of the closed door to Remi's ICU room. Cody's in the waiting room with Jackson, and I really appreciate that he let me go see his best friend first.

My knock is timid because I know what I'll find on the other side of the door—proof that this nightmare is real.

The door creeps open, and a puffy-eyed Kiara peeks out. I haven't seen her since I first interviewed Child Care Connection. She was poised with sleek straight black hair to her chin, accentuating the curve of her heart-shaped face and plush lips ... like Remi's. Her appearance is a stark contrast from when I met her. Back then, if someone had told me how bound she and I would be, I wouldn't have believed them.

Her forehead creases. "Miranda? Is Isabel okay?"

The steady beep of Remi's heart rhythm rings through my ears like a ticking time bomb. One I desperately want to dismantle. "S-she's good. I'm here..." Christ, this is hard. We were supposed to confront Kiara together. "Can I see him? *Please*. I just need to see him." I barely get the last word out before I burst into tears.

Brown eyes narrow and sharpen. "You're her," Kiara accuses, making my head spin.

"Huh?" I sniff.

"The one he was talking about. The one he's in love with." She slaps her forehead and clutches her hair. "Oh my God, why didn't I see it?" she asks no one.

"Um, w-we..." I clear my throat and compose myself. "We were going to tell you."

"Tonight. He called and said he was bringing the woman he's seeing to meet us tonight." Her face pinches, and her eyes well up. She pulls me to her and wraps her arms around me.

A modicum of relief at Kiara easily accepting us settles in my restless soul.

"He's pretty banged up. His head took the brunt of his fall." Her sigh is long and tired. "There is a fracture to his skull and a possibility of a traumatic brain injury."

"Oh God, *no.*" Those three words kick me right in the gut, knocking the wind out of my lungs.

"They said he slipped into a coma because his body is in shock. They are watching for swelling in the brain. The next forty-eight hours are critical." Kiara's chin quivers. "When he wakes up, he might be a little different." She drags her hand down her face. "But the important thing is, he *will* wake up. I know my brother. He's a little shit, but he's a fighter." She grabs my hand and squeezes. "Come on."

I need Remi to wake up like I need my next breath. "Whatever happens, I'm here." My severe voice cracks. "We'll get through it together." I'll take him any way I can get him. He's with us no matter what because that's what families are about.

Hand in hand, we approach Remi's bedside. Even though my brain conjured horrible images of him when I found out about the accident, nothing prepared me for the actuality of seeing him like this.

He has a wrapping around his head, and the left side of his face is all bandaged up. His left arm did not fare better—it's wrapped in a cast, shoulder to wrist. The color of his skin is an unhealthy gray. Instantly, I miss his cheeky grin with winking dimples and the mischievous glint of his eyes promising fun and joy.

"Oh, Manny." Without hesitation, I grab his hand. It's limp, but it's as warm as always, and that gives me a shred of comfort. He's hooked up to IVs and tubes, and there is a machine helping him breathe. Kneeling on the floor, I rest my lips on his hand. I can't hold back my tears, so I let myself have a moment before I toughen up and be strong for Remi.

"I'll just be out in the waiting room." Kiara's voice floats over me, but a thought enters my head.

I turn to her. "Gram?"

"He took you to meet her, huh?" With a watery smile, she shakes her head as if to say, *how am I the last to know?* "She's on her way. One of the residents is dropping her off."

When she disappears behind the door, I wipe my face and buck the fuck up.

"Hey, I need you to know something, so listen to me, okay?" Grabbing a tissue, I dab my eyes and wipe my nose. "There's a little girl out there who believes you hung the moon. Her mom thinks you're pretty extraordinary too." I hardly recognize the person I was before Remi. It's certainly different from who I am now.

Thinking about how uptight, angry, and bitter I was makes me sad for that woman. She didn't believe in it at all. She was so caught up in her anxiety that she missed what was really important—giving quality time to the ones she loves. Being present and enjoying every moment because the next minute isn't promised.

"I was drowning before you. So very lost. You put me back together." My throat is sore from suppressing my tears, and my heart feels like dying. "You showed me how good real love could be." Thinking of him holding me together in my kitchen sucks the life force out of me, and I sag. "You, my love, truly are the Jedi Knight of Nannies." I brush my fingers across the top of his hand. "Oh, and I love you. I meant to tell you that." Irrational anger bursts through me. "I *should* have told you that."

The more I talk to him, the more consistent his heart beat is both in tone and across the monitor's screen. My eyes squeeze tight, and I take a moment of gratitude. He's here with me.

"I know you can hear me. Your heart gives you away." My smile is wobbly like the tentative hold on my emotions. "It always does." He's probably worried about Isabel, so I need to set his mind at ease. "Isabel is physically fine. She's missing you, but... You saved her life. Now, you have to save yours." I clench my teeth because I know a wail is making its way up my esophagus and I need to stop it. "Please, we need you. *I* need you."

Picking up his hand, I place his palm on my cheek. And close my eyes. "I'm imagining us kissing. You feel so good, like everything I always imagined I wanted when I was young. My very own Prince Charming." I brush my mouth against his palm. "I'm your queen, so I command you to get better." My voice is dressed in false bravado while my conviction is brittle.

He doesn't move, but the strong tone of his heart monitor tells me he's still in there, and brain injury or not, he can hear me. Better yet, he recognizes my voice. That's what I choose to focus on, and a whisper of hope stirs inside of me.

"When you open those beautiful browns, I'll be here waiting for you. I'll be the one taking care of *you* for a change." I enclose his hand with both of mine. "All you have to do is come back to me."

Because if you don't, I'll be as good as a walking corpse. My heart might beat, but my soul will be empty.

Chapter 24

Ready For Battle

Mae

THE SOFT KNOCK ON Remi's door makes me jump. I'm not sure how long I've been by his side—a few minutes or a few hours. Time seems to stand still when a loved one's life hangs in the balance.

I open the door and find a grim-looking Gram on Kiara's arm. Shoulders hunched and bones fragile, she looks so different from the feisty showgirl I met just a couple of days ago.

She finds Remi right away, turning white as a ghost. I step aside so she can go to him, but she grabs my hand.

Kiara nods at the question in my eyes. For some reason, they want me to stay.

"My sweet boy." Letting go of me, Gram circles the bed. Her weathered hands hover over her grandson's prone form as if to assess the damage or find a place she can touch that isn't bruised. "Oh, Remington, no." Her body trembles, and her lips quiver.

Hot tears sear down my face, and my stomach clenches with hollow aches. The irony that I control every aspect of my life but I cannot do a damn thing about this doesn't escape me.

"This shouldn't have happened to you. Not you." Granada chants, "Not you," over and over, broken and frail. She wobbles on her feet, and I rush to her side and pull her to me. Kiara isn't far behind, wrapping her arms around us both. Her sobs echo in the dark room.

"Gram, listen to me. He's going to pull through. Please." Kiara tries to hold onto faith for all of us. "He's still here, breathing. I'm focusing on that."

For the first time in my life, I feel like I have a true sister. It may be strange since I just met Kiara, but standing next to her in Remi's corner is comforting. Almost as though our unified thoughts have power. As long as we uplift him and believe that he's going to pull through, he will.

Layers of emotions ripple through me: sadness, gratitude, solidarity, but most of all … hope.

We all stay in the room until the nurse sees there are three in here and kicks us out. Remi needs his rest—that's the only reason I'm willing to leave him for a few hours.

I need to check on Isabel. Guilt eats away at my gut. I should be with her. She had a traumatic experience today, witnessing something no child should. I grasp my hair, pulling at the roots. Jay's taking great care of her, I know that, but I just need to hear her voice and I know she needs to hear mine. She is my strength.

Once we have Gram settled next to Cody and Jackson, Kiara pulls me aside. "I wanted to talk to you for a minute." She has a look of disapproval on her face, and I wonder if she's going to give me shit about being with Remi. I brace myself for a confrontation. "My parents are coming. I told them to wait until Remi wakes up because they will just add to the chaos. But my mother refuses."

I nod, unsure of what she's getting at. If that was Isabel laying there, a tsunami couldn't drag me away. "I understand."

"No, I don't think you do." She lets out a long sigh. "My parents can be … difficult. I'm not sure how much Remi has told you about them, but my mother's mental health isn't in the best shape, and my father…" Remi already warned me about him. She shakes her head, her features tightening. "He's an entitled asshole. He will come here, ranting and raving about *his* son, causing us all to want to kill him."

My hollow stomach twists. "I can keep a cool head if that's what you're worried about." This is not the time nor place to challenge his parents.

"That's not it. He just might say some really … awful things. He hates that Remi lives here, and I know he's going to blame me for Remi's condition." Her eyes search mine. "He might say something nasty to you too."

I rear back. "He doesn't even know me."

"He doesn't need to," she replies. "He sees anyone who will keep Remi here as a threat. It's not going to be pretty." A deep frown crosses her features. "He hits below the belt, Mae. I can handle myself, but I don't want you to take anything he says to heart."

Not likely.

"I won't." Nothing will keep me from being here for Remi. He'd do the exact same thing for me.

"Good. Just steer clear of my parents, okay?"

"Sure." But if his asshole father starts ragging on his son, I will take it as a personal affront and put him in his place below the heel of my stilettos—metaphorically, of course. I need to keep a cool head for Remi's sake, but I can still be a calculated player.

When Kiara goes back to join her family, I call to check on Isabel.

"Mommy!" she answers my video call with chocolate on her face and a sucker in her fist.

The sight fills some of the hollowness churning inside me. "Is Unty Jay giving you too much candy?"

"Don't blame me. I told Ian—he's bribing her so that he's her favorite," Jay defends themself.

Ian's surfer-boy looks appear in the frame. "I am her favorite. I don't have to bribe anyone. Isn't that right, Isabel?"

"Yeah!"

Ian gives Jay a look that says, *Told ya so.*

"I thought Unty Jay is your favorite?" I tease because I know exactly what she's going to say.

"Yeah!" she agrees, and Jay gives Ian a smug look.

"How about Remi, is he your favorite too?" I don't let my voice crack when I say his name.

"Yeah! Mommy too!" Thus, proving my point—Isabel loves everyone.

"It's safe to say, whomever is playing with her at the moment is her favorite. So, if she blows chunks later, Ian will have to clean it up."

Ian's nose wrinkles. "Okay, Isabelly, no more candy for you."

Isabel pops the sucker out of her mouth. "Emmie come?"

Speaking of her favorite people...

"The doctor had to give Remi some medicine that made him sleepy." My eyes sting, but I keep my voice light. "He's going to rest and when he's all better, he will go wherever you want him to."

Her bottom lip sticks out, slaying my heart.

"I know, baby. Believe me, Remi misses you too." This doesn't assuage her fears as her face pinches before her mouth falls open and a cry bursts out.

Jay rubs her back. "Shhh, darling. He's going to be just fine. Why don't we draw Remi a picture? I'm sure when he sees it, he'll get better fast."

Rubbing her nose, she nods.

"Thanks, Jay. I don't know what I'd do without you."

"I would say dissolve into a vat of self-destruction, but it isn't the right time, so I'll just give you a condescending smile instead."

This makes me laugh.

"There she is." My best friend grins back. "Everything is great here, so don't worry about a thing."

"I don't. Love you." I sniff.

"Love you too, Mars Bars."

When the line goes dead, I hold my phone to my chest and take a moment to give into my emotions.

My daughter almost died today. The thought sends me reeling. In a single second, I could have lost my reason for breathing. It's hard not to think about the what-ifs. Would this tragedy have happened had I taken the whole day off to be with them? If they'd been just ten minutes earlier or later, could they have avoided it altogether?

I think about all the times I spent working, my mind constantly running numbers, stressing about clients, and being bitter over temperamental, sexist investors. My body may have been home after work hours, but my focus never left the office. A sour taste coats my tongue, making me sick.

I used to think time was money, but if this situation has taught me anything, it's that time is a precious commodity—its monetary value priceless—when it comes to spending it with the people we love. I lost a lot of it with Isabel and Remi. The fact of the matter is, without the people we love, it's all arbitrary. It doesn't matter.

I close my eyes, picturing Isabel's chocolatey face. *She's perfect.* Relief does not come because I know Remi's life is on the line.

Happiness is a fickle beast. When I finally gave into it, it was stripped away just as fast.

The days ahead are bleak, and going back to the house without Remi is incomprehensible. Sure, it's still standing, held up by lumber and masonry, but it's as empty as I feel inside. Sad and hollow. How do I make it a home without him? *You make a mess of shitty breakfasts, sing out of tune, and you keep doing it with a goddamn smile on your face, no matter how bad you feel.* Isabel deserves the best of me, and so does Remi.

If he doesn't wake up, I'm... No, he will. He has to. My heart constricts and folds, causing a sharp, unrelenting throb in my chest.

I did it. I leaned on someone. I let them in. Gave him parts of me no one has ever seen, parts that I didn't even know I was capable of giving. Let my daughter love him. Let *myself* fall in love with him.

Staring at the ceiling, I want to scream, *Why?* The tears fall down my face, hot and relentless, dripping over my neck and evaporating into misty air. Every single one is a wish, a demand, a bargain, a reason.

Please give him back. He needs to wake up now. If he just opens his eyes, I'll never take time for granted again. He said he'd never leave.

"He promised," I whisper.

It seems like years of sitting in the waiting room on uncomfortable vinyl chairs. We all glance at each other every so often, but no one says anything. What *is* there to say? We're all in our own state of trepidation.

Kiara is fiddling with her paper coffee cup. Cody paces like a caged animal. Jackson is playing on his phone. Granada is praying.

My forehead is buried in my hand, staving off the headache that wants to tear through my skull. I haven't eaten since this morning, nor tried to.

"Going without meals won't help, Queeny," Remi's gravelly voice floats through my mind, and my lids slide shut so I can savor the sound.

I don't think I can swallow anything until I know you're okay, I respond to the ghost in my head. *Please, be okay.*

A man in scrubs enters the waiting room, his round face devoid of emotion. "Family for Remington Arison?"

We all jolt alert.

"I'm Doctor Raj, the patient's resident. If you'll follow me." He directs us to a small room off of the hallway. "As you know, Mr. Arison has suffered major trauma to his head, causing his brain to shut down. We need to stay positive but also be realistic in our expectations," he explains, folding his arms over his chest.

My breathing is choppy, and I feel like the walls are going to close in at any moment.

Kiara holds onto her husband. "Such as?"

Granada grips my arm.

"He may need extensive physical therapy. We are still unsure of the state of his mental faculties. If he wakes—"

"*When*, Doctor," Kiara interjects. "When he wakes."

Dr. Raj concedes, "When he wakes up, we need to be prepared if he's a different Remington than you've known."

"What are you saying?" Cody asks the question no one wants to think about.

"He could experience anything from agitation, irritability, amnesia, to physiological damage or mental impairment." The doctor speaks impassively while my insides shred and my dreams smash.

It's hard to imagine the grinning, happy man-boy—who whistles in my kitchen as he makes broccoli-apple cookies—bed bound, wasting away silent and stoic. Or worse, agitated and angry. That's not who he is.

Unable to hold the severity of the situation any longer, I collapse against the wall. I don't care how he comes back to me, just that he does. Come what may, we will get through it together.

"He's tachycardic, Dr. Raj begins again, and I want to cover my ears. I don't think I want to hear much more. "We can't get his heart rate down."

"What does that mean?" Kiara whimpers, her fingers pressed to her mouth.

"We're moving him into a bigger room that will fit all of you," he replies. "In times like these, a family's love does more than medicine can do. Your job is to stay positive and let him know you're there," he says. "The next forty-eight hours are crucial." Dr. Raj's tone is flat, factual. He leaves us as impassively as he came.

We slump in our respective chairs, crestfallen, until the nurse brings us to Remi's new room. It's spacious and smells like bleach covered with fragrance, but there's seating for everyone. I take the seat next to Remi's bed, and Granada sits on the other side.

"We're all here, Remi," I whisper close to his ear as my hand slides over his. I almost expect him to wrap his fingers around mine, and my chest pangs when he doesn't.

"You're going to get through this," Kiara speaks up. "Mae, Gram, and I will make sure of it." She swallows several times, trying in vain to compose herself before she can talk again. "We love you." Her voice cracks and chokes, stirring emotion to the surface for all of us.

"Remi," Gram calls. "Everyone at Hope Village is praying for you." A small smirk cracks through her sorrow. "Well, except for Charlie. He's cursing God for being so stupid. You're the only one who can sing a good Frank Sinatra."

Remembering the beautiful day of their concert and what happened after is both a blessing and pure heartbreak. I wasted so much time and treated him like a toy. If I could rewind the clock, I would have told him how I felt when he declared himself. He's so brave, more than I will ever be. Courage is something else he taught me.

Reaching out with the back of my fingers, I barely stroke Remi's exposed and unbruised cheek. Just feeling his warmth has a sedative effect on my brain. As long as he's breathing, I can too.

"I miss that devilish grin, love," I sniff, trying to keep my nose from dripping. "You've got to come back to us. We have so many beautiful memories left to make." Taking hold of his hand, I brush my thumb across his skin, giving him any amount of comfort I can. His heart rate progressively calms, and so does mine. I send a silent thanks into the atmosphere.

He knows we're here.

Cody takes his son home to grab an overnight bag for Kiara, so she pulls up a chair and sits next to me. "I hope you don't mind if I stay with him tonight." Her chin wrinkles. "He's my baby brother. I need to—" She breaks down.

Rubbing her back, I try to put her at ease. "I understand. He needs you too."

She gives me a grateful look.

Wheel of Fortune is playing low on the television. It steals our attention every once in a while, but no one is really watching. It's been a few hours of sitting, pacing, and holding Remi's limp hand. We're all a bit subdued until the door swings open and an older man whisks through it, startling a little when he notices me.

"Kiara," he greets in an even tone.

She jerks to a stand and allows him to give her a cheek kiss, although she's quick to distance herself after. "Hello, sir," she says in the meekest voice I've ever heard from her.

"Who's taking care of my son?" the man asks the room, but no one answers.

Following behind him is a bone-thin woman, with her arms wrapped around her ribs so tightly it's like she's holding herself together. Her chin dips further into her chest as she walks through the door.

Oh damn. Those are Remi's parents.

"I want the chief of staff, *now*." His conversational tone turns sharp, puncturing the bubble of serenity we created around Remi.

I can see where Remi gets his dashing looks. The man is a silver fox—there's no denying it. But where Remi's brown eyes are warm and kind, his father's are as black as coal.

Granada takes a cleansing breath as if preparing for war.

Kiara raises placating palms. "Father, please keep your voice down. Remi needs everyone to be calm." Her whisper is as strong as a rattle on a snake.

The man looks at his daughter with a sneer. "Don't you talk to me like that." He smooths out his features when he side-eyes me. "If it wasn't for you, he wouldn't be in this mess." He points his finger as if it's a gun threatening his daughter, but his demeanor is entirely too composed for the acerbic words coming out of his mouth.

"Please, sir. We're all upset. Can't we just be cordial for once?" Kiara's eyes round, pleading. "For Remi?"

It's as if the man finally remembers the reason we are all here. His lips thin as he approaches the bed. "Goddamnit, Remington. What in the hell did you get yourself into?" He scolds his son like Remi is some kind of a juvenile delinquent, when he's a fucking superhero. Something any father should be proud of.

Granada gets up and approaches Remi's mother hovering by the door. There's a slight hesitation, but they soon embrace. Gram squeezes her eyes tight as she holds her daughter close.

I stare at them with longing because I wish I had that relationship with my mother. I need her now more than ever.

The exact opposite of her husband, Remi's mother is gaunt. She has delicate bone structure, which would make a cover girl jealous. But her cheeks are sunken in and her eyes are hollow, revealing the turmoil she's fighting inside. Remi's plush lips that speak with such sweetness are his mother's.

"Come. I want you to meet someone special." Gram circumvents her son-in-law, not sparing him a glance, and pulls her daughter towards me.

Standing, I smooth down my shirt. "Hello." I hold out my hand, but the woman only looks at it. This is uncomfortable, to say the least.

Gram gives her daughter an encouraging nod. "This is Mae. She and Remi are close. He saved her daughter's life."

Remi's father whips his head up, freezing me with a cold stare, but he has yet to say a word to me otherwise. I don't crumble under men like him. Never have. Never will. If he thinks he can intimidate me, he's sadly mistaken.

"Mae?" Gram takes my extended hand and places it into the woman's. "This is Evangeline, Remington's mother."

Smiling, I give her hand a small shake. "I'm sorry we're meeting under these circumstances, Mrs. Arison."

Remi's mother sucks in a breath and snaps towards her husband.

"It's Fairchild," the man corrects as if he's rectifying a high school classroom. "Remington is a Fairchild." He doubles down, sending Granada a hateful look, and I want to step in between them as a shield. Remi's father isn't threatening, per se, but something is off. He's being calm and cool now, but something tells me he has a thin restraint over his simmering anger.

Gram shakes her head in disgust but doesn't address her indignant son-in-law.

"Here, Evangeline, take my seat."

Uneasy, Evangeline slides past me and sits where I once was. Granada stands behind her, both hands on her shoulders. Remi's mother looks so sick and lost, my heart cracks for her.

"You can talk to him if you want. He can hear you," I mollify the woman, who looks so defeated compared to the man ready to go on a rampage.

For a minute, the only noise in the room is the steady beeping of the heart monitor.

Remi's mother speaks, "Son, I'm here." Her voice is scratchy, like she's not used to using it. Her thin fingers stroke Remi's arm. "Mommy's here, my beautiful boy."

Remi's dad clicks his tongue. "Always with the coddling. He's a fucking man, Eva." He pulls Remi's chart off the wall and scans it, seemingly displeased. "They have my son under a goddamn resident," he scoffs, exhaling through his nose. "We should consider arranging a medical charter." The man scans the room, but he's addressing no one. "We should take him back to Los Angeles, to the best neurologists in the country."

While Mr. Fairchild's mouth is saying "should", his cold features suggest he'll do whatever he damn well pleases. Is this "reasonable guy" act for my benefit?

"Remi's is right where he needs to be," Kiara speaks up. "If you put him through transfer now, as precarious as he is, it could do more harm than good. You know that, Father." She's struggling to keep her tone in check. After a long-suffering sigh, she adds, "Your son is in the best place he could possibly be."

At Kiara's mild defiance, Evangeline clams up, and I want to fight for her. I know an abused woman when I see one. I have a sneaking suspicion her drug abuse is a direct effect of her husband's verbal and, possibly, physical assault. I scan her arms for bruises that I don't find, but there is a nagging intuition I can't shake. This woman is in as much danger as her son right now.

All artificial sincerity dissolves from Remi's father. It's as if his skin peels back, revealing the beast disguised as a man. Yep, he's a sadist. No wonder Remi changed his last name.

"I will do whatever it is I deem fit for my son. You, above all people, should understand." He flays his daughter with a glare. "I'd hate for something to happen to Jackson and *you* having to make such a difficult choice." His tone is conversational, but his words are menacing.

Evangeline visibly shakes as Kiara's stuttered gasp reverberates around the room. Something else is going on here. Something way deeper than a man upset about his son being in a coma.

"Stop that," Granada admonishes. "This is not the place for your condemnation." She points her crooked forefinger to him. "It's been a long travel day for you. You just found out your son is in a coma, so maybe you *should* sit down and ... reflect."

Again, everything seems just under the surface, but the air is thick with tension. A dull knife could still be used as a weapon.

"Listen to me, Granada. I will take my son and your waste of a daughter away from here, and you'll never see them again." He points at Remi. "Do you think he's in any position to protest?" My muscles tense, ready to jump in front of any danger. "This is an *opportunity*," he says. I want to vomit at the hint of elation in his voice.

I'm a black mambo ready to strike. If he tries anything with Remi, I'll fucking kill him first.

"You should take Gram's advice. You're not helping anyone." Even though he hasn't said a word to me, I want to make myself known. My voice may be as serene as his, but my spine is stiff, ready for battle.

Gram squeezes my wrist in warning.

Mr. Fairchild smiles, but it's the kind an alligator would wear before devouring its prey. Unfortunately for him, I'm no salamander. I'm a motherfucking lioness, and we're in my territory. I will happily tear up this asshole, limb from limb.

"What's not helping is your presence here. You're *not* family." When he sees I'm not flappable at his insults, he goes for the kill. "It should be your daughter laying in that bed. Not my son." This bastard likes to go for the jugular.

I smile imperceptibly. I've played versions of this game before. "If you think you're scaring me, you can save it." I keep my voice low and pleasant. Remi doesn't need to feel the stress in this room.

"I wouldn't be so flippant, darling. You have no idea what you're up against," he goads with a candied smile.

I won't waste my energy focusing on silly words from a lunatic. Refusing to engage, my attention doesn't leave Remi's form. I hear rather than see the asshole come closer to me. By the shrinking shoulders of his wife, I know he's too close for comfort. Yet I remain unflappable.

"If I had to run around with your brat all day, I'd throw myself in front of a moving vehicle too." He talks so conversationally, like we're discussing an arbitrary situation, not his own flesh and blood with a possible traumatic brain injury.

"Father!" Kiara scolds.

Bile burns up my esophagus, and my body shakes with rage. Again, I say nothing because I have no response right now. None that is appropriate or helpful to the situation. Remi needs positivity, and that's exactly what he'll get from me.

"You're despicable," Granada spits through her teeth.

"And you're a bitch past her prime and her worth. Not that you were ever worth much," he grumbles, odious. "I should have known addicts breed other addicts."

What the fuck is happening? Does this man really need to spew his vitriol next to his comatose son?

"Stop!" Evangeline finds her voice.

The bed starts shaking, and my heart collapses on itself. Remi's body is convulsing while his heart rate is going wild. His choked gasps are a thousand serrated knives piercing my skin. Clutching my chest, I start to hyperventilate. I need to do something, but my body is frozen in panic.

A rational thought cracks through the icy trauma. I cry out in anguish, rising to my feet and running to the door. "Help! It's Remi! Please!" A horde of medical personnel rush into the room and I stagger back, sliding against the wall. "Save him! Please!" I wail, tearing out my hair.

"Everyone out!" the doctor yells, but I'm immobile as I watch on in horror. "Two milligrams of Ativan!" he shouts.

Remi's body jerks and jolts like a ragdoll. It's terrifying to watch, but I can't for the life of me look away. I'm being shredded alive from the inside. *So much pain.* "God, no. Remi. No!"

My breath comes out in shallow pants, and I can't seem to take in enough oxygen. My vision goes spotty then blurry, and I physically feel the moment my legs turn to jelly.

Someone wraps their arms around me and pulls me out of the room. I try to reach out to my love, unwilling to leave him but unable to fight off the panic threatening to pull me under. "No, please!"

The room spins before everything goes dark.

Chapter 25

A Lioness Defending Her Pride

Mae

"I'm right here, baby." His beautiful form stands in front of me, happy, full of vitality, and more breathtaking than ever.

Oh, thank God. "Remi?" It was only a nightmare. A horrific illusion gripping my mind. But when I go to wrap myself around him, my arms swipe through nothing.

"That's not going to work anymore," he says with a smirk.

My brows smash together. "Why not?"

"Because I'm dead, Queeny."

Agony's fire blazes up my back, scorching my flesh and my resolve. There's a shrill ringing in my head. It crescendos into an ear-splitting pitch. I'm in utter hell.

Ice-cold water douses my face and I snap awake, wheezing and choking.

"You're okay, sweetie. Just take a deep breath." A loving British accent replaces the blaring torment. A woman wearing scrubs strokes my hair and helps me respirate.

"R-remi? P-please," I beg.

"Oh, honey, he's stable now." Compassion is written all over her face. My cheeks puff out in an exhale. "That's right. Let's manage your oxygen intake and calm your heart rate." When she sees the steady rise and fall of my chest, she smiles.

"I'm nurse Vicky, and I'm here for anything you need." She hands me a cup of cold water.

I take a greedy drink. "What happened? Can I see him?"

Her pretty eyes turn weary. "He had a seizure," she explains. "It's not uncommon for comatose patients to have an episode within the first couple of days of being under." She covers me up with a warm blanket, and that's when I realize I'm on a recliner in an empty hospital room.

"Why am I here? I need to get to Remi." I attempt to sit up.

She gently holds me in place. "They're not allowing any visitors until tomorrow. Another seizure could be devastating for him." Vicky wraps a cuff around my arm and takes my blood pressure. "One twenty-seven over ninety. It's a little high, but I'd expect it considering what you're going through." She pats my shoulder. "You're here for some privacy, and there are a couple of officers here to talk to you."

"Oh." I tamp down my panic over needing to see that Remi is okay with my own eyes.

Vicky gives me a watery smile. "Stay positive, love. I've seen patients worse off, and they pull through. Remi's youth puts the odds in his favor."

Nurse Vicky's reassurance adds to my feeble hope, making it stronger. Not as strong as before the dream, but not completely debilitated either.

When she leaves the room, Officer Taylor and Detective Gracyk enter. "Ms. Keller, we're sorry to bother you at a time like this, but we need to ask you a few questions."

"Is this about Mr. Fairchild?" I can't keep the disgust out of my tone. "Because I want to file a restraining order."

The women look at each other in confusion before turning back to me.

"That's not why we're here, though it's something we can discuss," Officer Taylor says.

Gracyk pulls out a notepad. "Do you know of anyone who would want to hurt Remington Arison?"

The question is shocking. "Absolutely not. He's the most genuine person you'd ever meet. I can't imagine..." After witnessing Mr. Fairchild's utter lack of humanity, I guess I can.

"Ms. Keller, if you have someone in mind, please speak up," Taylor urges.

"Mr. Fairchild. He said he saw this as an opportunity to bring his son back to Los Angeles." I spit out the words, desperate to cleanse my mouth of them.

The detective is taking notes as the officer speaks a code into the radio on her shoulder.

"One more question, Ms. Keller," Detective Gracyk says. "Does he know a Laurel Smith?"

My brows knit together. The name nags at the back of my mind, but I can't place it. "I'm not sure. He's never mentioned anyone by that name." I scrape my fingers through my hair. "You might want to ask Kiara or Granada—they are close family."

"We have, and they couldn't identify her either," Gracyk explains. "We're classifying this as attempted murder. Witnesses say that the car was aiming to hurt someone. We looked up the license plate, but it was a rental. The rental agency gave us the driver's information, which looks pretty generic. We're not sure if Laurel Smith is an alias."

"We do have video surveillance, and we're waiting for forensics to identify the face of the driver." Officer Taylor hands me her card. "We'll be in touch."

I'm rooted in shock as they leave. Who on earth would want to hurt Remi? Even if his father wanted his son back in California, would he really have him almost fatally wounded? It doesn't make sense.

It's then I remember all those times I felt like I was being watched. Maybe it wasn't about me at all. Each time, Remi was either with me or showed up right after, like when Isabel and I were at the fair. Maybe his father had hired someone to investigate Remi and it was a job gone wrong. So many things just don't add up.

Sitting here doing nothing makes me anxious, so I head to the waiting room to see if there is any news about Remi's condition. Kiara is pacing outside of her brother's room. From her creased forehead to her stooped posture, worry etches all over her demeanor.

Anxiety forms a thorny ball, lodging in my chest. "Any news?" I ask, approaching her.

The question startles her. "Oh, um... They stabilized him, but they don't want him to have any stimulation for twenty-four hours." Throwing herself in a seat, she buries her head in her hands. "I don't know how I'm going to do this, Mae," she says on a quiet sob. "I'm responsible for him. I don't know what I'm going to do." Her shoulders shake with the weight of the world setting upon them.

"Hey, he's going to get better." I pull her hands from her face. "You told me yourself, he's a fighter. Whatever happens, I'm here too."

"Thank you," she sniffs. "I know he will, it's just..." Kiara zones out, looking as if she's trying to solve a quantum mechanics equation.

"What is it?"

"While we have medical insurance for our employees, it's only going to cover a small portion of Remi's hospital stay. Not to mention the physical therapy he'll need when he wakes up." Kiara catches my stare. "Because he *will* wake up." She shakes her head. "I can probably mortgage the house." Her cheeks blow out. "Maybe sell a kidney."

Even though I know the answer, I ask anyway. "Your parents won't cover their son's medical costs?"

She recoils, and her lip curls. "Sure, my parents would pay for it all but then demand my brother move back to Los Angeles and become a fucking plastic surgeon." Her left eye twitches. "I'll not have him survive this so he can die a slow death under my father's control."

"Remi mentioned he had a brother. Have you talked to him?"

Kiara gives a harsh laugh. "Benjamin is the oldest and Father's flying monkey. He's always resented that my mother doted on Remi, her baby." A small smile graces her grim face. "He was the apple of our eye. Gram, Mom, and I were always huddled around Remi. He was just so sunny all the time. No matter how mean my brother was or how cruel my father was, Remi never let it dim his light." She's lost in memory—a good one, by the softening of her features. "I had to kick his ass a few times." Mischief glints in her eye when she turns to me. "He was my little brother, after all. He could be a jackass at times, but we were always close."

Placing my hand on Kiara's arm, I reassure her. "I'm in your corner. Whatever happens, I'm not going to abandon either of you."

She grabs my hands and squeezes in solidarity.

The weight of those words has been crushing me for the last few hours of sitting, pacing, and aching to see the man I love. Each minute feels like an eternity. We're stuck in purgatory, and that's given me a lot of time to think, search my soul for the purpose.

Remi and Isabel are my world—it simply won't turn if a part of it is missing. When he wakes up, he'll need to concentrate on getting himself better. Physical, speech, and psychiatric therapy, plus doctor's—possibly specialist's—appointments could put Remi into bankruptcy, ruining his whole future. Even if he gets a clean bill of health, his financial status will be in critical condition. Healthcare is a scam in this country. No matter the thousands we pay into it each year, it doesn't provide much when we need it most. I don't want him distracted and stressed about his medical bills.

From what Kiara said, there's no way I want his parents to pay one cent towards Remi's expenses. There's no way in hell he's going back to a place he hates, with people who don't love him. He needs to stay here, with us, where he belongs, and I'm going to do everything in my power to make sure he's taken care of. He'd do it for me without question.

Pulling my phone out, I head to the stairwell and call Jay.

"How's it going, mija?"

My throat prickles with tears I'm swallowing. It's so good to hear their voice.

"It's a big fucking mess." I finally break down. Loud sobs echo in the enclosed space as if the walls are grieving too. It amplifies my pain.

Jay listens to it all without judgment. Without nonsense commentary.

"His parents came and… Oh God, Jay. They're just awful." I wipe my hand across my nose. "His mom is strung out, yet you can see how much pain she's in. And his dad," I mutter, "makes Beelzebub look like jolly old St. Nick."

"Oh damn," Jay swears. "How's Remi doing with his parents there?"

Fresh hot tears roll down my cheeks. "He had a seizure a couple of hours ago. They're not letting anyone in to see him because of the stress. I swear his asshole father is what set Remi off. He was peaceful, and then all hell broke loose," I whimper. "I've never been so scared in my life." It's hard to finish that sentence as sadness steals my words.

"Oh, Mars Bars, I'm sorry. Do you need me to come? Isabel will be fine with Ian, but who is there for you?" I don't deserve them.

"Just the fact that you asked is enough for me." I run my fingers through my tangled hair and wince at the sting from the knots. "Can I stay with you tonight? I don't want to go home alone." I gnaw at my chapped lip, trying not to break down. "He's everywhere, Jay. He's all over that house. I just… I can't."

"Of course, you can always come here." Jay is my rock.

I sniff. "I need to talk to you about something else."

"I'm here," they reassure.

If this situation has taught me anything, it's made me realize what's important—the ones we love. People are more important than things … than my pride.

"It's about Pür's proposal. I was being stubborn. My ego was getting the best of me," I admit. "I'm sorry it took something like this to make me appreciate what really matters." Sitting on the step, I wrap an arm around my legs. "I'm on board with whatever you want to do, but I want to sell Ever Heart."

Jay's gasp is so loud it'd be comical if I was in a better mood. "I think it's a good move, Mae. I get to do what I love best. Everyone gets job security. And you will be able to have a life outside of work." They sound so reasonable.

I'm ashamed I wouldn't listen to them before. Tingles of chagrin creep through my cheeks. "Yes, and I want to help Remi. After all he's done for me, I need to." I rub my lips together, stifling another round of tears.

"Of course. Ian and I will do whatever we can to help too. You're not alone, Mae." Jay is unequivocally the best human—besides Remi—that I know.

"'Kay," I sniff. "I'll see you tonight. I love you, Jayden."

"Of course you do," they reply. "I'm your tres leches dealer. You'd be too salty if it weren't for my sweetness." Jay's humor cracks through the black cloud hovering over me.

Although I can't find it in me to be jovial, the tension twisting in my head loosens.

We hang up, and I take a minute to decompress. To figure out how I'm going to move forward and what my and Isabel's life will look like. As long as we have Remi, we can get through anything.

Opening up the stairwell exit, I head towards Remi's room to see if they have any more information on his condition. When I find Kiara sitting next to his closed door, she gives me a sad shake of her head. I give her a watery smile and decide to take a stroll outside. It's a nice night—the fresh air will do me good and clear out all the muck in my mind.

I watch the cars go in and out of the parking garage as I make my way around the building to the greenspace, and I wonder who else is grieving like me. Who else is aching to bring a loved one home? Who is leaving, knowing they'll never see their loved one again? My chest shudders as it releases a cry. It's all I seem to do anymore.

When I get to the end of the block, I start to turn back, but something catches my eye. A majestic statue of Mother Mary towers over the park. My mother half-heartedly raised me a Catholic, but I could never accept dogma that preaches hate disguised as love. Patriarchy and I have never gotten along. But as I stare at the statue before me, something stirs in my chest and I'm drawn to her. Maybe because she's a mother too. Maybe it's the look of sorrow on her face as she watches over the pigeons and squirrels. Standing in front of her, I realize how looming yet benevolent the statue is.

"Hey. Long time, no see." I wince at my lame joke. "Listen, I never believed that much in your kid." *Fucking A, am I really talking to a statue?* "Sorry. I just ... want him back. Please." My hands seek purchase on the base of the shrine as I double over in absolute anguish. "He means everything to us, my daughter. I can't—" A

318

gasp steals my words. "I'm asking, m-mother to mother. Give him back to us," I snivel. "He's the best person I know. So full of love and kindness. Everyone who meets him leaves a better person. The world needs Remington Arison. *Please.*" Sobs wrack my body, but a calm sedation unfurls inside of me. I tick off my blessings one at a time.

Isabel is healthy.

Remi is still breathing.

Kiara is accepting of our relationship.

And I found love.

Don't look ahead. Focus on everything positive at this moment. Be grateful for all you have right now.

A strange sense of inner peace fills my hollow insides. I look up at her. "I'm still a skeptic, so forgive me if I'm not magically converted, but whatever you just did... Thanks."

As I walk back to the hospital, my mind clears and a second wind breezes through me. Remi needs me to be strong because he isn't right now. I'm not giving up on him because he'd never give up on me. If it were me laying in that bed, I'd fight heaven and hell to get back to him and Isabel. He'd do the same. He's *doing* the same.

Hope's helium fills me with newfound optimism. I almost float up to Remi's floor, but as soon as I step through the hospital entrance, I'm yanked into an empty office.

Mr. Fairchild has a vise grip on my arm, and the look in his eye is alarmingly cold.

"Let go of me," I grit and tug my body away to no avail. His hold only tightens, and I know I'm going to have bruises.

I'm going to have bruises. Something clicks in my mind, and I have the where-withal to see this for what it is—an opportunity. I struggle some more for good measure as I blindly press buttons on my cell in my other hand, hoping it calls the last person I spoke to. I turn down the volume at the same time, so as to not alert the unhinged asshole holding me hostage.

"Get your hands off me, Mr. Fairchild." I speak loud enough so Jay can hear me if they picked up.

With one last rough shake of my arm, which I verbally react to, Mr. Fairchild lets me go. "Listen to me, you fucking whore."

A spray of saliva hits my cheek, and I suppress a gag. I want to wipe it off, but I don't want him to know I'm affected whatsoever.

"I don't know what you think you mean to my son, but it doesn't matter. You are not and never will be good enough to even breathe the same air as us. You're a piece of trash, and your spawn should be the one dying in that bed." Gone is the conversational yet cold demeanor. The evil Mr. Hyde takes Mr. Fairchild's place. "If something happens to my son, your bastard will meet the same fate." The vitriol spitting out of his mouth is astonishing.

Bile surges up my esophagus as he says the most vile things about my baby. A red haze falls over my vision, and I feel claws grow out of my fingers. I'm going to fucking rip his face off.

He's goading me. He wants me to react, but I'm stronger than that. My head takes over because my heart wants blood, and that won't help this situation. He might be a rich bastard who uses threats to get what he wants, but I'm a mother who would fight to the death for her child. I'm stronger than he'll ever be.

Mary's serene face pops into my mind, and a switch is flipped.

A maniacal laugh escapes me. "You seriously think your balls are bigger than they actually are." I tsk, feigning indifference and purposely inciting the demon. My heart pounds against my ribcage, and I stiffen my joints. He doesn't need to see me tremble. "I'm not scared of your empty threats." I'm well aware I'm trapped by a psychopathic narcissist, but my hunch is that there isn't much he can do here, as staff could come our way at any moment. I pray my hunch is on point.

"Oh, sweetheart, they're not empty at all. You have no idea what I'm capable of." A psychotic grin twists his face. It almost makes me wonder if he's truly Remi's father. They're emphatically different.

"You're so full of empty hubris," I provoke. "A bitch past his prime and his worth. Not that you were ever worth much." I mock the nasty words he said to Gram earlier. "Not to your children, anyway." Steadying my feet, I shift closer and stand tall like a bird of prey ready to attack. "Or your wife. She self-medicates because she's trapped by you." I ball my fists and jut my chin. "You are nothing but a coward, trying to intimidate everyone with your turpitude. Save it for the weak because it's not going to work on me." I go to push past him, praying my incitement works. Men's lips have sunk empires when their ego got a boo boo.

My calculation is correct because delight paints this snake in the grass poised to strike. My arm is once again in his clutches. *That's it. Make that bruise nice and black.*

"A woman crossed me once. She went behind my back, contacted a lawyer, and tried to leave me, thinking she'd take my children too."

Shock rips through my gut. Oh my God, did Remi's mom try to get away? I can't take a moment to examine his story because he keeps the information flowing and I'm paying attention to every word.

"She's regretted it every day since." He smiles, back to discourteous conversing—a mild demeanor with harsh words. He holds his free scaly hand in the air, flexing his fingers. "I hold her life in my hands. I am her god." His voice is so deep on the last word, it reverberates around the room and threatens to make my teeth shatter. "Every day, I make it my personal mission to make her suffer. To make her sorry she ever existed. I took her life away from her, and her children followed."

Things are starting to fall into place and I need to keep him talking, so I roll my eyes and try to pull away again. "You're so full of shit. Let me go."

Right on cue, he shakes me by the arm, and it feels like broken glass is digging into my skin where his fingers are locked. I make an "ouch" sound. *Please be listening, Jay.*

"She thought she was smarter than me, but she's just another worthless whore. I relish in her pain." As predicted, he keeps talking. "I see the way your calculated eyes study me. You think you're clever, don't you?" He gets in my face. "If you even attempt to undermine me, I'll ruin you too. I'll celebrate the day your daughter gets taken from you. I'll make sure she gets lost in the system, never to be found again. She'll be a fucking statistic, and you'll be just another junkie deadbeat parent, begging on the streets. Go away."

Blood leeches from my face as more puzzle pieces snap together, painting a very dark picture. *Remain calm.* This guy is a certified psycho. If we weren't in a public place, I'm certain he'd kill me and parade around with my head on a platter. I tamp down the hornets stinging my stomach.

His head tilts ominously side to side. It's eerie, and my skin crawls with a million tiny spiders. This whole exchange is terrifying. I'm facing a truly evil man, in dark waters without a life jacket, so I calm my heart and pray not to drown.

"Don't believe me? Just ask my wife." He lets go in a half-assed attempt to push me away.

But I'm not done yet. We're almost there, and I just need a little more. So I cackle, spurring him on. "Like you have any control over her addiction." I continue to laugh and wipe my eyes. "Oh God. That's good stuff." Pointing a finger at him, I go for the kill. "You, sir, are a real comedian. 'I'm her god'," I mimic his words in a deep voice before chuckling again. "You don't have any more control over her addiction than she does."

"Oh, honey, that's where you're wrong." He grins widely, showing off his coffee-stained teeth. "I'm her dealer."

I widen my eyes because once he sees that I fear him, he'll let me go, thinking he's the victor. Thinking he has me under control.

With a smug smile and a puffed chest, he walks out of the room. My shoulders sag in relief because I am actually scared of him and what he's capable of. I just need to remain one step ahead.

Luckily for me, I know how to strategize against an adversary. Unfortunately for him, I have evidence of assault, and pretty soon the police will find out he's been drugging his wife.

Then he'll know what it's like to mess with a lioness defending her pride.

Chapter 26

A Queen With A Broken Crown

Mae

Between rehashing what happened between me and Mr. Fairchild, reassuring my best friend and their boyfriend that I was physically fine, and having nightmares about the whole damn thing, I did not get an ounce of sleep last night.

I did, however, get the recording I was hoping for. It's all there, as clear as day and just as horrific as I remember.

Jay's face pinched like they were sick to their stomach. I could tell they were trying to keep their anger under control by the way they mashed their molars, clenching their jaw. Thank Goddess for Ian and his effective soothing techniques. Jay and Ian are complements of each other—Yin and Yang. Two parts of a whole, where one does not function properly without the other.

Watching them together reminded me of how Remi is with me. The perfect calm to my madness. The sweet compliments to my self-flagellation.

As we sat on the floor with Isabel, making things out of Play-doh, I could see Remi here, and my heart ached. He just fits seamlessly.

I rocked Isabel, trying my damndest to sing Remi's song for her without choking up. I failed, but she drifted off into dreamland peacefully. Instead of placing her in the pack 'n play, I brought her to bed with me, all the while smelling her hair and rubbing her back. Isabel isn't used to sleeping with me, but I think we both needed it last night.

I look like hell trudging into the hospital early this morning. From the looks of Kiara lying knees-bent across a small vinyl couch in the waiting room, she's fairing worse than I am. She sits up when I approach, and I hand her a coffee.

"Thanks." Her voice sounds thick and groggy.

"How was last night?" I ask. "Have you seen the doctor yet this morning?"

Setting her coffee down, she scrubs her face to perk her up. "Last night was uneventful, which is good news. And no, he's supposed to update me around eight."

I nod. "Your parents?" I keep my voice low in case the boogeyman pops around the corner.

"I'm not sure where they are, which is the scary part. I'm worried that my father will try for medical power of attorney." Her tone is laced with disgust.

Over my dead body. Just the thought has my stomach seizing in trepidation.

"I wouldn't put much past him."

Me neither. I want to discuss what he told me last night, but now isn't the time. Kiara is barely holding it together, and this will tear her apart. I will, however, talk to Detective Gracyk and give her the recording as she's supposed to meet me here this morning. I called her about the incident and sent her pictures of my arm, which have dark purple bruises in the shape of fingers around it. She's coming here to take her own pictures and see if there is any video surveillance footage.

Kiara pulls her bag to her lap, rifling through it. "I'm going to freshen up in the bathroom real quick. Will you call me if the doctor comes?"

"Of course, take your time. I'll be here all day."

She gives me a grateful smile. "How's Isabel? I'm sorry I didn't ask sooner, but with everything going on..."

I grab her hand. "She's doing well. Misses her Emmie, but she's making cards and drawing pictures, and planning out the next forty-five years of his life."

A small chuckle comes from Kiara. "She's really precious. We can all learn a thing about optimism from children." She gets up, hoists her bag onto her shoulder, and waves as she disappears down the hall.

I'm going through my emails in the waiting room when I spot Mandy. My heart speeds because Kiara isn't here and I don't know how much I should say to her. The last time I saw her, she was on a date with Remi that ended early because of me.

"Hey." Mandy approaches, her face somber. "Kiara messaged me about Remi. How is he?" She takes the seat on my other side.

"He had a rough day yesterday, but he's been stable since," I say. "They're not letting anyone visit yet. It was … tense."

We sit in awkward silence. How do you tell your boyfriend's ex, *Surprise, we've been in love all along*? You don't.

"Listen." She turns to me. "I just want you to know that I care about him." *Oh fuck. Please don't plead your case to me.* "We only went on a couple of dates, but … he sure knows how to make a lasting impression."

"That, he does," I agree, biting the smile that wants to sneak out. "Remi spreads sunshine to everyone he meets. The world is a gloomy place right now." My chin quivers.

"You're not just here as a concerned friend, are you?" She levels me with a stare, and I feel like a hot spotlight is burning over my head.

"Uh, well…" What the hell do I say?

She gives me a sardonic smile. "I know, Mae."

"Know what?" I'm well aware I'm playing dumb.

"I saw something when we came to your house the night of our first date," she acknowledges. "I didn't want to believe it, so I blocked it out and agreed to a second date." Sighing, she runs her fingers through her dark hair. "And that was going well until he saw you."

"I'm so sorry. You have no idea."

Mandy holds up her hand. "Don't be sorry for falling in love with an incredible person. It's not like we were exclusive." Picking at a thread on her cuff, she continues, "I knew, though. It wasn't that he ran to help you and Isabel. Anyone worth anything would." She catches my stare. "It was the way he held you both in his arms, like you were his whole universe." Her smile is wistful if not a little sad.

I know this, and for some reason, hearing someone else say it makes me break down. I bury my face in my hands and try to silence audible sobs.

A hand rubs my back, warm and comforting.

"He saved my little girl," I say through my fingers. "The car was coming for her, and he pushed her out of the way so it hit him instead."

"Oh no, Mae. I'm so sorry. Do they know who did it?" There's something strange in the tone of her voice. I can't quite put my finger on it, though.

"They're investigating." It's all the info I'll give her. Anyone can be a suspect at this point.

She touches my shoulder, and I turn towards her. "He'll wake up, Mae. He'll come back to you. I don't think there is anything in this world that could keep him away."

We hug and I cry some more, surprised that I'm being this open with a practical stranger.

That's how Kiara finds us. "Hey, Mandy." I can tell by the tone of her voice just how depleted she is.

Mandy stands and embraces her friend, who starts crying like I did. Does this woman have some magical empathic powers to get us to open up so easily? Or is it that our sadness rests just under the surface of our skin, and any abrasion—good or bad—bleeds it out?

"I just stopped at the nurses' station. The doctor is making his rounds now." Kiara folds the hospital's threadbare blanket and sets it on top of a flat pillow before slumping into a seat.

"Okay, I'm going to go, but if either of you need anything, don't hesitate to ask." Mandy gives us both a hug before she leaves.

Kiara nudges my side. "How'd that go?"

"She said she already knew. That she saw it before he eluded there was someone else." Kiara knows about us, so I'm not sure why my belly is flipping at telling her about it. "I apologized." I catch Kiara's eye. "We tried to stay away from each other. Really tried. It was just so…" I shake my head.

"Cody is my ex-boyfricnd's best friend," she cuts in, taking me off guard.

"What?"

She nods with a small grin. "It's true. Sparks flew the day he was introduced to me."

Picking up her lukewarm coffee, she tells a story about two people fighting against all odds to be together. She didn't want to hurt her ex, but they could not deny their feelings any longer.

"It was selfish of me to restrict Remi like that. But things could get messy." She raises her eyebrows on a sigh. "For one client, things got really messy. Not only did I have to clean it up but the ex-wife tried to defame my company and me. I had to fight her in court." Indignation paints her features. "We won, but I strictly forbid it after that. Any caregiver caught having an affair with a client faces automatic termination with grounds for a lawsuit."

My chest seizes. Surely she wouldn't sue her brother. "Kiara, please. I love Remi. There is no ex on my end." She gives me a skeptical look. "Okay, there's Isabel's father, but he made it pretty clear he wants nothing to do with us." My tone is still bitter about it.

"Listen, I'm not going to rake either of you over the coals. I understand." Crossing her arms, she gives me some attitude. "But if you hurt him, I'll have to kill you." Her serious face breaks into a chuckle.

"You're a good big sister. He's lucky to have you."

"Damn right he is," she asserts.

I frown. "I wish my step-sister and I were close."

Her eyes widen. "I didn't know you had a sister."

I nod. "'Step' is the operative word. 'Psycho' is the other."

"Tell me how you really feel." Kiara chuckles. "I take it you two don't get along."

"When your sister, step or not, sleeps with your boyfriend, I'd say that's grounds for getting cut out of my life," I mutter.

"Oh damn! That really happened?"

"I wish I were lying." I palm my stomach. "I found them in our bed after my first ultrasound appointment."

Kiara sits up. "Holy shit!"

"Yeah." My laugh is harsh. "He was supposed to meet me at the doctor's. Even though Isabel was a surprise, he seemed excited about the baby." I shrug. "It was all an act. I got home early and heard them." Disgust churns my stomach. "It was bad enough that he was cheating, but when I walked into our bedroom, I realized how low he actually stooped." I rub my forehead, staving off the headache that always punches up when I think about this stuff. "He tried to scramble out from under her, but it was too late." I'll never forget the looks on their faces. His eyes were filled with shame. Hers were gleeful, along with the snicker that marred her face. "His promises to us were broken, and my faith in him obliterated," I say, painting the full picture.

"That must have been really tough," Kiara commiserates. "I'm sorry that happened to you."

"It was. Not because of my relationship with Brad, though. That night, I lost any hope of redeeming my relationship with my step-sister, Aubry, and Isabel lost a father. Something that has haunted me ever since."

"Until my brother, the super nanny, came to save the day." She bumps my arm. Her humor eases my angst over the past, and we both laugh.

"Yep, he gave us so much more than I ever expected." My nose stings. I would give anything to see his beautiful brown eyes right now.

We sit in silence, fiddling with our phones, until Dr. Raj meets us in the waiting room.

"I need to be transparent with you: the seizure Mr. Arison had yesterday wasn't a good sign. Statistically, patients that suffer a seizure while comatose have a poor morbidity prognosis."

A tonne of bricks land on my chest, and my heart crashes to the floor, shattering.

"What does that mean?" Kiara practically shrieks.

"It could mean anything from poor motor skills to intellectual disability. The neurologist is running some tests, but so far they have been inconclusive. The patient will have a full assessment when he wakes up. The longer he's under, the more detrimental it is." His mouth turns down as he speaks. "It's up to Remi now. I'm giving the clearance for him to have one visitor at a time." *Oh god, I'll get to see him.* I'm relieved but it's short-lived. "Soft sounds and positive words only. Another seizure would be bad."

"Doctor, how can I stop my parents from visiting?" Kiara wrings her hands. "My father set Remi off yesterday, I know it. He's not good for anyone."

"Mrs. Razzine, you are the only one on the patient's HIPPA record. While you can request it, you can't enforce preventing a parent from visiting an adult child. My advice is to seek legal counsel and push for guardianship. Though, that could take months."

Kiara glances at me, our stare saying the same thing—it's as if every odd is against us.

I want to curl in a ball and hide until all of this is over and we're back to where we were—happy, healthy, and bursting with love.

Doctor Raj leaves us like he met us, with little information and wavering hope.

Kiara excuses herself to make some phone calls, and I walk to the hospital atrium for different scenery. As soon as the coast is clear and I'm alone, I break down.

This can't be happening. This can't be happening. My thoughts scatter, and my memories burn through the dark recesses of my mind.

Remi's radiant smile. His boisterous laugh. His velvety voice. The touch of his hand. The first time we kissed. The first time we made love.

"Oh God, please." I slide down the wall and hug my bent knees. I can't do this alone, so I do the one thing I thought I'd never do. Fishing my phone out of my pocket, I dial a number that only ever calls me.

She answers on the first ring.

A blubbering mess, I admit the one thing I refused to ever acknowledge. "Mom, I need you."

Two hours later, I'm permitted into Remi's room and it's like sunshine after a horrific storm. I know we're not out of the woods yet, but I'm not making any assumptions until Remi wakes up. I refuse to believe he's going to come out of this anything other than perfect.

Kiara is at Remi's apartment, gathering any legal documents she may need to keep from her parents. Cody talked to a lawyer about a protective order, but unless we can prove Mr. Fairchild is the one that put Remi in danger, there's nothing we can do.

I contemplated giving Kiara the evidence of her father threatening me, but I don't want to put that on her shoulders unless I absolutely need to. I know once I meet with Detective Gracyk, she'll give further instruction. So I'll hold back for now.

As I sit here and run my fingers down Remi's forearm, I take in every inch of his beautiful face. There is a blue tinge to his eyelids and a purple hue underneath. Even with all his bruises and bandages, he's the most breathtaking man I've ever laid eyes on.

"Hi, Manny." I speak low and sweet, hoping my voice gives him comfort. "You had quite a day yesterday. I'm sorry that happened, and Kiara and I are doing everything possible to keep your father away." Disgust roils my stomach when I think about yesterday. To control my anxiety, I watch the trail I make on his arm and drift to the palm of his hand. "Your skin is really soft." Pressing my lips together, I fight the stinging of tears. "I talked to Kiara about us. She understands." A soft laugh escapes through my nose. "She warned that I better not break your heart. I told her I never would." My eyes burn. "I won't. No matter what." My voice is fervent because I need him to understand I'm not going anywhere. "I'm going to be here for you, Remi. Isabel too." My mouth quirks a small smile. "She's making plans for you, you know. She'll probably have the next four decades of your life planned out by the hour." I play with the back of his hand. "Takes after her momma."

Nurse Vicky walks in with a pleasant demeanor. She's just the type of person that sets everyone at ease. I'm glad she's Remi's nurse. "Hi, lovely. I'm sorry to bother you, but Officer Taylor and Detective Gracyk are here to see you."

My stomach dips. I feel like I just got in here and now I have to leave, but this is important. It cannot be put off. It's still difficult to let Remi out of my sight because as long as I can hear his heartbeat, I know he's alive, fighting his way back.

Vicky must sense my hesitation. "He's still on restrictive visitors, Mae. I'll make sure no one bothers him, except Mr. or Mrs. Razzine." She pins me with a knowing stare, saying without words that she knows exactly what's up. Though I don't trust many, for some reason, I trust her.

"I have to take care of something really quickly, Manny," I whisper close to his ear. "You're in good hands, and I'll be back before you know it." Leaning in, I give him the lightest kiss on his cheek. "I love you."

Nurse Vicky grabs and lovingly squeezes my hand on the way out. "I'll be right here."

I nod and go find Taylor and Gracyk at the nurses' station.

Gracyk tilts her head, asking me to follow her into an empty room. "I need you to make a written statement on what happened, then we'll take pictures." She pulls out some forms for me to fill out. "This other document is for the restraining order. It's a deterrent, but if Mr. Fairchild knows the law, you can't keep him from seeing his son unless Kiara has a court order of protection."

"I understand." I hand over the flash drive with my recording. "I have audio evidence of the incident." I wince. "It's disturbing, to say the least."

Detective Gracyk puts the device in her chest pocket. "Good work. Although we can't use it against him in court, it's surely enough to get him banned from the hospital."

Officer Taylor gestures to my arm, and I lift my sleeve. "Hopefully by this evening, he'll be detained," she says, examining my upper arm. "Jesus." A harsh breath escapes her lungs. "This happened last night?"

"Yes, he grabbed my arm and yanked me into an empty office right outside the hospital entrance."

"We're going to ask for access to video surveillance. Hopefully the hospital complies, or we'll have to get a warrant," the detective explains. "Which will take a bit longer, but either way, we can pursue the restraining order."

Once I wrap up with Officer Taylor and Detective Gracyk, I hightail it back to Remi's room. Just as she promised, nurse Vicky is standing sentry at the door. Her lips turn up when she sees me.

"Kiara isn't back yet?" I ask before heading in.

"Not yet, but Mr. Fairchild stopped by."

All the blood drains from my face as I rush to open Remi's door.

Vicky lays her hand on my arm. "I told him Remi was still on restriction and he'd have to come later."

"Are you okay? Did he threaten you?" If my voice sounds a bit panicky, it's because I am.

"He ranted a little bit, but I reminded him that security was right down the hall and if he gets thrown out, he won't be allowed back in." She looks past me, searching down the hall as if to make sure the monster left. "I just hope I bought you and Kiara some time. That man gives me the creeps." She shivers.

"Thanks, Vicky. I owe you big time."

"Nah, I'm just a romantic at heart. I do want an invite to the wedding, though." She chuckles, and my mouth drops in surprise. "Please, these are things I know." She winks at me before letting go.

Just as I sit down, my phone vibrates and Kiara's name pops up. Crossing my fingers, I plead for good news. "Hey."

"Hi." She sounds out of breath. "I found it, Mae."

The excitement in her voice makes me sit up. "What?"

"Remi, my brilliant shithead brother, filed papers for me to have medical power of attorney should he be incapacitated."

My mouth pops open. "Why did he do that?" It's almost like he knew something was going to happen.

"Because he's that weary of our father. But he never gave it to me to sign, so Cody called his friend, Sal, to help us file it. Turns out, the judge is a personal friend of his. We got it, Mae." Her voice cracks, but it's more relief than sadness. "The paperwork is notarized, and I have a copy for the hospital. My father doesn't stand a chance."

My chest opens, and I take a deep breath. "That's great news. What about your mother?"

"Well," Kiara hesitates. "That's a little bit different." I wait, biting my thumb nail, for her to continue. "This could be my chance to get her away from my father. If she spends time with Remi, maybe she'll want to get better. My father won't be looming over her, using every move she makes as a transgression against him. If there's any possibility, I have to take it. Please understand."

A thread of trepidation tightens around my throat. While I'm pretty sure Mrs. Fairchild only wants her son happy and healthy, could she be persuaded to sneak her husband in? Especially if what he told me was true.

"I do. But I need to tell you about something." I move to just outside Remi's room because I don't want him to hear what I have to say.

I tell her about yesterday. About the bruises on my arm and what he said regarding her mother. About filing a restraining order and writing a statement of the incident, with audio evidence.

She gasps and chokes, "No." I hear her quiet sobs through the receiver. "I've always known he was cruel, but this ... this is a new level of evil."

My heart goes out to Kiara right now. Her brother is in a coma, her mother is addicted to opiates, and her father is the dealer. I'm not sure how much more she can take.

"I'm sorry."

"It just sucks, you know. I hate the man," she grumbles. "It's why I moved across the country as soon as I could and persuaded my baby brother to do the same. But in spite of everything, he's still my father and there's a very small piece of me that loves him and wants to see the good in him." She sniffs. "That fantasy is gone now. There's no redeeming him after this."

It's true, but it's also really sad. "I know," I whisper. "I wish circumstances were different."

We end the call with a promise that Kiara will be here in a couple of hours with Cody, who is insisting on bringing dinner. It's sweet, but my stomach cramps at the thought.

Taking Remi's hand in mine again, I run his fingers across my lips, giving little kisses to his knuckles. "We're all waiting for you. Come back to us."

Helpless, I smooth Remi's blankets and make sure he's warm, hating that I can't do more. That I can't make it all better with the click of my heels. Why is life so brutal? First, the betrayal of Brad and my step-sister. When I finally find the love of my life, he gets hit by a car. Not to mention, his lunatic father.

"It's so fucking unfair." I fist the liquid pouring out of my eyes. "Please don't leave me," I choke, lifting my head to the ceiling, pleading with the universe. "I'll do anything, please." My chest caves in with a tsunami of anguish. "I know I haven't been the best kind of person. I'm mean, abrasive. Impatient. Egotistical. Not to mention, a terrible mother."

My ribs crack wide open and my heart spills out, flopping like a dying fish on the floor. Gasping for air. For life. For Remi.

"There's so much I regret. So many things I wish I could take back." My words are strained by the lump of sorrow in my windpipe. "But not him. Don't take him. He's done nothing but put his life on the line for someone he loves."

As if Remi's telepathically communicating, his voice floats around my mind. *"I promised you I wouldn't leave Isabel, and I keep my promises."*

"You promised me, Remi." My shoulders tremble, and my stomach quakes. "You said we'd never be without you. I didn't say I had enough. That was the bargain.

Remember?" I beg in vain. "I haven't had enough yet. I'll never have enough of you."

The decimated organ on the floor is tempered glass, cracking with every pulse, fragmenting into a million tiny pieces. But I don't have it in me to pick up the debris. I'm not sure I'll want to if Remi doesn't wake up. I'll be a queen with a broken crown, reigning over a kingdom of misery, as empty as any figurehead.

"You *promised*." My voice is a strangled whisper, slowly suffocating me. My body is heavy, and it takes great effort to keep me sitting straight, so I slump.

I'm half draped on Remi's side when I feel it. It's faint, but it's there.

I fling upright in a shock of hope. "Did you just squeeze my hand?"

While I don't expect an answer, I get one anyway. His fingers attempt to tighten around mine again.

My heart jumps back into its rightful place, pounding a dubstep beat full of electricity and ecstasy. "Ha!" My lids are wide open, just like my mouth. "You can hear me?"

Movement again. It's small, but unmistakable.

My tears of despair flip to elation. He can hear me, and better yet, he understands.

"I'm here, Manny," I reassure. "I love you so much."

I get a response of three tiny flexes around my fingers, telling me he loves me too.

Chapter 27

Narnia is Real

Mae

I yell for Vicky as I smash my thumb on the nurse call button. "Come quick! He's responding!" Air whooshes out of my lungs, and my body vibrates with violent anticipation. "Open your eyes, love. It's time to wake up."

The flexing of his hand becomes more fervent, and I know he's fighting his way back. A slew of nurses and Dr. Raj burst through the door. My lungs seize at the thought of letting go of Remi's hand, but I give them room and zero in on the doctor's assessments.

"His pupils are responding. Normal oxygen level. Blood pressure is stable," Dr. Raj rattles off Remi's vitals, and every word paints my world in a kaleidoscope of bright colors.

My hand presses against my mouth, and my heart feels like it's breaking my ribs to escape. To flee to its home lying on the hospital bed.

"Remi," I whisper, urging him to open his eyes.

"What's going on?" Kiara runs in the room, breaking my focus.

I turn to give her a genuine grin. "He's waking up. I was talking, and I felt something." I swallow, my mouth dry. "It was Remi, trying to squeeze my hand." Every bone in my body is trembling in excitement.

Kiara links her fingers around mine just as Cody walks in the room in a stupor. He drops the bags he had in his hands. "Kia?"

She reaches out to her husband, and we all stand in equal parts of hope and joy. With our hands linked, we form a semi-circle at the end of Remi's bed.

"Let's go, Remi. Wake up, kid," Kiara encourages.

"Come on, dude. Your sister is a basket case. Do your boy a solid," Cody hoots.

I squeeze Kiara's fingers so tightly I'm surprised I'm not breaking her knuckles. Though hers are just as tense around mine.

There's a frenzy of activity in the room, but I stand rooted, transfixed on the object of my affection, willing him to lift his lids. I watch on, waiting for Remi to wake up. Waiting for the sun to rise and warm this cold summer day.

Remi's body jerks, and we all gasp in horror. *Oh no, not another seizure, please.*

"Relax. You're intubated. Don't try to pull it out," Dr. Raj instructs as four nurses hold Remi's limbs.

The organ behind my ribs is killing a drum solo. "He's awake," I gasp. "Remi!" The bubble of hope in my chest grows so big I'm afraid I might float away.

His body jerks again like he's fighting a war, and nurse Vicky pulls us as close to his bedside as she can while letting the staff do their job. We all hold our breaths as we focus on the rapid movement of Remi's pupils under his closed eyelids.

"Keep fighting. You're almost there," Kiara cheers her brother on, her cheeks red and her eyes glassy.

"I've got a cold IPA waiting for you, man," Cody crows.

Kiara looks at her husband like he farted in church. He gives her a sheepish grin as if to say, *what?*.

I lick my lips and taste salt. "You can do it, Remi. Isabel is waiting for you."

The dark lashes fan against his cheek, fluttering before opening, and it's like finding out that Narnia is real and magic revived our hero, Aslan. It's fucking incredible. His eyes dart around the room as if he's terrified.

"Remi," the doctor practically shouts. "Stay calm so we can take the intubation tube out. I'm going to ask you to exhale on three. One." He starts, and each second is like an eternity. When Dr. Raj says the number three, they swiftly pull out the tube and Remi immediately breathes on his own.

God, I missed those beautiful browns. I grab his hand. "You're okay, boy scout. You're safe."

His gaze lands on Cody, flitting to Kiara, and then settling on me. His terror softens, but his breathing is still rapid.

Running my fingertips gently down his arm, I soothe him. "There's nothing to be afraid of."

His tongue dips out of his mouth as he licks dry lips that I want to lose myself in.

"Do you think you can talk?" Dr. Raj asks.

I give Remi an encouraging smile and his stare doesn't leave mine, blinking once, twice, then a small sound comes out of his mouth. He swallows, his demeanor turning earnest.

"I know, love. Take your time," I reassure because the last thing he needs is pressure.

As if he suddenly remembers my hand in his, he gives me a gentle grip, communicating the best way he can.

"Me too," I murmur.

Fright colors his gaze as it widens. "Isa." It's a hint of her name, but I know exactly what he wants.

"Isabel is absolutely perfect. You saved her life."

His eyes slide shut, and the rise of his chest softens. I almost panic that he's going under again, but when his lids open wide, they are clear and aware, and loving.

"You're still an asshole, but we're so happy you're back." Kiara ribs her brother.

The corner of Remi's mouth lifts slightly.

"Don't you smirk at me," she warns, her words more playful than threatening.

We all laugh, giddy and excited. Aside from giving birth, this is probably one of the best days of my life.

"Can you tell me your name?" Doctor Raj steals Remi's attention.

I want to scream, *He just woke up! Give him a break!* I'm about to tell him to back off when Remi peaks.

"H-hot." It's a scratchy whisper, but it's something.

"Are you hot? Nurse, check if he has a fever." Dr. Raj backs away to make room for Vicky.

Remi shakes his head, seemingly frustrated. "H-hot m-ma."

I wait with bated breath, hanging on every utterance that comes out of his mouth. Unease unfurls in my stomach because he's not making sense.

"Dude, say your name," Cody demands impatiently, like it's the easiest thing in the world for someone with a traumatic brain injury.

Remi takes a deep breath. "Hot." Cough. "Ma—Mann-y."

My mouth falls to the ground while everyone else is in various states of confusion. The side of his mouth lifts. I fall to my knees, crying out in relief, euphoria, and gratitude.

A hand falls to my head, and I peer up at Remi with so much adoration. His thumb makes small circles in my hair. He's the one hurting, yet he's trying to comfort *me*.

"Okay, before I have a flipping heart attack, please tell me you know what he's saying," Kiara harps.

"Yes, that would be helpful." Dr. Raj pulls us back to reality, where other people exist outside my Remi bubble.

"It's my term of endearment for him," I explain, not wavering my stare from Remi's. "He overheard me saying he was hot one day and has never let me live it down."

Everyone around the room takes a collective breath, releasing the building tension.

Cody starts belly-laughing. "Oh, this is classic cornball Remi."

Kiara's face morphs from surprise to bemusement. "Alright, flirt, tell the fine doctor your real name so he doesn't think you're incapacitated."

He clears his throat, still smiling at me, before he turns to the doctor. "R-r ... emingt-ton." He swallows, forehead creased in concentration. "A-ar ... ison."

"That's right. Are you in any pain?" the doctor asks, and my spine stiffens.

In all the celebration, I forgot that Remi might be in immense pain.

His forehead creases as if he's testing his limbs and joints. "Just my head." His pupils float to the left. "My side." His chest pumps quicker with exertion. "My left arm."

He nods. "That's because you're in a cast. Can you move your fingers on that side?"

Remi winces, successfully performing the task.

I rub his shoulder. "You are doing great."

"That's good. We'll give you some pain meds and run a few tests, but it looks like your cognitive thinking and motor skills aren't inhibited. Though, we won't know to what extent until we get you up and walking."

"H-how long?" Remi's voice is still rusty, but hearing it is a balm to my chafed nerves.

"A little over twenty-four hours, which is quite frankly a miracle. If you had been hit an inch to the right, you wouldn't have fared as well." Dr. Raj's lips flatten. "You're lucky to be alive."

Remi's eyes drift back to me. "I know."

My heart swells and bursts, spreading the tingling sensation of blissfulness throughout my body. It's like a star exploding, throwing tiny diamonds across the galaxy—something rare, priceless, and beautiful. My world rights itself.

"What the hell is going on?" A voice I never want to hear again booms into the room.

I practically place my body over Remi's. His skin pales, and I feel his body tense under me.

"Hey, look at me," I say to divert Remi's attention. His gaze locks on mine. "He isn't allowed to be here. We're going to protect you, and everything is going to be okay."

There's a bit of commotion going on behind me. It's loud. Abrasive. Acerbic. But it doesn't matter at this moment. My manny is my *only* concern.

Even though he's still with me, the quick rise and fall of his chest builds to a gallop. Panic, swift and unwelcome, returns back into the room.

I block it out and focus. "Remi, love, you have to calm down. You could still have a seizure, and that would be bad."

His lips thin as he nods. "'Kay." It's a gravelly mumble.

I rub his sternum with a gentle touch. "That's it. Just pretend it's you and me here."

It's hard, but Remi fights to slow his heartbeat in time with mine.

"You remember the last time I was sitting beside your bed while you recovered?" His stare warms. Yeah, he does. "Guess what, I actually *will* give you a nip slip this time."

All tension leaves his body as he grins. "Yeah?"

"Yeah." My voice turns husky.

"I'm sorry, Remi." Kiara's apology is thick with distress, and that's when I realize the room has cleared out except for her, Cody, and me. I shift away so Kiara can update her brother on the situation. "They came. Father tried to bring you back to California. I found your medical power of attorney and filed it. I won't let him anywhere near you," she explains, pointing her thumb towards the closed door behind her. "He's just pissed he can't do shit about it."

"Thanks, you're a good sister." His signature smile makes an appearance, and a wave of emotion falls over me, realizing just how much I missed it. "But you're still a booger face."

Kiara reals back in mock offense, flicking her wrist in his direction as if giving him a playful smack. "Do you want me to break your other arm?"

Remi's laugh is half-hearted as his blinks become slower. The pain meds must be kicking in. Soon, he's fast asleep. It's a little unnerving considering what we just went through.

Nurse Vicky comes in and checks on us, offering refreshments we gladly accept.

"The bag that dinner is in is probably a mess, but I bet the food is still salvageable," Cody says, picking up one of the containers. He opens it, and it looks to be some kind of pasta. "Yeah, completely fine." He hands a container to Kiara and then me.

My stomach grumbles but is still uneasy from stress. I manage to swallow a bit of the cold cavatelli anyway, remembering how much Remi doesn't like it when I skip meals.

"I just want to put your mind at ease," Kiara says, turning to me. "My father was escorted out of the hospital by the police. Officer Taylor was taking him in for questioning, and he'll likely have to stay in jail a few nights for aggravated assault and reckless conduct. Either way, he's banned from the hospital." She takes a healthy sip of water. "Investigation on the claims he made about my mother are also underway. If found true, he'll lose his medical license."

Cody kisses the top of his wife's head. She had to do a very difficult thing today while under tremendous duress. She kept a level head and got shit done. The way strong women do.

"I'm sorry you are going through all of this. I know it's not easy," I acknowledge because without her, I don't know what we'd be facing right now.

"Thanks," she says. "I just have one request."

"Of course." I'm not sure why she's asking me anything. She's next of kin and can do whatever she wants.

It's nice that she sees me as someone important to her brother, though. This fills me with a warm feeling of contentment. Kiara is significant to Remi, and her acceptance of us is valuable to me.

"We put my mother up in the hotel across the street." Kiara gives me a minute to let that sink in before continuing, "I told her the only way we would have her in our lives is if she got off the drugs and left our father. I don't think she was expecting the possibility of her children ever forgiving her."

"What about your oldest brother? Will he have something to say about it?" The thought of him still makes me uneasy because he's the unknown variable in all of this.

"That guy is such a dick. Honestly, I have no idea where you and Remi came from," Cody chimes in.

If Kiara is offended, she certainly doesn't show it. "If he wants back into our lives, he'll have to change his ways too," she grumbles. "Anyway, my mom is going to rehab, and Gram is trying to convince her to file for divorce. With my father in custody, this is our chance to get her away from him."

My mouth pops open. This is huge and if all works out, I'll be ecstatic. It's clear Remi loves his mother, and I think having her back in his life will fit a missing piece of his heart.

What would it be like if I reconciled with mine? My heart twists. I'd like to find out.

"There is a nurse with her now, mitigating her withdrawal symptoms." Kiara takes a deep breath as if bracing herself for a battle. "As long as Remi agrees, I said she could come and see him before she has to leave." She levels me with a look. "Mae, I need you on board with this."

"Me?" I'm stunned. "Why would you need my permission? It's your family."

"Yes, but you're a big part of our family now." She nods towards the bed. "If Remi was awake, he'd say you're the most important part." Her demeanor is full of acceptance and not a hint of jealousy.

Moisture builds behind my eyes. If it's this easy with a practical stranger, why is it so difficult with my step-sister?

"I'm... I don't know what to say." I blink several times. "Of course, I want Remi to have his mother in his life. If she's willing to get help and not victimize him all over again, I'm all for it." My thoughts turn wistful. "We all need our mothers, no matter how old we get." Why did it take for something like this to happen for me to figure it out?

"I don't know." Kiara's face matches my thoughts. "I really think it's going to work out this time. For some reason, I'm optimistic."

"Me too," I agree with a smile in my voice.

"Right on, ladies." Cody fist-bumps before digging his fork back in his container.

Halfway through the dinner I'm not really tasting, there's a knock on Remi's door. Kiara and I freeze, but Cody sets his food down and walks over with purpose. When he opens the door, my heart leaps, falls, and leaps again.

There's no mistaking her blonde hair and signature red lipstick, looking like she just stepped off a pin-up calendar.

"Mom." I jump up and run into her arms. We're not huggers, but I've grown to love affection and it feels good to have her here.

She tenses in surprise, but her arms immediately wrap around me. "Baby," she coos.

All the stress, despair, and intensity of the past few days bubble up to the surface, and I bury my head into my mom's chest and sob, audibly, my whole being shaking with the force of my tears.

She rubs my back, just like I do with Isabel. "Let it all out, honey. It's okay."

Cody and Kiara slip out of the room, granting us a moment of privacy.

I'm not sure how long I bawl like a baby in my mother's arms, but eventually my chokes turn into sniffles and my body relaxes.

She pulls back a little and brushes the hair off my face, before cradling my chin. "Oh, my sweet girl." She wipes away the wetness from my cheeks, just like moms do.

"Thank you for coming so soon," I hiccup, gaining composure.

"Of course, Mae." Her eyes glaze with emotion. "Thank you for calling."

I swallow the ball of shame forming in my throat. "I'm sorry for not calling sooner."

"Oh, honey. You never have to apologize to me." She wraps me up again, and I let her. It feels nice to lean on someone.

"I know it's under strange circumstances, but I want you to meet Remi." We walk over to his bed, where he's peacefully sleeping.

"My, my. Handsome *and* a superhero." She turns towards me, smiling. "You've done well, Mae."

"Yeah." My cheeks heat. I'm not sure why I'm so coy about it. Maybe it's the compliment or that I finally stopped criticizing the things I'm failing at and focused on the things going well.

My daughter is safe. Jay and I have job security, as do our employees. Remi is awake, and I will have the means to take care of him, just like he's always done for me. And best of all, I'm in love. Turns out I'm pretty good at it, regardless of what Brad did.

After a while, Cody and Kiara come back, and I introduce them to Charlotte. We all sit around, getting to know each other better through whispered stories of childhood memories and life in general. It's not long before visiting hours are over, and we all have to leave.

Kiara must see the longing written all over my face when I kiss Remi goodbye because she makes a difficult concession. "Mae, do you want to stay tonight?"

My head swivels in her direction. "Is that okay? I know how close you both are."

"Yeah, but I bet he'd rather wake up to you than my resting bitch face." She laughs.

"I don't think it would matter, but..." The thought of sleeping by him all night gives me a sense of comfort. Like we'll never have to sleep apart again.

But then there is Isabel. I've already been away from her more than I ever have in the past. As much as Remi needs me, she needs me more.

"Isabel needs me. She's been staying at Jay's." I scrape my fingers through my hair. "I don't know."

"Baby, how about I go to Jay's and stay with Isabel?" Charlotte comes to me and rubs my arm. "Or I could bring her home. Either way, we can video call you. You can tell her that Remi woke up and you are staying to help him get better."

My nose stings at her tempting offer. I turn to Remi and contemplate my decision. It's like I'm being ripped in half.

"It's okay, Mae. Isabel is cared for by people who love her. Sure, she's missing you, but she'll be okay for one night." Charlotte sounds so reasonable, it's a wonder I never spared her an ear before.

Isabel is probably having the time of her life. She'll have three people doting on her. *And* I'll get to say goodnight.

Will this mother's guilt ever subside?

"Yeah, okay. For tonight." I turn to Charlotte as I pick up my bag and hand her my keys. "You can stay wherever, but I know she would love to spend time with her grammy." Grabbing my phone, I send a quick text to Jay, giving them a heads-up that she's coming.

With a beaming grin, she nods and puts my keys in her purse. "Do you have a toiletry bag you want me to bring you in the morning?"

I explain where my stuff is, and I'm so much lighter having her to lean on.

We all hug in goodbye, and I'm left alone with my hot manny.

The man in question wakes up twenty minutes later.

"Hey, sleepyhead."

His lips quirk up when he realizes it's just me. "Queeny." He crooks his finger, calling me to him.

I bend over his prone form.

"Closer." His voice is thick and rough.

I oblige, lowering until my lips brush his. "Yes, Manny?"

His chestnut orbs heat and swirl with a vortex of desire and urgency. "I love you." It's a gravely whisper that wraps around my body and binds me to him.

I grin on an elated laugh, and liquid leaks from my eyes.

"I didn't realize me professing my love for you would be so upsetting." He smirks.

"I'm just so happy you're awake to tell me." I wipe my cheeks and kiss his lips. "I love you too."

Serenity replaces the intensity of his gaze, but I can see a glint of mischief in the gold flecks of his irises. "Now, about that nip slip I was promised…"

Chapter 28

Redemption and Revenge

Mae

A MAN'S BASIC NEEDS are food, sleep, and sex. Remi, who just woke up from a coma after getting hit by a car, is no exception. His head is wrapped along with the side of his face. There's a black bruise on his angular chin, his arm is elevated in a cast, and yet he's eye-fucking me from the bed.

I giggle at his request, thinking it's a joke, but the heat of his stare tells me he is dead-serious. "C'mon, Queeny, what's a man got to do?"

Standing, I plop my fist on my cocked hip. "Are you seriously using your injury to manipulate me into taking off my shirt?" I ask with an incredulous laugh.

He shrugs. "Man's gotta eat."

I drop my head back in laughter, remembering the first time he said that looking irresistible with his finger pointing to his cheek. Why does he have to be so damn adorkable?

With an eyebrow raised, I slide my hands down my torso and play with the hem of my t-shirt. "I can't believe I'm doing this," I say, mostly to myself.

Remi just lays there with a dopey smile, like a juvenile about to see his first set of tits.

Swiveling my hips, I do a little dance. "If Vicky walks in, this is going to scar her for life."

He chuckles. "Makes it more exciting." He wags his eyebrows.

My lips purse in mock indignation. "You're incorrigible."

"I am what I am," he quips.

I love who he is, so I wouldn't change it for the world. If he wants to see some boobage, I'm going to give it to him.

Slowly, I reveal the skin of my belly inch by inch, all the while keeping an ear on his heart monitor. While I don't mind having a little fun—after all, he deserves it—I don't want it to jeopardize his health. But right now, all is well, so I continue my sensual moves.

When my top clears my head and my hair swishes through the collar, the heat in Remi's gaze turns blazing. A starving man, he licks his lips. I toss my shirt on the chair and strut towards him, with only one thought in my mind: he's awake, he's perfect, and he wants me.

His face hardens to stone and his burning stare is doused in cold water. "What the fuck is on your arm?" His heart rate starts climbing, along with mine.

This was a mistake. I forgot all about the blue watercolor Mr. Fairchild imprinted on my skin.

I rush to his side. "Remi, listen. It's nothing. I handled it. It's fine." My words jump like a dinghy in choppy water.

Steam flows out of his flared nose. "If you don't tell me who gave you those marks, I will get out of this bed and tear this place apart until I find out." The beeping becomes more frantic, like my panic.

"Okay, I'll tell you everything, just... You have to calm down. I can't lose you because of this." My hands are shaking, and tears build in my eyes. If something happens to him, I'll never forgive myself. "*Please.*"

He makes an effort to control his temper. "Give me your arm." His voice is low, deadly.

Anxiety creeps up my chest, reaching for my throat. Fidgeting with my fingers, I don't move. How do I tell him his father did this? He'll become enraged.

"Miranda!" he demands.

I startle at the sharp tone of his voice. *This is okay.* The doctor told us he'd be irritable.

"I will, but you have to calm down." My palms are up in a placating gesture.

He narrows his lids, and his lip curls. "What are you going to do when they find out who hit me?"

Fury shoots through my veins, my hands tightening into fists. "Touché." I will cut them up in teeny tiny pieces, killing them slowly and painfully.

Sitting on the side of his bed, I give him full view.

Sucking in a breath, his free hand lifts and his fingers phantom over the marks. "Tell me."

My eyes slide shut, and I take a deep breath. "I had a small altercation with your father," I start with a calm voice. The one I use on Isabel when she's throwing a tantrum.

Remi's hand trembles, and his face becomes purple. I'm so afraid he's going to do damage to his heart, so I pick up my shirt and swiftly put it back on, covering the mess his father made.

"I'm going to fucking skin him alive," he vows.

I understand, but it's not something he needs to worry about right now. "That's going to be difficult because he's in custody." I play with his blanket, wishing I wasn't so thoughtless. "I did it on purpose. He was threatening to take you away." I sniff. "I saw an opportunity and took it, goading him into marking me." When I turn to him, his eyes and nose are red-rimmed.

"What?! Why?" The ferocity behind his words slaps me like a whip.

I recoil, stunned by his tone. "Evidence," I shoot back, aggrieved. "He said some pretty awful things, and I wanted him as far away from you as possible." I wipe the tear falling down the sharp plane of his cheek, but his face remains stony. "I recorded him. Jay was on the phone the whole time, and trust me, they were ready to come with military force." My mouth quirks, trying to lighten the situation.

It doesn't work. "I met with the cops the next day. Gave them a report and filed a restraining order." I shrug. "It worked."

Remi is quiet for a while. His mood seems to have evened, but he holds my stare with such sorrow. I rub his arm like I did when he was under, trying to keep him relaxed.

"I love you, Mae," he starts, voice full of gravel. "I'm grateful for the lengths you'd go through to keep me safe." He grabs my hand, halting my touch. His irises are a cyclone of anger and anguish. "But don't you *ever* do that shit again."

Outrage slithers through me and I stand, pulling away from him. "I can handle myself. I did it because the man I love was being threatened, and I'd do it all over again." My chest heaves with my words. How dare he get so upset?

"I didn't say you couldn't handle yourself. I said don't put yourself in a situation like that again." He scrubs his face, the last of his tears drying. "My father is a sociopath. Who knows how long I would have been under. If something happened to you, where would that leave Isabel?"

I press a hand against the stab in my sternum as my lungs turn to ice, freezing my heart. An earthquake of regret rips into me, and shame shakes through my limbs. How could I have been so careless?

"Baby, I know you'd fight heaven and hell for me, and I would for you too, but..." He sees my chin quiver. "She comes first."

"I know. You're right," I whimper, slapping the moisture off my face. "I just... I was so scared of losing you, I wasn't thinking," I admit. Because of my recklessness, Isabel could have lost us both.

I've been so worried about neglecting her while I work. Where was that concern when I put myself in the line of fire? I just made myself a prime target. If things hadn't gone as planned, Isabel would have lost her mother completely. It could have been a devastating error and egregiously unfair to my baby.

Her silly grin pops into my head, but it quickly morphs into deep melancholy—her cheeks gaunt and gray, her glinting eyes dull with sadness.

My hand flies to my gut as it wrenches.

"Hey, come here." He points to his mouth, and I give him a shaky kiss. "You and Isabel are my world. You will never lose me. No matter what happens, God himself—"

"Herself," I interject.

He smiles. "God *her*self couldn't keep me away."

Part of the night, I slept half sitting on Remi's good side, until Nurse Vicky came and insisted someone bring me a recliner. While only marginally better than the stiff chair, I fell back asleep easily.

Around seven, they bring Remi his breakfast and with it, a sick-looking Evangeline and a hopeful Kiara.

Remi's eyes crack open and widen when he sees his mother. His face contorts in pain before he remembers himself. The nurse lifts the bed, so Remi can sit partially upright, and pulls the table closer to him.

The nurse takes the lid off the tray. "Jello, apple juice, and chicken broth. If you can keep that down, we'll bring you some solids."

Remi takes one look at his breakfast and turns to his mom cowering behind her daughter. He gives her a warm smile. "Breakfast of champions." His sweetness breaks the tension in the room. "Hi, Mom."

Moving out of the way, I lift my hand, gesturing for her to come closer. She must be in agony. The desperation and adoration in her gaze tell me—despite the disease she's fighting—the woman loves her children. I'm not perfect either, but I would die for my baby.

"Hi, Remington." Even though her words are soft, I can hear the elation in them.

Clearing the blanket and pillow off the recliner, I turn to Evangeline. "Come and sit."

Kiara gives me an appreciative smile, but I need no thanks. She's a mother who misses her child. I'd never stand in between that.

"I'm going to freshen up," I tell Remi before giving him a kiss on the cheek and leaving the room.

Five minutes later, Kiara follows, tears streaming down her face.

Alarm steals my breath. "Everything okay?"

She nods. "She couldn't help herself. She took the bowl of broth and started feeding him. I know it's silly and possibly a bit weird, but he let her and was gracious about it."

Because that's Remi—he sees the good in everyone, and that's the only thing that matters. Does he want his mother to spoon-feed him? Probably not. But he saw the meaning behind the gesture—a mother needing to care for her child. And maybe he needed his mother's love too.

My stomach grumbles. "Why don't we go to the cafeteria and get some breakfast ourselves?"

"Sounds good," she agrees.

Kiara and I grab our food and sit down, making small talk about the cafeteria's food that doesn't look half bad.

"Have you spoken to the police? Any leads on who was driving the car?" I hope Kiara has a little bit more information because I haven't heard anything. If it was Remi's father, is the threat over or did it escalate? These questions spin like a hurricane in my mind.

"Officer Taylor said they had a few leads and when she finds something concrete, we'll be the first to know."

I look up from slathering my bagel with cream cheese, chewing my lip, hesitating. "Do you think it could have been your father?"

"While nothing would surprise me anymore," she grumbles, "I just don't see it. Gram called my mom, said she had a right to know." She wrinkles her nose as she takes the tomatoes off her egg sandwich. "If it was Jackson, I'd want to know too, so I can't fault her for it." She sighs. "From the shell-shocked look on my father's face, it seemed like he didn't have a clue."

My hand flies to my stomach, where the bite of bagel I just ate expands and churns. It's unnerving to know the person responsible is still at large. Are they planning on finishing what they started? "Then that means the person is still out there. We need security posted at Remi's door." I fish my phone out of my bag, ready to call Detective Gracyk.

Kiara stills my hand. "I don't think calling is necessary."

My eyes fly to her face in disbelief.

She nods towards the cafeteria entrance, where Officer Taylor and Detective Gracyk stand searching the area. Kiara wipes her face, and we both clear the table before meeting the women at the door.

Their faces are grim. "Kiara." Taylor nods. "Miranda. Follow us."

Kiara and I look at each other because the women are all business, almost as if we're in some kind of trouble. Wordlessly, we make our way up to Remi's room, where we find him and his mother having a pleasant conversation.

Evangeline looks more relaxed than she did before. Her skin isn't as ashen, like Remi breathed some vitality back into her. They both look up at us with a smile when we enter, until they see the set of the officers' faces.

"I'm sorry to interrupt, but we need to speak with Remi, Kiara, and Mae alone."

Panic colors Evangeline's face, and she turns towards Kiara with questions in her eyes. "It's okay, Mom. Just some police business," she reassures before typing something on her phone. "I let Sandy know you're coming out. She's in the waiting room."

Evangeline's gaze dims, and she looks at her son with such sadness that the tentative stitch holding my heart together splits.

"Mom, you need to get healthy. It's time." Remi speaks to her as if he's soothing a child. "When you get out, we'll be right here waiting." He holds his hand out to her, and she doesn't hesitate to take it. "There is a very special little girl I can't wait for you to meet."

My tears well up again. I swear I never cried this much in my entire life.

Remi's grin is hopeful. "She's amazing, and she's going to love you."

"Jackson too, Mom. He needs his grandmother, just like we did when we were growing up." She walks over and holds her mother's free hand. "You can do this." Kiara's voice cracks on the last word. "Please, we need you."

There isn't a dry eye in the room. My peripheral sight catches Detective Gracyk discreetly wiping under her eye.

"I need you too." Evangeline volleys between her children. "Both of you." Her face crumples. "I'm so sorry for everything. I know I tried to get clean before, and I know I let you down." She takes a cleansing exhale. "I think I can do it this time. Without Arthur around, feeding into my addiction." Eva musters a small smile. "When all I have to look forward to... You are my strength." A sob concaves her chest. "My whole heart."

We all hug Evangeline before she leaves. She takes a moment to cradle my chin, and although she doesn't say a word, gratitude swirls in her brown irises.

When Mrs. Fairchild leaves the room, she takes all the heavy emotion with her. Though, the air is still charged with tension.

Detective Gracyk pulls a folder out of the messenger bag she's carrying. "After forensics examined the footage of the street cam, we found a primary suspect. But no motive." She surveys us with a keen stare. "We're hoping you three can help fill in the blanks."

Gracyk opens the folder and hands a document to Remi. "Do you recognize this woman?"

His forehead creases, and his brows smash together. "Yeah, she tried to pick me up at the grocery store. She got too close to Isabel, and I basically told her to back off." He studies the picture a little more. "She said her name was Bree."

Officer Taylor gestures to Kiara and me to come closer to view the image. I only need to see the signature sweep of hair, and all the blood drains out of my body, the floor dropping out from under my feet. Anguish rips through me, stabbing and slashing at my flesh. Every cut stings like I'm being eaten alive by angry hornets.

All her abominations hide behind a pretty smile. The longer I stare at the image, the more inventive I become planning her demise.

Rage ignites in my gut, and every gulp of oxygen I take in stokes a fire for vengeance. The blaze will not subside until it gets blood. I realize the only difference between me and a cold-blooded killer is the right provocation. And I just found it.

"It's Aubry Laurel Laughtin." My voice is monotone, my mouth dry. I shudder, enraged. "She's my step-sister. She wasn't going after Remi. She wanted Isabel." My legs turn into cooked spaghetti and I go down, my whole being shattering on the bleached linoleum floor.

It's been said that the best way to get back at an adversary is to move on and be happy. While Remi's recovery is remarkable and Isabel is healthy, it's difficult for me to not think about all the ways I could annihilate Aubry.

I gave Remi quite a scare when I passed out. In the small midnight hours when we whisper our secrets across his pillow, he asked me to forgive my step-sister.

At first, I was pissed. How could he ask that of me? She wanted to hurt Isabel. She almost *killed* him. For what? Jealousy? Revenge? Fun? I'll never wrap my head around it.

But he didn't want what happened in the past to oppress our future, which is bright and full of happiness. He said that forgiveness is for *my* peace, not my step-sister's.

He's right, of course, but every time I think about it, I thirst for blood.

I made a promise to never be reckless again, and I intend to keep it. As much as it pains me to sit aside and let the law take over, I will. For Remi and Isabel.

Officer Taylor and Detective Gracyk ensured that Aubry would be prosecuted to the full extent of the law. Her crime showed premeditation. She had been stalking me for a while. Just the thought sends tremors through my joints. There were so many times we were vulnerable, and I'm not sure how I'll be able to move forward without constantly watching my back.

My mother vomited when she found out, then apologized—profusely.

In another life, I would have felt some sort of satisfaction that I'd been right, but now, it just feels petty. When you've been through true trauma, everything else is unnecessary grief.

I couldn't blame her. There is some part of Aubry that's broken, and the crack started way before Charlotte and I came along. A guilt-ridden Randy offered to pay for Remi's medical expenses, but I declined. As long as I have the people I love in my life, I don't need anything else.

Except, there is just one more thing...

Chapter 29

Two Months Later...

Remi

IT WAS A WEEK before I was finally discharged from the hospital and Mae brought me home. To *her* home. Which, I guess, is now my home. I have zero complaints about it.

We turned half her living room into a temporary bedroom for both of us since the stairs are still a challenge. I'm not as steady on my feet since the accident. I have physical therapy five days a week, and it's hell but necessary. I'm determined to get back to a hundred percent. If only to take over the kitchen before Mae really does poison me.

She insists on making me breakfast saying, "Someone told me it was the most important meal of the day," with a saucy wink. I laugh, remembering the second time apology pancakes made it onto my plate. It makes me love her that much more because she's willing to do things she hates in order to take care of me. I ate every burnt, soggy bite and asked for more with a smile. The look of happy surprise on her face when I asked was worth it.

Mae has been very, um, hands-on with my care, and I'm enjoying every second.

"Daddy," Isabel shouts when she comes home from nursery school, running up to where I'm sitting and hopping on my lap.

"Hey, Isa-bea, how's my sweet girl?" Hugging her, I kiss the top of her head.

She started calling me that the day Mae brought her to the hospital to visit me. My sweet girl broke out in tears and crawled into my arms. My ribs ached, but there was no way I was going to let her go. I consoled her through it, telling her how brave she was and how proud I was of her.

While I was incapacitated, Isabel was a very busy toddler. She made a card for me every day and brought a stack of her drawings, each one showing me the plans she's made for us.

Lots of cats are involved.

But it was the last picture she held up that absolutely slayed my heart. She drew the house and her, Mae, and me holding hands outside of it. She pointed to each stick figure, telling me exactly who we were—Isabel, Mommy, and Daddy Emmie.

My eyes shot to Mae, wondering if it was an overstep. She just smiled and shrugged like, *As long as you're okay with it.*

A feeling of elated wholeness filled my soul, and I cried like a baby.

Isabel saying, "Don't cry, Daddy. I wove you," in her cherub voice did not help.

I plant a kiss on top of her head. "What did you do in school today, kiddo?"

"Painted with my fingers." She holds up her hands, with blue and yellow paint still stuck under her nails.

"Isabel," Charlotte calls from the kitchen. She's been staying here to help Mae with Isabel. While I'm glad she's here, I miss rocking my baby and settling her into bed at night.

She pops up from my lap. "I'm here, Grammy."

Charlotte comes into the room and scoops her granddaughter up. "We're going to go to the park. Do you need anything before I leave?"

"I'm good. You two have fun." I look at the clock. Mae should be home at any moment. She's working half-days at Pür, and the company has been more than accommodating with her schedule. The best part about it is that when she comes home for the day, she's all ours. No more staying up all night to crunch numbers. No more coming home as if the weight of her life is crushing her.

"You also." A knowing smile forms on her face. "Isabel and I will be gone a *long* time." Charlotte winks, and I toss my head back in laughter. She's always trying to give us alone time, which is nice. Especially when Queeny is feeling extra frisky.

"Mom! Remi!" Mae calls when she walks into the kitchen door and comes into our living room slash bedroom. Heading straight for me, she plants a big wet one, and if we didn't have an audience, I would have pulled her on top of me.

"Hello to you too, Queeny," I greet, staring like a dope as she picks up Isabel and smooches all over her chubby cheeks.

Isabel squeals in delight, and my love grows too big for this room.

That right there is everything I ever wanted. It's my dream come true. The reason I breathe. The reason I fought like hell to be alive.

"Bye, Daddy." Isabel waves as Charlotte whisks her out the door.

"Have fun with Grammy, sweetie." I wave back.

There's a look in Mae's eyes that instantly makes my pants tight. She sashays over with a feline smile and takes my face in her hands. "I love you."

I'll never get tired of hearing it. "I love you."

She pulls me in for a decadent kiss, but before I can pull her to me, she backs away.

"I'll be right back," she says with a smirk planted on her gorgeous face.

I smile and shake my head, anticipation building as I wonder what she has up her sleeve.

Fifteen minutes later, I find out.

"How are you feeling, Mr. Arison?" she says with a flirty pout, dressed in the skimpiest nurse outfit I've ever seen, her tits barely contained by a measly button.

My mouth waters. "Mmm, I'm a little hot. I might be running a fever."

"Is that so? I need to take your temperature." She climbs on top of me on the couch, her knees straddling my legs, and she runs her fingers up the back of my neck, lightly gripping my hair.

"Do you want to kiss me, Mr. Arison?" She rocks against me, and my eyes roll back in my skull.

"God yes."

Soft apple-candy lips take hold of my mouth, and she swirls her silky tongue around mine. She swallows my moan.

Fuck, I'll never get enough of her.

Running my hands up her luscious legs, I squeeze the ample cheeks of her ass, pressing her to me. "Why, nurse, you're not wearing any underwear. Are you trying to take advantage of me?" Peering up at her beautiful face, I smile.

I get a wicked grin as she slowly nods. "There's nothing you can do about it." Queeny leans back and her fingertips glide down her ample cleavage, and my salivating mouth dries. Every time I see her naked is like the first.

My erection becomes painfully hard. I want to rip that hot but silly scrap of fabric off her, though I sit tight. She's got plans for me, and I'm a willing participant.

"Do you want to see my breasts, Mr. Arison?" Her finger rests on that ridiculously tiny button.

"I'm not sure that's appropriate, nurse," I tease, knowing that she likes a little reluctance.

Green eyes flare with want, like I knew they would. "Well, there's no one here to stop me, now is there?"

"N-no, there isn't." I add the nervousness for effect, knowing that it spurs her arousal.

She flicks the button loose and my eyes widen, ready to feast on her flesh. "*Shit.* You're so innocent, aren't you?"

I bite my lip and nod, saying anything she wants to get her warmth around me.

Queeny takes my hand from her ass, draws my index finger into her mouth, and I almost blow. She closes her eyes as she sucks and moans, torturing me. Drawing out my pleasure. She guides my wrist until I'm cupping her soft breast, my wet finger teasing her tightened areola.

"That's it," she hisses.

I start plucking and flicking her pebbled nipple, becoming more daring in my approach.

That grants me a reward. "You're such a good patient." Holding her breast, she feeds it to me. "Bite."

I do as I'm told, savoring her flavor of sugar and Mae.

"Harder," she growls.

With my teeth scissoring her puckered flesh, I pull and tug over and over, until she's writhing on my lap. I pull her other globe out and switch back and forth, giving them both equal attention.

"Jesus, you're good at this." Her moans become fevered, but before she gets off, she wraps her hand around my neck and squeezes, pushing my head back.

It makes me goddamn wild when she handles me like that. Standing, she giggles, and I want to grab her and pin her to me while I spear my dick inside her incessantly, but I restrain my impulse. Mae's plans are always way better than mine.

She laughs at my frustration. "Silly me, I forgot to take your temperature."

My chuckle sounds more like a pant. I stare, transfixed, as my beauty kneels before me—strawberry lips swollen and tits out like an offering. I've never seen anything more erotic.

She pulls my erection out of my gray sweatpants and watches it like it's the ninth wonder of the world. "Let's see how hot you run, Boy Scout."

Queeny snugs my length in between her tits and, holy shit, tingles spread through my chest to my groin as goosebumps dimple my skin. She spits on my tip, rubbing it around her tight buds and cleavage, and it's like I'm inside an X-rated movie I never want to end.

"That's fucking hot," I rasp, my need growing exponentially.

Queeny holds her soft breasts around me and slides down my shaft in a tit fuck. Her tongue swirls over my crown with every downward pass, and I see stars. My stomach dips and twists with every stroke. My pulse throbs in my neck and cock.

"*Christ.* So sexy, baby." My hips can't help but thrust, and my scrotum tightens.

She doesn't take her eyes off my length as it slips in between her flesh. Warmth rushes through my veins like a hit of heroin. My dick twitches, begging to be inside of her, fully seated and whole.

"Baby, I need you," I whimper.

That does it. With one last kiss to my crown, she stands. Her eyes are dilated and her mouth is open, crazed with lust. One by one, she flicks her buttons loose. There's only, like, five, but it's taking an excruciatingly long time.

"You want my pussy, Manny?" Her tone is thick with desire.

"Yes," I breathe, pulling off my shirt. "I want it all." I want to devour every fucking inch of her.

Queeny helps me with my pants because my legs are still recovering. She's sensual and loving, never making me feel less than I was before the accident. She tells me I'm her superhero, but I just did what anyone would do for a child, especially one who's like their own. There are days I get frustrated with my slow progress, but she soothes my agitation, telling me I'm perfect just as I am. Reminding me that she almost lost me.

Mae stands and props her leg up on the couch, widening her stance and giving me a perfect view of her slick pussy as her fingers glide through it. "You're so fuckin hot," she murmurs.

Me? She's the one who could melt Antarctica into a hot spring right now. But the way she's half-lidded, staring at me as if I'm Adonis incarnate, tells me she means it—no matter my fractured state.

I draw her hand away from where my dick wants to be and suck her fingers into my mouth. Flavors of sex, honey, and Mae explode on my tongue. "So good."

Pulling her on top of me, I caress and savor her silky skin.

Mae shifts, and I notch inside. We both moan, savoring our connection.

"You feel incredible. The stretch is..." She sighs, closing her eyes and rocking a slow, sensual pace. "Mmm." She eases back on my lap, and her hand slides down her torso and flicks her swollen clit. She moans. "You're all I thought about while I was out. Scheming about what I wanted to do to you when I got home. Mmph." She flicks her tongue at my mouth while she rocks against my pelvis.

My hands dig into her hair, holding her to me. "Yeah? Tell me."

"I was so wet at work today. I wondered if anyone could tell."

Jesus, I don't know why that turns me on so much. "Were you aching for me, baby?"

"So much." Her voice is thick, sounding like she's on the verge of tears, and I get it.

I get her. I understand her need is more than sexual. She needs reassurance that the nightmare is over.

"I'm right here. I'm not going anywhere," I murmur. I'd take a blood oath if she asked me to. "Never again." My poor Queeny. God knows what she went through when I was under. She had to be out of her mind. I certainly would have been.

With a small sniffle, she nods against my forehead.

With one arm around her back and one cupping her head, I hold her to me. "I love you, baby, and I'm right here." I'll tell her every day of our lives if I have to.

"Love you." She pants, her hips swiveling faster. A beautiful flush spreads from her chest to her cheeks.

My legs shake and my diaphragm quakes, winding a tight coil in my gut, burning through my cock. I'm not ready to come so I lift her off me.

Her chest heaves, and a small smile forms on her face. "You learn fast."

That gives me another fantasy. "We'll have to explore that, Ms. Keller. I want an A, for sure."

She giggles, calming her breath. "I like that idea, very much. Only..." She bites her lip and looks at me through her lashes. Coy and fucking sexy.

"Only what, baby?" I peck her lips, sliding back inside her. Christ, it's perfection.

"I'll need you to teach me, Sir," she purrs like a leopard.

"Jesus." My head drops to her shoulder in a haze of lust. I can just imagine her in a slutty little plaid skirt and a tight button-down shirt, her nipples poking through the semi-sheer fabric and her doe eyes begging me to fuck her raw. "Gonna come."

She grunts and picks up the pace. "Hmm you like that, don't you?"

"You have no idea."

Shit, I love everything with her. My balls tighten, and my muscles brace for an orgasm hauling in like a freight train.

"Remi!" She throws her head back, screaming my name as she clenches around me.

I hold her to the hilt and, with a decadent groan, empty deep inside her, not letting her go until I'm wrung dry. My eyes roll back from the intense pleasure vibrating through my body.

Mae clings to me like I'm going to disappear, and I rub her back. Soothing her through the emotion that builds when we're together. She dots tender kisses all over my face, showing me without words how much she adores me.

"Same, baby. Same," I breathe into her mouth.

Two months after that...

Mae

"Miranda Keller," a woman in uniform calls my name, and I step up to the counter. "You're here for Aubry Laughtin." She barely looks at me as she slides a piece of paper my way. "Sign."

When I scribble my name, I notice the shakiness of my handwriting. This isn't nerves. It's rage, and it's taking everything in me to keep it under control.

I follow the officer down a hall and into a locked vestibule. From there, she uses her badge to enter another portion of the building. There is a corridor of steel doors to my left, and she knocks on the first one.

A male officer opens the door, and she waves me inside. "You have fifteen minutes and will be supervised the entire time."

"I'll only need five," I say, purpose squaring my shoulders and empowerment straightening my spine.

When I enter the small room, my eyes land on her immediately. She's slouched in the metal chair, swimming in the orange jumpsuit she's wearing. Her hair is greasy and her skin gray, hands bound in metal cuffs.

"Well, well, well, if it isn't Little Miss Perfect. How's that stud of yours doing? I heard he's still in physical therapy. Can he get it up yet?"

My face remains passive at her goading. Her remarks don't cut under my skin like she wishes they would.

She's wearing a smug smirk, like she got one over on me. It's the same one she gave me when I found her fucking my boyfriend. It's just ... sad.

This beautiful woman, who has all the money and opportunity in the world, projected her self-loathing onto me—a poor girl from a trailer park, who pulled herself up by the second-hand bootstraps and made something of herself.

"You're always so self-contained," she spits, like that is a bad characteristic. "Dull and principled. It's fucking annoying." She ran over the love of my life because she was aiming for my daughter, and *I'm* annoying? "Get that self-righteous look off your face. You're no better than me. Fucking trailer-trash bitch," she curses under her breath.

Again, her words mean nothing. I'm not the one going to jail for the next twenty-five years.

Aubry jerks back, her chair screeching across the floor. She's trying and failing to get a rise out of me. "No matter what I did..." Her lips curl under. "No matter how much I gave of myself…" she seethes. "My father, Brad … fucking everyone…" Her sharp shout echoes around the room, and the guard places his hands on his belt next to the taser. She cocks her head, and her eyes narrow. "They always loved you more."

Ah, there it is, her petty motive—jealousy. All the havoc she wreaked because of the little green monster festering inside of her. It's vile.

She has no Remi. No one who will love her unconditionally and unselfishly with all that they are.

She has no Isabel. Not one person to love more than herself. To show her how amazing love can feel when you give it away.

She has no Jay. No best friend that will stand by her side through thick and thin, no matter what. Jay also offered to help me hide her body, but that's beside the point.

She has absolutely nothing but her hate, festering inside her like a cancer, her heart rotting away while her soul blackens. Her new home will be in a six-by-six concrete cell, where she'll have to take a piss in the corner next to the thin mat she'll sleep on. Far away from her three-thousand-square-foot penthouse in the sky. I have a sneaky suspicion poor little rich girls don't make it far in prison.

It's then that I feel sorry for her.

Turns out, forgiving her isn't difficult at all. I have everything I've ever dreamed of and more. I have no purpose here.

There's no meaning in a conference room either. Especially when dealing with misogynistic assholes who underestimate the value of a woman.

My purpose is out in the bright big world, waiting for me to harness it.

I don't sit. My parting gift is a look of pity before I walk out the door. Towards my daughter.

Towards my love.

Towards the rest of my beautiful life.

Epilogue

Two Years Later...

Remi

TODAY STARTED NORMAL, LIKE any other. Wake up, shower with my wife, and get Isabel and me ready for school while Mae gets ready for work. Reconvene at five, when Mae comes home from Pür.

But when I slammed my hand on the alarm clock and scrubbed my face alert, I was completely clueless that this day would change my life forever.

When Isabel started kindergarten, I took a job teaching music at her school. We usually get home a couple of hours before Mae does, but not today. When I walk through our door, I'm surprised to find my wife sitting at the kitchen island, eating a cookie.

"Mommy!" Isabel runs to her mother and Mae scoops her up, sending me a beatific smile. I swear she's glowing from within.

Walking over to my girls, I wrap my arms around them and give Queeny a smooch on the lips. "Well, this is a pleasant surprise, Mrs. Keller."

She looks up at me from under her lashes, coy and fucking edible. "I was anxious to see you, Mr. Keller."

Although it's not how it's typically done—when we got married last year—I took Mae's last name. We discussed it, and since she is well known in her industry—her career in full swing—she wanted to keep her surname. I didn't feel threatened by it, but I did want my name to be the same as Queeny's and my daughter's.

Mae practically jumped in my arms when I told her my wishes. "You are one in a million, you know that?'" she said, kissing every inch of my face.

Mae sets Isabel down so she can go change into play clothes. Isabel and I usually romp around in the backyard before I start dinner. Something tells me that's not going to happen today.

Mae pulls me in and seams her lips over mine. One hand digs into her hair while I pin her to me with my other arm. God, I've been waiting for this all day. Heat simmers just under the surface of my skin. My mouth travels to her jaw and neck, licking and sucking, and tasting the intoxicating drug that is Queeny.

She pushes me back slightly with a wicked grin. "I have a surprise for you."

"Yeah?" Fuck, I love her surprises. They usually involve scorching seduction and her clenching around my cock multiple times. But Isabel is home, so I'm not sure what she has up her sleeve.

"Yeah, why don't you sit and I'll go help Isabel change." She winks before extracting herself from my arms and sauntering out of the kitchen.

My eyes don't leave the bounce of her plump ass as she walks away from me. It's times like these that I wish I had X-ray vision.

I pull a cookie from the cake dome on the counter. It's a new recipe I'm trying to perfect, made with broccoli and chocolate. This is the best batch yet.

Ten minutes later, I hear little feet tromp down the stairs.

"Daddy!" Isabel shouts. "I painted you a picture." She runs towards me, waving a paper in her hand.

Bemused, Mae walks in right behind her.

Isabel hops up on my lap and holds her masterpiece up, so proud of herself.

I suck in a breath for dramatic effect. "It's beautiful. You paint so well, Isa-bea." It looks like a house, a few stick figures, and a cat? Turning the picture this way and that, I'm trying to figure out why the cat has a spoon in its hand. "Who's in the picture?" I smile, looking towards Mae, who's standing by the island.

There is a grin she's trying and failing to hide.

"There is our house," Isabel says, pointing to the square topped with a triangle. Her little chubby finger goes down the line. "That's Mommy, Daddy, Isabel, and the baby."

I'm a little confused. "Is the cat your baby?" I ask, thinking she wants to play house with the furball.

"No, silly, it's your baby." Jumping off my lap, she runs to Mae and pats her belly.

In life, you have moments where you kind of know what's happening but your brain is too excited at the possibility, so your thoughts jumble and scatter, and it doesn't compute. I'm in that moment.

"The baby is in Mommy's belly," Isabel explains like I'm an idiot and should have known all along.

My heart freezes and then pounds as my jaw drops to the floor. "Are you?"

Mae nods, and her face beams. "Congratulations, Daddy."

In awe, I stand slowly. As if liquid caramel is dropped over my head, a warm, tingly sensation drips down my body. "Baby?" I breathe.

"Baby," Mae repeats, laughing with all the love in the universe shining in her eyes.

Or maybe it's my reflection because the love thrumming through my veins is too big for my body. It's too big for this house. It's infinite. Like gods and goddesses. Miracles and *new life*. So immense that it leaks out of my eyes in big fat tears.

I stand in front of Mae, my hands pantomime over her form. I want to touch her everywhere, but I don't know where to start. "Our baby."

Queeny wipes her cheeks. "Are you happy?"

A half-cry, half-laugh whooshes out of me. "Ha! Am I *happy*?" I don't think there's a word to encompass all I feel right now. "If we're speaking English, I suppose 'happy' works, but... *Oh my God*!" I pull her to me and bawl in elation as we swing a jubilant dance. I kiss her head, cheeks, mouth, and then kneel, nuzzling her belly. My hands grip her hips. "Hi, baby."

Mae's fingers run through my hair, and Isabel skips around us singing, "Baby," over and over, oblivious to my absolute meltdown.

I peer up at my love. The woman who's made my dreams come true. The woman I never thought I'd have a chance with. The woman who will forever own my heart. "I love you so much."

She pulls me up and gives me a decadent kiss. "I love you more."

I shake my head, vehement. "Not possible."

Isn't it funny that someone could want something their whole adult life, hoping and praying for it almost every day, and then when it finally manifests, a pound of shit drops straight to their gut. Because they are totally unprepared.

Reality dawns on me. I'm going to be responsible for raising a tiny human from infancy, doing everything possible to not mess it up, which I most likely will at some point. It isn't any less thrilling, but...

I grab the top of my head with both hands. "Oh fuck."

The months pass by fast, and yet not fast enough. Mae had a fairly sick pregnancy. There were many a midnight I went out for pickles and ice cream. Back and foot rubs were abundant, but anytime I get to put my hands on Mae is a good time.

Even though it's not something I ever gave much thought to, pregnancy sex is hot. How could it not be? The woman of my dreams swelled with our growing child, rocking on top of me. Her heavy breasts bouncing with every thrust. It's heady.

My only primal thought is how do I get another one inside her.

As responsive as Queeny always is, she's electrified pregnant. The hormones raging inside of her made her ravenous for me. She'd kill me if I said it, but it was the best nine months of my life.

But today is the day. I'm currently on my way to the hospital. I just dropped off Isabel at home with Charlotte, who is giddy with elation, kissing both my cheeks and hugging me enthusiastically.

Mae and I have filed papers for step-parent adoption, claiming parent abandonment for Brad. I will celebrate the day I can truly say Isabel's my daughter.

God, I'm going to have two kids.

As I drive, I get lost in my head, preparing myself to become a dad, even if it's for the second time. I'm feeling a bit overwhelmed. But then...

An excited laugh jumps out of my mouth. Images of Christmases, school plays, and children's laughter swirl around in my mind, and I can't get to the hospital fast enough.

Jay called about ten minutes ago, explaining that Mae's water broke at work. I could hear Mae screaming obscenities in the background. Jay reassured me they've seen it all before and that Queeny will be fine when the baby comes.

When I drive into the parking garage, my tires squeal as I fly into the first available space. I jump out of the car and run across the street to the front entrance. It's not long before I make it to the delivery floor. I'm quickly disinfected, suited up, and ushered into Mae's room.

Her feet are already propped up in stirrups, and her wet hair is plastered to her face. She's cradling her swollen belly. *Our baby.*

Jay is at her side, helping her breathe through her contractions. They exaggerate expulsion and I almost laugh, until I take in Mae's distressed state.

"I need an epidural," she whines, though it's most likely too late for one. When she sees me, her head rolls back in relief. "Remi, *ahh*," She cries out.

"Baby." I rush to her side and kiss her forehead. "How far apart are they?" I ask Jay as I smooth her hair back.

"Seven minutes. Doctor's on her way now. This kid is ready to pop out." Jay looks at the clock hanging on the wall.

Doctor Haily pushes through the door thirty seconds later. "Alright, let's have a baby," she cheers, sitting in front of Mae's legs.

"Epidural!" Mae demands.

"It's too late for that. Mae, this baby is coming," the doctor explains, organizing the tools she needs to deliver.

"No, *argh*. Give me a fucking epidural." Queeny is about to lose it.

"Baby, you didn't want one, remember?" I speak low in her ear, hoping to calm her.

"I can change my mind! It's the twenty-goddamn-first century, for chrissakes." She huffs a few breaths. "A woman can change her mind," she shrieks.

"Not when you're fully dilated," Doctor Haily explains, reaching under Mae. "The baby is crowning." She looks towards me. "Do you want to see the head?"

I jump at the opportunity to watch this miracle, not really thinking about what I am actually going to witness. *Big mistake.* These moments are precious and life-changing, I know, but I'm not sure I'll ever get the image of my wife's hoo-ha stretching over a basketball out of my mind.

"Oh." I gulp, shifting towards Mae, trying to keep the contents of my stomach in place. I may be ecstatic about my kid being born, but I don't think I would stay upright if I watched it.

"Yaaaah," Mae wails. "Get it out. Get it out!"

"Mars Bars, you have to relax. See? Breathe like me." Jay starts their expulsion again, and I swear Mae's head rotates like she's possessed.

"You fucking relax. I'm the one having to push a whale out of a goldfish and shit myself in the process."

Jay's face scrunches in perplexity. "That's not actually possible. You see, whales come from—"

"Are you shitting me right now?" she yells.

"No, but you will be." Their grin wanes when they see the murderous look in Mae's eyes.

"Okay, Mommy's helpers, hold her legs. The baby is coming," the doctor announces. "Mae, start pushing."

I cannot get over the image of the crowning head pushing through my wife's vagina, but I do as I'm told and try not to pass out.

Jay starts singing Salt-N-Peppa. I join in for encouragement. The nurses rap, poppin' it in their scrubs.

"Are you fucking serious right now?" Queeny shrieks. But she's been screaming for the last ten minutes, so it's more like a pleasant whisper. "My body is being ripped in half, and you're gettin' jiggy with it." She's incredulous.

"That's The Fresh Prince," Jay corrects, unphased by the Mommy Monster that is ready to strangle someone.

Queeny grabs my t-shirt and yanks me down. "I can't believe I let you talk me into this."

It's me. Hi. I'm someone.

Her lips curl, revealing clenched teeth. "Look what *you* did. I hope you're happy with yourself." She throws her head back with a guttural growl derived from the gates of hell.

I'd be scared if I wasn't so excited. The baby is coming. *Our* baby.

"You're doing so good, love," I coo.

"Fuck off. Just fuck right off."

Okay, then.

"Keep pushing. You're almost there," the doctor instructs.

Jay and I hold Mae's legs as she gives it all she's got.

"Motherfucking bullshit in a candy wrapper."

I look at Jay, who just shrugs their shoulders.

Mae's head rolls from side to side. "I wanna go home." She jerks me down again. "Take me home."

"Uh—"

"Now, Manny. Fucking now."

Panic sets in my chest because I know I can't give her what she wants. Indisposed or not, I would not put it past Mae to rip my balls off. Adjusting myself, my feet shift and I glimpse at the doctor. "Help." My plea is weak.

"You can't go home, Mae. One more big push," Doctor Haily says, unaffected by the monster possessing my wife's body. "Come on, you got this."

"Baby, we gotta push," I soothe, rubbing her leg where I hold on for dear life.

This was the wrong thing to say.

"*We* aren't doing anything! I am!" she wails. "All *you* had to do was come. I have to rip through my vagina opening."

She has a point.

"Mija, just one more push and you can have alcohol." The doctor raises her eyebrow at Jay. "After you're done breastfeeding," they amend.

Queeny bears down and gives it all she's got. "Graaaaaah. Gah!"

The only sounds in the room are Mae's labored breaths, monitor beeping, and nurses scrambling. My lungs seize up until … a baby's cry, sweet and sharp, falls over the space like a million resplendent stars. Ethereal and majestic.

Mae's sobs turn into overjoyed laughs.

"You did so good, baby. So good." Tears fall fat and furious out of my eyes. I don't know that I've felt this much love. I shift on my feet, anxiously waiting for the medical team to check the baby's—my baby's—vitals.

It feels like an eternity before the doctor approaches with a broad smile. "Congratulations, it's a boy." Doctor Haily hands the tiny bundle in my arms.

The moment I lay eyes on him, something happens in my chest that I can't quite describe. The love I have in my heart grows too immense. It's overwhelming and awe-inspiring. Like I'm seeing the glory of the divine for the first time. I don't remember my life before this minute. I only know how much I feel. I'm going to love and protect this child for the rest of my life.

I place the baby on Mae's chest and wrap my arms around them both.

Mae is bawling, checking over every inch of our son. Once she's satisfied that he's got all his fingers and toes, she smooths her hand over his tiny head. "He is staring at you, Daddy."

He is. I can't take my eyes off of him either.

Jay takes our picture, and Mae gives her best friend a look that would kill a ghost.

"What? You're going to want this picture, and I want to commemorate the day you shit the bed."

Now that the intense pain is over, Queeny finds her laugh.

"Do you have a name?" Doctor Haily asks.

Mae and I look at each other because it's something we couldn't agree on. She wanted Remington, but I told her how I got wedgies until I was a sophomore in high school. I wanted Lukas, after my grandfather. But ultimately, she did the work, so it's up to her.

My wife looks at me with a beaming grin. God, she's beautiful. "Lukas Remington Keller."

"Woo hoo, Lukey!" Jayden hoots.

We all laugh. It's joyous and exciting, and humbling.

In a few hours, we're in Mae's assigned room, waiting for Charlotte to come with Isabel. I can't stop holding Lukas and making silly faces at him. He can't see much, but it doesn't stop my overzealous dad streak.

When the door finally opens, my Isa-bea runs inside but halts when she spots the tiny bundle in my arms. I start crying like a chick all over again.

Our daughter fidgets and hesitates until I sit, waving her over. She gives me an excited smile and runs to me, wanting to meet her baby brother. She's been planning for her little sibling to come home. Drawing pictures and making a list of dos and don'ts, she is taking her big sister duty very seriously.

I let Charlotte hold the baby while Isabel sits on my lap. She wants to know all about "Mommy pushing the baby out of her belly". I try to describe it as delicately and kid-friendly as I can. Mae giggles at my fumbling story.

"He looks just like you, Remi," Charlotte says, swaying the bundle in her arms.

This surprises me. "You think? He's got Mae's button nose," I point out.

"Yeah, but the rest is all you." Mae smirks. "I'll be warding the girls off with black magic."

Charlotte chuckles before giving Lukas to Queeny. "I'm going to step out and call Randy."

When she leaves, Isabel climbs on Mae's bed to get a better look at her brother.

"Do you want to hold him?" I ask, knowing that she'll bond with him right away if she does.

She gives me a look of wonder. "Can I?"

"Sure, baby. Come sit against Mommy," Mae says, handing Lukas to me as she gets Isabel into position.

I lay the baby on Isabel's lap, and the three of us cradle him together.

I realize money and power don't make a man, like my father thinks. I didn't need to become a medical doctor to find success in life. This right here makes me the richest man on Earth, and the happiest too.

That's pretty damn exceptional.

The End

Afterword

DEAR READERS, IF YOU enjoyed this book, please consider leaving a review. As authors, we put so much blood, sweat, and tears into our craft, and every review heals our fractured souls. Or, really, it feels good to see something that I've created resonate with someone else. With a million other brilliant books out there, thank you for reading this one!

- Website: www.ninabloomauthor.com

- To get the latest news on new releases, arc opportunities and bookish giveaways, subscribe to Nina's newsletter: https://forms.wix.com/r/71 56428591163507095

- Stalk Nina on socials!

- Facebook: https://www.facebook.com/profile.php?id=10008240734 6649

- Facebook Readers Group: http://www.facebook.com/groups/shadeso fromancereadersgroup/

- Instagram: http://instagram.com/nina.bloom.author

- TikTok: https://www.tiktok.com/@nina.bloom.author?lang=en

Other Works

The Weight of Our Hearts

A Standalone Enemies-to-Lovers Romance

Blurb:

Sticks and stones may break bones, but words will break hearts.

Lucy, an introverted college student, left her troubled past with hope for the future. But soon, she finds old wounds can still bleed, taking away the little bit of spirit she has left. When a powerful company threatens to bulldoze her home and the small unhoused community she looks after, Lucy refuses to crumble in defeat. She enlists the help of a friend, who has one condition—work for Lucy's nemesis.

Marco, an ambitious real estate developer, knows the price of desire. As he tries to right the wrongs of his past, he becomes tenacious in his agenda. The last thing he wants is a relationship, but when he comes face-to-face with his best friend's stubborn sister, he doesn't know what to make of her. And he certainly doesn't understand her frustrating ability to shut him out while she lets everyone else in.

Sparks fly as they both fight against the pull of passion. But after they've been hurt in the past, can they learn to trust again? And could that trust build into something bigger?

The Weight of Our Hearts is a stand-alone, steamy, contemporary romance. If you love angst laced with raw emotion and sprinkled with a dirty talking hero, you'll love this debut by Nina Bloom.

Warning: Not suitable for ages under 18 due to graphic language and adult content, see full content warning inside. Reader discretion is advised.

POV: Heroine 1st

Angst: High

Humor: Low

Spice: High

Happily Ever After: Always

Read it here: https://books2read.com/u/4N7Y8W

Acknowledgements

To Mr. Bloom, you are my why. Why I wake up with a smile on my face every morning. Why I Love as deeply as I do. Why I'm embarking on this crazy journey—to spend more time adventuring with you. I know romance because you are the most romantic man I've ever met. The best characteristics of my Heroes will always be inspired by you. Thank you for always supporting every cockamamie idea I've ever had—including this one. Thank you for Loving me as I am. I Love you more than life.

Mom, I would've never taken this chance if it wasn't for you. Thank you for always loving and embracing me, your weirdy child, no matter what. Thank you for loving this book more than I do and cheering me on every step of the way. I get knocked down, but I get up again because of you. Thank you for teaching me what quiet strength truly is. You are the Bonnie to my Clyde. I love you infinitely.

To my sister and best friend, thank you for always sharing the best books and igniting my love for passionate, angsty, romances. For helping me to always land on my own two feet and most of all thank you for helping me clear out the bullshit in my head. Thank you for planning the most epic adventures which will inspire more stories to come.

Nina, you have been in my corner since I started and I'm excited for the years to come! From your impeccable editing skills, to your full understanding of story structure, and the hours of therapy I should pay you for. You always know exactly what I'm trying to convey, even if I don't know it myself. You, my sorceress, are one in a million! And I'm truly blessed to have you in my life. This book is inspired by you and your strength—a true Queen and amazing mother.

Dream Team, my unwavering cheerleaders and sisters, you girls are good for the soul. This book—or anything I write really—would be absolute shit if it wasn't for you. Thank you for always giving me the truth, even when it was hard to give. I've learned so much from you. You both are so talented and I'm humbled to be in your circle.

Beta Readers: Michelle, Susy, Pattie and Tina – You ladies ROCK! Thank you so much for taking a chance on this book baby. I hope you know how much I love you and how much I respect your opinion. Your suggestions are invaluable in making this book the best version it could possibly be.

Shades of Romance Authors: Angela, Blye, Charissa, Corissa, MK and Vicky, you have no idea how much I love you. How was I to know that meeting seven strangers would change the course of my life forever. From strangers to sisters & lifelong friends. I can't wait until we're all together again!

Nikki Tubery: This book would not even exist if it wasn't for you. Thank you for asking me to write you a nanny story. I hope I made you proud.

Aisling from Pretty Indie - You are a dream to work with, even when I can be a pain in the butt. Thank you for creating the most beautiful cover for my book baby.

Thank you Sarah Clark for your thorough sensitivity analysis. Your advice was invaluable to making this book everything I wanted it to be.

Aunties, your spirit is in everything I do. I love you all so much.

Shades of Romance Shaders, you are the most supportive group of people. I love sharing my work with you and I love when you share your words with me. I'm so honored to be a part of this great community of romance lovers.

Facebook groups The Smuthood, BANG Book Club and Cliterature Book Group, Thank you, THANK YOU, for giving us readers a safe place to talk about our favorite deviant books with no judgment. I have nothing but gratitude for the communities you've built and the acceptance you've given to horny little readers like me.

Aspiring authors, if I can do it, you can too. Your story is important, it's valuable and it's meant to be told. Sit down and write, even if it's only a sentence at a time.

Eventually you will hit that publish button. Readers are hungry for your story and I am one of them.

About The Author

Raw, Angsty and Spicy Contemporary Romance

Nina Bloom is an independent author, who is also a voracious reader. Her unique skills include reading and daydreaming and reading some more. Occasionally she writes. After earning a bachelor in fine arts, Nina floated her way through life doing this and that and then a little more of this, until she decided to make something of herself. And, so, here we are. When Nina is not daydreaming, she's chasing around her two obnoxious boxers or snuggling with her seriously handsome husband, who feeds her waffles and calls her 'good girl'.